THE DARK LANTERN

GERRI BRIGHTWELL

THE Dark Lantern

A NOVEL

CROWN PUBLISHERS + NEW YORK

Copyright © 2008 by Gerri Brightwell

Published in the United States by Crown Publishers,
an imprint of the Crown Publishing Group,
a division of Random House, Inc., New York.
www.crownpublishing.com

CROWN is a trademark and the Crown colophon is a registered trademark
of Random House, Inc.

Library of Congress Cataloging-in-Publication Data

Brightwell, Gerri.
The Dark lantern : a novel / Gerri Brightwell.—1st ed.
1. Women domestics—Fiction. 2. Great Britain—History—Victoria, 1837–1901—
Fiction. 3. London (England)—Fiction. 4. Impostors and imposture—Fiction.
I. Title.
PR6102.R54D37 2008
823'.92—dc22   2007020759

ISBN: 978-0-307-39534-4

Printed in the United States of America

DESIGN BY ELINA D. NUDELMAN

10 9 8 7 6 5 4 3 2 1

First Edition

For Cam, with love

ACKNOWLEDGMENTS

This book is a work of fiction. Although it refers to some historical people and events, my intention was to create a compelling story rather than to write history. I have therefore allowed myself to reimagine them for the purposes of this novel.

I am indebted to many people in writing this novel. I must thank the many members of the VICTORIA discussion list for their generosity in helping with information about late-nineteenth-century Britain. In particular, I'd like to thank Judith Flanders for her willingness to answer tricky questions or point me to sources that would help.

For taking me on, thanks to my wonderful agent, Zoe Fishman, and my insightful editor, Allison McCabe. For their support and encouragement, thank you to Derick Burleson, Anne Caston, David Crouse, Melina Draper, Amber Flora Thomas, Len Kamerling, Anne Carter, Louise Doughty, and Fadia Faqir. For getting me to the point where I could write this novel, thanks to Frank Soos, Don Ross, Gordon Hirsch, Lois Cucullu, and Anna Clark.

Thank you to Conor, Ross, and Callum, who patiently put up with a mother who must have seemed always to be writing. Lastly, for plot fixes, the time to write, and his love, thanks most of all to Cam Esslemont.

By the late nineteenth century, two new technologies appeared which promised to streamline the process of criminal identification. One, fingerprinting, is familiar to us. The other, an identification system based on anthropometry, the physical measurement of the size and proportions of the human body, has become a historical curiosity. Yet the two techniques were once well-matched rivals, which vied for ascendancy for forty years.

— Simon A. Cole, *Suspect Identities: A History of Fingerprinting and Criminal Identification*

THE DARK LANTERN

She sits stiffly on the seat of the cart, her whole self held in against the tumult of the city. It is too much: the carriages that clog the roads, the raucous cries of costermongers pushing barrows, the shabby children that hold limp bunches of flowers and cress out to her and, when she shakes her head, run off through the filth of the street in bare feet.

Beside her the driver in his shapeless hat urges the horse on with flicks of a whip. They slip into a gap between a hansom and a four-wheeler, around a corner into a narrow street of frowning houses where the *clop-clop* of the horse's feet echo. On and on they go, through murky streets where men and women are little more than shadows. She waits for grass to appear, or fields, but this is a world where such things do not exist. So many buildings, so many people—she fears she will be swallowed up by it all.

Her breath trails in plumes behind her, then fades into the darkness of the afternoon. Night is creeping out of alleys, out of courtyards, and it's only half past four—as they turn a corner she hears bells ring out close by, then those of another church, and another. She grips the seat with both hands. She thinks how down in Teignton she'd be bringing in the tea, how every day when she opened the study door Reverend Saunders would huff, "Oh, it's you, Jane," and glare at her from over his books, as though she was determined to disturb him.

Does she regret it, leaving his warm house, his vinegary wife, the daily round of scrubbing and scouring? Of course she does. Now as she's driven through these streets by a man who smells not of horses—that she could have borne—but of gin, she wonders if she is safe here, and suspects she is not. She has thrown herself out onto the world, enticed by an advertisement in a newspaper, and a letter written in an elegant hand by a Mrs. Bentley saying that yes, her character is acceptable and for fourteen pounds per annum plus room and board, she will take her on as second housemaid.

Such a step seems folly now. But to have stayed was impossible. The way Mrs. Saunders would go out visiting on Jane's half days off, and not return until teatime, when there was no time left for Jane even to walk into the village. The way she counted out Jane's wages every month and slid the small pile of coins across her desk with the very ends of her fingers, as though there was something dirty in the whole business. The way she fed prim spoonfuls of custard into her flat line of a mouth at dinnertime and, with the smell of it still on her breath, called Jane and Mrs. Phelps up from their work in the kitchen for evening prayers and warnings about extravagance.

That place had closed in around Jane like a wet sheet, and it wasn't until this morning, when she found herself on the station platform with her box at her feet, that she'd realized: she had left it behind. She'd pressed her hand against her pocket and Mrs. Bentley's letter inside it. A sheet of paper—that was all she had to see her safely through the world. Her breath felt hot in her chest, and she couldn't help looking back through the station's archway to the road and the sullen winter sea beyond, though who she thought was going to walk in and tell her not to get on the train she couldn't imagine. Not the Reverend or his wife, that was for sure. They'd already taken on a new girl, who'd arrived four days before she left. Another girl who, like Jane, had been taken from the orphanage to be trained up. But a girl unlike her. Not the daughter of the murderer Martha Wilbred, who'd been hanged by the neck until she was dead. Not a girl they would watch with wariness when she took up the poker to stir the fire, or carried the carving knife to the dining table. Not a girl whom no one else would take on, whom even the matron had given up hope of hiring out until she'd resorted to the unfair means of appealing to the Saunderses' sense of Christian charity.

Now she has fled from their resentment and suspicions, far away to London. Nearly five hours by train, a wagon waiting for her, a man in a dirty hat and a pipe gripped between rotting teeth to drive her to Mrs. Bentley's house at thirty-two Cursitor Road. She's afraid that she remembers none of the lessons Mrs. Saunders tried to instill in her—or, more accurately, that she left to Mrs. Phelps to instill in her between preparing lunch and dinner. How to polish brass. How to air a bed. How to clean stains from a carpet. But nothing on how to manage all the work of cleaning and waiting at table and answering the door on her own, or how to stay clean and tidy through it all so that she wouldn't show in Mrs. Saunders's guests with soot on her apron or her face flushed and sweating.

When the wagon stops she is caught by surprise. The street lit by the sour yellow of street lamps is grander than she'd expected. Stretching above her is a tall wall of houses like the side of a castle. Here and there slits of light break through where curtains have been drawn and lamps lit. Above hangs a flat sky—no moon, no stars, as though she has come so far that she has left them behind. She holds more tightly onto the wooden seat, but it is too late for that: the man is reining in the horse. With a grunt he climbs down and heaves her box onto the pavement. Even in the dim light she sees that the ground is filthy—with dog dirt, horse dirt, scraps of vegetables—and that he has set down her box in the middle of it.

He holds out a thick hand. She takes it and he helps her down, but he doesn't let go. Instead he ducks his face towards hers until all she can see are his wet eyes and the pitted skin of his nose. "You better watch yourself, little maid," he says. "Take my advice—keep yourself to yourself, and keep yourself inside there where you'll be safe." He nods to the house.

She pulls her hand away and he snorts. He doesn't move away, though. His hand is out again, not for hers—it takes her a moment to understand. From deep in her pocket she pulls out her purse and searches for a coin. She has so little—the half-sovereign Reverend Saunders gave her, the two more sovereigns she's managed to save, a few small coins. Her fingers pull out tuppence and she drops the coin into his hand. Before his fingers have snapped shut around it she regrets it—he is scowling, disappointed, and she has tuppence less in her purse, and nothing more to put in it until the end of the month. He lumbers back onto the wagon and spits onto the ground. "Which house is it?" she calls out, but he doesn't even turn his head. Instead, with a snap of the whip at the horse's bony back, his cart rattles away.

In the light the street lamp casts she stands shivering. She peers around, one foot against her box—she has heard stories of boxes being snatched away and girls like her left with nothing—and sees the silhouette of a gentleman coming towards her. She opens her mouth to ask him to direct her to number thirty-two, but as he steps into the pool of light he remains a shadow cut against the brightness. He is black, from his hat to his face to his ragged jacket, black in everything except his eyes, which stare back at her as white as eggs. She closes her eyes against the sight of him and turns away. A carriage passes. From a street close by a dog barks shrilly. Then comes the slurred singing of a drunk man. She sees him, tottering between the islands of light that stretch the length of the street. Closer he comes, his hat crooked, the silver top of his cane glinting coldly, his unbuttoned coat flapping around him like wings. When he sees her he spreads his arms and calls out, "Little bird, come here, come over here," and she takes flight up the steps of the nearest house.

The carter didn't do such a bad job: she finds that the door she has run up to is that of number thirty-two. The Bentley home. Hers too now, in a manner of speaking, for she has no other. But here already is a problem. She comes back down the steps, looks to the left and the right: there is no gap between these houses, no way to get to the back entrance. Down below her feet, in a sunken area fenced off with metal railings, is a window bright with light. It has been jammed

open with a piece of wood, and she hears angry voic
ing: "You took half the afternoon and you still have
servants? Are they the Bentleys' servants? She can't

From out of the darkness comes a young man w
and plain as a loaf. He leans against the railings an
into his hand. For a moment he looks at her, looks
on the pavement, then heaves himself off the railin
thing, the words hanging on the air all twisted in
she realizes that he has said, "New maid, are you?'
until he's standing over her box.

"You leave that, you hear?" she calls out.

He doesn't, though. Instead he crouches an
along it, touches the scar where one handle used
this box belonged to her. "Where you from?"

A stranger in this city, that's what she is. Her v
away—it stretches her vowels, and caresses the
hear. It has marked her out already. Her mouth
tips up her box as though he means to lift it. She
It's all I have."

The door is right behind her. She grabs the h
and sends it thundering against the plate. She's
the warmth has been washed from her thin coa
from Mrs. Saunders's youngest sister, yet it's no
makes her tremble. She knocks again and the str
rat-a-tat-tat. From the other side of the door
must be in, though. There's always a servant at l

The grate of wood on stone, and she turns. F
onto its end and has his arms around it.

"You!" she shouts. "No—no, you mustn't.
with it."

He tries to lift the box higher and grunts wit

"Put that down. Please." Her voice turns ir
peats, "Please."

From behind her comes light and a rush o
has opened and there, in a black suit, stands a s

hite hair combed back, and a chin so small he seems barely to
 one.

Oh sir." She stumbles towards him. "Sir—"

e raises one finger for silence, and stares down to where she
ds on the step beneath him. Then he flutters his hand at her.
ay, away. You must use the other entrance," he says, pointing
n to the sunken area behind the railings. He leans towards
conspiratorially, one fat hand on his belly. "And if you ever use
front entrance again, you will be dismissed immediately. I
I see to it."

'es, certainly; yes, sir."

distant voice comes down the corridor, and he lifts his head to
"Merely the young person who—" and pushes the door closed.
the sudden darkness she spins around to see what has become
er box and steps back, missing her footing and falling hard
nst the railings—so hard that she will have bruises across her
for days to come. She saves herself only by grabbing hold of the
ls that top the railings, though the sharp edge of one scrapes
skin of her palm. She snatches for her hat too late: it sails over
railings and into the area.

he young man is waiting, her box balanced on his shoulder.
uld've told you that was a mistake, knocking on the door. They
t want to see the likes of you on their front doorstep, now do
?" With that he starts down the steps and leaves her to follow as
she can.

With all the laundry that hangs from the ceiling racks, the
en feels like a ship about to set sail. There's nothing fresh about
ir here, though. No, it's swollen with steam and the hot smell of
ing beef. Jane stands at one end of the table with her hat in her
Is. The brim is damp and covered with something dark that may
ud, or mold, or worse. In the light of the gas lamps it's hard to tell.
he cook bustles between the stove and a set of serving dishes.
r all she has said is, "You'll just have to wait. I'm right in the

middle of getting dinner started and I can't be dealing with you right now. Albert"—that, it seems, is the name of the young man who carried her box down the stairs—"you'll catch it if Mrs. Robert knows you've been hanging around again. But I'll thank you for moving that box out of my way." She talks a little like Albert, and Jane has to hold the words, just for a moment, to make sense of them.

The box is by the door that opens onto the area, and the cook's dress has brushed against it a couple of times. Albert obliges. He leans down and hugs it in both arms, then carries it over to the corner, between a dresser and the wall. "Good enough, Mrs. J.?" he calls over.

She has a ladle raised to taste the soup. "None of your cheek," she says. Then she glances over to a girl at the sink, sullen and bow-shouldered, who is halfheartedly peeling apples. She's lanky and pale, like a plant grown up without enough light. "You can't still be working on those apples," the cook barks at her. "You need to shift yourself, Elsie. There's a sinkful of pans waiting for you in the scullery. Come on now, put a bit of effort into it."

But the girl just goes on peeling, sleeves turned up on her thin arms, her apron stained and drooping with damp. She hasn't glanced at Jane, not even once.

Albert leans against the dresser and starts picking at his nails. The cook sets down the ladle and turns to him. "I told you—you'd better be off."

"Sarah busy, is she?"

"Out on some errands." She wipes her forehead with a cloth hanging from her apron strings and rests her thick hands on the table's edge. "Now, you're not going to wait for her. I can't have my kitchen cluttered up like this. Besides, if Mrs. Robert catches you here again, you'll be sorry."

He lifts a hand, about to say something it seems. Then his face closes in on itself and he lets himself out without a word. Behind him the door swings closed and a gust of cool air sweeps into the kitchen. In moments it has dispersed. Jane fans herself with her hat, says, "I'll take off my coat, then."

From over by the stove the cook eyes her. "You wait a moment. I don't want coats and boxes and all God-knows making a mess of my kitchen."

So Jane waits. Not leaning on anything, not standing with her legs crossed, but as she's been taught: heels touching, back straight, chin up but not jutting into the air. Above her the sheets swing gently, and a cold drop of water falls on her head. Is there nowhere outside this closed-in place to hang laundry? She shivers, not just from the drip sliding across her scalp but from the thought of it—being trapped in this house with no garden to go to for a breath of fresh air.

Elsie picks another apple from the bowl beside her. Her knife rasps as she cuts away the peel in a ragged ribbon, then the apple slips and it's out of her hands, bouncing from the edge of the sink to her hip to the floor, rolling towards the table. But Elsie's fast—she spins around and crouches, stretches out her arm, and she's snatched it up. There's something animal in her quickness, something familiar. Oh yes, Jane recognizes it—a girl brought up in an institution learns to be fast, to grab what she must, to hold it to her without giving herself away. Already Elsie's back at the sink peeling the apple, hair dangling into her thin face. The cook hasn't noticed a thing.

The cook dips her hand into a pot. She sprinkles salt into the soup, then pulls open the oven and peers in. The roast hisses back at her. Even from where Jane stands she feels the lick of the heat. Already her back is uncomfortably sticky, and despite the fact that she has been sitting most of the day—in carts, in trains—she would do anything to pull out one of the chairs ranged around the table and let herself down onto it. Her stomach is roiling, and she has the strange sense of herself as being less substantial here than she ever was in Devon. How is it, then, that she feels her presence is a nuisance, when she's doing nothing more than standing at the side of a long wooden table loaded with plates and cutlery and trays?

The kitchen is smaller than she'd expected from outside, and grimier. Soot clings to walls that must once have been white but now are grey and hung with cobwebs. The gas lamps shed a sallow light that catches in the laundry overhead and leaves the corners dark. In one corner she catches a flicker of movement—beetles, or something larger. She shivers. More than anything she'd like to take off her coat, to lie down and close her eyes to shut out this new place that she's sold herself to—because that, she thinks, is what it comes down to. She has sold herself for fourteen pounds a year to clean up other people's dirt. Ladies are ladies because they don't get their hands dirty—it didn't take her long to understand that. As for the likes of her, they're not to expect anything better, not being born to it.

The door on the far side of the room opens and the stout man who opened the front door comes in. "Ah," he says. "I see you found your way to the right entrance." He shuts the door behind him in a manner both graceful and final. "But how long did it take you, my dear? I find you still in your coat." He glances at her, and at her hat, which she's holding.

What a sight she must look, she thinks—her head uncovered, her hair untidy because she hasn't had time to put it straight, and who knows what soot motes on her face from the train and this filthy city.

He comes towards the table, light on his feet as though about to dance. "My dear—" he starts. Then lifts one pale eyebrow. "Your name?"

"Jane, sir. Jane Wilbred."

"Wilbred? That's a familiar name. Now, why is it familiar?" He lets his eyes rest on her face as though he will find the answer there.

"It's a common enough name in Devon, sir."

"Ah. Indeed." He presses his lips together in a way that signals he is not convinced. "Well, Jane Wilbred, if you want my advice, you'll make yourself useful. You are here to work, not to—" he pauses "—not to stand about or be waited on. Maybe Mrs. Johnson needs a hand preparing dinner. Maybe the table needs to be laid for our evening meal." His voice is gentle but his eyes are not. They hold hers uncomfortably long.

"Yes, sir; yes, of course. I'm sorry."

For a moment she thinks Mrs. Johnson—for that must be the name of the cook—will explain that she told Jane not to take off her coat, that she should wait out of the way. But Mrs. Johnson busies herself with the soup. She doesn't even turn around.

Jane has to tug at her coat to get it off her arms—it's tight, meant for a slightly smaller woman, though God knows, she's not exactly large herself. Indeed, it would be hard for anyone to have become large on the meager food that the orphanage provided all those years that she was growing into a young woman.

Then she unwinds a woollen muffler from around her neck, and together with her coat lays it over her box at the end of the room. Now she feels naked, despite her print dress. It has a design of tight rosebuds and leaves. It's not one she would have picked. The fabric was her Christmas gift from Mrs. Saunders the year before, but what kind of gift was that, to be given fabric for a work dress, and to have to pay out of her wages to have it made up? She wouldn't have had the time to sew it herself, even if she'd known how, and though they'd been taught sewing at the orphanage it hadn't amounted to much. Hemming, darning, making aprons—skills to fit them for a life of serving others.

Her aprons are packed in her box. Still, once she has smoothed her dress with her hands, she approaches the cook. "What needs to be done, Mrs. Johnson?" she says, and glances behind her at the table, at the piles of plates and the trays waiting to be laden.

Mrs. Johnson is lifting a pot of potatoes from the stove. "Elsie," she snaps, and the girl steps to the side, wet hands lifted high. In the gaslight they look huge—red and glistening, bent at the joints like an old woman's, as though she has been peeling and scrubbing for so much of her young life that they have grown into the shapes best suited for holding knives and brushes, but not good for much else. Elsie closes her eyes as Mrs. Johnson tips the potatoes into a colander, then shakes it vigorously. Steam swells around them, gathering on the windows, which show nothing except the darkness outside.

When Jane sees her slide the potatoes back into the pot she says, "I'll mash them for you. I can do that to help."

"No you won't. There's the table to see to."

From over at the table the stout man calls out, "Mrs. Johnson is particular about her potatoes. You wouldn't want to be taking over her work, now would you? Not unless you have aspirations." He lingers over the last word in an unpleasant way.

She makes herself look from him to the table, to make her tired thoughts come together. "How many will we be for supper, Mrs. Johnson?"

Mrs. Johnson is working the masher through the potatoes, but she looks up. "Five. Only five, as you can see." She nods to the pile of plates and the cutlery heaped on top. But there's no room to set them out—the table's taken up with a chopping board and a long fish dressed with herbs waiting for the oven. The cook watches her, and gives a sigh that billows out with the steam from the potatoes. "The bread—cut the bread. Fetch the butter. And bring out the rest of the pie—Mr. Cartwright likes a bit of pie after his dinner." As though surely Jane should know all of this already, from where the bread is kept, to the butler's name, to his liking for pie after dinner.

She cannot do this, she thinks, she cannot work in this place, with these people. Her cheek twitches and she presses her fingers against it. Think, she tells herself, think. Yet even as she looks around the kitchen for the bread box, the knife drawer, the pantry where the pie must be, she notices—dinner, not supper. This is a whole new world, one she doesn't know her way around. She wants to ask—where is the bread? The knife? But Mr. Cartwright has unfolded a newspaper, and Mrs. Johnson is cutting chunks of butter into the potatoes. As for Elsie, she has retreated to the scullery.

The clock above the stove is so grimed with soot and dust it has faded into the grey of the wall. Mrs. Johnson glances up at it, then tips the soup from the heavy pot into the tureen, clicking her tongue against the roof of her mouth.

When the door to the area swings open she spins around, the pot pressed against her apron, her face flushed with effort. "Sarah," she hisses, "Mr. Cartwright has already sounded the gong for dinner. You're going to catch it if you're found out, and you know it."

In the doorway stands a young woman with a delicate face, and a small hat pinned above blond curls. "Oh, Mrs. J.," she says in a singsong, "you *know* I always make it back in time."

She gives a smile, but Mrs. Johnson isn't looking; she's shaking the last drops of soup into the tureen. So Sarah turns her smile on Jane. Tugging off one glove, she holds out a hand. "You must be our new housemaid," she says, giving Jane's fingers a squeeze. "I've been waiting for you to get here—it's been more than I could do to get everything done by myself this last couple of weeks." She looks past her to the corner of the room where Jane's coat and hat lie across her box. "Goodness, Mrs. J., haven't you even shown her up to her room yet?"

Mrs. Johnson wipes her hands on a cloth and snaps back, "With you out all this time, just when did I have the chance? It's an early dinner upstairs tonight, as I've told you a dozen times—we've been all in a rush."

Sarah gives a laugh. She whisks off her coat and tosses it over Jane's, lifts off her hat, and takes her cap and apron from where they're hanging behind the door. "Well, here I am now, ready and willing," she announces. She takes the soup tureen from Mrs. Johnson, then sweeps out of the room and up the stairs.

Mrs. Johnson runs the back of her hand over her forehead, and it comes away glistening with sweat. "Elsie," she calls. Then again, "*El*sie. Get in here."

Elsie comes through the doorway from the scullery and leans her hip against the table. A smell of soap and hot grease hangs about her.

"Now," says Mrs. Johnson as she nods at Jane, "let's get your box upstairs." By which she means that Jane and Elsie must carry it, large and heavy though it is. For a moment Jane suspects that Elsie will do nothing more than look down at it with her hands knotted together, for she stands like that until Mrs. Johnson swats at her bare arms with a cloth and says, "We can't be waiting all day."

Jane reaches down behind her back for one end of the box, and Elsie picks up the other. She expects that the girl will not be much help, but all of a sudden she feels the other end lifted high. Of course, she thinks. For although Elsie is thin, like her she must have spent years carrying scuttles of coal and buckets of hot water.

Together they follow Mrs. Johnson out of the kitchen and up the narrow stairs at the back of the house, up past the main floor, past the first floor, on up to a dimly lit corridor that must be right under the roof. Mrs. Johnson opens a door at the far end and tells her, "You're sharing with Sarah. Your bed's the one beneath the window." She steps back to let her in. "You'll want to tidy yourself up. I'll see you downstairs in ten minutes."

Between them she and Elsie get her box to the end of her bed. Jane dusts off her hands and opens her mouth to thank the girl. But already Elsie's skirts are disappearing around the door, then she's gone.

*E*ven with her knees hugged up to her chest, Jane can't get warm. She pulls the sheet over her head to hold the warmth of her breath close to her body. It isn't just the cold that is keeping her awake, though God knows, with a draughty window above her bed and no fire in the hearth, this room is icy. Nor is it the ache in her ribs from when she fell against the railings. No, what keeps her awake is the quick-quick squeezing of her heart. Her muscles—in her arms, her legs, her neck—all feel stiff, ready for her to flee this place. She wonders if the Saunderses would have her back. Maybe their new girl isn't working out. Maybe she's already broken some of Mrs. Saunders's best china tea set.

They'd keep her, though. That's the point—to train up girls and make them useful. It's Mrs. Saunders's favorite word: girls like Jane need to be *useful,* and they need ladies like Mrs. Saunders to make them *useful.* Maybe, thinks Jane, that's the only way in which Mrs. Saunders is *useful,* because she wouldn't dream of carrying a tray or putting coal on the fire, or even washing out her own teacup.

I'm ungrateful, she tells herself. If the Saunderses hadn't taken her on, what would have become of her? The thought of it makes her feel smaller and more miserable.

She would stretch out her legs to relieve the cramp in them but she's only now begun to feel warm. So she holds herself and listens to Sarah's soft breathing in the bed only a couple of feet away. She doesn't seem ill at ease. In fact, she seems content in this strange household. But if everything here is as it should be, then is she the one who is all wrong? She has tried telling herself so since she lay down in this cold bed an hour ago, but she can't make herself believe it.

Her last evening in Teignton—only yesterday!—Mrs. Saunders asked her into the parlor. Jane stood on the edge of the rug, careful not to block the warmth of the fire from her mistress. Mrs. Saunders said, "You be a good girl, now, you hear me? I've given Mrs. Bentley a fair idea of your character, and your history. She must be a true Christian woman to bother with you." The words hung there, like a cobweb between them. "Now, you listen to your new mistress, you obey her in everything. And when you are not in her presence, you must obey the upper servants because they are her surrogates." The word sounded new on Mrs. Saunders's lips, straight out of one of her books that told her what to say to her servants, as though if only you talk in the right way you can persuade them into working more hours than there are in the day. "And if," continued Mrs. Saunders as she looked into the fire, "things are not as they should be, you must stand firm." She shifted her gaze to Jane. "Do you understand me? Because your character, Jane, will be at stake."

She'd thought she had understood. Now, though—now things are less clear. The Bentley household is not what she expected, yet what does she know? Only the orphanage, the vicarage, what little Mrs. Phelps told her of her previous positions. Still, this is what she has noticed so far, and this is what keeps her awake: there is something upside-down about this place. After the early dinner upstairs, the servants sat down to their own meal. Mrs. Johnson served them some of the soup meant for the family, but that wasn't all. They had thick slices of the roast, too, and mashed potatoes with gravy.

This is not how things should be. Didn't the servants have their dinner at midday? Wasn't an early supper of bread with cheese and some cold meat more than enough in the evening? And to eat the same food as upstairs—to Jane this is beyond decadent. It is almost obscene.

As she lies curled into the warmth of her own body she wonders: here in London are servants not a different class of people from their employers? Maybe Mrs. Saunders was wrong for having made her and Mrs. Phelps eat two-day-old bread and cold, boiled mutton, while the good food—the roast veal and new potatoes, the milk puddings and jellies—that Mrs. Phelps made and Jane carried upstairs was kept for her and the Reverend.

No, she tells herself, that's not right. Mrs. Phelps would have known if they were being hard done by, and Reverend and Mrs. Saunders were religious people. Even having such a thought is unforgivable. Still, she remembers the words she caught one afternoon as she closed the door behind her, Mrs. Saunders saying to her niece, "I just love silk—how could one not?" The hallway was empty—the Reverend in his study, Mrs. Phelps plucking chickens down in the kitchen—so she'd pressed her ear against the door. There was talk of Mrs. Vincent's ugly new dress, of Miss Foster, who'd just got married and could speak French and play the piano beautifully but who had not the slightest idea how to run a household, let alone manage her servants. "They'll rob you blind," Mrs. Saunders trumpeted. "They get through tea and sugar like nobody's business. People of their class simply do not understand it all has to be paid for and..."

Jane's hands had clenched into fists, her nails had bitten into the flesh of her palms. "You bitch," she said softly. "I'll get you back, I will, even if you never know it."

There was a cough, and she turned to find the Reverend standing a few feet away.

"Is there something the matter?" he said. "No? Then I'm sure you have better things to do than standing around listening at doors." She'd hurried off, holding down the urge to cry, because God had intervened, hadn't He? Hadn't He brought the Reverend out of his study to catch her?

Outside a cat is yowling. Its cries echo between the high walls as though it's trapped in a well. There are voices, too, small and far away. Pulling down the covers, she listens, but from up here it's hard to tell if they belong to men or women. Plus the coldness of the air clings to her skin now that she's warmed herself under the blankets, so she buries herself beneath them again.

It's late and she should sleep—she's tired out and tomorrow she'll have to be up at six. She tries to still her mind, but it courses back through the evening. After dinner was finished she was sent upstairs with a tray to clear the dining room. She hoped to see her employers, to catch a glimpse of them, to hear their voices at least. She opened the door an inch or two and listened to the sounds in the hallway. There was nothing save for the dull ticking of a tall clock by the stairs. No voices, no music, no laughter, no creak of feet on floorboards. She wondered where they had gone out to. Were they sitting in a crowded drawing room under chandeliers? Were they playing cards, or listening to music? Isn't that what ladies and gentlemen did?

She had set down the tray on the sideboard and loaded it with the dessert plates and glasses, removed the candelabra, the fruit bowl, the top-heavy glass tazza of nuts in the center of the table, everything from the tablecloth. There'd only been two people for dinner, sitting at opposite ends of a table that could have sat six. One of them— Mrs. Bentley, she thought, for it was at the place setting where the bare branches of a small sprig of grapes were left behind, not the broken shells of nuts—had laid a napkin over a spill on the tablecloth. The stain of red wine already showed through it. Somehow this made her feel for this lady she had not yet met, whom she knew only through the sinuous handwriting of her letter. She imagined her graceful in a green silk gown, with her hair piled up on top of her head, laughing and listening to her husband. A couple, she thought, as elegant as this room with its high ceiling and molded plaster cornices, its intricate Turkey carpet, its dark red wallpaper and curtains so long and wide they looked like the folds of a dress.

By the time she'd cleared the table and folded the cloth and swept up the crumbs from the carpet, she was sweating. The fire had died down to embers, but the embers were fiercely hot. Maybe it was the heat, maybe the tiredness that gripped her suddenly, but as she lifted the tray it knocked the tazza, and with the tray in her hands she could do nothing as it tipped off the sideboard. By a miracle it missed the bare floor and hit the carpet. And there it lay, apparently undamaged.

She set down the tray and crouched to pick up the tazza. A warning, she told herself, and she deserved it—oh yes, because she was a liar. A miserable, sinning liar who had already deceived this new mistress of hers. It hadn't seemed like a sin. There was Mrs. Saunders's letter on the hallway table, and in her large, loose hand across the front she'd written, "Mrs. R. Bentley, No. 32 Cursitor Road, London." Jane's character. The shape of her future folded into an envelope, a malignant genie about to be released. Almost without thought she'd slipped it into her pocket and hurried downstairs. Mrs. Saunders was off visiting in the village, the Reverend in Exeter until the next day. She'd told Mrs. Phelps she was going to see to a hole in the study curtain and fetched needle and thread. She couldn't help knocking, though she knew the room was empty—the autumn sunlight dreary, the fireplace cold. There was paper in the top drawer of the desk, and pens, and pencils, and India rubber, and she set them all out on the top. Then she eased a knife under the seal of the envelope. She had to read the words over and over to convince herself of what they said. And though a cold hard fury swept through her, she wouldn't let herself tear up the letter. Instead she beat her fists against her legs, over and over, until they stung. Then she set to work, the letter held up against the window, each line traced in pencil onto a fresh sheet of paper. Each line except "the child of a brutal murderer" and "her unfortunate parentage, from whose influence, one can only hope,

Jane has been saved." There her pencil paused. After staring beyond the plump letters into the garden with its forlorn bushes, she simply left them out. She moved the paper over so that the words lined up differently and the stain of her past was gone. Then she sat at the desk to trace over the words in ink, and gently erased the pencil marks. At any moment Mrs. Saunders would be home, so she hurried— finishing the letter and folding it back into the envelope; ripping a hole in the curtain that she could repair because Mrs. Phelps might check; slipping outside and running to the village to drop the letter in the pillar-box without asking Mrs. Phelps. Afterwards she was blamed for being gone when she was needed, and for making a slip-shod job of the curtain. She hung her head, not from guilt but to counteract the heady sensation of having been relieved of a burden she'd carried for as long as she could remember.

In the heat of the Bentleys' dining room she had closed her eyes and whispered, "I'm sorry for what I did. I won't deceive again, I promise, Lord; oh yes, I promise. You'll see. I can be a good and faithful servant to my new mistress, and to You." However, when she glanced at what she held in her hands she felt a rush of panic: the pedestal of the thing was intact, but the glass dish had broken in two. Where was it? Her skirts were in the way, so she moved, stepping to the side, her foot coming down just as her eye caught the shiny surface. Too late. It cracked beneath her boot like an egg. Not into two big pieces that might have been fixed, but into a hundred jagged bits. She got down on her knees and there, in the shadow of the table, began to sob. So much for bettering herself. So much for making a fresh start.

A creak of the door handle and she jumped—Sarah, her smile falling away as her eyes caught Jane's. She saw the remains of the tazza and said, "Oh my—what's happened here?" With a glance over her shoulder she pushed the door shut. Coming close she said, "Oh dear. Not much we can do to fix it, is there?"

"I've ruined everything."

"You've ruined the tazza, that's for certain." She crouched down.

"Don't worry—it'll be our secret. I know where Mrs. Bentley buys her tableware. We can get another."

"How can I pay for it? I don't have enough."

"You have something saved, don't you?"

She took a small breath. To tell the truth would be to leave herself with no money at all between this strange household and ruin. So she said, "Two pounds. It's all I've got."

"You can give me your wages every month until you've paid me back the rest." Sarah gave a small smile, then laid a hand on Jane's shoulder. "All right?"

She could have said no. She could have gone downstairs and told Mrs. Johnson what she'd done and endured whatever punishment was her due: having to work on her half days off until she'd made amends; being sent away because, on her very first day, she'd failed the Bentleys. Instead she'd let Sarah help her gather the pieces of the tazza into a napkin and take them away.

In this cold bed, in this cold room, her relief now wears thin. Already she has resorted to deception again. And not only has she lied to Sarah, but worse still she's in her debt. She presses her cheek into the pillow. She remembers how Sarah's fingers closed over the two sovereigns, and the tightness she felt in her chest. Now she wishes she'd at least asked how much a new tazza would cost. All she has left is the half-sovereign, a sixpence, and a few pennies, and those she has hidden in a slip of paper at the bottom of her box.

It grieves her to think that she is spoiling her chances of doing well, as though Mrs. Saunders was right: with a mother like hers, who stole and murdered, she will have to fight her criminal tendencies. *Criminal tendencies.* She imagines them as shadows that slip out of her bodily self and take on a life of their own: a wanton self with rouged cheeks, a hard-eyed self with quick hands, a sneaking self that hides in the dark and glints viciously when it moves. Maybe she should have burnt the photograph of her mother that lies at the bottom of her box. Maybe it has set a curse upon her: her mother in her best hat with a feather drooping from it, her chin raised, one end of her mouth lifted. If you look carefully, there's a hardness to her eyes and faint lines around her mouth that suggest a cruel nature. Or is that a trick of the light? Still, it makes her afraid to look too closely at herself in the mirror.

It takes her a long time to fall asleep. Eventually, though, the shadows slip away and leave her in a dream: she is clearing a dining table so long that the candles at its far end look distant as stars.

In a chair by the fire, Mina Bentley brushes her hair. She is still a young woman, a beautiful woman even, though there is something of the fox about her—in her nose, which is a little too sharp; in the point of her chin; in her hair, which glints orange in the glow of the fire and the candles that light this room.

This has long been a habit of hers—to end the day with a cup of tea and the strokes of a brush against her head. Except, until a few weeks ago, it was Marie who brushed her hair. Robert has told her to send up for Sarah, or for Price—what else is that woman, if not a lady's maid?—but she never has. What pleasure would there be in having that sour-mouthed woman wait on her? As for Sarah—she doesn't trust her. Sarah's eyes slide away at the wrong moments, and she has a tendency to tilt her head in a manner that is almost insolent. As it is, she has had no choice but to call her upstairs to fasten her into her dress every morning, to help her out of her dress each night, to bear away her soiled clothes and replace them with those that have been cleaned.

Tonight she sent Sarah away early to see to the new maid. An excuse. But better that than catching the way her eyes flit around the room. She is sure that Sarah takes advantage of the times when she is alone in here to rummage through her drawers, to try the lid of her jewelry box and her portable desk. And Mina has noticed her taking off up the area steps at odd times of the day—to post letters, apparently, or take a message to Beecher's about the meat. Always some explanation, given reluctantly because Mina is not the mistress of this household, she's not *the* Mrs. Bentley. She can see the servants' resentment in the way they stand so stiffly when she calls them and in the clipped way they reply to her. Ever since *the* Mrs. Bentley's seizure, they've been a law unto themselves—at least until she and Robert arrived.

Let them hate me then, she thinks. Just let them see who is going to win.

There is a click, a squeak of hinges as the door opens, and she turns. Robert. He comes over and rubs her shoulder, then presses a kiss against the side of her neck. He takes the brush out of her hands and runs it through her hair. "How's that?" he says.

"Delicious." She lifts her head a little, even though he presses too hard and the bristles scratch her scalp.

"I'm sorry," he says. "I was too abrupt." He stands against the side of the chair and she leans over so that her shoulder rests against his hip.

"You talk about it as though it wouldn't make any difference to me."

"Must we live the rest of our lives in France? Bertillon can't pay me for my work—sometimes I feel I should pay *him* for all the trouble he's taken with me." He sighs. "We've always known that your inheritance would only be enough for a few years." He pulls the brush through her hair again. "And we haven't been as careful as we might."

She glances up at him. Even in this soft light he looks tired out with worry—their money fast disappearing, his mother ill. She wants to cup his face in her hands and press her mouth against his—it will be all right, she wants to tell him, somehow, if only they can leave this city soon. Instead she turns towards the fire and says, "I've grown used to Paris. I feel at home there."

"As though the city I was brought up in can't be your home, too?" He gives a small laugh, then leans closer. "Is London really so dreary? You have it laid out at your feet—all the museums, the galleries. The shops, too. But you sit in the house, day after day."

"Not every day. And your mother—"

"She has Price to nurse her. Mrs. Longman has offered to take you around. She said so again tonight. She'd be only too happy to introduce you, and yet you stay home."

"It hardly seems worth it when we're only here a few weeks." She takes the brush from his hand and sets it down on the table beside her.

For a moment his hands hover, empty, then the weight of them settles on her shoulders. "If we stay you'll need friends like her."

"With your mother so ill, someone needs to keep an eye on the household."

"Oh Mina." He gives her a squeeze. "I'm certain the household runs itself. Mrs. Johnson and Cartwright have been here so long, is there much for you to do other than look over the menu?"

She presses her hands onto her knees. "There was that business with the housemaid, and a new one to be found." She takes a breath. "And no one had gone over the books in months. The bills are far higher than they should be. Servants can't be left to manage things without supervision. They get careless—after all, what does it matter to them how much the bill from the butcher is, or how much butter is being used? I've done what I can, but I'm not their mistress and they know that. It makes a difference, you know—it makes everything more difficult."

He bends so low that she feels his breath on the side of her neck. "Who'd have thought you'd turn into such a tyrant?" He kisses her just below the ear. "When Mother recovers she'll be grateful for all you've done, I'm sure. Plus you've smoothed the way for when Henry gets here."

She watches the flames shifting amongst the coals. "Then will we go home?"

His voice is low, his mouth close to her ear. "How much longer can we live there without an income? Mother can't help—she has barely enough to keep this place going."

"I know," she says gently, and turns her face to his. It is all she can see—the old-wood brown of his eyes, the thick arc of his moustache, the surprisingly delicate pink of his lips just beneath it. She lays a hand on his cheek, his moustache prickling her palm. "Robert," she says, "I do understand. But you could find yourself a position in France, surely." She slides her nose against his and lets her eyes close. "I think I would die here. I really do."

"Is London so bad?" He shifts his head a little, whispers. "Does it remind you of him? Is that it?"

Him. Her first husband. The man who haunts the edges of their marriage, because they barely speak of him.

She could tell him *Yes, that's it*, and they would not have this conversation again. But she can't bear to. To think about him, to mention him even—it conjures up the man and their life together. "It's not that. I've grown so used to Paris. Life here—it wouldn't be much of a life at all."

He laughs and stands straight. "I should be grateful you never took it into your head to move to Bombay, like Henry did. You'd be wearing a sari and eating curry three times a day, and I'd have a devil of a job to civilize you enough for London society."

She gives him a smile. "I'd have caused a sensation—and maybe you'd have rather enjoyed that."

"You are the most provoking woman I know."

"Maybe your brother's taken on all sorts of Indian ways. Maybe he's bringing an Indian servant or two with him."

"You don't know Henry. No wonder he's never found a woman to marry him—he's as inflexible as a cricket bat. I'm sure he demanded oxtail soup and suet pudding from his Indian cook, just as if he were at home." He sighs and walks over to the bed and sits on its edge. "I think it would be best if we stayed until he's settled in. Besides, Sir Jonathan is interested in my work. I should make the most of the opportunity. It may lead somewhere—he can get me into other prisons. The more research I do, the better."

"We agreed to stay six weeks at the most." She tries to keep her voice light, but it comes out strained.

"Darling, if it's not a matter of..." His voice hangs in the air. "I mean, if it's simply a matter of you feeling at home in Paris, it can't make a great difference if we stay here a little longer. And it would offer advantages, don't you think?" His voice slips away as she twists around to look at him. Her hair is still loose and falls around her shoulders. But her face has a severity to it, an expression that he has only rarely seen in the four years they have been married.

"I realize that it is not easy to live in another woman's household, even if she's sick and unable to manage it herself. I realize that you'd rather be anywhere than London. But I need to be here—and I need you at my side. What would I be without you?" His eyes hold hers for a moment, then he looks down at the carpet.

The start of a sigh leaves her mouth, but she's careful not to let him hear it. Instead she smiles. "My love, you are a terrible flatterer."

"Is that so bad?" He leans back onto the bed, his head propped on one hand.

She walks over to him. "You know that I can defend myself, don't you? I might even retaliate."

"I doubt it." He reaches for her hands and pulls her to him. "What weapons could you have hidden away?

She lets him draw her down onto the bed on top of him, and she laughs.

"Oh my darling," he says into her ear, "how I wish I'd been the first to find you." Then he presses his lips into the soft skin under her chin and licks it longingly.

There is a knock, a subdued if businesslike *rat-a-tat-tat*. Barely do they have time to sit up, to swing their feet to the floor, when the door opens. Cartwright, his face stiff, his eyes fixed on Robert's as though he cannot bear to understand how they came to be sitting on the bed together. "Sir?" he says. "I have finished locking up. Will you be needing anything else tonight?"

CHAPTER 3

In her fitful dreams she has loaded trays with plates and glasses and heavy tureens, straining her arms against their weight, on and on so that when Sarah wakes her at six o'clock, she is as tired as if she has worked all night.

The candle throws startling shadows against the walls of the stairway. Down she walks, candle in one hand, chamber pot in the other. Her boots thud against the wooden steps and she wonders—should she have waited to put them on until she got downstairs? Can the Bentleys hear every footfall, and will they complain? She's already late, what with having had no time to unpack her box the night before and trying to find her dress and an apron and a clean pair of stockings by the shifting light of this small candle.

Her bladder is tight and painful. She couldn't bring herself to crouch over her chamber pot again while Sarah watched from her bed. The pressure makes her go a little faster, but she doesn't know these stairs, and going around the corner, her heel catches on the edge of a riser—she stumbles, wax drips onto her fingers, the chamber pot tilts and sloshes. Just in time she steadies herself against the wall. To have fallen—she imagines the pot tumbling from her hands, tipping its contents down the stairs, breaking apart with a crash that wakes the whole household—what humiliation! She stretches her fingers to loosen the wax hardening on them, then, despite the burning urge in her crotch, puts down her feet as gently as she can, one step after the other, down one flight after the next of unfamiliar stairs, all the way to the sudden hardness of the basement's stone floor. From the kitchen she hears the scrape of a chair pushed back. Someone is up. Someone who coughs hard and long. She creeps away down the dark corridor, all the way to the water closet at the end. And there, in the tiny, dank room, she lifts her skirts and settles herself onto the seat with a flood of relief.

Afterwards there's nowhere to leave the emptied chamber pot except in the darkness under the stairs, so she pushes it out of sight. Later, she'll carry it back upstairs. Later, whenever that might be.

In the kitchen she finds Elsie crouched at the stove, breathing life into a sickly flame. The light shifts over her bony face. She looks as though she has never had enough to eat. Next to the table waits a cinder pail and a housemaid's box.

"Them's for you," Elsie says over her shoulder. "And keep it quiet on the stairs—Mr. Cartwright don't like being woken up too early." She jerks her head to the doorway and the stairwell beyond, and Jane understands: Mr. Cartwright sleeps in the room under the stairs. Maybe she's already woken him and will find out how bad his temper can be.

With the box set on a chair, Jane lifts the lid: blacking and blacking brushes, emery paper, a dry leather. "What do I do about sweeping the carpets?" she says. "Is there a back garden where I can get grass?"

Elsie swings her head towards her. She lets out a snort of laughter. "Garden? A garden? Not likely." She bends back to the fire.

"Then what should I use to keep down the dust?"

Elsie's cheeks fill out as she blows on the flames dancing through the kindling. "Tea leaves, like everyone else. Didn't you rinse out the used ones from yesterday before you went to bed?" She sighs, then lifts her chin towards the scullery. "Jar of them in there."

As she steps away from the stove, Jane catches a movement at her feet, something small and quick scurrying across the stone floor. Beetles. Small ones like dark fingernails, fat ones as long as her fingers. She stamps at them and doesn't care if she crushes them or not as long as they are scared into running off. In their confusion they turn this way and that. One runs onto her boot and she kicks wildly, but who knows if it has been sent flying? In the dark it is impossible to tell. She shakes her skirts hard, for all the good it does—no beetle drops out, and now she cannot rid herself of the idea of it clinging amongst the folds.

"Don't have beetles where you come from?" Elsie asks.

"All over the floor like this? No."

"Had them every place I've worked." She lets out a sharp laugh. "It doesn't mean nothing and the light gets rid of the bleeding things." She sniffs. "The thing is, they creep all over you in the night if you sleep down here. You learn quick to keep your mouth closed."

Jane's disgust shows—the thought of it, quick legs and feelers reaching into her mouth, touching her tongue, testing the damp warmth as a place to hide.

Elsie lets out another laugh. She pulls her skirts around her and crouches at the fire again. Tenderly, she blows on the flames. "Come on, now, come on, my chicks," she says, and feeds them some small pieces of tinder.

In the scullery Jane finds tea leaves in a jar by the sink. The water she uses to rinse them is cold enough to sting her hands, but she keeps going, handful after handful, squeezing them out as hard as she can. Of course they're wet and stick together—what use will they be on the carpets? Maybe, she thinks, she'll have to manage without. Maybe the dust won't be that bad.

Elsie has her hands held out to the fire. She calls over, "You'd better get a move on. Lizzie was never this late getting started."

Lizzie. Until this moment Jane hasn't given much thought to the fact that she has taken over this situation from another girl—but of course she has, just as the young girl from the orphanage came to take over from her at the Saunderses'. She's only the most recent of a succession of maids whose bodies have made a hollow running down the center of the hard, narrow mattress upstairs, whose hands have rubbed dirt into the wooden handle of the housemaid's box as they lugged it from room to room. "And where did Lizzie start?"

Elsie breathes hard into the fire. Jane watches the way her cheeks billow out, the shine of the light on her eyes. She's just about to ask her again when Elsie turns around. "With the dining room, seeing as the family'll be needing it for breakfast."

Jane lifts the box. She should get going, up to the empty rooms upstairs to clean grates and lay new fires. She hesitates, though. She asks, "Is this a hard place?"

"Hard? They're all hard." There's a twist to Elsie's mouth. "Isn't a mistress in the whole bleeding city who doesn't think she's paying you too much, never mind how hard you work. And there's not one of them'll let you work your way up. Can't bear it, can they? Can't bear the idea of paying you a bit more than before."

"Is that why Lizzie left? To better herself?"

Elsie sits back on her heels. Into the half-moon of light around her creep the shiny bodies of beetles. "This place didn't use to be so bad. But that's all changed for now. Lizzie found that out."

From somewhere close by comes the groan of hinges. Jane glances towards the doorway, but she doesn't step away, not yet. Instead she asks, "So she left?" She hopes she doesn't sound too eager to know. This is not her business—that's what Mrs. Saunders would have said.

Elsie lets herself down on a chair and gives a grin that shows teeth all tilted this way and that. "Oh yeah," she says. "We've got two mistresses here. One of them never minded us as long as we did our work. But this new one—she says we're all wrong." She shakes her head. "Oh Lord yes, we need to be put right. Lizzie found that out. Mrs. Robert said she had a follower, and next thing we knew Lizzie had packed her box and was gone. Didn't even have time to eat the dinner set out for her."

"That doesn't sound fair."

"Fair? Isn't a matter of fair. Them upstairs do what they want. And as for the likes of us, we're not supposed to even look at a man. But *they* do, don't they? How else do they get themselves husbands? Have you thought about that?" She lets out a hoot of a laugh. She rocks herself forward, her grimy hands gripping her arms. "They get to have their fun, don't they? Making themselves pretty for the men, all those dresses and ribbons, and going to dances, and stealing kisses whenever they can like they—"

"You're forgetting yourself," Jane says quietly, and she feels like Mrs. Saunders. It's exactly the sort of thing she used to say, all prim and proper, the meaning skewed, since what did it mean except that you'd forgotten to pretend to be someone you weren't?

In the doorway stands Mrs. Johnson, a candle in her hand. "I'll thank you to keep a civil tongue in your head, Elsie. And you, Jane, you can't be standing around gossiping when there's upstairs to be getting on with. Get yourself up there or you'll still be at it when Mr. and Mrs. Robert come down."

And so a morning of sweeping and blacking and starting fires begins, a morning that seems to go on forever. By the time Sarah fetches her down for breakfast the sky has lightened to a sullen grey and a miserable rain is falling. Already the bottom of her apron is filthy from when she stumbled in the coal cellar, and her hands are so black that she has to wash them three times before she can sit down to eat. Bread and butter, sugared tea. She is hungry, but her stomach is so tight she can barely eat. Instead the bread slips around her mouth, and the tea when she drinks it leaves a scorched trail down to her stomach. Across the table Sarah is watching her. "Drink it up," she says. "You've earned it." Then she gives a funny laugh, and Jane realizes how she means it: she's worked hard, all right, but tea and sugar are part of their wages. Not the good tea the family drinks—no, the sort of tea that leaves dust at the bottom of the cup.

There's a knock at the door and Elsie pulls it open. It's the baker's boy with a basket on his arm. "All right, Mrs. J.?" he calls. "Got your bread and buns, nice and fresh." He stares at Jane from under his cap. "Got new help, have you then?"

Mrs. Johnson swats at him with her cloth. "Any business of yours, is it?" she snaps. Elsie goes to carry the bread to the pantry, but Mrs Johnson clucks her tongue at her. "Put it on the table where I can see it. Haven't had a chance to write it down. You're going to mess up my accounts, you are."

The Dark Lantern

Even after Elsie has pushed the door closed a coldness lingers in small currents that curl around the room, making Jane shiver, swaying the laundry above her head. Mrs. Johnson glances up at the clock, then lifts the lid on a pan. Soon the air is thick and warm again and filled with the smell of hot kippers. "Get a move on," she tells Sarah. "They'll be down before long. It'll be your hard luck if you're not finished."

Mr. Cartwright opens the door and glances in. "Let's be having you," he says.

And so Sarah stands, adjusts her cap, smoothes her apron. Then the silver domes that have added a touch of brightness to the room are gone, and Jane is left staring at the dull gleam of copper pans hanging from the racks along the walls.

At the stove Mrs. Johnson bangs her spoon against the edge of a pot. "You've got the bedrooms to do, love," she tells Jane. *Love*. Yet coming out of Mrs. Johnson's mouth it is a hard word, empty as a husk. "Up the stairs to the first floor. Quick now."

From outside Jane hears the rattle of a carriage and the cries of a costermonger, though what he is selling she can't make out. The world outside is large as the sea, and that at least is something she is familiar with: the English Channel that can turn grey as stone, that can heave and crash and blur into the clouds or settle into a sharp line against the sky. As she brushes crumbs off her apron she remembers the smell of it, that mix of fish, brine, and wet sand. Her eyes prickle and her throat tightens. Stupid, she tells herself, to feel sad about leaving Teignton. She forces herself to remember the way Mrs. Saunders would call her up to her sitting room to read to her from a book called *The Servants' Friend,* would read from it as though she were in a pulpit, instructions on keeping oneself clean, and scorning pomps and vanities because they were the road to ruin. Jane would sit there, sewing and listening, glancing at the bottom of Mrs. Saunders's silk dress, the full skirt of it that must have taken yards and yards to make, at the slim waist she had thanks to a corset, at the lace she wore around her neck, at her hair coiled up all fancy on top of her head. It was all she could do not to jump out of her chair and throw the socks she was darning into Mrs. Saunders's face.

Even the memory of such humiliation is not enough to stop her tears now. She gets up quickly and rushes out of the kitchen before Mrs. Johnson sees her lips trembling—if nothing else, the orphanage taught her not to show weakness, because others will use it against you, whether they mean to or not.

Out of the kitchen and into the stairwell she hurries, straight into a woman carrying a tray. A spoon clatters onto the tiles, and she reaches for it. This woman is not Sarah, not Mrs. Johnson or Elsie. It's a large-nosed woman in a dark dress. Jane places the spoon back on the tray, says, "Excuse me, ma'am, I'm so sorry."

The woman laughs, not all held-in like Mrs. Saunders but like a crow. " 'Ma'am'?" she says. " 'Ma'am'? That's a fine one." She goes cawing into the kitchen. "Oh, Mrs. Johnson," she calls, "did you hear that? I must be looking my best today, that's for sure."

Jane doesn't wait to hear what follows. She lifts her skirts and runs up the stairs, tears cold against her face here where the air is chilly. Of course that wasn't the mistress—carrying a tray downstairs, and at this time of the morning—what was she thinking? She retrieves the box from where she left it on the landing and carries it upstairs, though it bumps, bumps, bumps against her knee and the weight of it pulls at her sore ribs. Up through the dim light she goes—for who uses this staircase except the servants?—out into the brighter light of the first floor, where she emerges, blinking. The door of one room has been left ajar. She pushes it open: a bedroom. She carries her box over to the fireplace, then ties on her rough apron over her cotton one to catch the worst of the filth. At least it is warm in here, though the fire looks sickly in the light coming through the windows. Sarah must have lit it early this morning to take the chill off the room—it's not for the likes of the family to have to get dressed in the cold.

She flings open the windows to let in the air. She should get started on the bed, but instead here she stands, in a cold breeze peppery with the smoke of coal fires, her hands tucked under her arms as she looks out at the city. The rooftops have turned silver in the rain, and when she leans forward she can see down to the street. With both hands she holds onto the window frame to watch the gleaming tops of carriages sliding behind horses, and the dark circles of umbrellas floating beside them like strange, burnt flowers. Between them, in hats and coats and shawls, carrying baskets, holding children by the hand, move the figures of shabby people. People like her. The ones who work for a living. She has to correct herself—Reverend Saunders, Mrs. Saunders reminded her more than once, worked too. Though from what Jane saw when she brought coal or tea into his study, he spent a lot of time in an armchair by the fire with a book open on his knees. However, that didn't stop him from complaining when he sat down to dinner that he was weary to his bones.

The city is all black carriages, black hats, black umbrellas, black coats, grey sky, grey horses and, on the other side of the street, tall pale walls with dark windows. At one doorstep a maid is on her knees scrubbing, at this time in the morning—people all about who can see her ankles, and the shape of her behind as she crouches. Thank goodness, Jane tells herself, that she doesn't have to scrub the doorstep here. That must be Elsie's job. Despite the sick feeling in her stomach at being so far from everything she knows, she realizes that she has bettered herself, that at least here there is someone below her in the household to whom the very worst jobs go.

The windowsill is down by her knees, and she leans her weight on it. Her eyes follow the rooftops that roll away into the near distance like waves, spires showing amongst them like the masts of ships, before it all disappears into a pale obscurity of fog that even the rain has not washed away. So this is London. And one day soon—when she has her half day off—she will go out into its streets, and she will not be afraid, not in the daylight.

For now she sighs and turns away to the bed. On one pillow a woman's nightgown is lying limp, and on the carpet on the other side, a man's has been dropped to the floor, as though he just pulled it over his head and let it fall. She drapes them both on chairs by the window to air, then tidies the dressing table. Pots of face cream left open, a hand mirror dirty with fingerprints, a brush tangled with hair. The woman she ran into downstairs cannot be this woman's lady's maid, not when there is so much left to be done.

She sets to work tugging the hair from the brush and coiling it into the small pot on the dressing table. Next she turns her attention back to the bed and its sheets, which are already smudged with the blacks that have come through the window, then to the carpet and the grate, where the fire has shrunk to a few livid embers.

In the course of her work, this is what she discovers: that the woman who has slept in this room has long, brown hair, that she has a liking for lavender scent, that she sleeps on the left side of the bed by the window and has been reading a book in French—at least, Jane suspects it is French, because she cannot make out a word of the title—and that she is having her monthlies, because there are dark clots of blood in the chamber pot.

From the landing she hears voices on the floor below. A woman's raised in a question, a man's answering. A door closing. Then nothing more.

She carries the chamber pots down to the basement to empty in the water closet—Sarah has warned her not to use the one on the half-landing. Servants mustn't go in there except to clean. She brings down the cinder pail and carries up coal for the scuttle in the bedroom. Next she gathers up her box and the bucket she used for the coal. There's a door standing closed. Another bedroom? She isn't sure. How many people are there in this family? Are there children? She hasn't heard a baby crying, hasn't heard young voices or quick feet thumping hard across the floor. She's asked Mrs. Johnson, but she hushed her and told her to keep her mind on her work. As for Sarah, she was quicker with her own questions—Where was Jane from? Why had she left Devon?—until Jane was relieved to be sent back upstairs to sweep the drawing room.

So now she leans towards the door and listens. Nothing. To be sure, she raises her hand to knock, but it meets with air as the door jerks open.

The woman with the long nose. "Well," she says, "what's this?"

"I'm on the bedrooms. Does this one need doing?"

"Oh you are, are you?" She gives a smile that shows only her front teeth. "Fancy that. And you just happened to be cleaning by the door. Well"—she leans close, her breath full of a strange, fishy smell—"don't let me catch you with your ear up against any more doors or I'll be having a word with Mr. Cartwright. You hear me?"

There's a weak cough from deep in the room, and the woman glances over her shoulder. If she meant to keep Jane from seeing, she has failed, for between her head and the door frame Jane catches sight of an old woman—at least, she thinks it is an old woman—lying in a large bed. The room is dim, the air stale. A chair by the bed holds a tray with a bowl and a spoon and a jug of water, and brown-glass bottles of medicine.

In the couple of seconds it has taken Jane to see all of this the woman has turned back. "Already sticking your nose in where it's not wanted?" she snaps, and she pushes the door closed in Jane's face.

At two o'clock Jane is summoned to meet Mrs. Robert Bentley—not *Mrs. Bentley,* who is ill in bed, Mrs. Johnson corrected her, but her daughter-in-law, Mr. Robert's wife. She hurries to change into a clean dress, to put on her only other apron, to make sure her cap is spotless and set straight on her head and that her hands are as clean as they can be. Traces of soot and blacking are caught around the nails, and although she knows that they are faint enough to be invisible from a distance, she closes her hands around them as she stands at the drawing room door, ready to knock.

The first time she taps too softly and there is no answer. She waits, but her neck prickles. If Mr. Cartwright sees her standing here like this, he might think she is eavesdropping. So she raises her hand and raps more loudly.

"Yes, yes, come in."

The room is so high and long that it takes Jane a moment to see that on a sofa by the fireplace sits a woman in her late twenties. Her face is a little browned by the sun, as though she has only recently arrived in London; and she has a small nose; a stern, flat mouth; and long brown hair pulled up so that, somehow, it makes a gentle halo around her face. So this is the woman who likes lavender scent and books in French, who is having her monthlies. Knowing what is going on in this woman's body seems terribly wrong, and Jane looks away from the light brown eyes that are watching her.

Mrs. Robert gestures her to come closer. She stands on the rug by the fire, amongst all the pretty things of the room, feeling large and not quite clean enough. She half expects that when she moves her feet she will see dirty marks left by her boots. But she can't look down now. Mrs. Robert is talking to her. Her journey—how was her journey?

"It was fine, ma'am."

"And Mr. Smee found you without any difficulty? The stations can be so crowded."

"The carter? Yes, ma'am."

"Isn't he from your part of the country? He has an accent like yours."

She frowns. "Oh, I don't know, ma'am. I didn't ask."

The woman gives a small nod. "I'm sure you had other things on your mind. Now, have you settled in a little?"

"Yes, ma'am." Though even as she says it she thinks how very unsettled she feels, how she does not know anything, not even who lives in this house. "Yes," she says again because the enormity of having left Teignton and coming here, to London, to this house-hold, swamps her. A tremor that begins in her gut and rises through her chest threatens to reach her throat and make her voice shake. She swallows and tries a smile.

"And is this situation to your liking?"

"Oh yes, ma'am." But this doesn't seem enough—Mrs. Robert is waiting for more. "Not that I wasn't happy with Mrs. Saunders," she announces, "but I wanted to better myself."

Her mistress gives a small smile at that, a smile that seems more for herself than for the young maid standing on the rug in front of her. She says, "Ambition is a worthy motivation. Still, I hope this does not mean that you will be thinking of leaving us anytime soon."

"Oh no, ma'am, of course not." She realizes that she sounds too horrified to be sincere, and that she cannot imagine staying. This place feels too far from everything she knows to be her life, or how life should be.

"Well, then, Jane, if you work hard and are obedient and loyal, I will be a friend to you for as long as I am here."

"Thank you, ma'am."

"I'll see to it that you are trained up properly so that you are a credit to this household, and to yourself. And of course"—she smiles—"to your husband one day, should you marry."

Jane's face turns hot and she looks down at her feet. "Thank you, ma'am, I'm sure."

When she lifts her head her mistress is gazing through the window. She looks sad, Jane thinks, as though she is weighed down with worries. "We have had a difficult time of it of late," she says.

"Yes, ma'am?"

She touches the side of her face with one hand. "You don't have to flatter my sense of propriety. I find it difficult to believe that the other servants have not told you everything they think you need to know about this household."

"Oh no, ma'am. There hasn't been time for that sort of thing."

For a moment Mrs. Robert simply stares at her. "I see. Well, before there is time for that sort of thing, let me make a few things plain. Since Mrs. Bentley fell ill, this household has slipped into lazy ways. To take advantage of an elderly mistress who is unable to seek out deceptions—that is the worst sort of dishonesty, wouldn't you say?"

"Yes, ma'am."

"A mistress can only do so much. She can set an example, she can have high expectations of her staff. But she cannot watch them from sunup to sundown, nor should she. Servants who cannot be trusted cannot be kept."

Jane's shoulders stiffen. Her breath catches, and it is all that she can do to reply, "Yes, ma'am."

Mrs. Robert leans forward. In the pale light coming through the window, her face looks strangely eager. "You are to be my ally below stairs, Jane. You will tell me if you come across anything in this household that strikes you as—as not as it should be."

"How do you mean, ma'am?"

"You will be my eyes and ears. I'm putting my trust in you, do you understand?"

"Oh yes, ma'am." But even as she says it, Jane wonders what she has promised. To tell tales on Elsie, Sarah, Mrs. Johnson, and Mr. Cartwright? And if she does, will they tell tales on her?

"You're a good girl, Jane." Mrs. Robert nods for her to understand that she should leave now.

Jane walks unsteadily through the doorway and along the hall. Then she sits abruptly at the top of the stairs that lead down to the kitchen and presses the weight of her chest onto her trembling legs.

Mina lets her head sink back against the chair and closes her eyes. The girl, she thinks, is scared of her—of her! But then she is barely sixteen and new to London. And she embarrassed the poor girl with talk of a husband when she only meant to be kind. The next time she will have to tread more carefully, for this Jane is not like Sarah, whom nothing seems to embarrass. Sarah. She has seen her march boldly up the area steps, then along the street in a hat with too many feathers, at times of the day when she should be helping with the mending or cleaning the dining room. Even this afternoon—when Sarah should have been helping this new maid—Mina saw her push the area gate closed and stroll off as though the afternoon was hers to do with as she liked. Maybe she has a follower, probably one of the young men who delivers meat or bread to the house.

She has said nothing. Not yet, not like with Lizzie. But then Lizzie was more dangerous. Not a flirt, not a girl likely to have a follower, yet Mina had seen her at the top of the area steps talking to a thin stick of a man in a tall hat who'd thrust something into her hand and hurried off. There was something about the way their faces had been tilted together: this was not love but business, she was sure. Lizzie had hidden whatever he'd given her in her apron pocket and had glanced about her as she came back down the steps. Guilty. Mina was certain of it. Guilty of selling the secrets she'd found from prying through her things.

Yet what was there to find? After she had thrown Lizzie out of the house, she couldn't think what the girl might have discovered. There was nothing of her old life here, nothing to give her away. Now Mina worries that dismissing Lizzie so suddenly and for so little reason looks suspicious, like the actions of a woman with something to hide.

She will have to be more careful with Sarah. She knows Sarah goes through her things too. But what of it? Don't most servants pry? And perhaps her outings are innocent enough. Still, she must say something. No mistress can turn a blind eye to servants taking advantage. She'll mention it to her. Tonight, when Sarah is unfastening her dress and can't escape until the job is done. She'll catch her eye in the mirror and tell her what she's seen of her jaunts down the street. Maybe she'll deny it—or maybe she'll explain that Mrs. Johnson sent her out on an errand. What then? Will she call Mrs. Johnson upstairs to her bedroom? Or will she give Sarah a warning that will mean nothing? Even with a new maid just arrived, Sarah knows she can't easily be dismissed, especially since Price insists that Robert's mother is fond of her—of Sarah!

She'll watch her. She'll have to be careful. But she will not let herself be brought down by a maid who spies on her, all for a little bit of money.

From the mantelpiece the clock—an ugly thing, all gold and curlicues with a self-important tick—chimes the quarter hour. With a sigh Mina gets up, glances at herself in the mirror, then leaves the room. The silk of her dress rustles as she crosses the hallway and starts up the stairs.

She knocks gently. Without waiting for Price to answer, she opens the door and walks over to the bed. "How is Mrs. Bentley today?"

Price comes close. "She took half a cup of broth. And she has a better color today, thank the Lord."

Mina opens the curtain a little and looks down at her mother-in-law asleep with her dry lips slightly parted and her grey hair spilled around her face. "In my opinion she looks much the same. We can't expect much."

"Oh yes, ma'am," says Price. "But we can hope—and we can pray. The Lord can work miracles and we should appeal to Him for Mrs. Bentley's recovery." She reaches down and tucks the sheet more snugly around her mistress's shoulders.

Mina lets the edge of the curtain drop. "We should never forget our place so far as to ask the Lord to grant our own wishes. We must all of us accept when our time here is over. Don't you agree, Price?"

"Oh yes, ma'am." She gives a cold smile. "We should all of us accept our place in His order."

"This room needs fresh air, Price. And a thorough cleaning. We cannot expect Mrs. Bentley to do well with dust everywhere like this. I will send Jane up directly."

"Not Jane, ma'am—Sarah, I think you meant."

It happens this way every time: her instructions countered, her warnings to Price that the doctor holds out little hope ignored. This woman is like a gnat, always too close, her thin voice whining, relentlessly stinging as though it's part of her nature.

"No." She walks to the middle of the carpet. "I meant Jane. Cleaning grates and such like are the duties of the second housemaid, now that we have one to replace Lizzie."

"You must excuse me," says Price, "but this room has always been the work of the first housemaid, on the specific instructions of Mrs. Bentley. She has taken a liking to the girl." She knots her hands together. They look pale and blind, like strange sea creatures. "What's more—excuse me taking the liberty of mentioning it—but the new housemaid was not hired by Mrs. Bentley. To have a person who—"

"I looked into her character myself. So far I have been very well satisfied with her work."

"Mrs. Bentley is very particular."

"Then we should not take advantage of her illness to let her room deteriorate." She points to the cinders choking the grate, the carpet specked with ash, the blankets heaped on the sofa.

"Mrs. Bentley cannot be disturbed. The doctor said—"

"I know perfectly well what the doctor said. Yet that is no reason for her room to be in such disorder. And you would do well," she says, "to remove yourself to your own room at night."

"Thank you, I'm sure." She comes so close that Mina is obliged to take a step back to avoid the feel of her breath on her face. "But I'd prefer to obey my mistress's wishes and stay close at hand."

Mina holds the woman's gaze. "Your constant presence means the air is more quickly becoming foul. You will air the room, as I instructed, for the health of your mistress."

Before Price can respond she turns and opens the door. Behind her the lady's maid calls out, but she pulls the door closed and walks away, down the stairs, her heart thumping wildly in her chest.

At half past three in the afternoon there is a knock at the front door. Mr. Cartwright is out on an errand, and as for Sarah— well, the trip to the shop was not supposed to take more than half an hour, yet she has not come back. Mrs. Johnson looks up from her pastry.

"You," she tells Jane. "Quick. Make yourself presentable and answer the door."

Jane pushes her needle through the edge of the shirt close to the button she is sewing back on. "Me?" she says. "But I've never—"

From upstairs comes the sound of the knocker again.

"Now, Jane. Get yourself moving."

So she rushes from the room and up the stairs, setting her cap straight as best she can. Once she opens the door into the main hallway she slows—it wouldn't do to be heard rushing like this. But then, it wouldn't do to answer the door without looking as clean and tidy as she is able, and she isn't sure she looks either. A large mirror hangs on the wall by the hat stand and she steals a glimpse at herself. Her face looks flushed, and she still has a needle threaded with black cotton pushed through the bib of her apron. She plucks it out and drops it into her pocket.

Whoever is at the door is getting impatient. There's another knock—a *rat-a-tat-tat* that Mrs. Johnson will scold her about, no doubt, because how could she have taken so long to get upstairs? So she hurries to open the door and swings it wide.

There, on the doorstep, stands a large man in a hat and a black coat, an umbrella swinging from his arm. A thick beard hides the bottom half of his face. "Good God, girl," he grunts, "how long does it take to answer a door?"

"I'm very sorry, sir."

He makes to step forward but she doesn't move. She knows that much—she must take his name, then show him in and announce him if the family is home. "Who shall I say is calling, sir?"

"Mr. Bentley." He watches her as she blinks.

"Oh, sir, I am so sorry. I didn't—"

"If I could come in, if you please." All stiff formality now.

She steps back out of his way and bumps a small table behind her. He hands her his hat and umbrella, then tugs off his coat. "Where's Cartwright?"

"On an errand, sir."

"And Sarah?"

"I don't know, sir. I think she went to the shops."

"You think?"

"Yes, sir." Her voice is quavering now. She grips his hat, feels the heat from his head still on it.

He hands her his coat. "And my wife? Is she in this afternoon?"

"I don't know sir, I—"

But he walks away, announcing, apparently not just to her but to the household at large, "This is not good enough. There will be repercussions, mark my words."

Her arms tremble as she reaches up to hang the coat and hat on the stand, right behind what looks like an identical hat. There is a brass umbrella stand, and she drops his umbrella into it. Then she makes for the door behind the stairs that lead to the servants' stairway back down to the kitchen. There she hides in the darkness, out of sight of Mrs. Johnson and Elsie. Maybe they hear her sobs coming down the stairs. Probably they do. But they do not come and see what is wrong, and she is thankful for that.

CHAPTER 4

U_{proar.}

Mr. Cartwright out sending a telegram to summon the master home, Mrs. Johnson banging her pots at the stove, and upstairs the police treading to and fro. All except one young constable who has been put on duty in the kitchen and who is sipping a cup of tea that Mrs. Johnson has made for him. Every now and again he looks up at Jane to make sure she is still there across the table and, she thinks, to impress on her that he is *watching* her. She looks back just to show him she can. Of course, it might be taken the wrong way. Maybe she doesn't look innocent and able to meet his eye, but saucy or even brazen. Aren't these the words that are used about women of her class who go bad?

She has been sitting this way for over half an hour now, her back too straight, her fingers twisting together in her lap. No tea for her and, though no one has said as much, she knows they believe her guilty. The policeman who questioned her certainly seemed to think so, though he tried to hide it by being both stern and encouraging at the same time.

"And how would you describe this man, this 'Mr. Bentley' you opened the door to?" So she told him.

"Didn't you find him suspicious?" he wanted to know.

For wanting to come into his own house? What gentleman carries his keys with him when he knows there are servants to open the door? She said as much and he cut her off with a wave of his hand. "You realize the gravity of what has happened?" he said. "And that it looks bad for you? Very bad. Not even a full day in the position and you've let a burglar into the house. We'll have to make enquiries, you know."

Where will those enquiries lead? To Mrs. Saunders, and to the truth that she is the daughter of a murderer? Yet she did not feel panic at the thought of it as she watched him write in his notebook then slide it into his pocket. He stood, looming towards her over the table to say, "Think things over, or it will be all the worse for you." With that he jerked his head at the younger policeman so he'd know to stay and keep an eye on her.

Now the young policeman glances at her again. His hair is a reddish blond that makes his eyebrows and lashes almost invisible. It gives him a curiously blurred look around the eyes, as though his features have been pencilled in, then erased. He blows noisily on his tea, then turns towards Jane. His pale eyes linger. Does he expect her to collapse under the power of his gaze and confess that she let in a burglar to break the lock on Mr. Bentley's desk and rifle through his papers? How can he not understand that she doesn't know a soul in this city—no one to let into the house, no one to help her out of this misunderstanding?

She stares back at him for one second, and another, then forces herself to look away to the window. I haven't done anything wrong, she tells herself, even though that's not exactly true. After all, this is a respectable household and she got herself a position here under false pretenses, didn't she? He's still watching her, and beneath the table she presses her knuckles together until they hurt.

Down the stairs come feet heavy against the treads. The woman from upstairs—Price. From the way her eyes flicker past her, Jane knows she has spoken against her to the policeman. Most likely she's told him she found her listening at Mrs. Bentley's door that very morning. Price whispers something to Mrs. Johnson, and Mrs. Johnson tilts her head, says, "No no, not yet."

As for Elsie, she's got her head down amongst the parsnips she's peeling at the sink. When she's looked over at Jane it has been with awe.

Yet all Jane did was answer the door, as she was told to do. There was the knocking, and Mrs. Johnson telling her to hurry upstairs, and the man who said he was Mr. Bentley, who gave her his hat and was angry with her. She'd cried on the stairs, then she'd gone back to her mending in the kitchen, was still at it when there was another knock at the door. Half an hour after the first? Surely not that long, but she isn't sure. Mrs. Robert back early from an outing. Jane took her coat and hung it up, asked if she would be needing tea. Mrs. Robert didn't reply. She was pointing at the coat already on the stand. "Do we have a visitor?"

"No, ma'am. Mr. Bentley came home a little while ago."

"Mr. Bentley? That's not possible." Her voice was thin, and she held out a hand, touched the wall as though she might fall. Her mouth looked suddenly stiff.

For a moment Jane had not known what to say. Then she told her, "He's in the study, ma'am."

"Very good. Please ask him to come to the drawing room." Then she walked away unsteadily.

Hardly had Jane knocked when the man himself opened the study door. He stood right there in the way. "Yes?"

"Mrs. Robert would like to see you in the drawing room, sir."

"Many thanks. And would you be so good as to order up some tea?"

She'd only just started downstairs when she heard the rattle of the knocker as the front door closed. Hadn't she shut it properly? When she went up to check there was nobody there; the door was closed. Mrs. Robert had come out of the drawing room wanting to know who was at the door. Then she'd glanced at the stand: the coat and umbrella were gone, and only one hat remained.

Mrs. Robert rushed to the study and swung open the door so violently that it knocked against the wall and sent a picture crashing down onto a cabinet, where its glass shattered. Such an accident merely added to the disorder of the room. Boxes and boxes of papers torn open and strewn around, the drawer of the desk lying on the floor, the front broken where the lock had been forced. Mrs. Robert walked into the room with her hands outstretched as though she could dispel this disaster. Then she held them up to her mouth and mumbled through her fingers, "Send for the police, Marie; we've been robbed."

Marie. But she remembered Jane's name well enough when the police arrived.

Only when the older of the two policemen broke into her account of who Jane was did Mrs. Roberts stop and let Jane be escorted out of the study. Now Jane has no idea what her mistress might have said about her, or what Sarah might be adding because now it is she who is upstairs being questioned. Still, it can't look good. Even in Teignton such stories made it into the paper, the sort of thing to catch Mrs. Saunders's eye and for her to read aloud when Jane brought in the tea. A warning, Jane had always thought it, in case she'd been thinking of stealing Mrs. Saunders's pearl earrings, or letting a young gentleman into the house when the family was out and allowing him take off with the silver plate. But she'd noticed: when the old newspapers were sent downstairs to be rolled into spills for the fires, there were other stories too.

Mrs. Phelps would cluck her tongue in horror and say, "Listen, Jane, listen to this," then, between mouthfuls of bread and dripping, would read out stories of maids who'd put arsenic in their mistresses' tea, or valets who'd beaten their masters senseless with candlesticks, or a cook who'd bludgeoned her old mistress, boiled down her body, and sold the rendered fat to the neighbors.

Over at the stove Mrs. Johnson is straining a stock, her back to Jane. She is, Jane thinks, keeping her back turned on purpose, shunning her for bringing down this disaster on the household. Disaster or not, dinner will be needed this evening, and Jane wonders: Will she be here to eat it? Or will she have been taken away to the police station?

When the butcher's boy came with the meat, the policeman set to watch her glared at him, then stared from Jane to the boy as though to gauge if there was some secret communication between them. Now there has been no knock at the door for so long that he's getting bored, she can see it. He has started to fidget. So, she thinks, let him fidget. All she did was answer the door. It was Mr. Cartwright's job. Or Sarah's. As luck would have it, they were both out.

Or, she thinks now, not luck. Design. Someone knew them by name and knew they wouldn't be answering the door. Someone knew it would be her, and that she didn't yet know Mr. Robert by sight. Who would know such a thing? She watches Mrs. Johnson, busy with the stock, and Elsie at the sink. Who would have known except for someone in the house?

Mr. Robert has not yet returned, nor has Mr. Cartwright, who was sent to summon him. She wonders what will happen when he arrives. Already she knows the blame for the robbery has settled on her for letting the man into the house. As if she could have known! As if she has ever seen Mr. Robert Bentley! Whose fault was that? Yet somehow the policeman who took down her story thought it remarkable that she didn't know the man was a burglar. Was she supposed to have questioned him? What were the chances that he wasn't who he said he was? After all, who ever heard of such a thing?

Sitting here, she has had plenty of time to hear the knock again, to remember Mrs. Johnson telling her to hurry, to get herself upstairs. She'd been nervous. She'd looked at herself in the mirror for a moment, taken the needle out of her apron, and stepped over to the door. And there he was, angry at her for taking so long, setting her all at odds by telling her he was Mr. Bentley. How could she have noticed anything strange about him? She'd had her head down. She'd only looked up to take his hat and umbrella, and to put them away. Then he'd said—what was it? That there would be *repercussions*—and had taken off for the study.

He knew which room it was, she thinks now. Had he been in the house before? Or had someone told him where the study was? Plus there was something curious about the way he walked, bowlegged, on the edges of his feet.

She looks towards the policeman and opens her mouth to speak, but she lets out a sigh instead. There is nothing to be gained by remarking on this. It will only look worse for her.

She must wait. Mr. Cartwright will return, and Mr. Robert, and her fate will be decided. Now she wonders about the sort of man Mr. Robert might be. The sort to send her away without a character just because he suspects her? The sort who thinks too highly of himself to do such a thing, yet who will find fault with her from now on and soon, in a few weeks, or maybe a few months, dismiss her over some other small matter?

The policeman sets his cup back down in its saucer. With a loud sniff he strokes his chin and stares towards the door.

"Fancy a slice of pie?" asks Mrs. Johnson.

"Meat pie?"

"If you like."

"Thank you kindly. We were just about to eat when we were called off on another case, and then what with this right when we got back to the station—" He looks across the table at Jane as though this is her fault.

Mrs. Johnson fetches a pie from the pantry and cuts a generous slice. When she passes it to him he says, "Having a run of bad luck in this street, aren't you?"

"Not more than anywhere else, I'm sure," Mrs. Johnson tells him tartly.

He picks up a fork but holds it almost accusingly at her. "That maid that fell from the window—that was near here, wasn't it."

It's not a question. Mrs. Johnson wipes her hands carefully on the cloth hanging from her apron. "A terrible accident," she says. "Those young girls—they step onto the ledge to clean the windows. I've seen them do it—mop in one hand and the other on the frame like it's nothing to them that they could slip."

"That was the second in a week, that one was. Had another do the same thing just a few streets away. We had an awful job trying to get her off the railings. Stuck fast on them she was." He gives a low chuckle. "Thought we was going to have to cut her off."

He's just about to put a forkful of pie into his mouth when the door opens. Mr. Cartwright. Even as he unbuttons his coat his eyes swing over them all—Elsie at the sink, Mrs. Johnson at the stove, the policeman with his pie, Jane sitting rigidly across the table from him. He looks back at the policeman. "What's all this then?" he says.

"Keeping an eye on the young person here." He puts the piece of pie in his mouth and points his fork at Jane.

Mr. Cartwright shrugs himself out of his coat. Jane watches him—the careful movements, the way he folds the coat over his arm, the way he catches Mrs. Johnson's eye and hands the coat to her like a man about to fight. "Well, now," he says, coming close. "In my experience"—he sits down at the end of the table—"and I've been in service now—oh, let me see, going on forty years—young maids straight up from the country aren't known for being part of criminal gangs. I'd say"—he rests one finger at the corner of his mouth, as though he is thinking—"that somebody had been watching this household and found out a new maid had just taken up a situation here."

"Would you, now?"

"Yes, I would. That wouldn't have been difficult, would it? We're a private household, but our affairs aren't secret."

The policeman is now hard at work on his pie. "Sounds to me," he says, "as though you're in the wrong line of business, being in service." He chews. "Maybe you should think about a change. With all your *experience*"—he wipes his mouth on the back of his hand—"they'd be sure to take you on at Scotland Yard."

Mr. Cartwright smiles. He leans forward in a friendly way. "Tell me—how did our young maid here know she'd be the one answering the door? After all, it was only by chance that I had to go out on an errand just when Sarah was at the shops. And seeing as Jane was in the kitchen doing the mending—right, Mrs. Johnson?"

"Right, Mr. Cartwright."

"—ever since she cleared away luncheon, even if she *had* known, how could she have given a signal to her accomplice? Isn't that how it's done?"

The policeman's pale brows stand out, light smudges against a face that is growing more heated. "The tales I could tell you of the craftiness of criminals—"

"Well, this one wasn't so crafty. He left his hat upstairs. I noticed it straightaway."

The policeman tries to hide his surprise with a cough, but Mr. Cartwright smiles.

"Yes," he continues, "the hat on the stand upstairs is not Mr. Bentley's. I'm intimately acquainted with all his apparel. And that hat is not his. Indeed, Mr. Bentley's hat that was hanging there is gone. So I should say that the burglar took off with the wrong one, wouldn't you, Constable?"

Only now does Jane lay her hands flat on the table and say, "Yes—that's right. There was already a hat on the stand."

"Mr. Bentley's second best."

Above them on the wall a bell rings. The labels are so dark with dirt that even if Jane turned around she would not be able to read which room it was for. Mr. Cartwright purses his lips. "Mrs. Robert Bentley," he announces, "needs me." He stands. "If you would like to view the hat—"

With a grunt the policeman pushes away his plate and gets up. He takes a moment to brush the crumbs off the front of his uniform, then he follows Cartwright to the stairs.

Mrs. Johnson takes up the plate and the half-eaten slice of pie. "Well, now," she says to Jane. "I daresay you're getting thirsty, love. How about a cup of tea?"

*U*pstairs Mina Bentley goes to the bedroom window and lifts the sash. The air is cold and smells of soot, but she leans both hands on the sill and takes deep breaths anyway. Her eyes are on the street below, but she doesn't see the people and horses and carriages moving through the deepening dusk. No, she's breathing in painful lungfuls of air to calm herself. This ridiculous burglary— one of the servants must be involved, for how else did the man know it would be the new maid who'd answer the door? Was it Sarah? If not, then who?

He was in the morning room too, she is sure of it. Going through the papers. That mess in the study as though a storm had blown through—a ruse. Because whatever he wanted wasn't in there. No. The papers in the desk in the morning room must have been gone through. She imagines him carefully picking through them and wonders what he read, what he might have taken away with him that will not be discovered for weeks. For months even. Only, she thinks, he might use what he found before then.

But there's nothing of her old life here, she tells herself, nothing that could have stowed away with her to London. Does this mean that Lizzie was innocent? Or that she didn't find anything and this man had to come to finish the job? She leans her head against the wooden frame of the sash. Maybe that's not what he's after. Yet what else could he have hoped to find?

This morning she was going over the accounts, calculating how much money she and Robert have left, how long it will last them if they move to a smaller apartment in Paris. Was it her account book he was after? It is still safe in her portable desk upstairs. But she remembers using an old envelope for her calculations—names on it of her landlord in Paris, and her dressmaker. Where is it now? Taken away by one of the maids to be thrown on the fire? Or folded into his pocket? She cannot know. Such information seems suddenly dangerous. Would a little cleverness be enough to pull on such a small thread and unravel her life? Could he trace her back not only to Paris but from there to who she was before? She hadn't thought it possible. And yet, if he's clever—

She looks up. Across the street a woman is outlined against the brightness of a window. She wears a cap and, as Mina sees as the woman steps back into the light, a white apron—a maid. It takes Mina a moment to understand that she must be visible to anyone who chances to look over to this side of Cursitor Road, and she straightens herself. Slowly, she lets down the sash. She is merely a woman who needed a breath of fresh air. She makes sure to close the curtains, too, then sits back on the bed. It is hard, and too small for two people, for this is the room Robert had growing up. She lifts her fingers to her mouth and catches the edge of a ragged nail in her teeth.

When she and Robert arrived here the house felt hollow—his mother keeping to her bed, the rooms ghostly in their dust sheets. Mrs. Bentley used to be a formidable woman, by all accounts. Maybe that's why the servants have taken liberties. It's their revenge. She imagines them like mice that creep out at night, or when doors are closed. Nosing around in places they should not be; looking for crumbs, for secrets to feed their curiosity with, or their greed. She has tried her best to scare them back into their place, but they hold her eye a little too long when she talks to them, as though they have uncovered a truth: that they are every bit as good as her.

The house doesn't feel hollow anymore. Instead it has pulled in so uncomfortably tight around her that she finds it hard to breathe.

*N*ight has fallen, the lamps have been lit, and the rooms look more splendid. Gone are the faded patches of wallpaper, the grime in the corners of the ceilings, the paleness of the carpets where threads have started to show through. As Jane opens each room she sees the gleam of polished furniture, the dance of light on the glass domes covering clocks and stuffed birds, the rich reds and oranges of paintings that had looked lifeless in daylight. But she does not have the time to be admiring anything. There are fires to be laid, and the whole frantic business of dinner for Mr. and Mrs. Robert to be got through.

Did she arrive only a day ago? Weariness has settled deep into her bones, and she could believe that she has spent half her life in this place, treading up and down the stairs with buckets and mops, emptying ashes and cinders out of fireplaces, washing her hands again and again so that they are clean enough to smooth sheets and carry trays. Was it only this afternoon that she was sitting at the kitchen table with a policeman keeping an eye on her? It feels as though weeks have passed since then.

She gets onto her knees to lay rolls of newspaper and splints of wood across the grate in the drawing room fireplace. Then she picks lumps of coal from the scuttle and lays them on top, one by one. She is tired, and the next lump slips from the tongs and falls into her lap, and she could cry to see the dark trail it leaves across her apron when she'd thought to wear it another day at least. And her hand—without thinking she grabbed for the coal with her bare hand, and it is smudged too. Now she will have to be careful not to touch her face, or the paintwork of the door. She will have to go all the way downstairs to wash before she can turn back the bed. The very thought of it—of all those stairs—makes her long for this day to be over so she can curl under her blankets and give herself up to sleep.

Her stomach murmurs and she presses both hands against it. Mrs. Johnson served beef and potatoes, but her stomach was so clenched she barely ate a mouthful. A hot meal for supper—Mrs. Saunders would have called it an extravagance, because didn't they have a proper meal at midday? Only, thought Jane, if you call the leavings from the upstairs dinner a proper meal, and only those leavings not good enough to be served again as soup or a stew.

She loads more coal onto the fire—too much, perhaps—and takes a match from the mantelpiece. It catches easily enough and, with the fireguard in place, she sits back on her heels with her hands held out to catch the first flare of heat.

There's a knock at the door. Sarah. "Mr. Robert wants to see you in the study," she says.

"Me?"

"Of course *you*." She doesn't smile, just pulls the door closed again.

Jane wonders: Is this it? Has enough suspicion clung to her that already he wants her gone? Or, now that the question of her honesty has been brought up, has he asked to see her letter of reference and seen something wrong in it? But then, wouldn't it be Mrs. Robert who'd have asked to see her? Jane's hands are shaking as she gets to her feet and pushes a strand of hair back from her face. Too late, she realizes she must have left a smear of coal dust across her cheek. So she stands and peers into the mirror above the mantelpiece, a mirror not intended for such a purpose, evidently, for it is so high that she must strain to see herself. The heat of the fire laps around her ankles. She stands there anyway, rubbing her cheek with a corner of her apron until her skin is so red that it's hard to tell if there's any trace of coal left. From her dress rises the unpleasant smell of hot cotton.

The slow ticking of the grandfather clock fills the hallway. It needs dusting—she notices that as she passes it and turns under the stairs to the study. Talking to Mr. Robert will only delay getting her work finished. As it is, she has been behind ever since she was made to sit idle at the kitchen table, watching the policeman eat his pie.

She knocks on the door. Three gentle raps.

"Come in." The voice is sharp, and from it she expects a small man, but the Mr. Robert she finds standing by the fire is tall and slim, and at most in his thirties. His face is all straight lines, from the crisp part through the middle of his hair to his trimmed brown moustache. The rest of him is in disarray—his shirtsleeves rolled up, his collar crooked, his jacket slung carelessly over the arm of a chair. He is intent on the sheet of paper in his hands. Papers lie everywhere—over the floor, on the desk, caught in the aspidistra by the window. On the armchair by the fire sits an untidy pile that he sets the sheet onto, then he glances over at her.

He is, she thinks, nothing at all like the intruder. "Sir?" she says.

"Ah. Jane, isn't it?"

"Yes, sir."

"Yes." He stoops to gather up another handful of papers. "Quite a mess this burglar of ours left behind him. No doubt he was looking for something of value and all he found"—and here he spreads his hands—"are these papers. He must have been somewhat disappointed."

"Yes, sir."

He perches on the edge of the armchair and holds his hands out to the fire. "I hear you were the one to open the door. He must have been an audacious fellow to have presented himself as me."

"Yes, sir."

He looks at her. "I know the police officers spoke to you, asked you questions, that sort of thing. But let me put this question to you again: What did the man look like?"

"Oh, sir." She sucks at her lip as she looks towards the wall, bringing into her mind's eye the man she saw so briefly. "He had a beard, a brown beard going grey."

"So do half the older men in London."

"Sir?"

But he waves at her to continue.

"He was older than you, sir, by quite a way."

He nods. "So, he was nothing like me at all, by all accounts. This is really quite remarkable."

Jane looks down at the carpet and the pattern of roses woven into it. It is not her fault, she tells herself. How could she have known that he was not only an impostor, but a bad impostor at that?

Without looking up she senses him stepping this way and that, no doubt exasperated. "Well," he says at last, "anything else you noticed?"

"No, sir. There was nothing much to notice. He was dressed like a gentleman."

"*Like* a gentleman? Do you mean he wasn't a gentleman but still you let him into the house?"

Her breath catches in her throat. "No," she says, "that's not what I meant." For what else can she say? Yet there was something not quite like a gentleman about him, though she cannot decide what it was.

Mr. Robert is watching her. "Well? What is it you *did* notice?"

"He was in a black coat, a hat, and a white shirt, like a gentleman." She thinks, thinks. "His eyebrows were thick. His lips were full. He was a little stout, so that his waistcoat gaped." She is pleased with herself for all of this. Yet evidently Mr. Robert is not.

"Yes, yes," he says. "But is there anything to distinguish him? Any mark that would set him apart from the many gentlemen in this city—other than the fact that he patently is no gentleman?" He sighs. "His voice? His accent?"

She presses her arms against her sides to keep herself calm. "I don't know, sir—maybe his voice was a little rough."

"Rough? How so? Uneducated?"

"I don't know, sir, really I don't. He just didn't talk exactly like you."

Letting his head fall forward into his hands, he sighs. "Try to think clearly. Close your eyes. Picture him to yourself. Let yourself hear him speak."

So she closes her eyes, but that doesn't help. She sees the same man standing there, his thick beard, brown eyes beneath a black hat. An umbrella held uneasily in one hand. The stretch of his waistcoat over his belly—his coat not buttoned. A gentleman's clothes, but not quite clean and tidy enough for a gentleman: a dark smudge on the edge of his collar, his collar badly pressed. His beard unkempt. His voice when he said, *There will be repercussions, mark my words.* The sounds strangely flat, not round the way Mr. Robert talks. The way he took off down the hallway in long strides as though he was used to walking great distances—and his boots. The heels worn down on the outside because he walked a little bowlegged. But how to explain all of that without Mr. Robert suspecting she's to blame for letting in a man so obviously not a gentleman?

She's so tired that she can't concentrate. Her head is spinning and she has to open her eyes.

"Nothing?" he says in a tired voice.

"Sir, when he walked—"

"Did he limp?"

"No, sir."

He lets out a sigh and flicks his hand through the air. Enough. As though she couldn't have noticed anything useful, as though he should have known. "It can't be helped. I don't suppose the majority of us have a distinguishing feature that the common populace would notice." He reaches for a sheet of paper by his feet and glances at it. "Most likely we will never catch him. But he learnt his lesson, didn't he? It wasn't worth his while to risk so much only to find all these papers."

There are papers close to her feet, and small cards. She bends down and gathers the cards together. Columns of numbers in a tight hand. Numbers upon numbers. She comes close. "Here you are, sir."

"Thank you, Jane."

He lets his eyes run over them, then stares back into the fire. "Not an auspicious start to your career here. For that I'm sorry. The police officers are—the police officers have seen too many cases where servants have deceived their employers. Their view is jaded."

"Yes, sir."

"Thank you, Jane."

But she doesn't leave. Instead she says, "Sir, he knew the house."

"He knew the house? What do you mean?"

"He walked straight through to your study. As though he knew the way. And"—here her heart presses harder because something else has just struck her—"he didn't go into any of the other rooms. Did he, sir? But he was here for close to half an hour. Wouldn't a burglar want to take jewelry? There's none of that in a study. Maybe there was something in here he particularly wanted."

He stands, his hands flying up to his head, fingers combing through his hair. "By Jove, you're right. You're exactly right."

He looks around him as though seeing the disordered room all over again. "This sheds a new light on the matter." He takes her hand and shakes it. "You're a good girl. We'll see through to the truth of this business, yes we will."

"Sir?" she says again.

He looks up at her, impatiently this time.

"He must have known, mustn't he? That it was me who was going to answer the door."

"I suppose he would."

"So how would he know?" She bunches up her apron between her fingers because his eyes are on hers.

"Ah," he says at last. "Ah, I see." He smoothes his moustache and looks away. "There could be a number of explanations—but tell me, do you suspect any—any wrongdoing? From inside the house, I mean?"

"Oh no, sir," she tells him fast. "That's not what I meant." A lie, of course, but to hear the suspicion coming from his mouth scares her, for it gives it a life of its own.

He raises his eyebrows. "Well, I suppose there are all sorts of ways information can be obtained. Tradesmen come to the door, delivery boys—without even thinking, it could have slipped out and been passed on."

She watches as he moves around the room picking up papers and cards that have fallen on books, on the desk, on the carpet, even a couple in the coal scuttle. She wonders if she should help, but he seems intent on something.

Then he pauses and looks back at her, as though he has just remembered that she is still there. "I'm sure you're eager to get back to your work. It has been a long day."

He has already turned his attention to his papers when she closes the door. The hallway echoes under her boots, then she takes the dim stairwell down to the kitchen. It has, she thinks, been a very long day.

*T*hrough dinner that night Robert Bentley often catches his wife's eye but says little. He asks how his mother is—"Much the same." He asks if she has read the letters to the editor in *The Times* today—she has not. He grunts and bends his head over his beef consommé. Mrs. Johnson's best, despite the interruptions and distractions of the day, but neither he nor Mina says as much. Indeed, they barely say another word, despite Cartwright and Sarah standing at attention by the sideboard, listening to their silence. The quiet magnifies Cartwright's quiet tread, Sarah's sniffs and sighs, the delicate tap of serving spoons against serving dishes, Sarah's whisper to Cartwright—"Should I fetch the roast?" When a piece of coal suddenly spits, they all jump.

In the wake of the burglar's intrusion, silence hangs like cobwebs. What is it waiting to catch? The small buzzings of suspicion? Inklings about who and what and why that might flit through the air? But Mr. and Mrs. Robert are too cautious to talk in front of their servants, and as for their butler and their maid—they have to stand quietly until dinner is finally over, a dinner endured from soup to nuts so that, to all appearances, nothing has been upset by the events of the day.

Then, with a glance to Cartwright, Mrs. Robert orders tea in the drawing room, and they are gone. Napkins left beside plates, chairs pushed out from the table. Sarah bursts out with, "Bloomin' heck, Mr. Cartwright, they didn't say a word about it, not a single word," and is reprimanded, for Cartwright's own nerves are becoming unstrung.

It takes a while for the tea to come—no water had been set to boil downstairs. While Mina Bentley settles herself in front of the fire and her husband stretches his feet towards the fender and opens the newspaper, Mrs. Johnson is snapping at Elsie to fill the kettle. Robert Bentley reads out a letter to the editor, a letter about the pressing need for an efficient system of identifying recidivists. His wife says, "Oh really?" and, "How interesting," though it is clear that her interest is somewhere else entirely.

But then, as she knows full well, so is his.

Twenty minutes later there is all the bustle of the tea being brought in. Sarah putting down the tray, straightening one of the cups and saying, "What a day it has been, ma'am." All she gets for her trouble is Mrs. Robert glancing up at her with, "Yes, Sarah, what a day. Thank you." And that *Thank you* is enough to make her bite her teeth together and close the door just a little too hard on her way out of the room.

They listen to Sarah's footsteps fading along the hallway, and the squeak of the door down to the kitchen. Only last week Robert re-marked that they should have it oiled, but Mina shook her head—squeaking hinges, she said, have their uses. Now she sighs, reaches for the milk and pours a little into the cups. "She is growing unbearable."

The tea gurgles into the cups, leaving a tail of steam rising through the air. He lets the newspaper drop onto his knees. "Mother likes the girl."

"I'm sure your mother wouldn't put up with impertinence." She spoons sugar into the cups and holds one out to him.

"The servants are curious. How could they not be?"

"Yes." She lifts a cup off its saucer and holds it between her hands. "How could they not be?"

Later, she is sure, Sarah will be rough unfastening her dress. She is easily made resentful—for being told not to leave the house without permission, for not learning anything about the burglary this evening. But she's also not the sort to give up. Perhaps while she's folding the dress she'll offer up a little of what's being said below stairs in the hope of learning something new. There's that about Sarah—not cleverness, but tenacity and a certain lack of scruple.

The cup is deliciously hot against Mina's palms. In the fireplace, flames are swaying through the coals, but inside the layers of her dress and petticoats, she is still cold. She lifts one foot high enough for the warm air to flood in around her ankles.

"English houses are an abomination," she says. "You get burned on one side, and freeze on the other. Look at that." She nods at the fire. "All that heat going straight up the chimney." She glances at Robert, but he's paying no attention. His cup is forgotten on the arm of the chair. He's bent forward, eyes closed, squeezing the skin between them. This is how he will look as an old man, she thinks. His nose thinner, his shoulders bowed. She imagines herself beside him, a little stout perhaps, and her hair bright with grey. For a few moments she lets herself believe that this can happen. A quiet life together. A dull life—how wonderful! Then the weight of all that's balanced against it presses back down.

The heat wraps itself around her. The fire splutters and spits. She draws back her feet. "What do you make of our intruder now?" she says. "I know you have a theory—I can see it on your face."

"Oh." He gives a slight smile. "That new housemaid pointed out something interesting. The police might have noticed if they hadn't been so intent on suspecting her."

She nods. "The poor struggling police. They never get it, do they? And then people have to call in the likes of Mr. Holmes."

He sucks noisily at his tea. "Where else do you think Doyle gets his ideas? The police see nine cases of domestic burglary in which servants have robbed their employers. They are called in on the tenth case, and they assume it's the servants again, but instead it's something quite different."

"Such as?"

"Our man was a burglar."

"Darling, only a couple of hours ago you announced that he wasn't. He didn't take a thing."

"That was before I talked to the new housemaid." He takes another sip of his tea and scowls. "My love, you are a clever woman who has chosen a clever maid."

"You see?" she says. "There is more to domestic management than meets the eye."

"And more to this burglary than met my eye. The maid noticed something peculiar. Not only did our burglar go straight to the study as though he knew his way there—"

"Whoever told him all the other servants were out could have told him that, too."

"Yes, yes. But what is more interesting is that he was here for half an hour and didn't venture into any of the other rooms. How long could it have taken him to prise open the desk? How long to realize that the room was full of papers and more papers, and nothing of any other sort of value?"

"Oh." She settles her cup in its saucer and grips both tightly. Her hands feel flighty.

He doesn't notice. "That's right," he says. "I've been thinking—what could he have been after?" He nods to himself. "Well," he says, and lifts his eyes to hers, "it only just occurred to me—the work of the Troup Committee is not secret, and neither is the fact that while I am in London I shall testify before them."

She pulls a lungful of air into herself before she can speak. "Robert," she says, "oh, Robert—he was after your work, then?"

"There's precious little else in that room."

Maybe he is right. After all, she has found no sign that the burglar was in the morning room. And yet—a careful man wouldn't have left any sign, would he?

She lifts her cup to just beneath her chin, then glances up at Robert. "What could be gained from someone looking at it? Someone who's not an expert in the field?"

Staring into the fire, he shakes his head. "That's the problem. I don't know."

CHAPTER 5

Only two days since the burglary, and the servants' frightened look has disappeared. Now they merely resent her once more—Mina sees it in the way Cartwright stands stiffly beside his chair, and the way Elsie peers at her from the scullery. Worst of all is Mrs. Johnson. "Well, Mrs. Robert," she says, "I don't know about that. The mistress doesn't much care for veal."

"Your mistress is ill in bed and taking little more than broth. I am merely requesting a dish that is one of Mr. Robert's favorites."

Mrs. Johnson won't hold her gaze. Instead she sucks in her cheeks and takes a dirty cloth from beside the stove. Then—the cheek of it!—she pulls open the oven, forcing Mina to step aside. Hot, buttery air rises out of the oven. Pies—two of them. Yet when is there pie for the upstairs table? Not more than once a week.

"More pies, Mrs. Johnson?"

"Yes, ma'am. Mr. Cartwright likes a slice of pie with his dinner." When she stands her face is flushed and strands of grey hair are stuck to her forehead. "Don't you, Mr. Cartwright?" she calls over.

Cartwright leans forward. "I do indeed, Mrs. Johnson."

"Your mistress cannot afford all of the butter and meat that this household gets through each week. Indeed, I can't imagine how it's possible for so few people to eat so much."

Mrs. Johnson links her hands together over her belly. "Well, Mrs. Bentley has never complained. She wouldn't want us to live on bread and cheese as some mistresses might." For a moment she stares right into Mina's face, then she bends towards the oven again. "Excuse me, ma'am, but I need to get the pies out before they're overdone, and there's luncheon to start. Next time I'll be happy to come upstairs rather than putting you to the bother of coming down here. That's how the mistress has always done it."

"Then you'll be so good as to bring up this week's bills from the grocer and the butcher, and be ready to explain where exactly so much butter and meat have gone. I'm sure Mrs. Bentley will also be eager to hear your explanation when she recovers." She stands perfectly still to let her words hang in the air. But Mrs. Johnson dips a cloth into the oven and pulls the pies out from the racks and slides them onto the table. "Did you hear me, Mrs. Johnson?"

"Oh yes, ma'am." She wipes her hands on the cloth and twists her head towards Mina. "Next time I'll come to see you upstairs."

Mina's hands lift, of their own accord it seems. What do they intend? To slap the broad face of this woman? To shove her, hard, against the table? However, they stop in midair, fingers curved, wrists bent back. Perhaps Mrs. Johnson notices, for she hurries away to the sink and Mina is left looking at the pies, and at Mr. Cartwright standing just beyond them.

"Mrs. Johnson is used to having her kitchen to herself," he says, and gives a slight nod.

"Yet it is not her kitchen, is it? It is her mistress's, and must be run according to her mistress's wishes."

"Yes, ma'am," he says flatly.

What good is it? She has got nowhere with these servants. Worse than that—she hasn't even left the room and their attention is elsewhere. Mrs. Johnson washing her hands at the sink. Cartwright tapping his fingers on the back of a chair. Elsie tugging at a loose thread on her apron.

She walks out, pulling the door closed behind her. She doesn't walk away, though, not yet. No, she leans her head towards the door and listens to Mrs. Johnson's voice curl up in annoyance, hears, "think we were thieves," and "back to Paris." The audacity of the woman, when in all likelihood she has come to some arrangement with the grocer and the butcher for the household to be charged for more than it uses, and to make a profit by it. How to catch her, though? How to watch when she cannot spend her days down here overseeing what is delivered and what is charged for and what is actually cooked?

Jane has noticed nothing. But this is not what Mina intended Jane to look out for.

She makes for the narrow stairs, her shoulders uncomfortably stiff and her dress damp under her arms, up to the morning room, where she will sit and stare out at the gloom hanging over the city.

*I*t's a cold morning, thick with fog, and Jane's called upstairs, up to Mr. Robert's study. She hasn't seen him in the two days since the burglary, but she's been thinking: Is there something she overlooked? Something that would explain the whole incident? The sensation that no one in this household quite trusts her has lingered. Maybe, she thinks, Mr. Robert wants to question her again, but what more can she tell him? As she knocks at the door she can't help but bite her teeth hard together.

Of course she's been in this room since the last time Mr. Robert called her up, because there was the grate to clean and the fire to lay. This time, though, Mr. Robert is here and he seems out of place, something that doesn't belong in a room that she is used to seeing when she is the only person in it.

"Ah," he says when she comes in. "Ah yes." He doesn't put down the document he is reading, and she understands that she should wait. The papers that the intruder left lying about have all been tidied away, back into the boxes that give the room a moved-in look. But then, she thinks, he and Mrs. Robert are only here for a few weeks. That's what she's learnt downstairs. With his mother sick and Mr. Henry coming back from India soon, this world she's been pulled into could soon break apart.

She has stopped herself from asking more. That way Mr. Cartwright's eyes do not search hers out, and he doesn't say, "Wilbred. Not such a common name, is it?" or "I know that name from somewhere. I'm certain I do," as he has so many times already. Instead during meals she keeps her head down and her eyes on her plate while Mr. Cartwright tells them about what he's read in the day-old newspaper Mr. Robert lets him bring downstairs. A report of the burglary in *The Times,* herself as the unnamed maid who opened the door, the police still investigating when in fact they have not been back.

When she raises her eyes now she finds Mr. Robert watching her. It startles her, the intensity of that stare, and she looks away to the window and the backs of the next street's houses. Surely, she thinks, he must notice something not quite right in the way she doesn't want to meet his eye.

Instead he only shifts in his chair, says, "Very good, very good." He comes around to the other side of the desk, where he stands so close that she catches the scent of Macassar oil on his hair. Then he grasps her chin and lifts it, turns her head this way and that. Inside she shrinks. This is not right. This cannot be right. But before she can think what to do he has let go, and she watches as he treads across the carpet to a cabinet where a wooden box waits. He carries it to his desk, then fetches a chair that he sets down beside her. "Please sit," he says. Not a request. A command. So she sits.

He is rummaging behind his desk, and without glancing up tells her, "Remove your cap, if you wouldn't mind."

But she does mind. Her cap? No. Her eyes are blinking fast, and her hands are twisting together in her lap. She wonders, is this how it is to be ruined?

There come the thin sounds of metal on metal, of instruments of some kind knocking against the wood of the box, but she won't look. She'd run from the room except it would do no good. She has nowhere to go except downstairs, and what would she say? Why would they believe her? Or maybe—and her head twitches around in panic because he's coming close—this is what Mrs. Saunders meant by telling her that her character could be at stake. And if she resists? Will she be dismissed?

He is carrying a large metal device like a pair of tongs designed to lift a very large egg, and the sight of them makes her whimper out loud. She presses a hand over her mouth.

"Your cap," he says. When she doesn't move, he reaches for it himself. She hears a thin wail, and it takes her a moment to realize it is coming from her own mouth. He steps back, and she sees surprise in the arch of his eyebrows.

"I'm a good girl, sir," she cries out. "Please. Please."

He sits on the edge of his desk and lifts his hands, the device in one, the other palm out to her. "Calm yourself," he tells her quietly.

She's not listening. Now that she has dared to speak, she can't stop. "I can't be ruined like this, sir. Have pity on me, sir, please, please, I can't—" Her voice breaks. Unable to say more, she brings her apron up to cover her face and, in the privacy of its white cotton, lets sobs rise through her chest.

She's so caught up in her misery that it takes her a few minutes to realize that he has not said anything more, and has not come close again. In fact, it is so quiet that she wonders if he is still in the room. Has he left? Or is he watching her, silently? From the mantelpiece a clock chimes the quarter hour. Her crying has a halfhearted quality about it. She should be clearing the dining room and making a start on the stairs. In one go, she lets the apron drop.

He's behind his desk, head bent, writing. Now that she has uncovered herself he looks up. "Ready?" he asks, and the dread creeps back into her.

In the end it wasn't so awful, at least not in the way she'd imagined.

Still it took time—so much time. What's more, it has left her with the strange sensation that a part of her has been taken away and might be examined by Mr. Robert or anyone else who cares to see it, anytime they wish. All those notes he made on that small card, then tucked it away with so many others in a special box full of drawers upon drawers of cards. She even got up the courage to ask him what it was all for and he said, "To keep track of people. With this"—he tapped her card—"you'll never be able to pass yourself off as someone other than Jane Wilbred without me knowing."

He smiled, but she didn't.

Now she has to hurry to get the carpet swept. The tea leaves she sprinkles over it clump. While she was in the study fresh leaves must have been added to the ones she'd squeezed out, and now not only is she an hour behind in her work, everything is going wrong: the too-damp tea leaves, Mrs. Robert in the morning room just when she needs to give it a thorough going-over, her box short on blacking and Mrs. Johnson too busy to get more, the hem of her dress snagging on the sharp corner of a side table and ripping. She'll have to stay up late tonight fixing it. There'll be no time before that, what with having to catch up with all that has to be done this morning.

Through it all—all this sweeping and carrying and polishing that make up her day—she feels the cold grip of the device he put on her head. What had she been expecting? Not that, that's for sure. Something more along the lines of the tales she'd wasted her money on when she first started at the Saunderses', at least until Mrs. Saunders found them at the bottom of her box. What a lecture she got. Stories rot the brain, they flatter a girl's vanity, they lead her astray. Mrs. Saunders had held up one of her magazines by the corner, as though touching it would contaminate her. "Priscilla's Adventures," she read out loud, then she looked up at Jane. "Is this the reading that our Lord sanctions? Will it make you modest and obedient and satisfied with your station in life?" Jane had to admit that no, it wouldn't. So Mrs. Saunders dropped the magazine into the fire, then the next, all of them one by one, and it had seemed an act of needless cruelty. At least she'd read them all except the last one, and as it curled up in the flames she resigned herself to never knowing what happened to Priscilla Tremault and Lord James. In the weeks afterwards, this was the story that lived on in her. Pushing a bucket of water and her candle across the floor as she scrubbed, she'd find all manner of ways for Lord James to rescue Priscilla from the count, and to marry her, and to keep his inheritance despite his uncle, because after all, she wasn't just a maid, she was the daughter of a French nobleman.

Now, as she shakes the carpet brush free of the tea leaves sticking to its bristles, she thinks how those stories, and Mrs. Saunders's warnings, too, prepared her to protect her modesty, but did not tell her what to do when her master sat her in a chair and measured her head every which way, as though he was planning to make her a hat. Even after she thought he must be finished he kept measuring, with a whole boxful of instruments: her ears, her nose, the position of her eyes and mouth, the length of her arms, her fingers, and then, making her take off her boots and stand flat against the wall, her height. Afterwards he didn't tell her to move, so she stood there while he wrote on the card and filed it away, staring at her boots where she'd left them on the carpet, those ugly worn things, thick and heavy, sitting on a red carpet laced with designs of leaves and flowers that was so pretty you could have hung it on the wall and looked at it like a painting.

Eventually when he turned around he seemed surprised that she was still there. He said, "You may go," in such a way that she felt caught out, as though she should have known. She gathered up her boots in one hand and her cap in the other and hesitated. Should she put them back on here, when he'd dismissed her? Or did she dare carry them out into the hallway when anyone passing would see her like that, cap missing, boots in her hand, creeping around as though she'd been up to no good? He must have seen her falter, for he told her, "Thank you, thank you for your time," though without really looking at her. So she stepped out into the hallway. A noise from the stairs—of feet shifting? Of someone leaning against the banister? She wasn't sure, but she hurried away to the dining room, where her brushes and dusters waited for her.

From under a glass dome on the mantelpiece a clock strikes the hour. She's hopelessly behind, and the chimes send her whirling around the room with her duster. Over the mantel and the clock's dome, over the vase on the far side, over another glass dome with an arrangement of dried flowers beneath it, then to the side tables.

Gritty dust everywhere, as though no one has dusted in weeks, when in fact she dusted in here only yesterday. Then the door opens. Sarah. It's always Sarah, as though she has the time to be looking in on her like this. She has a curious smile on her face as she presses the door closed behind her.

"You're not finished?" she says. "You're going to catch it."

"I got called in to see Mr. Robert."

"Mr. Robert? Again?" She comes closer. "Did he tell you anything about the burglar? Is that what it was about?"

She shakes her head. "Not that. No."

Sarah walks over to the window and looks out. "Lost your tongue this morning, have you?"

Her face is burning. She turns away, but not quickly enough.

Sarah laughs. "What on earth have you been up to?"

She rubs the arm of a chair with her duster, though she should shake it out—it is grey with dust.

"We mustn't keep secrets—at least not from each other. Come on—out with it."

With the duster squashed into her fist she looks over at Sarah. Against the window she's little more than a silhouette. "He measured me."

"Oh—that." Sarah wraps her arms around herself. "He's called us all in there. It gave me the creeps." She turns back to the window and leans her hip against the frame. "What I wouldn't give to go out whenever I liked. Wouldn't that be the best thing about being a lady? You could just leave and there'd be no one to say you couldn't." She lets out a sigh and comes over to Jane. "Anyway, this afternoon I'm going to fetch the new tazza."

"You haven't got it yet? Hasn't anyone noticed?"

"Haven't had the chance, have I? Cartwright said something about it being strange it was gone—don't worry about him, though. He's not going to make a fuss, not when he owes me a favor or two. Now, I've still got the hallway to finish—you can do that for me, can't you? Just skimp a bit here and there along the way, and you'll fly through it all."

"All right then," says Jane. But the thought of having more to do weighs on her. There is more than one person can manage, far more.

Sarah shakes out her apron. "If Mrs. J. asks why you're so behind, you can tell her Mr. Robert wanted you for his measuring." With that she spins on her heel and heads for the door. As for Jane, she stands on the edge of the carpet, holding her duster and looking about her at all there is left to do.

*I*t's so late that Mr. Cartwright has locked up the house, and Mrs. Johnson wished her good night and left the room in the swaying light of her candle. Jane listens to her footsteps fading down the corridor, then the groan of her door as she pushes it closed. That morning lost in the study, and having the hallway to finish, set her behind the whole day. Now when she should be going to bed she is still down in the kitchen sitting over a slice of bread and dripping because she missed dinner. Elsie has pulled a small folding bed out from the pantry and is sitting on the edge of it to unlace her boots. Both of them glance around as the door squeaks, but it's only Sarah. In her hands she holds something wrapped in a cloth. She sets it down on the kitchen table and plucks off the cloth, like a magician doing a trick. "Look," she says. "Not a perfect match, but close to it."

The new tazza. Jane snatches in her breath. "How did you manage it?" She bends her chin almost to the tabletop, her hands on its edge, not wanting even to touch the thing.

"I know where the missus shops," she says, and she pauses. "It isn't a cheap place. Five pounds, this cost."

"Yes," says Jane, and she lifts her head, "yes, of course. I'll pay you back." Does her shock show on her face? She hopes not. Five pounds. More than a third of her wages for the year, for what's hardly more than a fancy plate on a pedestal.

"Well then"—Sarah takes up the tazza—"all that's left is to put it back where it came from."

The closing door leaves a shudder of cool air in her wake, and Jane shivers as she takes another bite of the bread. The dripping slides across her tongue, greasy and slick, and for a moment she thinks she might gag. No, she tells herself, you can't—not when you've barely eaten all day. If you can't keep your strength up, you can't work, and if you can't work, you'll be on the street. So she forces herself to open her mouth wide and tear off another piece of the bread and to lick the dripping from her lips. Butter, she thinks—butter would have been so delicious. But after Mrs. Robert came downstairs and warned Mrs. Johnson about using too much—she heard all about that, saw the way Mrs. Johnson's mouth set like a trap afterwards to hold in her anger—they've had to make do with dripping. As for Mrs. Johnson, she's been quiet ever since, as though she is weighing things in her mind.

Jane chews with her eyes closed and her arms flat on the table beside her plate. They feel so heavy that when it's time to take another bite she has to tell herself to lift them, to make them reach for the bread, to bring it to her mouth. Then she lets her eyes close again. Her hands smart from where small splits have opened up—so much of the day with her hands in water, or polishing with silver sand, or bringing the furniture to a gleam with a mixture Mrs. Johnson makes up that stings her raw skin. As for her joints, they're swollen and aching. It's almost enough to make her cry, but she doesn't. Every night since she can remember her hands have pained her like this. Not just at the Saunderses' but before, at the orphanage, where training up girls meant having them scrub floors and pans and clothes from sunup to long past sunset.

A little dripping has smeared onto her fingers, and she rubs it in. Five pounds, she thinks. It'll be spring before she's paid Sarah back. She sees those weeks upon weeks laid out before her, filled with fetching coal and emptying slops. All for nothing. All because she was tired.

There's a strange gurgling noise. It intrudes far enough into her tiredness to make her open her eyes. Elsie, rocking herself on the edge of her bed, her dress down below her shoulders so that Jane can see the top of her chemise, laughing, laughing.

"What is it?" says Jane. "What's so funny?"

"Oh Lord," says Elsie. "You're in for it now, well and good." She almost chokes on the words. "You owe her, don't you? A favor here, a favor there—it all adds up, don't it?" She stands and pulls down her dress, then steps out of it. Beneath it her flannel petticoat is patched and stained.

"I'll pay what I owe."

"Oh no." Elsie drapes her dress over the back of a chair. "You won't—you won't ever be able to do that."

Jane pushes her plate away. "That's enough of that foolish talk."

"Oh, la-di-da." Elsie sits back down and brings her feet up onto the bed, then arranges the covers over herself.

She should mend the rip in her dress, but she can't bring herself to, not tonight when it takes such an effort to move. So instead she hauls herself to her feet and takes her plate over to the sink. She busies herself washing and drying it and putting it away. Now that the room is dim the vermin are out. When she turns shapes scatter across the floor before her like spilled beans.

Elsie has laid her head on a thin pillow. In this light it looks filthy, her blanket too. Her eyes are closed, but she's not asleep. "I'd watch yourself," she says softly.

Jane stares down at where Elsie lies, her bony face all shadows, making her look like an old woman on her deathbed.

She lights her candle stub from Elsie's—maybe she should blow out Elsie's for her, but she doesn't. After all, what does she owe her? She lets herself out into the corridor and starts up the stairs towards the room on the second floor where Sarah is already in bed, and where she will lie so close that, if Sarah sighs too heavily, Jane will feel her breath on her face. She has done wrong, she tells herself, letting Sarah replace that tazza. She should have taken the broken pieces to Mrs. Robert and shown her what she'd done, and borne the consequences—one of Mrs. Saunders's favorite words, *consequences*. Because even if she'd been dismissed, maybe that would not have been so bad. Maybe she could have found herself another situation.

Nonsense, of course. Without a character no decent mistress would want her. Besides, if she wanted to admit to what she'd done she could still do it—though now, of course, it would mean admitting that Sarah helped her cover up the breakage, and that would mean trouble for both of them. So what is there to do except climb the stairs, up to where Sarah is probably already asleep?

As she lifts her tired feet from one step to the next with her shadow looming over her from the walls, the idea of lying down in that bed, so close to Sarah, fills her with dread. Five pounds for a tazza. Who would have thought that Sarah had five pounds saved?

Silly, she tells herself, letting Elsie make her afraid like that when Sarah has been a good friend to her. And yet, the farther up the stairs she climbs, the smaller she feels—small as a cat, small as a mouse, small as a creature that seeks out dark corners and lives in fear of its life.

CHAPTER 6

The hat, when Robert Bentley gets his hands on it on Monday morning, is nothing remarkable. Yet it took all the weight of his letter of introduction from Monsieur Bertillon of the Paris Police Prefecture's Department of Judicial Identity to obtain it: the hat that was left in his house—in his possession!—by the intruder five days before. The police offered it up reluctantly, although, as they admitted, they'd found nothing more than the stains of Macassar oil belonging to a man with a head larger than the average—they had, they told him, all tried it on and it fit none of them. As for the name of the hatter—a popular establishment among gentlemen, they told him, though Robert could have told them that himself, for it is the same shop from which he bought his hats when he lived in London. Had they, he asked, been to the shop and asked to view their records? The officer who handed him the hat had scoffed. "Are you aware of the number of crimes daily reported to this station, sir?" and he'd leant forward onto the counter, his eyebrows raised. "Although the intrusion into your house was disturbing, as you yourself have admitted, nothing is missing. Am I right, sir?" It certainly was right, and he admitted as much. Were such intrusions to be overlooked, then? Good God—what a state of affairs!

At home he sits in his study and stares at the hat, turning it this way and that in the feeble light coming through the window. The crown is dusty, and is marked by a greasy spot that might have come from a candle. Inside, the red silk lining is a little stained. The owner has not taken good care of his hat, but what else is there to deduce? An hour later, when he steps into a hansom, he has the hat under one arm and his other weighed down by his box of instruments.

He should head straight for the prison to be sure of arriving in good time. Yet barely has the cab reached the end of Cursitor Road when he calls out to the driver: "Oxford Street. Not the prison, but Heath's on Oxford Street."

When he arrives at the hatter's there is only one other gentleman there, a thin man with flushed cheeks who is in deep discussion with the more senior shop assistant. A young man comes towards the counter. "Good morning, sir. Can I help you?"

All of a sudden he feels a little foolish. He had, he realizes, been imagining himself as a sort of Holmes who could, from this one hat, glean everything he needed to know about its owner. After all, he is a man of science, and has been trained to extract inferences and information from the scantiest of details. However, as he sets the hat on the counter between him and the young man, he cannot find the words to begin. Together the two of them stare down at it.

"This hat," he says, "was left in my possession."

The assistant pulls a large handkerchief from his pocket. "Yes, sir?" The end of his nose is red. He dabs at it, giving a loud sniff.

"Yes." Robert turns the hat over so they can peer inside. "It is from this shop, as the label indicates—as you can see." He points with one finger. "The initials were once marked here, but they have been worn away and are illegible."

"Yes, sir." The young man holds his handkerchief bunched in one hand. His eyes narrow as he swallows, as though it pains him to do so. "Do you wish to purchase another similar in style to this one?"

Robert looks up. "No. I wish to find out who the owner is."

"I see." He looks down at his handkerchief and folds it. "Would not the owner find that he is missing his hat and come to claim it? Or wouldn't a small advertisement in the newspaper alert the owner to his loss?"

"Unfortunately, this hat was left in my house by a person who intruded himself into my home and apparently wished to keep his identity to himself."

"Ah," says the young man. "Then is it not going beyond the call of duty to want to return it?"

Robert straightens himself up. He is ready to snap at this young man, to tell him that he isn't a fool—but instead he lets out a burst of air from between his teeth. "I am trying to discover who it was that forced his way into my house during my absence, and this hat is all I have for my information. I am, in short, doing the work that the police have chosen not to do."

He realizes as he finishes his explanation that the shop is largely silent. From behind a curtain steps a short man with slicked-back grey hair and small features. There is something of a seal about him. "May I be of assistance?"

And so Robert is escorted into the back of the shop—not into the area where gentlemen have their heads measured in curtained privacy but beyond, to an office piled high with papers tied with ribbon and ledgers leaning drunkenly against one another on the shelves. Here he explains his problem again, then lays the hat on the ledger open between them.

The man—Mr. Heath, as it turns out, the proprietor of this shop—presses his fingers together and listens. "I see," he says. "I see."

"And I am myself one of your patrons," he finishes.

"But not recently." He gives a smile that shows small teeth.

"Exactly right." Robert smiles back, but only with some effort.

"Your hat, you see," says Mr. Heath. "The flat brim—it's more the French style."

"You're right. I've lived in Paris for some years—working, in fact, with Monsieur Bertillon of the Paris Police Prefecture."

"Ah, the famous Monsieur Bertillon, who would have us all measured up from the crowns of our heads to the length of our feet."

"All criminals. In the case of the criminal element, it is all too easy for the name to become separated from the person." He lifts the hat. "An article such as this might bring the two back together, at least in the case of my burglar."

"I see." Mr. Heath leans forward excitedly. "If we measure the hat for its size, we can compare it to the list of the gentlemen who have purchased such hats from my shop." He lifts the hat out of Robert's hands and holds it up to the light. "In the last three years, I'd say, from the curled edge to the brim. But its owner has not treated it kindly." He taps the dusty crown with one finger.

Then he stands and runs his pale hands over the ledgers on the shelf behind him. "Yes, yes," he mutters to himself. He lifts two of the big books onto the desk, and pauses with one hand flat on the cover of the top one. He licks his lips. "You must understand that under normal circumstances I wouldn't—"

"I quite understand."

He nods as though this is good enough and moistens his finger on his tongue to turn the pages. His body is all angles, as though he is so excited by the prospect of this investigation that he can barely contain himself. He snatches up a pencil and pulls out a sheet of paper and starts to write.

At first Robert can scarcely believe his luck. This man is as eager as he is to get to the bottom of this matter. But as the clock on the mantelpiece ticks out the seconds, then the minutes, and more than twenty have passed with Mr. Heath turning the pages and occasionally making a note, his foot starts to tap the air and he looks about him with vexation. If he does not leave in the next five minutes he will be late arriving at the prison, and the governor does not take kindly to his visitors—visitors who are there, after all, only under his sufferance—arriving late. So he clears his throat and sits a little farther forward. "Mr. Heath—are you getting close to the end?"

"Oh yes, very close." He runs his finger down each line, on and on until, with a hiss of a sigh like a train coming in to a station, he holds out a slip of paper. "I have four names for you, Mr. Bentley. This hat size and this style—they are not often found in combination, as my records show. The hat size is somewhat larger than the average. We can assume, if we follow Mr. Holmes's methods, that your man is of above average intelligence, but of a rather retiring nature."

"Retiring? I would hardly think so. He had the audacity to have himself let into my house and to rifle through my belongings."

"Oh yes, retiring," repeats Mr. Heath. "Only the more shy of our customers would choose a hat so unlikely to draw notice to itself."

The clock on the mantel strikes the hour, and Robert Bentley pushes back his chair. "Your help has been invaluable." He extends his hand.

"A pleasure." Heath shakes it. "A pleasure, sir. Though I do have a couple of small requests."

"Certainly."

"If you are successful, would you be good enough to let me know who out of our four men is the culprit? You see"—he taps the side of his nose—"I have my own theory. Also, there would, of course, be no need to mention how you discovered his identity."

"None whatsoever, I'm sure." Robert puts the folded paper into his pocket and takes up the hat.

Outside the sun has taken the dampness off the air. His hansom is still there, the driver with a pipe sticking out of the corner of his mouth and a grey cloud of smoke hanging about his head. "As fast as you can, now," he calls, and climbs in. The slip of paper is in his right pocket, and his fingers tremble slightly as he pulls it out. For a moment he fumbles with it—the paper is folded so precisely into quarters that with his gloves on he cannot open it. Then it spreads like a butterfly, a small white butterfly on which the hatter has written four names: Joseph McDonald, Michael Danforth, Richard Dupont, and David Tate.

He doesn't recognize any of them.

Flyte is there, as usual. When he sees Robert enter the room his creased face brightens into a smile, and he presses his small hat more firmly onto his head. It is the same drab color as his uniform, a slant of badly starched fabric that looks like a child's paper hat. On the other prisoners the outfit looks forlorn; on Flyte it somehow suggests an optimistic spirit, as though his time here is something he can take pride in.

Isn't that the point, thinks Robert—to transform convicts? To make them want to earn positions of trust? To make them useful to society once more? And yet—and yet Flyte's eagerness annoys him, for in it he can't help but detect a note of insincerity.

Flyte steps forward, head tilted towards Robert's. "I was beginning to worry, sir," he confides. "You've not been late before."

Robert points for the guard to set down his box close to the table. Another stands by the door and looks on. They have a way of standing that sets him ill at ease. Is it the way they watch him? Yes, he thinks, because unlike normal men their heads do not turn when they want to look to the side, as though they're forever trying to catch you out by watching out of the corners of their eyes.

Who can blame them? In this place there are murderers and men who have committed outrages on women—on children, too. There are men who must be locked away forever and who might have grown desperate at such a prospect. And they have ways—the governor told him this on his first visit—they have ways of secreting sharp objects on their persons, and the cleverest of them can fashion a weapon from the simplest object—a comb, a pencil even.

Of course, Robert is used to such things. He knows that the governor has not mentioned the knives and money and other contraband that surely makes its way past the guards. He has been in French prisons, and their prisoners seem neither better nor worse than the English variety—he has seen fights in which men's throats were slit, and the way one man can leap on another and puncture his eyeball with a weapon that is never found.

Yet at least the French, thanks to Monsieur Bertillon and his anthropometry, have a better idea of whom they have in their prisons. Should thief Marcel Desjardins be released and shortly afterwards a man calling himself Thierry Martin be caught breaking into a house, they will know them to be the same man. For a French recidivist there is no longer a sporting chance that a change of name and a shave of his moustache will be enough to make a different man of him. No. He will be betrayed by the length of his ears, the length of his fingers, by every measurement taken by Bertillon and the men he has trained.

This is part of what Robert is here to do—to help train the guards in this prison who are responsible for processing new prisoners. An experiment of his own devising. A trial to see if such a method "works"—though it has been shown to work elsewhere. A chance to convince the Troup Committee that must soon decide: anthropometry or fingerprints? As though most of Europe hadn't yet decided, or the United States. As though there still remained any real debate.

"So," he says as he tugs off his gloves and drops them into his hat, "are we ready to begin?"

"Oh yes, sir," says Flyte. He lifts a hand and lays it along the length of his face in a way that he has. "The guards have been dispatched to bring today's men. As for Mr. Jessop and Mr. Arthur—" he glances at the clock high on the wall "—I expect they will be here shortly."

"Thank you, Flyte." Robert sits.

The guards are still by the door, stiff as posts, the two of them. They could safely leave him here with Flyte, but maybe they have been instructed not to. After all, Flyte is a prisoner, albeit hardly a dangerous one by the look of him. Robert watches as he fusses about the room. He gives the impression of being a small man, though in fact he can't be much less than average height. It's his stoop that does it, and his odd little ways with his hands, as though he is forever trying to find a good place to put them and has not yet come up with the right one. Even as Robert watches him, Flyte lays a hand on his belly—like Napoleon, he thinks—then, as he checks the pens and the ink pots, he lifts his hand and places it at the top of his chest, as a woman might.

Maybe he's conscious of Robert's gaze, for he turns and smiles again. His face is thin like a mouse's, and his skin is tinged yellow against his uniform. "Is there any news from the outside, sir?" he asks. "Is the queen still poorly?"

"Indeed she is, Flyte."

"Well, I'm sorry to hear that, sir. I've always been a devoted subject of Her Majesty."

At that one of the guards lets out a snort, and Flyte darts a look at him. His hands curl into fists, not like a man about to fight, more like a child who has been willfully misunderstood yet must hold back his frustration.

Robert knits his fingers together and watches as Flyte comes closer.

"I remember her jubilee." He glances behind him to where the guards are standing and lowers his voice. "Of course, that was before my present troubles. My wife and I held a little celebration in Her Majesty's honor."

"Your wife?" says Robert, before he catches himself. Without giving it much thought, he had assumed that a man like Flyte, a man so womanly in his gestures, would not have a wife.

"Yes, sir," says Flyte. "A beautiful woman, sir, even if I say so myself. And quite the one for organizing dinner parties."

"I see." He nods. For what else can he say? This woman—this Mrs. Flyte—momentarily finds his sympathy. He imagines her: a small woman who chatters away in a hushed voice, who has cluttered her house with porcelain statuettes of shepherds and shepherdesses and the like, a woman who arranged dinner parties for her husband's colleagues—dismal affairs, probably, ill-afforded out of a small budget. For what else could Flyte have been before his fall except a clerk or something of that nature? And now—well, now most likely she would be earning her own keep for the first time in her life. She'd have had to give up the house and the servant, and spend her days taking in sewing or, even more pitifully, painting on porcelain and trying to sell her work, when London is awash with the handiwork of thousands of such ladies.

What has Flyte done to ruin her life and his own? Some sort of fraud, Robert suspects. A slow draining of a bank customer's account into his own, or the sly redirection of a commercial house's funds when he thought no one would notice—and all because Mrs. Flyte needed a new dress for their next dinner party, and a new set of silverware, and another servant, not out of the workhouse, but one who could lay a table without disgracing them. Curiosity pricks at him, but it will pass. Better not to ask—he learnt that in Paris. One of the prisoners there had been a funny fellow, always ready with a joke, and a quick way about him that made him invaluable in getting prisoners measured. One morning Robert had asked a guard about him, and after that could hardly bear to be in the same room as the man. On Christmas Eve he'd beaten his sister so badly that her head had caved in, then had taken her body to the river, sawn it up, and tied it into sacks. Afterwards he'd washed and changed and gone to midnight mass, where he'd told everyone his sister had run away with the baker's apprentice. He'd only just escaped execution. His cousin had spoken for him, had maybe even bribed the judge.

Footsteps, then the door opens. Two guards: Jessop with his small prow of a chin that rises so easily in indignation; Arthur with his eyes that look forever on the verge of closing in sleep. These are the guards Robert must train.

Flyte is sent off to collect the first batch of new prisoners. They arrive sweating, fresh from the treadmill, though rather than the pointlessness of it wearying them, the exercise seems to have invigorated them. One man refuses to spread his arms, another to hold his head still. Only when the guards by the door come close do they allow Jessop and Arthur to measure them.

And so the afternoon passes, with each man put through the Bertillon method, or as close to it as Robert has managed without all of the specialized equipment. He watches Jessop and Arthur do the measuring—three times for each measurement to make it accurate to the millimeter. That is another difficulty: these men confuse centimeters and millimeters, and he has to explain to Arthur yet again that there are not sixteen millimeters to a centimeter, but ten. Between writing down measurements and fetching prisoners, Flyte finds time to bring him a cup of tea. He drinks only half of it, for, horrified, he spots Jessop measuring a prisoner's foot with his shoe still on and springs out of his chair to intervene, then must rearrange the cards in the small cabinet he has set up for the purpose, since no matter how many times he explains, Arthur cannot seem to understand that a card misfiled is as bad as a card lost.

When he gets back to his tea it is cold. He drinks it anyway, his mouth pursed against the unpleasant feel of it. If the fate of anthropometry in Britain rests in part on these men, then his efforts, he thinks, might all be for nothing.

*I*t is not until Robert is on his way home, reading the evening paper between the jolts and swings of the hansom, that his eye catches the name Michael Danforth. For a moment he lifts his head, trying to place it. Then he plunges his hand into his pocket and pulls out the paper Heath gave him: it is the second name on the list. Michael Danforth has just testified before the Troup Committee, making the case for the use of dactylography, not anthropometry, as the primary means for England to keep track of its criminals. The weakness of the case for using fingerprints must be evident even to its proponents if Michael Danforth risked everything to break into his house! He lets out a burst of laughter and punches his leg with glee.

CHAPTER 7

From the window Mina Bentley can see nothing but the backsides of the houses behind Cursitor Road and a band of dingy sky. A thin rain is falling. She puts down her pen and stretches first her arms, then her back. Her chair creaks and she gives a loud yawn. "God," she mutters to herself, "what a dreary town." As much as she can, she has kept inside. She has excuses for Robert—there are the household accounts to look over, there are the servants to supervise while his mother is ill.

She would give anything to be out in London's streets, in the life and bustle of the place—not a street like Cursitor Road, walled in by high, blank-faced houses, but in a part of the city where there is life. But she must not risk that more than absolutely necessary. It would be dangerous. Two days after arriving here—her first time to step foot outside this house!—she caught the eye of a man leaning against the railings across the street. A quiet bulk of a man with a thick beard that hid his mouth, and shabby gentleman's clothes. He seemed to have nothing better to do than to smoke his pipe and occasionally stroll about with a newspaper under his arm. She was certain he'd been there since breakfast time—what could he be doing? He didn't belong in a street like this. As she came down the steps his gaze hung on her, and she felt a clutch of panic in her chest. Since then she has seen him out there from the dining room window and decided she would not go out. Is such fear ridiculous? Perhaps. But then there was Lizzie, and the thin man who'd taken off up the street, and Lizzie's face looking so thoughtful.

It's easy to tell yourself you're making too much of such incidents. Isn't it?

She forces her attention back to the papers on the desk. Even with Marie and Madame Pépin on board wages for the time being, expenses have not gone down substantially. There is still the rent to be paid. Bills have been coming in—for the new dress she bought before leaving Paris, for the boxes the carpenter made for Robert's equipment to transport it safely to London, for food from the butcher and the baker that has already been eaten and forgotten. Now what is left in the bank account has withered away. She's known for months this would happen. Of course—they have no income as such, only expenses. Her money could not last forever. Yet to see it so reduced—to know that they must do something, and for Robert that means finding a position here in London—fills her with dread.

There is hope, though, and she sits back and lets the pen roll across the open flap of the desk. It comes to rest against papers and account books shoved carelessly into the pigeonholes at the back. Or not so carelessly—the burglar must have sat here, picking through the papers, replacing them carefully. But what might he have found out?

Nothing more than she knows: that Robert's mother has little else now beside the house, that all the property his grandfather once owned has been sold off over the years because his only son was determined to be a gentleman. Now Robert's father has long been dead, and his older son has taken off for India and the civil service, and the younger one—well, maybe Robert isn't so different from his father. When she met him he'd been living in cheap lodgings, using what money he could save from the allowance his mother sent him to buy equipment. A man of twenty-seven! Yet, she'd loved him for his lack of interest in money, and for the way he'd been shocked by her suggestion that he use his knowledge and education to earn a decent living. How could he, when he had so much to learn at the side of his beloved Monsieur Bertillon? To her, though, Bertillon seemed a cold fish. Besides, as she pointed out, Bertillon earned his living, didn't he? He was chief of the Department of Judicial Identity for the Paris Police Prefecture. Robert had thought about that, had turned serious. One day, he said, he'd persuade the British government to do as the French had, to adopt anthropometry, and then they'd need someone—a Monsieur Bertillon, of sorts. And maybe that would be him. She'd nodded, said, *One day*. As though that day would never come, or else by the time it did she'd be ready for London. Ever since they'd married she'd found reasons why they couldn't visit—she was ill; she'd arranged to have people over for dinner after the Christmas concert; she'd accepted Monsieur and Madame Martin's invitation to stay in their villa in Nice—Madame wanted to teach her to swim. Robert was to have come to London on his own to testify before the Troup Committee, but when the news arrived that his mother had taken ill she'd had no excuse for why she could not accompany him.

And now? Even if Robert's testimony does sway the Troup Committee, there'll be no position for him before her money is worn down to nothing. Is that what it will come down to? Living here on the thin hope of Robert's prospects, hiding herself away as best she can? No. They must return to Paris. They must have money.

She props her chin on her hand. Upstairs her mother-in-law is lying in the expanse of her bed. Beside her, Price might be dozing, or measuring out her medicine. Or, more likely, reading a magazine she has taken without permission from the drawing room and that she will say she wanted for her mistress. How long might Robert's mother live? Another few weeks? Surely not even that. Then she and Robert will dismiss the servants, put the furniture up for auction, sell the house—such a house for one old woman! Henry will have to agree, of course. If he doesn't? He can buy Robert's half of the property—he will be here in a day or two. And once the dreadful affair of what promises to be a slow death is over, the business of the funeral and executing the will and finding a buyer for the house will unroll.

She leans over the paper, but she isn't thinking about her letter. She's thinking about what kind of man Mr. Henry Bentley must be. A careful man. A man who takes control, who organizes. After all, wasn't it he who insisted on having the water closet installed on the half-landing? And the new stove down in the kitchen? And wasn't he the one who after the chaos of his father's dying without a will, would not let his mother make a similar mistake? Mina picks up the pen and lets the end of it rest against her lips. She will have to be cautious around him—a man who looks off into the future and sees consequences, a man who arranged his own mother's will. A will that not only makes him and his brother beneficiaries, but is careful to lay out what should happen should he or Robert marry and die, so that under no circumstances will their widows or children be in doubt as to their inheritance.

She makes herself lean back over the papers. There are still the bills to be paid, and a letter to be sent to Marie with instructions for her and Madame Pépin. She writes the date at the top of a new sheet of paper but finds herself looking out the window. Hard to keep her attention on the desk when a coldness has gripped her gut. There's a dinner tonight, despite her protests that there is little use in socializing here when they will be leaving again so soon. For some reason Robert has insisted this time. So they will go out—to the Fosdykes'. Robert and Mr. Fosdyke will talk about the dreary business of identifying criminals, all the measuring, the photographing, the difficulty of using fingerprints, leaving her to Mrs. Fosdyke and whatever conversation they can find between them.

It will all happen without incident, she tells herself. A four-wheeler will arrive, she will keep her head down as Robert helps her into it, and they will be closed into its privacy. By the time they return it will be dark.

Yet she can't rid herself of the sight of that man loitering in the street, a newspaper rolled under his arm, smoking a pipe and looking about him as though he was simply waiting for someone. What if he was waiting for her?

Ridiculous, she tells herself. More likely he is the follower of the cook across the street, or the impoverished uncle of some butler who lives nearby and is hoping to borrow money from him. Besides, has she seen him in the last few days? No, though a few doors away she's seen a man in a brown hat and a smooth chin—the man who took his place? Or the same man with an altered appearance?

Neither. It's all nonsense, the result of an imagination gone wild. Really, she tells herself, she must stop reading those detective stories in the *Strand*.

From the hallway she hears the chiming of the clock. Three o'clock already, and she's done little this afternoon. So she forces her pen back to the paper, writes a few lines, tells Marie that London is dreary and she hopes they will be back within a month or two. There's a knock at the front door, a double *rat-atat, rat-atat,* but she pays it no attention. She's gripping the pen hard, and though it makes her fingers ache, she keeps going. If Madame Guillaume should call, pass on her regards and ask about the baby. Be sure to clean the apartment thoroughly. Don't let the Bonzons' young maid persuade her to buy any more hats—she must be sensible with her money.

The knocking comes again, louder this time.

One floor below in his basement room, Cartwright puts down his glass of port and yesterday's newspaper. Only the postman, with a telegram by the sound of that insistent double knock. He straightens his tie and heaves himself out of his chair. He breathes a few times with his mouth open to clear the smell of alcohol. Where are the maids? Where is that Jane Wilbred? He walks up the stairs— Wilbred, the name makes him think of the police and a hanging, but over what? He can't remember exactly—he walks up the stairs and feels his breath tight in his chest and his head light. He has to hold on to the handrail to steady himself.

The postman sees nothing of this confusion, though. When Cartwright swings the door open he holds out a telegram and says needlessly, "Telegram."

At the back of the house, in the morning room, Mina Bentley is still bowed over the letter, her face close to the end of her pen. Along the hallway comes Mr. Cartwright, in his hands a salver holding the telegram. His tread is light enough for her not to hear his approach. Just before the door he stops for a moment. This has long been a habit of his. He has found out all manner of information this way: that after the master's death his mistress, despite her stiff face, wept when she was alone; that she was upset over Mr. Henry's decision to go to India; that although Mr. Robert wants to stay in London, Mrs. Robert is determined not to, that she hates this city. It made him like her less to hear her talk about London in that way, as though it is not good enough for the likes of her.

This afternoon, though, he hears nothing at all.

Mina lets the end of her pen rest against her lips. There's a knock at the door of the morning room this time. The servants have been told not to disturb her when she is working in here. She does not want their eyes wandering across her accounts, or noticing that their mistress's papers have been tugged out of their pigeonholes. She frowns and looks over her shoulder. This is not the first time— far from it. In the week after she arrived Price would come knocking with her demands that the doctor be called right away, although her mistress was no worse—and no better—than on the day before when he'd visited her. As for the maids—Sarah burst in three times in as many days and Lizzie, before she'd dismissed her, had the habit of rapping on the door then marching in as though determined to catch her at something. So now she simply calls out, "Yes?"

Through the door Cartwright tells her, "A telegram, Mrs. Robert."

"For me?"

"For Mr. Robert."

"He is out this afternoon, Cartwright."

"It is a telegram, ma'am. I thought you would like it brought to your attention." There's silence for a moment, and he scowls at her through the wood of the door.

"One moment."

He hears a chair being pushed back, the rustle of her skirts, then the key being turned. She has been in there most of the afternoon with the door locked—what, he wonders, does she have to hide? Sarah said she's been going through Mrs. Bentley's papers, and he'd had to hush her. It doesn't do to have the lower servants talking about the family like that. Still, he's taken to going down the back stairs more slowly, listening for what Sarah tells Mrs. Johnson, though that hasn't been much of any substance, as though there has been nothing at all to find. That in itself, he thinks, is strange—who hides the details of her life so carefully?

When Mina opens the door she sees only his jowly face, his flushed cheeks, the salver between his hands. Around him hangs the heady scent of alcohol. That, she thinks, she must mention to Robert, because it's not the first time. "Thank you," she says, and plucks the telegram away before pushing the door closed.

It is not, in fact, addressed to her husband. It says simply, "Bentley Residence." Despite her curiosity, it is not for her to open it. Instead she presses the envelope against the window and brings her face close. To her disappointment, the afternoon light is not strong enough for her to make out anything of the message. With a sigh she props the telegram against the desk lamp and goes back to her letter.

*H*e is dead. Henry James Bentley, drowned at sea in the foundering of the steamer the *Star of the Orient,* off the treacherous coast of France.

There is more news: he had a wife. And she has survived.

CHAPTER 8

Already the room feels haunted, stale with old smells, its furniture covered with dust sheets. The first thing Jane does is to push the sash up as high as it will go and fling the shutters open. Then she leans on the sill, breathing in the dirty air of London. Even on a morning like this, when frost glints on the roofs in the first sunlight of the day—hazy though it is—the air smells of coal, as though no wind is ever strong enough to sweep it away. She closes her eyes and tries to imagine the prickling smell of the sea that she has lived with for so long, but even after only a fortnight in this city, it can't be done.

This is the first time she's seen this room: Mr. Henry's room, not that he'll be needing it. He's already two days dead. After living in India, after coming all that way, to drown in the English Channel! And now they've put him in his coffin for what's left of the journey. That's what Mr. Cartwright said at breakfast. Jane wonders how it must be for his widowed bride to travel with her husband in a box, as though he were a piece of luggage.

With the window open the room is cold enough for her to see her breath, and it hangs in ghostly shapes. The covered furniture has a sinister look, as though Mr. Henry Bentley is here somewhere, lurking. It takes all her nerve, but she tugs off the dust sheets, one after the other, holding her breath until she sees beneath them only chairs, a dressing table, a washstand. The air is full of dust now, but she doesn't care. Better that than what she imagined beneath those sheets—Mr. Henry with his eyes rolled back and his clothes still damp from seawater, his cold, dead hands reaching for her.

She's shivering. She wraps her arms around herself and looks over what needs to be done: the mattress to be shaken and brushed, the bed made up with fresh linen, the curtains taken down, the rug taken up and beaten, the carpet swept, the floorboards scrubbed, the furniture polished, the trophies on the mantelpiece—what are they for?—dusted. By the time Sarah comes in she has already shaken out the top mattress and fed the feathers that escaped back through the seam of the tick. Over one arm Sarah has sheets and a blanket. She lifts her shoulders, says, "It's freezing in here."

"It smelled stale."

"Opening the window for half an hour isn't going to make any difference." She drops the linen on the bed and puts her hands on her hips. "If I were you, I'd close the window before I caught my death of cold."

"It's not so bad."

"Not so bad?" She shakes her head. "You've got no sense. No point making things harder on yourself, is there? Besides, when you're finished up here you'll have to give Elsie a hand with the laundry. Come on." She starts unfolding the under-blanket. "Let's get on with it."

"But I haven't swept yet."

"Who's going to know? If you want a hand, take it now before I change my mind."

This day is all wrong, her routine, such as it is, bucked and twisted. Today, laundry day of all days, there is Mr. Henry's room to do, on top of everything else, and Sarah's to do the other rooms as quickly as she can. Early this morning—at a time when the servants usually have the house to themselves—Mrs. Robert came downstairs and stood in the kitchen doorway to talk to them all, and she asked them for their greatest effort because, at a time like this, they all needed to help one another keep the household running as it should.

Sarah seems not to have listened. Mr. Henry is dead, but from the bright look about her you'd think that today was Christmas: not a day off, but a day of excitement and pleasure nonetheless. While Jane unfolds her end of the blanket and flaps it to loosen the creases, Sarah holds her end tight in her hands and says, "I wonder what she's like. Mrs. Johnson reckons Mr. Henry was a bit of an old stick-in-the-mud, and then he goes and gets married all of a sudden without telling anyone. Maybe she's a beauty and he couldn't help himself."

"Sarah!" It comes out more as a hiss than a word, and she glances around her. To speak so lightly of the dead—the very recently dead too—isn't right.

"Oh, come on." Sarah laughs. "You've been wondering too, I know you have."

Instead of saying anything, Jane presses her lips together.

"See?" Sarah sounds delighted. "You can't deny it."

But that's not it at all. Last night when she'd heard enough of Mrs. Johnson's stories about Mr. Henry as a serious young man, and Sarah's speculations about the widowed bride, and Elsie bursting out with "It's a bloomin' *tragedy*," she'd taken her candle and gone up to bed. When she heard Sarah come in she'd kept her eyes closed and her breathing slow. The darkness behind her eyes had lightened—Sarah standing close with her candle. She'd felt the tickle of Sarah's breath on her cheek.

"I know you're only pretending, orphan girl," she said and laughed softly.

Jane had to hold herself in, to concentrate on not letting her eyelids twitch until, eventually, she heard the floorboards creak under Sarah's feet, the soft rustle of Sarah pulling off her clothes, the gentle thud of her boots being put on the floor, the groan of the bed as she lay down, then with a whisper the room went dark. Jane let herself imagine the rush of wind against her face: a storm at sea, the tops of monstrous waves catching the moonlight, a young woman on the deck of a ship—her hair torn loose, her dark dress flapping in the wind. Then her mouth wide with horror as the ship lurches, and a wave crashes over the deck. She is alone. She calls for her husband, but he is not there, and a member of the crew—where has he come from?—must force her into the lifeboat, for she is too distraught to think for herself. Then she changed the details—the woman is not on the deck but in a cabin—and she spun the story around, this way and that until she fell asleep and the tragedy of it all swallowed her.

"Well," Sarah is saying, "we'll see her soon enough. Then we'll know all about her." She opens her arms to hold the sheet straight, and together they lay it across the bed. Then there's a second sheet, a heavy blanket, a counterpane, and a bolster that Sarah wraps her arms around to lift.

Jane shivers again—it looks like a body wound in a sheet. She says, "All about her?"

Sarah tosses her head and gives a smile. "A bit of kindness can go a long way towards getting someone to talk. She'll need a bit of kindness, even from the likes of me—all on her own and her husband drowned."

Jane grabs the other end of the bolster and pulls so it lies across the top of the bed. With both hands she smoothes it. "I don't see when you're going to talk to her."

"Why, the new Mrs. Bentley will need someone to do for her— and there's nothing like those moments when you're brushing their hair for them, or doing up their dress, that ladies don't mind talking."

The pillows are piled on a chair, the pillowcases draped beside them. Jane opens one and pushes the end of a pillow into it, then shakes it down. She looks as though she's concentrating on the pillow, slapping it with the flat of her hand, but when she looks back at Sarah she says, "I don't know about that. I can't imagine what you'd have found out about Mrs. Robert."

"You'd be surprised." Still, she tilts her head away from Jane, adds, "You're going to have your work cut out for you."

"How's that?" She lays the pillow against the bolster.

"If I'm busy with the widow, you'll have to shift yourself to get the rooms done."

She hadn't thought of this. "But they can't—" she starts. "I can't do all—"

Sarah walks towards the door, swinging her hips. "Yes, they can— just watch them."

The door closes behind her, and the room is still.

The Dark Lantern

On her own Jane works fast, though now there is a nervousness to her movements. How will she be able to get it all done? How can she work any harder than she does already? As it is she must rush through her days to have any hope of getting to bed before ten o'clock at night. Any small thing that gets in her way—Mrs. Robert calling her upstairs, Sarah taking off and having to cover for her—can send her day out of kilter and mean that at eleven o'clock, or even midnight, she is still sweeping or polishing or fetching coal.

Maybe Sarah is wrong, she tells herself. What is Price, if not a lady's maid? Wouldn't she be the one to do for the widow?

She works the broom over the bare floorboards around the carpet. Sweep, sweep, sweep, then again, sweep, sweep, sweep, gathering fluff and hair and the gritty dust that covers everything in London. With her hands moving, her thoughts can drift away. Today she thinks of Mrs. Henry Bentley sitting on the deck of a ship next to her husband's coffin, a tragic figure in black, a delicate handkerchief pressed to her eyes. Of course, the coffin is probably down in the hold where the widow cannot sit next to it, but this image satisfies Jane. She doesn't notice that Sarah has carried off the carpet brush until she crosses to the door where her box and bucket wait and she reaches out her hand for it. Gone. Sarah must be in Mr. Robert's room next door and so, with a sigh, Jane steps into the corridor. She knocks and opens the door almost at the same moment, for Mr. and Mrs. Robert are out of the house this morning.

Sarah is sitting on the bed, and that alone should be enough to make Jane hesitate in the doorway. But what she notices is this: over the sheets of the unmade bed lie papers. Letters by the look of them, and bills, and even some photographs. On the dressing table a portable desk gapes open.

"Just as I thought," Sarah says, looking up. "Forgot to lock it today, didn't she? Too much on her mind." Then she waves one hand. "Close the door or we'll catch it for sure—Price has been creeping around all morning. You know what she's like."

Jane pushes the door closed. "Put it away," she urges. "You'll get found out and that'll be it for your character."

"Well, you're not going to tell on me, are you? Us lot have to stick together. And she's not going to notice a thing." She goes back to the papers, leafing through them, then holding one up to read.

"I only came for the carpet brush," Jane says. It's leaning against the wall by the bed and evidently hasn't been used yet.

"Then do me a favor and give the carpets in here a going-over." She doesn't even look up.

Jane doesn't move.

Sarah glances at her. "Go on—what are you waiting for? I've done favors for you, haven't I?"

Jane steps forward, her hand reaches for the brush, and she bends her head away from Sarah as she sweeps. It's not right—she knows that—doing Sarah's work while Sarah sits on the bed reading through Mrs. Robert's things. How to refuse, though, when there's the matter of the tazza? Those two pounds she has paid, the entirety of her wages that Sarah held out her hand for just three days ago, the rest that she still owes? She was a fool, she tells herself.

Sarah's made herself at home on the bed. Jane wonders: Does she do this often? Does she check drawers and cupboards and desks when she's alone in a room? She thinks of her own box upstairs, and the times she has left it unlocked. As though there is anything in it to find—her spare aprons and caps, two dresses, her stockings and underthings. The half-sovereign she lied to Sarah about. The photograph of her mother. What could a photograph of a young woman in her best things mean to Sarah? Nothing much, surely.

She works her way across the room towards Sarah, who raises her feet so Jane can sweep beneath them. The long hairs of the carpet brush make only the slightest whisper against the rug, and Jane finds herself listening—for footsteps, for voices in the corridor. Sarah sighs. "Everyone has a secret," she says. "It's just a matter of winkling it out." She picks up another letter.

Jane keeps her head down, her eyes on the dust and hair that the brush is gathering.

Before long Sarah pushes the papers together. "Who locks a desk when all they've got in it is a few old dress bills, letters from her husband that don't say much of anything, and photographs of the two of them together?" She dumps it all back into the desk.

"Aren't you going to put it back how you found it?"

"What's she going to do—dismiss me for finding out she doesn't pay her dressmaker on time?" But she bends over the desk and re-arranges the papers. "I've waited so long for the chance and now—there's nothing to find out!" She lets out a laugh. "More fool me." She's still laughing as she carries the desk over to the dressing table and sets it down. When she turns around her smile drops away, for there's Mr. Cartwright standing in the doorway, watching.

"Laughter at a time like this?" he says.

"Have to keep your spirits up, don't you?" She smiles at him. "I mean—"

"I do not want to hear what you mean. None of us has time for idle conversation, today of all days. The two of you should be ashamed of yourselves." He shifts his gaze to Jane. "Since you are in here, can I presume that you have finished in Mr. Henry's room?"

She shakes her head.

"Then if I were you I would get back to my own duties." He steps close to her. "Don't think that, even at a time like this, I would not intrude a report of misbehavior on Mrs. Robert's attention." His eyes, small and hard, hold hers before she bows her head.

"Yes, Mr. Cartwright."

He leans so close that she feels his breath on her cheek. "I'd have thought that with such parentage as yours, you would want to make every effort to prove yourself worthy of the trust Mrs. Robert has placed in you."

Does she give a cry, or does she only imagine it? Either way, her hand goes to her mouth and she looks up into his face, into the self-satisfied roundness of his jowls, the mean slant to his lips.

He spits, "Get along with you."

She hurries past him, her fist pressed against her mouth. Even with the door of Mr. Henry's room closed behind her she cannot calm herself. She uses her sleeve to wipe the tears from her face, then kneels at the hearth to lift out the arrangement of dried flowers that must have been there for months, so dusty has it become. She dumps it in the bucket and sets to cleaning the hearth. She keeps her mouth closed to hold in her sobs as she dusts, as she fetches kindling and coal from beside the door. This is a precipice, and she is on the edge of it. She imagines being turned out of the house—what would there be for her then? No respectable mistress would hire her, not if she knew the truth.

What's more, she deserves it. She has betrayed Mrs. Robert. She has helped Sarah pry into Mrs. Robert's things when she promised—didn't she?—to be her eyes and ears below stairs. And what has she told Mrs. Robert? Nothing more than what Mrs. Robert surely has noticed herself: that Mr. Cartwright has a liking for port, that Sarah is often out on errands, that all of them below stairs eat far too well. What will Mrs. Robert think of her when she hears that Jane has hidden the fact that her mother stabbed a gentleman and killed him?

Slowly her crying wears itself out, as it must. Her face still feels hot, her eyes gritty from the salt of her tears. But she thinks: Cartwright talked of Mrs. Robert's trust. What can that mean except that he thinks she *already* knows? If that's what he believes, he won't tell her himself. So she's safe. For now.

The inside of her head feels light somehow, as though it has been flushed clean. She starts piling lumps of coal onto the kindling in the grate, lifting the black chunks out of the scuttle with the tongs. Her hands move without her seeming to direct them. She thinks: how odd it is that a woman like Mrs. Robert would have so little in the way of correspondence in her desk. It is almost as though she doesn't know anyone—not just in this city, but beyond it. And how could that be? Does she have no family? No friends? How is it possible to go through this world without ties, unless you are an orphan? Or unless you have cut yourself off because of some shame in your past?

Outside, the sun breaks through the clouds and the room brightens. She crosses to the window. There's a fluttering of wings, and a pigeon lands on the sill. It swaggers up and down, then stares at her with eyes as small and hard as seeds—like Mr. Cartwright's eyes, she thinks. "Got nothing for you," she tells it. "Go on—get going." She waves her hand at it until it takes off across the street.

*T*he assistants at Mortimer's General Mourning Warehouse have the serious look of undertakers. Of course, considers Mina Bentley, their profession is not so different. They too deal with the recently bereaved, death after death, day after day. The woman who lays out black silks and bombazine for her on the counter has a face that has set itself into a look of exaggerated sadness. Her mouth sags, her eyes blink too often, and when she speaks to ask if madam would like her dress made up in this fabric or that, her voice is smooth and heavy as lead.

"Yes." Mina lays a gloved finger on one of the black silks. "This one will do."

There is still the undertaker's to visit, but they cannot do that until Mrs. Henry Bentley arrives. After all, it is her husband whom they will be burying. Up above the shelves of fabric and trim hangs a clock adorned with black streamers tied in a bow, like the prey of an untidy spider. Nearly half past ten already. The maids will be having a hard time of it, with their routines thrown off and the extra work of making Henry's room ready for his widow. And in the middle of it the doctor will be calling, for the elderly Mrs. Bentley has not taken the news of her older son's death at all well. As for the fact that she has a new daughter-in-law, Robert has been unable to convince her of it.

Beside her another customer coughs into a handkerchief. A young woman, her belly bulging out from under the seaweed green of her dress. Soon she too will be wearing black. The woman lays her hands on her belly, then walks slowly, so slowly, to one of the chairs that wait by the windows, ready to hold up the grieving whose emotions overwhelm them. She lowers herself onto the one farthest from the door and hides her face as best she can in a small handkerchief.

Mina picks at her gloves. Already they are looking a little shabby, not that it matters since now she'll have to wear black ones. A delicate ring of chimes announces half past ten. The maids should have finished with the bedrooms, and she wonders: Has Sarah found her desk unlocked? Did she look through it? Of all the days for her to leave it open, today surely seemed the most credible. After all, with the confusion of Henry's death, with so much to do, she could so easily have forgotten. What could be more natural? But the larger question is this: Will it teach the girl a lesson? When she finds nothing of interest, will she stop prying?

She glances over at where Robert is being shown hatbands. Already he seems impatient, but they have had to wait. Several other customers were ahead of them: the loss of a ship as large as the *Star of the Orient* must be good for business, and the thought of it—of the proprietors of this shop reading the news of sinkings and influenza outbreaks and railway accidents with satisfaction—makes her pull her hands away to the edge of the counter.

"Yes, yes," she hears Robert say. "If four inches is customary, I'll take it." He turns away as though that is the end of the matter. But the assistant has not finished with him. There are black gloves to be bought, and she catches his sigh of annoyance.

They will be here for a considerable portion of the morning. After all, although Robert only needs a hatband and black gloves, she must be measured for her dress, her hat decided upon, her gloves chosen. And for the house too—crape tied with white ribbon for the front door to show the city that the household is in mourning.

The shop assistant is back, and she lays samples on the counter. It is a tedious business, not helped by Robert pacing up and down behind her. When she senses someone at her shoulder she turns, expecting him, but it is not Robert. Instead she finds herself looking at a man whose face still has the round cheeks of a child, though he must be at least forty, and what hair is visible from under his hat is so pale that it is almost white.

"Good heavens, it *is* you." He slaps his hands together. "You're so changed, and I was standing there trying to decide if—"

"I'm sorry," she says. Her voice trips only slightly. "You're mistaken. I don't know you."

He blinks at her. "Why, you must remember—our circle was so small. And your father—"

"My father has been dead since I was an infant." She gives him a small nod. "Now, if you will excuse me."

"Of course." He steps away, looking about him as though no longer quite certain where he is. "I'm terribly sorry."

She hears footsteps behind her, and she feels Robert's hand on her shoulder. "Mina?" he says.

The gentleman seems ready to flee, but one of the shop assistants approaches him. "Mr. Popham? I will attend to you shortly. This morning we have been unusually busy."

"The *Star of the Orient*," says this Mr. Popham to Robert. "My cousin was returning from Bombay."

"Ah," says Robert. "My brother, too. But by a miracle his wife has survived."

Popham fiddles with his moustache. "A terrible business," he says. "And so close to home—off the coast of France. After coming all that way! It is extraordinary."

He looks away, through the windows at the traffic in Regent Street. Then, just as Mina is about to take her husband's arm and lead him away, Popham turns back to them. "I'm sorry," he tells Mina again. He shifts his gaze to Robert. "It's quite uncanny," he tells him. "For a moment I believed your wife was a lady of my acquaintance from a few years ago. The resemblance is quite striking. But of course—" he gives a small bow "—now I see my error."

Such a remark cannot go without comment from Robert.

It *is* extraordinary, he tells Popham, how people who are unrelated can so closely resemble each other that even their relatives can be mistaken. He himself has come across numerous instances of men wrongly accused of crimes because of a remarkable resemblance to the actual culprit. In his experience photographs are especially misleading, and as for using them to identify recidivists—why, any criminal could shave a beard or grow one, or dye his hair and comb it differently, so that even his own mother might be unable to recognize him. It is imperative—absolutely imperative—that the Troup

Committee act with alacrity if it is to address this problem, for who knows how many recidivists truly are among the convict population and are being released on an unsuspecting public?

On and on he talks, Popham nodding, while Mina feels her hands growing damp inside her gloves. She nods too; she adds her own exclamation of, "With our cities grown so large, such mistakes are inevitable!" Throughout, she is careful to keep her voice low, and to hold her body still and a little bent, not quite like her usual self.

But what is incredible, she thinks, is that David Popham can stand only three feet from her, talking to her husband, and apparently be persuaded that she is not the woman he once knew.

Surely he knows better than that.

She finds him standing by the fire in the drawing room. His hands are on the draperies of the mantelpiece, his head bent so that he seems intent on the flames. He doesn't turn. Coming close, she reaches her arms around to his chest and presses her face against his back. "No, darling," he says softly, then plucks her hands away.

So she sits in the armchair and watches him. There is despair in the curve of his spine, in the angle of his shoulders. The fire must be scalding his legs, but he doesn't move.

"I didn't imagine it would come to this," he says. "Not this quickly, at least. A few days? That's all she has left?"

She says gently, "The second seizure was too much."

He doesn't look at her. "I blame myself. I should never have told her. It was the shock of it."

"How could you have kept it from her? Besides, if *you* hadn't told her—"

"Yes, yes. Price." He lets out a sigh. The coal in the fire crackles and spits, and an ember arcs to the carpet. He stamps on it, once, twice. "Her husband dead, her mother-in-law dying. What a welcome for *her*."

Already Henry's widow has become *her*. They do not know her name. Indeed, they know nothing about her except that she exists and that soon—in a day, or two at the most—she will be here.

Mina leans forward. "She'll go back to her own family, surely. She doesn't know us. What comfort can we offer her at a time like this?"

He stands up straight and holds his hands out to the fire. "Yes, you're right. I hadn't thought of that. I was expecting that she would stay here for some time."

"Of course," says Mina, "if your mother passes on, it will be her right to stay here for as long as she pleases."

Now he lets his hands drop and looks at her.

She says quickly, "As Henry's widow, she'll have as much right to this house as we have. Isn't that the way the will is written?"

He looks startled. "Ah," he says, then he runs his fingers over his moustache as he looks back to the fire.

He is thinking, and she watches him. Maybe she seems heartless to be concerning herself with such matters. Is that why he won't look away from the flames to where she sits? My poor love, she wants to tell him, you must be on your guard, even at such a terrible time as this. But how to explain? The Bentleys aren't rich, yet there's the house, and his mother's jewelry, and Henry's insurance money. It's enough to catch the eye of the unscrupulous. She must teach Robert wariness, or soon there might be little left of the Bentleys' money, and certainly not enough for them to return to Paris.

The mantelpiece clock ticks under its glass dome. In the hallway, footsteps approach, then pass. She says, "No doubt she'll want to sell, unless she has the means to keep up this house."

"Perhaps she's an heiress," he says, and gives a faint laugh. Then he rocks on his feet, back and forth, back and forth. "I doubt Henry would have left her badly off. Life insurance—he had a policy, and she'll be the beneficiary now. He was farsighted enough to plan for any eventuality, even the unlikely event of his own marriage."

"So she should have enough to ensure a comfortable life for herself. Perhaps more comfortable than she's had before. Though of course," she says, looking up at him, "she won't have her husband. Poor thing. They couldn't have been married long."

She lingers a little on that last word so that it hangs on the air like warm breath on a cold morning, but Robert is intent on the flames curling through the coals. Rain spatters against the window. She shivers. Pulling her shawl around her she stands beside Robert, her shoulder just touching his arm. She holds her hands out to warm them. The thin skin at the base of her fingers turns a dull red with the light of the fire shining through it. She keeps her eyes on her hands, keeps her voice flat as she says, "I wonder what she's like."

"We'll find out soon enough."

"Yes, we will." She takes a newspaper from the table. Today's, but it is still folded. With all the business of buying mourning clothes and the house to prepare, it has lain unnoticed. She turns past the classified advertisements to the main stories of the day. Of course, there is more on the loss of the *Star of the Orient*. A gale, an attempt to seek shelter in a French port, a young captain, the loss of all but two dozen of the passengers and crew. Bodies washing up on the shore of France, and Monsieur Bertillon called in to photograph faces and do what else he can to identify them. She is about to read out the passage to Robert but stops herself. Later, she thinks, and lets herself sink back in the chair. There are more important matters at hand.

"Is it so extraordinary that he'd have done something as impulsive as this marriage?" she asks.

"Henry? Good God, yes." He gives a brief laugh. "Henry is the perfect administrator. He plans so far in advance that I always suspected he knew what he'd be eating for dinner a fortnight on Tuesday."

"Then"—she looks at him—"she must be quite the woman, to have captured his heart."

"She must indeed."

"Or perhaps under the surface he was a passionate man."

"Henry? I can't imagine that."

She tilts her head. "Well, how do you explain it?"

"I'm sure I don't know." He lets himself down into his armchair. For a few moments he stares at her, a distant look as though he cannot quite place who she is, then he sits back with his legs out-stretched and closes his eyes. He looks suddenly young, his face all delicate curves, his moustache out of place.

Has she gone too far? Instead of planting the seeds of suspicion, has she suggested too much? Someone has to alert him—this unex-plained and unexpected bride, this woman who will inherit enough to keep her in reasonable comfort for the rest of her life. It is—strange. And she is suspicious of such inexplicable strangeness. With all the confusion of the sinking of the ship, exactly how sure can one be that a person is who they say they are? It's possible that over the course of a three-week voyage from Bombay, a young woman could have learnt enough about Henry to cast herself as his wife. If no one raises an objection—why, what could be easier than to collect all that is due to his widow and disappear?

She looks over at Robert. His eyes are still shut, but from the way his lips are pressed together she knows he is thinking. At last he says, "It *is* odd, I'll grant you that."

He still hasn't opened his eyes when the gong sounds. The ring-ing pulls him out of his thoughts. "Come on, my love. Let's put on a brave face and eat what we can of Mrs. Johnson's lunch."

*T*here is an excitement below stairs: coming down for tea, Cartwright announced a telegram had just arrived—the widow is on her way. Her ship from France has docked, and she will be in London by evening.

Above their heads the hanging laundry shifts slightly. At least it has stopped dripping, not that they'd mind particularly, today of all days. Sarah talks faster than usual and sits a little straighter in her chair. Mrs. Johnson hurries about the kitchen, chivvying Elsie to clean the fish for dinner, to sit down for her pie, to put the dishes from the upstairs lunch away, until poor Elsie stands at the sink and says, "Can I sit down now? Can I? Can I?" Even Price joins in, taking pursed-lipped sips of her tea and saying, "Goodness gracious, what a tragedy for the young lady. Barely married and a widow already."

Shaking her head and enjoying every minute of this, for, if truth be told, they know that most likely the widow will soon be gone, back to her own family once the funeral is over.

And then? Will the household sink back into its usual routines? Or will it be caught up in the windstorm of a greater change? The day before at dinner Price told them that although Mrs. Bentley had taken a turn for the worse, the doctor held out hope—oh yes, there was *great* hope she would recover, and she'd nodded her head like a puppet. The rest of them had looked down into their plates. At any moment their mistress could leave this world and her household be broken up. They'd be released from its cramping routines: from hours spent alone in rooms with a brush or a mop; from meals hurried through but interrupted nonetheless because there was always something to be fetched or taken away; from the need to always think of the family—always the family—before themselves. But to be freed from this household wouldn't be freedom, not really. After all, paying for lodgings and food is costly, it eats through savings, and soon each one of them would have to find a new situation, maybe less comfortable than this one, maybe with a mistress more demanding than old Mrs. Bentley has been.

For now, though, the thrill in the air comes from the prospect of the widow who is soon to arrive. Jane feels it, this promise of a disturbance in their lives. Of course, another person in the house will mean more work: another bedroom to be cleaned, more laundry to be washed, more food to be cooked and carried upstairs. Jane takes hungry bites of her pie and doesn't say much beyond "Yes, a terrible shame" and "It's awful," even when Price catches her eye and seems to be asking her opinion. For once Cartwright doesn't put a stop to their gossiping but sits at the end of the table with his coat hung over the back of his chair and his pie waiting on his plate in front of him. Even when Albert appears at the kitchen door he doesn't send him back into the chilly grey of the dying afternoon, doesn't do much except give him his cool stare, so Albert comes in, and soon he is leaning against the sink with a cup of tea in one hand and a slice of pie in the other.

"It's the talk of the whole street," he tells them. "That poor lady what's lost her husband when they'd only just got themselves married. Coming home for the honeymoon and all that." He takes a loud sip of tea. "It's a tragedy, in't it? A bloomin' tragedy. Everybody's talking about it."

Over by the stove Mrs. Johnson pauses with a strainer between her hands. Price looks around her, and Sarah comes close to smiling. Even Elsie is not immune to the enormity of this—the household's sudden, tragic celebrity—and her hands fidget over the tabletop between her cup and her plate. Only Cartwright seems above it. He has yesterday's paper held up in front of him, but, as Jane notices, his eyes are fixed on one spot, and that spot lies far beyond the paper.

"Mr. Robert is taking it well," says Sarah. "He ate most of his lunch. And so did she. But they only talked about how quiet the funeral should be and where the new Mrs. Bentley is going to have Mr. Henry sent."

"Sent?" Elsie sets both elbows on the table. "Sent how?"

"To the you-know." Sarah drops her voice. "The undertaker."

Elsie grips her cup with both hands. "Undertaker?"

"Well she's not going to bring him here, is she?" Sarah gives a small laugh. "Besides, that's not how it's done anymore, not if you have the money."

"That's not right," says Elsie, and her voice is loud. "That's not right to have him sent away like that to people who are paid to do for him."

"It's better than having him here." Sarah shivers. "It makes my skin creep, the thought of a body in the house like that, just lying there, and the family not knowing what to do except to just sit there and stare at it."

A bell jangles and their heads turn towards it. "Morning room," says Cartwright. "Off you go, Sarah—it'll be Mrs. Robert wanting more hot water for her tea, I'll bet."

Sarah sighs. "Barely got started on my own." She catches Jane's eye. "You go—you don't mind, do you? Besides, you've finished most of yours."

She hasn't finished most of it. For once she has let her tea cool rather than hurrying to drink it, too caught up this afternoon to think ahead. "Oh," she says. "I don't know—"

Sarah waves her hand at her. "Go on, you'd better get a move on."

She looks at Cartwright, but he doesn't say anything, doesn't lift his head from the newspaper. As for Mrs. Johnson, she's swatting away the heat from the open oven with a cloth so she can lean close and ladle fat over the ducks she has roasting.

So Jane goes, but her chest feels tight. The last time she took on a chore not hers she opened the door to a burglar. And although she only has to walk upstairs to the morning room and enquire from Mrs. Robert what she would like, the job seems fraught with danger. Indeed, as she climbs the narrow steps, the thought of being alone with Mrs. Robert alarms her. What if Mrs. Robert wants some account of what she has seen and heard downstairs—what will she tell her? That all the talk is of Mr. Henry's widow, she decides. No need to mention that a few days ago she saw Mrs. Johnson selling butter to a large man lurking outside the kitchen door. Surely Mrs. Johnson would guess who had told, so why risk having less on her plate for dinner, or the tea leaves for the carpet being inexplicably thrown away?

Mrs. Robert is at the desk, looking through papers in the feeble north light that comes through the window. "Oh," she says, "they sent you, did they?" She nods to herself, and turns her chair around. "I should have guessed."

"Ma'am?"

"Come here, Jane."

"Yes, ma'am." She comes closer and stands just off the edge of the carpet that she brushed clean only that morning, and that already is flecked with flakes of ash from the fire.

"How are you getting on, Jane? Are you being worked too hard?"

"No, ma'am."

She raises one eyebrow, and Jane almost smiles. "I do hope you are telling me the truth."

"Oh yes, ma'am."

She raises the other eyebrow too. "Well," she says, "for the time being we'll say that you are finding this position satisfactory."

"Say, ma'am?"

"To Mrs. Saunders. Apparently the matron of the orphanage is concerned for girls who leave for London and likes to be assured that they are doing well." From the papers on the desk beside her she pulls a letter and unfolds it. "Mrs. Saunders wants to reassure her."

Jane feels her blood turn sluggish. It has thickened all of a sudden, and everything from the blink of her eyes to the lick she gives her lips is slow and awkward. I won't cry, she tells herself. I won't, not in front of her, even if this is the end of it all.

"It's a curious thing," Mrs. Robert is saying. "She refers to *the stain of your past,* but I don't understand what she . . ."

Mrs. Robert's voice grows faint, and her mouth—the only thing that Jane looks at—moves too quickly for the words it is producing. The sensation lasts only a few moments, then all of a sudden the room shifts around her and she feels very cold.

She has never fainted before. It is something one associates with ladies—they are more easily overcome. By repugnant sights and strong language, by walking up stairs too fast or getting out of a chair without the aid of a gentleman. But when the darkness wheeling in front of her eyes clears she finds her head close to the fender and the heat of the fire on her face. Mrs. Robert is holding smelling salts beneath her nose. An awful, sour smell. She turns away and takes a deep breath. Mrs. Robert is saying something. She has to force her attention to the words to make any sense of them, then she hears, "I didn't mean to shock you. It was only my intention to see if you had—an explanation."

She strokes the side of Jane's face—her hand is warm and soft, and Jane catches the scent of lavender, a light, summer smell of the country that makes her close her eyes. Her life with the Saunderses was plagued by injustices, but this other life—her attempt at bettering herself—how it has gone wrong! She will have to resort to more lies now, and where will they lead?

Mrs. Robert's skirts rustle. "You are a resourceful girl," she is saying. "Illegitimacy—is that this *stain*?—need not hold back a girl like you."

Jane nods, but she doesn't open her eyes.

"It was a passable attempt. Come on—look at me."

She doesn't. Her head swirls, as though it has been filled with water that shifts when she moves.

She feels the slight brush of breath on her cheek, hears, "Jane—look at me."

This time she does look. Mrs. Robert is crouched beside her, and when she sits back a little Jane sees what is in her hand: Mrs. Saunders's letter. She would know that writing anywhere, those elaborate tails curling from her *y*s and *g*s, the flattened *e*s that look like squinting eyes. Did hers look so different? Surely not—she'd copied them so carefully.

Mrs. Robert takes her hand and holds it against the silk of her skirts. To be touched gently—it is almost more than Jane can bear. When has anyone touched her like this? Never at the orphanage, and certainly never at the Saunderses'. Mrs. Robert's chin is sharp, her eyes watchful, but her face does not have the pinched look of self-righteousness of Mrs. Saunders's.

"I couldn't bear it," Jane whispers. "None of that is my fault. I didn't do anything wrong. Why does it have to follow me?"

Mrs. Robert rubs Jane's hand with her thumb. "You did wrong in taking your mistress's letter, nonetheless, and in substituting your own. Nothing can excuse such behavior. It is a terrible betrayal of trust."

Of course, Jane thinks. The sin of her birth is not her doing, it should not be her burden, but trying to escape it puts her at fault. There it is, the predicament of a girl like her laid bare—she can be pitied but she must not help herself.

On the far wall, beside the desk, hangs a delicate painting in pinks and blues of the sun going down over the sea. She, too, is sinking, but not like that, not with any beauty. No, she is turning everything around her ugly—even by lying here, on this carpet, in this small room that is supposed to delight the eye: the luxurious drapery of the curtains, the rich wood of the desk, the delicate flowers of the wallpaper. This house is a beautiful shell, keeping the Bentleys safe inside, no matter the way the tide turns or the toss of the waves on the shore. For her, there will never be a home like this. And now—now even her lumpy bed in the cold room under the roof will not be hers much longer.

She wonders if it is still raining outside, and if the air is as cold as it felt when she threw open the bedroom windows earlier in the day.

Heat is creeping in around her, out from the fire, down from the room's low ceiling. The chill inside her retreats. Instead, she feels hot. Already sweat is gathering under her arms.

"Come on," Mrs. Robert is saying. "We need to get you up."

So she lets herself be settled into the armchair by the fire. She knows its curves well—she has swept ash and stray threads off it every day that she has been here—but she is surprised by how it seems to reach out to her, to hold her body as if it wants to offer her comfort.

Mrs. Robert turns away with a swish of her skirts. She drags the chair from the desk close, then smoothes Mrs. Saunders's letter over her knee.

"How did you do it?" she says at last. "Did you take her letter and trace the words?"

Jane nods.

"You used pencil, then ink to write over the words you'd traced. Afterwards you erased the pencil marks, no?"

"Yes, ma'am."

"I guessed as much—the flow of the ink looked uneven. And as for the color—all that careful rubbing turned the ink a little grey." She sits forward in her chair. The way her chin is thrust out gives her a predatory look. "But what I have been wondering," she says, "is where on earth you might have learnt such a thing."

"Learnt it, ma'am? I didn't learn it. It was the only way to do it—anyone could see that. I know I've done wrong—but I've never mixed with the wrong sort. In the orphanage they wouldn't even let—"

Mrs. Robert raises one hand. "Yes, yes. I'm not suspecting you of that. I wondered, that's all. Not every maid would be clever enough to manage a deception like this."

She has a kindly tone to her voice, and Jane shrinks from it. There was something of this tone in the policeman's voice after she let in the burglar.

Mrs. Robert's eyes catch the shifting light of the fire, shining like an animal's at night. Jane looks away, to Mrs. Robert's lap, where Mrs. Saunders's letter lies against the black silk of her mourning dress. In the midst of the tragedy of Mr. Henry dying, she thinks, here is Mrs. Robert having to concern herself with this matter. She thought she'd been so careful, and so clever! Then here came Mrs. Saunders's letter and ruined everything.

But that couldn't be right. It wasn't Mrs. Saunders's letter that showed hers to be a forgery—it was her own. The ink—that's what Mrs. Robert said. The uneven ink, the greyness of it. "Ma'am?" Her voice sounds thin in this room. "Ma'am—why did you hire me if you knew there was something wrong with the letter?"

Mrs. Robert's face doesn't move. Even her eyes are still. Then she presses her lips together in a smile. "Oh, you *are* a clever girl," she tells her. "Far beyond anything I expected. You're going to be very useful to me."

CHAPTER 9

S ince yesterday those words have been coming back to her: *You're going to be very useful to me.* They've spun around her head as she's scrubbed the back stairs, and filled buckets of water, and pressed a hot iron over sheets and tablecloths. No wonder when Mrs. Robert sent for her again she felt the shock as a physical pain, as though she'd burnt herself. And now she's been up here an hour and she still can't get the hang of what has been asked of her.

"Pull the hair tighter," says Mrs. Robert. "Grip it between your fingers or it'll all come undone."

Jane's voice trembles. "I can't do it, ma'am. I just can't." With a sob she lets the strands drop, but Mrs. Robert spins around and grabs her wrist. She holds her so hard it hurts.

"Listen to me," she says darkly. "You're a clever girl. You can do it. Try again." She lets Jane's hand drop and picks up the strands of hair herself, then deftly twists them. In a matter of moments she has her hair elegantly pinned up behind, and a fringe of curls left over her forehead. "Like this—see?"

Outside it is still raining, and a gust of wind sends a splatter of drops against the window. Jane shivers. Isn't this what she wanted? To be trained up? To learn ladies' tricks so that she can use them to better herself? To be a lady's maid—no more scrubbing floors, no more carrying buckets of water and slops. But this is something else entirely. To do for the widow, to dress her hair, and help her with her clothes, and all the while to be watching out for the loose ends of her secrets, to pull on them, to carry all that she finds to Mrs. Robert.

When Mrs. Robert undoes her hair and gestures for Jane to try again, she does no better. Doing the curls was difficult enough, for there was the danger of scorching the hair, or Mrs. Robert's skin. But this pinning up is impossible. The hair is unlike her own—not dry and coarse but so soft that it slips between her fingers, or catches on her rough skin. "I can't do it," she says miserably and looks up. In the mirror she sees her face, red and a little swollen from crying, her cap wilted. And there too is Mrs. Robert's reflection—Mrs. Robert in her peignoir with her hair loose around her shoulders, her lips thin with exasperation. When she's angry, Jane notices, two lines appear between the delicate arcs of her eyebrows, and she is angry now.

"Don't look away." Mrs. Robert meets her eye. "Is this the trouble? That I am sitting here in my peignoir? That you have to be the one to undress me, then dress me again?"

"Ma'am?" She says the word so softly that it barely leaves her mouth.

"I'm a woman like you. Look." She pulls at her peignoir until it is loose enough to show her chemise underneath, and the top of her breasts, then she raises one leg so that it appears, pale and naked, from between the folds. "It won't do to be embarrassed. For you this is simply work. Now"—she lets her leg down, then shakes her hair loose from the tangle Jane has left it in—"do it again."

So she does. She reaches for the long, warm hair and holds the heaviness of it in her hands. Pulling it hard—will Mrs. Robert cry out?—she rolls it around on itself and into a coil.

Mrs. Robert hands her some pins. "Put them in at a slant."

This time the hair stays in place. Mrs. Robert shakes her head, then smiles into the mirror, a smile that twists up one end of her mouth. She stands. "Yes. You've done it." She pulls out the pins and hands them back to Jane. "Now get me dressed, then do it again— faster this time."

Jane holds out the petticoats for her to step into, puts her weight into pulling the corset tight. She holds the dress for Mrs. Robert, then fastens it. Her hair, this time, she does more quickly.

Mrs. Robert stands back to look at herself in the mirror. "Good enough," she says.

The whole house has been holding itself in, waiting. And then it comes—the knock at the door. Jane leans over the banister just far enough to see down to the hallway. Across the black and white tiles comes Cartwright—from the study, perhaps—the long tails of his coat flaring out behind him. The door opens and Jane leans farther out. A bustle of skirts; a small, plain hat; one phrase spoken in response to something Cartwright says—"Thank you." It rises up the stairs to where Jane is listening, then the widow is gone and Jane is staring down into an empty hallway.

A murmur of voices, the squeak of a door. Footsteps. Before she can duck out of sight, Cartwright is back, staring up at her with one finger raised in warning. She scurries back to her brushes.

Mrs. Johnson has propped open a window to let out the steam, and she moves between the stove and the table, her face red and shiny. However, at the sink, where the cold air from outside is pouring in, Jane shivers. Her arms are wet up to her folded-up sleeves, and water has seeped through her apron to her dress. Elsie has been sent off to wash pots in the scullery—she knocked a whole leg of pork ready to be roasted to the floor, today of all days, and Mrs. Johnson shouted at her to get out of her sight—so of course Jane was told to hurry with turning down the beds and laying the fires upstairs because she was needed in the kitchen.

So, here she stands, soaked through from washing asparagus and potatoes and parsnips under a tap that spurts, washing her hands now to get rid of the butter she had to measure out for the dessert sauce. The cold water runs off her greasy hands; she must use the soap, and she grabs it up. As soon as the butter is gone, though, the soap finds its way into the cracks in her skin. They sting horribly.

But her thoughts aren't on her hands. After years of this sort of pain it is not so much that she is used to it, more that she can make herself think of other things. In Teignton, she'd stand at the sink with her raw hands smarting and imagine Mrs. Saunders brought low by a sudden reversal: maybe she'd discover that the Reverend already had a wife living in a madhouse and would have to go out into the world with the shame of it dragging behind her; or maybe her doddering father would be exposed as a swindler who'd bilked widows out of their pensions, and she'd never again be able to raise her head in public—and certainly not to talk of the stain of birth.

However, this evening it is not Mrs. Saunders that Jane is thinking of. She is remembering how it felt to close herself in the widow's room and, between turning down the bedcovers and building up the fire, to search it like a thief. There was not much to look through—no dresses in the wardrobe and so no pockets to let her fingers probe. No trunks, no jewelry boxes, no photographs, no packets of letters tied together with ribbon. All of that must be at the bottom of the sea. Instead, all there was to examine was in one locked drawer of the dressing table. From her apron pocket she took a key. She remembers that moment—the way it turned so smoothly in the lock. Then she slid the drawer open and pushed her arms against her sides as she stared down into it, for she was shivering. Inside she found only a pair of delicate silver earrings, and a small book whose pages were stiff and bent from being soaked and dried. It creaked when she opened it. In places the blue ink was blurred. A book of addresses, all in India except for *Mr. Henry Bentley—32 Cursitor Road, London,* and all written in the same tiny hand. Inside the cover, *Victoria Cecilia Dawes, January 1892.* She barely had time to put it all away before Sarah knocked on the door and told her she was needed in the kitchen.

Mrs. Johnson is making a racket with the pans. This, Jane knows, means she is nervous. There's a burst of air, and Jane tilts her head a little. Someone must have opened the door to the stairs. She hears Sarah say, "Well, Mrs. J., they're quizzing her something awful."

The Dark Lantern

"They are? They probably just want to know who she is."

"You should hear Mr. Robert—just before I came in with the soup he asked her how long her and Mr. Henry had *been acquainted*. That's how he put it."

Jane takes a cloth from the rack by the window and dries her hands gently, slowly, listening.

"Well," says Mrs. Johnson. "It's not like Mr. Henry to pick up and marry someone."

"You'd think she'd done something wrong, the way they're carrying on."

The rattle of a pan against the stove, and the creak of the oven door opening. The air from outside smells of coal and frost. No snow yet, though Jane half expects it. To be inside—even here, in the freezing draught from the window, half soaked from leaning against the sink, hands smarting—even that is something to be thankful for. If Mrs. Robert had thrown her out, where would she be now? She doesn't know a soul in this city.

"I pity her," says Sarah with a sigh in her voice. "She's not likely to get married again, I don't think, not unless she makes something of herself."

They have already heard Sarah's description of her, and now in her head Jane carries a picture of the widow. A slight woman with light brown hair and small features, eyes that are a nondescript blue, and a way of sitting with her hands in her lap as though to hold herself down when she'd rather run away. That's what Sarah had said— that she looked as though she'd scarper given half a chance, and that she for one wouldn't blame her.

"Ready for dessert now, are they?" asks Mrs. Johnson.

"Should be." There was a scrape as Sarah pulled out a chair. "My feet are murder today. And I'll just bet they'll take forever over the rest of dinner."

"She must be exhausted, poor love," says Mrs. Johnson. "Just imagine the shock of it all. After coming all that way and getting so close to home. Still, maybe in a few days she can get back to her family."

"Oh no, she doesn't have anyone here except a second cousin,"

119

Sarah tells her. "She's never even been to England before—can you imagine?"

"Never been here?"

"Never in her life. She was born out there; I heard her say so."

"But she's bound to feel at home, now that she's back here," says Mrs. Johnson.

"I don't know about that. She looks half scared to death by everything. From the way she poked around with her eels, I don't think she's seen the like of them before."

The cold air pulls more strongly past Jane, and she glances over her shoulder as Cartwright comes into the kitchen. "Have time to sit and gossip, do we?" He places the serving dishes on the table. "The family is waiting for dessert. And Price says she asked half an hour ago for Mrs. Bentley's hot water and still hasn't got it."

So Sarah loads a tray with dessert plates, and Jane is sent to Price with a kettle of boiling water that sloshes dangerously as she carries it up the stairs. She climbs them carefully, kicking out her foot so it doesn't catch the hem of her dress and send her flying. She thinks of Mrs. Robert and the small key she pressed into her hand only a few hours ago, and how she said matter-of-factly, "One has to be so careful these days. See what you find out, Jane, and once we're sure of this new Mrs. Bentley we'll be able to give her the welcome she deserves." This is the lady who has hired her—a lady who will set a servant to look through another lady's things. A lady who can recognize the signs of a forged letter. And just what kind of a lady is that?

She has had to go upstairs for a clean apron and brush her hair and wash her hands, though the smell of grease clings to them. Now she stands outside the door and knocks. There is no answer, but she is sure the widow is in there. She knocks again, then presses her ear against the wood. She can hear something—a small sound that could be crying, or laughter, or the soft voice a woman might use to talk to herself. A third time she knocks and calls out, "Ma'am? Mrs. Robert sent me. Can I help you get ready for bed?"

Footsteps. The groan of a floorboard just beyond the door, but the door doesn't open. "No, thank you. No." A thin voice, frightened, or fraught with grief—it's impossible to tell. "Please—I don't need your help."

"Very good, ma'am." She steps away from the door and heads down the first few stairs. Then softly, so softly, she creeps back and listens. There is nothing to hear, and though she waits until the clock downstairs strikes the half hour, her time is wasted.

On the toes of her boots she moves away as silently as she can. The dining room still needs to be cleared, the drawing room tidied, and it is unlikely she will be in bed before midnight.

CHAPTER 10

Mina waits until Robert has finished his breakfast and is gone before she pushes away her plate. She pours more tea for the two of them. "Does nothing about England feel remotely like home to you, Victoria?"

The young widow puts down her fork. Her sorrow has not much affected her appetite, Mina notes, for she has finished a second helping of kedgeree. Perhaps Mrs. Johnson's approximation of it is not so bad, despite her complaints that such a thing was impossible and besides, no civilized person eats rice for breakfast.

"I feel as though it should." Her voice is as insubstantial as she herself is. Her delicate egg of a head rests on a thin neck. Her ears, her nose, her mouth, all are small and nestled together in the center of her face, as though not wanting to intrude themselves. As for her pale hair, it is pulled back tight, leaving her head looking strangely exposed. For a couple of seconds she holds Mina's eye, then looks down at her plate.

So far breakfast—and dinner the evening before—has been punctuated with these moments, though up until now Mina has waited for this young woman to raise her head before addressing her again. But this morning she has this young woman to herself.

"Then I will take you under my wing—for at least as long as you are here. Of course"—she takes a sip of tea—"we need to make plans for you."

"Oh," says Victoria, "Henry and I had plans—"

"Now you need to make new plans. I don't mean to be brutal," she says, setting down her cup, "but you must consider what you will do. Do you intend to stay in England?"

"Oh—" Her voice catches. "Oh, I don't know about that. I don't know a soul here." She bows her head again to stare into her plate.

"Victoria, we are your family. Henry would have wanted us to care for you, and we will provide any sort of help that you need. If you don't want to stay, we'll arrange for you to return to India. Nothing could be more simple." There are crumbs on the tablecloth in front of her and she pushes them together with the ends of her fingers. "Why don't you explain again the nature of your circumstances before your marriage? Surely there must be someone you can go to."

"I was living with my aunt," she says miserably.

"And she would take you in again?"

She nods, then tugs a handkerchief from her pocket. Her cries sound like coughs, and her shoulders tremble. Her crying doesn't last long. Then she sits up straight with her handkerchief wadded into her hand. "How can I go back? When I left I was a bride—"

"You have to live somewhere. Naturally, you don't have to decide yet, and you can stay here for as long—"

"Oh yes," Victoria says. "I think that will be for the best. For the time being. I will stay here."

Mina gives her a gentle smile. "Of course."

Of course. For either this young woman is really as helpless as she appears, or she has intended all along to find herself a home and an income by playing the bereaved bride. She could even, Mina thinks, have been put up to this. She doesn't appear to be the calculating sort—but isn't that the perfect disguise? Deceptions only work if they are convincing.

From the mantelpiece a clock strikes the half hour, and Mina glances at it. Still time, she thinks, before they should leave, and then there will be the round of shops—hairbrushes and underclothes and shoes to replace all that were lost, then another visit to Mortimer's, for Victoria this time. She lowers her own head a little and keeps her voice soft to say, "Is your aunt a hard woman? Is that why you are reluctant to return to her?"

Victoria's lips part in surprise, then she catches herself and bites the bottom one. "It's difficult to depend on someone for everything," she says. "And she is a woman with strong opinions."

"Did she approve of your marriage to Henry?"

"Henry?" She hesitates, and her eyes slide from Mina's face to the table to her own lap. "No," she says at last.

"I'm surprised. What could she have found to disapprove of?"

The widow's face is a little pink now, and she picks up her fork and gathers the last grains of rice into a pile. "He didn't quite meet her expectations."

"She must have had high expectations indeed if a man like Henry was beneath them."

Victoria's fork scrapes against the plate, then she lets it drop with a clatter. She leans so far over it that for a moment it looks as though her hair is going to touch the remains of her breakfast. "I'm feeling a little unwell," she murmurs. "I think I'll lie down before we go out."

"As you like." Mina pushes back her chair. However, the young widow is quicker and reaches the door before she can, and takes off quickly up the stairs.

This is not grief, Mina tells herself. This is something else entirely.

A low, dirty sky hangs over the city. There will be snow today. Robert can feel it as he steps into the hansom, where he sets down his bag on the seat beside him. Already his hands are cold, despite his new gloves. He tucks them into his pockets. He should have worn a scarf, he should have picked out a thicker pair of trousers, but somehow the widow's arrival has set everything at odds, and here he is, hunched against the cold.

The driver clucks his tongue and the horse moves off. The tall houses of Cursitor Road slide past. When he was a boy they seemed like walls of monstrous proportions. He remembers running away from Nurse one day and these houses looming over him. He couldn't find his way home—they looked so much the same. So in the end he'd chosen one with an aspidistra in the window, though he knew that there was something different about the house, that it was not home, and had knocked anyway. Luckily it had been the Eliots' house and they'd sent a maid to take him back. And at home—Henry, sitting at the small table upstairs in the nursery, eating seed cake. Eating two slices, since Nurse, in her wisdom, had taken the slice off the plate laid for him and made him watch as Henry ate it. It had taken him a long time, and soon he'd had trouble swallowing it—but he'd finished it all, every crumb, for it was his duty to help punish his little brother.

Henry. Gone now. Henry, who'd always been one for playing it safe because he'd believed Nurse's warnings about what happened to little boys who ran ahead or disobeyed or let their hands explore the parts of their bodies that were *dirty*. He'd taken a job in the civil service because what could be safer than a government job? Then India—a surprise until Robert had realized that out there an Englishman could be more than he ever could in England. A clerk who'd have lived in a terraced house with a maid-of-all-work in London could afford houseboys and—what had Henry called it?—a *khansamah,* while an administrator like Henry could live like a prince. He'd have felt it was his due—he'd always had that about him, that sense of the world being there to serve him.

Hardly has the cab turned the corner when it comes to a halt. Angry voices, a horse's frantic whinnying. A carriage and a hansom are caught up, the two drivers shouting into each other's faces while around them the traffic gathers.

He sits back with a sigh. What, he wonders, did Henry think of him, going where he needed for his research—to university, to Paris. Had Henry sensed a flatness to his own work? Had he wanted something more than to oversee the paying out of pensions, a job that, after all, many a man could have done? In his last few letters he'd written about how his predecessor had started a successful system that he'd continued, using thumbprints to identify which men had been paid and which had not because, with so many Indian men with the same name, and his officials overwhelmed by the numbers of pensioners, it had become evident that the system was being abused. One man, he'd said, was found to be collecting eight different pensions, and might never have been caught if not for having to leave his thumbprint as a receipt of payment. Surely, Henry suggested, this system could be used in Britain. Were fingerprints not the ideal way of matching a man to his name, with no possibility of mistake?

He'd had to write back to explain—without a system to classify fingerprints, the vast numbers of records would be nothing more than a gigantic haystack through which officials would have to search. Galton had tried to develop such a system, but so far to no avail. It was the same problem presented by photographs—they were easier to take than Bertillon's precise measurements, of that there was no doubt. The trouble was, what did one do with all of the photographs—or all of the fingerprints—to make them usable? Monsieur Bertillon's system for anthropometry, with its drawers filled with cards classified by head sizes, arm lengths, and so on, meant that a person's data could very quickly be matched with an existing card, and any alias therefore uncovered. It had galled him—he had devoted his life to anthropometry only to have Henry think he was the one to understand the complex process of identification. Now he is sure that his annoyance must have seeped through his explanation, and his curt delivery of the news that Mother was failing. For why else would Henry not have told him about his engagement to Miss Dawes?

The hansom jolts forward, stops again, then sways as his driver climbs down behind him. Robert pulls his watch from his pocket. He is going to be late.

He brings his hands to his face and breathes on them. Maybe Mina is right. A woman possessed of a little knowledge and sufficient cunning would not find the deception a difficult one. The opportunities presented by the loss of the *Star of the Orient* might have been more of a temptation than a woman of few scruples could resist.

After all, Henry would have had no reason to hide the fact that he was returning to visit his sick mother, or that she might not live long. He might even have mentioned his life insurance, for he was always keen to encourage others to be as careful with their arrangements as he was with his own. For a woman in straitened circumstances that money could mean freedom from a life of penury and humiliation. Plus, one could not overlook the fact that Victoria had been found on the shore next to his body. Henry, facedown in the surf, by her account, and dead. After the three-week journey from Bombay, she'd have known who he was, would have known of his circumstances. Maybe she'd have known more than that. Enough to pass herself off as his widow.

Yet if Mina is wrong—if she is wrong, then this woman who has already been through so much does not deserve their suspicions.

He sees Victoria again as she was during dinner. Her thin neck bare and bent over her plate, her nervous way of blinking, the flush that crept up her face when she drank the glass of wine he insisted she take to bolster her spirits. A mouse of a woman, he thinks now. Does that explain why her answers were so short? Or why, when he enquired—delicately, he thought—how she and Henry had met, she'd said merely that everyone in Bombay knew everyone else, that everyone was thrown together? Or why, when Mina gently commented how romantic it must have been to have married so quickly, and so quietly, she'd looked down into her wineglass? Yes, she'd said, she supposed it was. When next she looked up a fragile smile had twitched across her lips, then fallen away.

He'd caught Mina's eye and given a shake of his head, so slight he doubted if even Cartwright had noticed. Mina raised her eyebrows before reaching for her glass, and even though she asked a few more questions about Henry, he knew she was only holding in her curiosity for his sake. When Victoria had excused herself after dessert and the two of them had moved to the drawing room for tea, Mina had sat forward so they could not be overheard through the door and said in a low voice, "It's not that we *must* doubt her. But have you noticed how little she's told us? There's something not right, I'm sure of it." He'd had to admit that yes, it was odd—the fact of her marriage to Henry that they'd heard nothing of, the fact that she said so little when given every opportunity to convince them of who she was. The fact that she arrived with little more than the clothes she was wearing when the ship foundered, and so could not offer proof of her story.

Perhaps he should make enquiries. It would not be so difficult—there must be someone in Bombay he can write to for information, and if the English community is as tight as Victoria has described it, her engagement to Henry could not have been a secret. If necessary, he could even ask for proof of their marriage, for there will certainly be a record of it.

He leans to one side to see up the road into the knot of traffic, but instead his attention is caught by the hansom's horse lifting its tail and letting soft, steaming pats of manure drop to the ground. A little way up the street stands his driver on the edge of a crowd, looking on with his hands in his pockets as a man with a florid face swings his fist at a coachman in red livery. "Driver," Robert calls out. "Driver. Get me out of here. There must be a different route."

It takes some time to attract his attention, and when he does it takes even longer to extract the cab from the tangle of carriages, carts, and omnibuses blocking the road and to turn it up a stinking alley that, the driver assures him, is the only shortcut available.

Half an hour later Robert takes the stairs up to the offices of the British Institute of Anthropology two at a stride, his bag knocking against his legs. But he discovers to his annoyance that not only is Sir Jonathan not waiting for him, he is not in the office at all.

"Not here?" he says to the secretary. "I don't understand. He requested a meeting at half past nine."

The secretary is a rather hunched young man with hair slicked down firmly from a middle part. He daintily licks one finger to leaf through an appointment book on the desk. "Well," he says, "it appears you cancelled the appointment a few days ago. Sir Jonathan is in another meeting this morning."

"I would remember if I'd cancelled our meeting, and I assure you—"

Beside them the door opens, and for a moment he imagines it

must be Sir Jonathan, that the morning will not be wasted after all. A rather dapper man with a small moustache and glasses glances from him to the secretary and back. "Oh dear," he says, "I hope I have not intruded onto some delicate matter."

"Merely some confusion over Sir Jonathan's schedule, Dr. Taylor," says the secretary.

"Again?" He stands there leaning slightly forward, as though he is about to lift himself high onto his toes. "This must be the third time in a fortnight, Stallybrass. Someone needs to set their house in order." He gives the young man a wink.

Stallybrass gives a weak smile that barely lifts the corners of his mouth. "Sir Jonathan is meeting with the steering committee. Perhaps you have some idea if he is likely to be detained the whole morning."

"The steering committee?" He turns to Robert. "I am afraid that if you hope to see him you will have a long wait." Then he lowers his voice. "They do tend to get into things rather."

"Then it seems I've had a wasted journey. Perhaps," Robert says to the secretary, "you would be good enough to present my compliments to Sir Jonathan. If he would still like to meet with me, then maybe he would be good enough to inform me."

"I shall pass on your message, Mr. Bentley."

The other man steps closer. "Bentley? Robert Bentley?"

"Yes."

"Well—of all the luck," he exclaims, "to meet you here. I am Sir Jonathan's colleague. Anthropometry has been my passion for years now, and I am familiar with your work with Monsieur Bertillon in Paris. Sir Jonathan will be most disappointed to have missed you. Now tell me, when are you presenting to the Troup Committee?"

"In ten days."

"Ah, and Sir Jonathan is leaving for Edinburgh this evening and won't be back for a week at least." He pauses for a moment, touching his lips with one finger. "I wonder," he says, "since you are here—" He looks down at his shoes, then back at Robert. "Would you be good enough to meet with me instead? It would be a great honor, and I would be able to pass on to Sir Jonathan the essence of our discussion."

"Yes, of course, of course." Robert's smile is genuine, for now, at least, the morning is not entirely wasted, and this man—this Dr. Taylor—seems barely able to contain his excitement at having Robert Bentley all to himself.

CHAPTER 11

By the time the snow has fallen to the ground it has a grey tinge.
Robert turns his gaze towards the prison gates. The guard carrying his
equipment is a huge fellow but stooped, as though his own weight is
almost more than he can bear, let alone that of Robert's anthropometric equipment. The snow doesn't help. It makes the steps slippery, and
gathers thickly on the man's eyelashes so that, though he hates to
touch him, Robert reaches out and guides him by the elbow.

It is a miserable business, getting into a prison, no matter that he is
known here now. The clang of the gates rings out unsettlingly loud,
and the grate of the keys in each set of locks as they pass into the
heart of the building sets his nerves on edge. How, Robert wonders,
must it feel for a convicted felon? To have the freedoms of life shut off
one by one as the doors swing closed? To know that inside is nothing
but the dreariness of bare cells, overcooked food, and the treadmill?
He pushes away such depressing thoughts by calling to mind the sight
of Mina that morning as he rose above her in their bed, her hair glinting auburn in the light of the candle he'd lit to see her better, her nip-
ples hardening to the touch of his fingers. She has a way of half
closing her eyes with a gasp when he enters her, as though each time
the feel of him is a surprise, and it is this that he sees instead of the
guard stumbling along the corridors with his boxes: Mina—the lift of
her chin, the hair that clings damply to her neck in delicate curls, her
ribs hard against his own as he pulls her to him.

"Sir?"

They are at the door. "Yes?"

"Flyte is waiting for you, sir. And the governor should be with you shortly."

"Ah. Very good."

After all the measurements they have taken so far it should be— indeed it *is*—possible to match a man against his record. And so, today, a test. Three prisoners to be brought in and identified by Jessop and Arthur by their measurements alone. Robert has seen Bertillon do it a hundred times. For these men it will be a different matter: Arthur still scratches his head over millimeters, and as for Jessop—Robert cannot rid himself of the sight of him about to measure a prisoner's foot in its shoe. If they fail him today, the case for anthropometry will be considerably weakened—for surely Governor Waite will not speak for it before the Troup Committee unless he can see proof of its efficacy here, today, in this room. Only fair, Robert reminds himself, because anthropometry will have to weather the confusions and inaccuracies of other Jessops and other Arthurs if it is to be adopted. Yet of all the men the governor could have given him, why these two?

Flyte is busy setting up the equipment. "Good day, sir."

"I hope it will be, Flyte, I certainly do."

"As do I, sir." He gives a small smile. "This may be our last meeting within these walls—I will soon be a free man again, and shall be able to reestablish my reputation."

"Good luck, then, Flyte." He nods encouragingly, though such hopes seem foolish—what reputation can an ex-convict have?

"Thank you, sir." He leans a little closer, says softly, "I hope I have been of help to you, sir."

"Yes, indeed you have."

"Then perhaps"—his grey eyes stare directly into Robert's—"you would be kind enough to be of help to me. To have a gentleman vouch for my ability to be of use, and so on—am I right in thinking that you have found me a resourceful man, sir?"

"Yes, very resourceful." He steps away and wipes melted snow from the top of his boxes. He even glances at the guards, though one of them is yawning and the other picking at his nails.

Flyte follows him, his shoulder almost touching Robert's. His voice is low and insistent as he says, "Just a brief letter as to my character, sir, if you wouldn't mind. I am a reformed man, and I—"

Robert rests his hand on one of the boxes. He says a little too loudly, "Surely the governor would be a more sensible choice. He knows you far better than I do. Now really, that's the end of the matter." Is it his imagination, or does a sudden sharpness flash across Flyte's face? Out of the corner of his eye he catches a movement—the guards shifting, looking his way.

Flyte has seen them too. He says, "Very good, sir. I'm sorry to have troubled you." He turns away, back to his work.

Robert rubs his hands together, as though he is still cold. Men like Flyte—they do not let a chance go by. No wonder, he thinks, they end up in prison.

Flyte is precise in his movements, like a doll that has been wound up to perform the same tasks over and over again. Already, then, Robert's visits, and this routine of measuring the prisoners, have been absorbed into the repetitions of his life. As for the guards, they look bored again. None of the days that they have stood here watching have been rewarded with prisoner misbehavior. No attempts to flee this room, no sudden attacks on the visiting expert in anthropometry. Not even any serious attempt to refuse to be measured.

Flyte has set out chairs for the observers, and now rubs the top of the small cabinet containing the anthropometric cards with his sleeve. Then he sighs and looks about him. There's a knock at the door, and one of the guards steps over to open it. A trolley with a tea urn, cups and saucers, and—no doubt because of the importance of the day—small cakes. The man who pushes it in has a gaunt face and massive hands, yet he sets out everything quietly and in order, as a woman would.

Flyte is at Robert's side, and he puts a slip of paper in his hand. "I thought you might need this."

Robert barely has time to glance at what he is holding before

Governor Waite comes in with his secretary and Foley, the Inspector of Prisons, Jessop and Arthur right behind them. Instinctively Robert reads what is on the paper, but it takes a moment for his mind to register what it is: written in small letters are three names. The names of the men who will be brought in, and whom it is Jessop and Arthur's job to identify. Names he should not know if the test is to have any validity.

"Ah, Mr. Bentley." The governor stretches out a hand.

Robert stuffs the paper into his pocket. With a quick smile he takes the governor's hand, then Foley's, squeezing both a little too hard. In his chest his heart is frantic.

Maybe Arthur and Jessop have the names too, he thinks. Maybe this test of the Bertillon system is nothing but a charade. It is too late to protest. So he sits and watches, and when Flyte comes close with a cup of tea he can barely bring himself to take it from him.

*I*t's dinnertime, and he wishes that the widow would excuse herself with a headache or whatever other maladies a lady can summon up, but she doesn't. He'd come home thrilled with success—in those few hours out of the house he'd let the fact of Henry's death slip away from him. Striding into the drawing room he'd barely acknowledged Henry's widow sitting by the fire with her fingers twisted together in her lap, had barely seen her, to tell the truth. She'd kept her head down and said not a single word, as though she'd been taught to efface herself. Mina had lifted a finger to her lips, and she was right: it would have been wrong to have crowed about how splendidly the test had gone, even if it was not all it seemed to be.

As for dinner, it lasts an eternity. The three of them would hardly have had a thing to say to one another if it were not for Mina asking about India, and the climate, and the servants there, and the customs of the Indian people, leading the widow's quiet voice through explanations and descriptions and, when it trails off, talking about France and the French way of life, and how in Paris servants are not so closely guarded as here—indeed, since the Parisians live in apartments, servants share quarters together at the top of the building. Whenever Mina pauses, the widow's eyes slide down to her plate, but his wife does not give up. How can she when Cartwright and Sarah are standing at the sideboard, watching?

After dinner the widow says she is tired, and Mina gently kisses her good night. It is enough to make him uncomfortable, the ease with which she presses her lips against the cheek of this woman, then, once the door is closed, says, "Well, at least we can be reasonably sure she has come from India."

He gets to his feet. "Mina!"

Her skirts rustle as she comes over to him, and the suggestion of what lies beneath is almost more than he can stand. He reaches for her, pulls her hard against him; there is fabric between his skin and hers, and a corset. "Come," he whispers to her, "come upstairs with me now."

He expects her to refuse—the widow has only just left the room, the servants are about, tomorrow is the funeral. But no—she turns his face slightly with hers and opens her mouth full on his while her hand slides down his belly, so far down that he grabs her hand and pulls her towards the door.

In the hallway they come across the new maid and sing out, "Good night, Jane." They are close to laughter, running upstairs like a couple of newlyweds when Henry's widow has barely closed the door to her room—what has got into them? They lock the bedroom door and undress each other, slowly, for Mina has layer upon layer to remove and he wants her naked beneath him, utterly naked. Then he lays her back onto the pillows and parts her knees. She is so soft, her skin so warm in the light of the fire, the hair between her legs opening to reveal glistening pinkness. He pushes himself hard into her until she starts to bend away, then with a hoarse cry she grabs his buttocks and lifts herself so he can enter her more fully.

Afterwards he rolls to his side, still inside her, his arms around her, the stickiness of their bodies between them. "Poor Henry," he whispers.

"Yes," she says, "poor Henry."

"Mother tried to persuade him not to leave. She thought India was too dangerous. She even invited the new neighbors around for dinner in the hope that he'd fall in love with their daughter."

"But he didn't?"

"He told me that Miss Pritchard had *a most unfortunate laugh.*"

"And did she?"

"She brayed like a donkey."

Mina strokes his cheek with one finger. "Poor Miss Pritchard."

"In the end she married the deputy governor of Dartmoor Prison." He feels Mina shift her shoulders. "Can you imagine? Your whole life spent in sight of a place like that? Even after a few hours, I have to get it out of me. To be locked up—it must be a living death."

"It's supposed to be, isn't it?"

"Can you imagine how it must be to work there? I don't know how those men bear it." He rubs his nose against the delicate skin between her collarbone and her neck. "As you go through the gates you feel all the joy in life drain away, and you wonder whether it will be there for you when you come back out."

"But it went well? The test?"

"Oh, a great success! I had my doubts about Jessop and Arthur. Of all the men the governor could have chosen for me to train—"

"Maybe"—she shifts slightly—"maybe he thought that if you could train them, you could train any men."

He nips at her skin. "You are too clever for your own good." Then he sighs. "But it went well. I'd had nightmares of Jessop measuring the men with their shoes on, but he managed. Not quite as well as I would have liked, but close enough."

"They got all three of them?"

"Each one in a matter of minutes. The governor and the inspector were impressed, I could tell. I don't think either of them quite believed anthropometry could do it."

"That's wonderful! Will they both speak to the committee? Surely they will now."

"Foley's *on* the committee, but he was adamant that anthropometry is nothing more than a means of negative proof; it can distinguish between two men but not conclusively match a man to his identity."

"Oh, but he's wrong, isn't he?"

He shrugs. "The chance of two men sharing precisely the same measurements exists, but it's infinitely small. Besides, what better method is there? At least Governor Waite understood that. As I was leaving he said he'd have a word with Foley."

"That's wonderful." She runs her fingertips along the ridge of his shoulder. "And yet?"

"And yet, my darling, I'm the one who's unsettled now." She pulls back to look at him and he feels himself slipping out of her.

"By the test?"

"Just beforehand, something odd happened. They were bringing in the tea, and the prisoner who helps out came over to me. He's a quiet sort, a forger or the like, I imagine, whose time is nearly up."

"What did he do?"

"He passed me a sheet of paper and there, written small, were three names. Of course I knew what they were."

"The prisoners for the test?"

He rolls onto his back, one arm still beneath her. "Exactly. I have no idea how he got them, or why he gave them to me, unless he thought he was going to ingratiate himself." He sniffs. "Or create trouble for me if they were found. He wanted me to write him a character for when he's set free, and I said no."

"Oh darling, some people love their own cleverness and think others will be impressed. If he found out who was going to be brought in, maybe he couldn't keep it to himself. Most likely that's how he got caught in the first place—being clever and wanting others to know it."

"He's not the showy sort. He has this way of seeming smaller than he is—I thought he was much shorter than me, but he isn't."

"That's one way of slipping beneath notice, isn't it? He could have committed the most atrocious murder and no one would have suspected him—and finally he couldn't bear for his perfect murder not to have been noticed." She laughs softly.

"You don't know Flyte. I think he's more the sort who takes a few shillings here, a few there, for years." He looks at her, but she's not watching him anymore. Instead her eyes are on the fire and she feels stiff in his arms. She shivers. "Poor darling," he says, and pulls the sheets up over them both, though he is still sweating.

"I miss our life in Paris," she tells him in a thin voice.

He lifts himself onto one elbow and kisses her shoulder. "Me too. But I can't see when we'll be able to go back. Not for the time being."

She twists around. "I don't want to live in this city, this house. It's—it's sucking the life out of me." Her voice is trembling and she stares into his face, shadows making her cheeks look hollow and her eyes sunken.

"Mina," he whispers. "Oh no, it won't be like that. I promise it won't." He follows the bones of her face with his fingers and she closes her eyes.

He doesn't tell her what he is thinking: that to return would be a step backwards, that in Paris there will always be the famous Bertillon, and no one will ever surpass him. But in England, who is there? As yet anthropometry doesn't have one star in its firmament that shines more brightly than the rest. There is Sir Jonathan at the British Institute of Anthropology, but from what Dr. Taylor said, he is beginning to lose his hold on the institute. What could one expect from a man in his seventies? And then there is Dr. Taylor himself, with his smooth, round chin and his plump cheeks, and his way of peering through his spectacles. He is a charming man, yet is he the man to guide the future of anthropometry and all it could mean for England? Robert stares into the shadows of the room and, for a few minutes, imagines himself making speeches, appointing committees, speaking to Parliament even. And why not? Why not him?

Soon the cold air seeps beneath the sheets he has pulled over them, and he sits up to arrange the blankets. Mina seems to be asleep. Such anxiety at the idea of staying in London—it's natural. This is the city in which she lived with her first husband. Not a happy marriage, one that haunts her, though he's never persuaded her to tell him why. He leans forward now and presses a kiss into the soft skin of her neck.

In a few hours, the funeral. A quiet affair with a few family friends, a colleague or two of Henry's from years ago, yet the prospect of it makes him rub his temples with his fist. He will have to introduce Victoria. After that, how will they be able to rid themselves of her, even with proof that she is not who she claims?

Poor Henry. He was coming home for Mother, but it is he who is being buried. "God help us," Robert mutters, and Mina turns over, her back to him now. He presses his body to hers, belly to back, knees tucked behind knees, and cups her breast in his hand.

Sometime after eleven o'clock, when the house is quiet, he falls asleep still holding her.

She stares into the hearth, where the embers glow a dangerous red. Eventually the gentle wash of Robert's breathing slows. Usually it is he who moves away, but tonight she cannot bear the weight of his arm on her chest. Carefully she lifts it and rolls away to where the sheets are cold.

Downstairs the clock chimes. Midnight already. Only ten more hours until the funeral, but it's not that that occupies her thoughts. Robert had said, "You don't know Flyte." Those words have been nudging her away from sleep.

Oh, yes, she knows Flyte. She knows him only too well. At least he has not yet been released, because the thought of him being a free man makes the world around her seem fragile as glass, as though she might fall through it and be lost.

CHAPTER 12

Here, ma'am," Jane says for the second time, and holds the dress ready—a dull black bombazine with black trimming. Everything about it is black, like a hole from which no light will ever escape. Fitting her into it is not an easy task, for the widow flutters and twitches, and when she does look at Jane it is with resentment.

Jane nearly apologizes. For being in this room at all. For seeing this woman, whose life has broken apart, in her undergarments—those, too, marked by her loss with small black ribbons. For being the one to have to persuade her into the deep mourning she will wear every day for the next year. Leaning towards Victoria, she closes the fasteners one by one. There is an awful dry smell about the dress, of dye perhaps, as though it reeks of death. Above the high collar the widow's face looks as small and pale as the kernel of a nut newly cracked, not yet ripe for the world.

From downstairs Jane hears the clock strike. "If you don't mind, ma'am." She points to the stool in front of the dressing table. The widow almost starts, looks down at it in confusion. "For your hair, ma'am." And Jane reaches for the brushes.

The widow sits like a nervous bird, on the very edge of the chair, and fidgets as Jane pulls the brush through her hair.

"How would you like it done up, ma'am?" Jane tries a smile in the mirror, but the widow isn't looking at her. Anyway, it would not have been enough to cover up the fact that she has little idea what she is doing, that the only way she knows how to style a lady's hair is like Mrs. Robert's.

"You've seen how I wear it." She drops her voice. "Haven't you?"

"Not really, ma'am. I could try, though."

"Yes." She blinks. "You could try, I suppose."

So Jane brushes the hair and divides it and sets to twisting the strands together and pinning them up. The widow watches her, so small and hunched on her stool that she looks as though she will topple off if Jane pulls too hard. She fiddles with the bodice of her dress, as though she never learnt to sit still.

When Jane has finished she stands to the side to see her in the mirror. "It's not quite what you're used to," she says.

The widow looks weighed down by the hair piled onto the crown of her head. She raises her hands to her cheeks. Her breath seems to catch, and she plucks out the pins and drops them onto the dressing table in front of her. "I'm sorry," she says, "I'm so sorry." Then she rests her hands on its edge and lets herself cry. She says something under her breath, and Jane steps forward. She hears, "I can't do this, I can't do this, I can't do this."

"Come on now. You don't want to be late."

The widow sits up at that. She closes her eyes, then, crying still, runs her fingers through her hair to rid it of Jane's work.

"We have to hurry, ma'am."

It only takes a minute or two for her to wind her hair into a tight ball that she pins to the back of her head. In the mirror she finds Jane's eyes. "Don't worry," she blurts out. "I'll say you did it for me. They won't know."

"Thank you, ma'am." She doesn't know what else to say.

On the table is a box holding a jet necklace. Jane loops it around the widow's neck. Then she busies herself with the room, though there is precious little to tidy—everything was already put away when she stepped in here half an hour ago, even the covers pulled up on the bed. But she doesn't want to look at the widow, who has a way of staring into Jane's face as though waiting for something, and Jane doesn't know what that might be.

When she does look back the widow is still at the dressing table. Crying has dappled her skin red, and against the black of her dress the marks stand out vividly. She is trying to calm herself, her chin high but twitching as she holds herself still, her mouth a little open like a split shoe. She's all angles—arms stiff, neck stiff, her movements jarring. It's hard to watch her. Soon the clock downstairs sounds the hour and Jane helps the widow to her feet. "It's time," she says softly, and leads her over to the door, and to the stairs beyond, then down to the carriage that will take her to Henry Bentley's funeral.

Mina stands at the window. More snow is falling, fragments of white scattering over the black of carriages and coats and hats. You'd think the whole city had been bereaved, the men especially. All Robert had to do for mourning was to add a crape band to his hat and buy himself black gloves. As for her, she'll be in this black dress for months. She leans closer to the glass and looks up into the dizzying swirl of flakes. A few miles away this snow is falling on the freshly dug earth of Henry Bentley's grave. By now the half-dozen mourners who'd braved the wind cutting through the cemetery must be home, bellies full of pie and brandy, huddled by their fires yet still unable to rid themselves of this day's chill. What, she wonders, did they think of Victoria? A widowed bride who in the church laid her head on the coffin as though asking forgiveness, who turned away even the most gentle question by bowing her head? Most likely she merely seemed overcome with grief. And now that she has been seen, how much more difficult it will be to stop her from taking Henry's money and vanishing.

Cold air is sliding down the glass—Mina can feel it, leaking down and pooling by her ankles. She stands there anyway, her breath clouding the glass, and watches the street. To lose the money—to be trapped in this city—she would have to always be on her guard. How long might she manage it? There must be some other way. Yet what are they to live on? Robert is a sensible man, and that might be their downfall, for how is she to convince him to let drop so sensible a plan as finding work here?

A charwoman hurries by in a shawl, three small boys in caps run up the pavement, a man in a great coat leans against the railings of the house opposite with a tail of tobacco smoke flaring from his mouth—the man who is often there, doing nothing but watching. Then she sees him. He steps down from a carriage and looks up at the house. Even from this distance she'd know him anywhere—the round jaw, the flushed, full cheeks, the way he stands with both hands gripping his cane and his shoulders back. David Popham. At the church she'd turned and he'd nodded to her, sitting at the back by himself. Later he'd made a show of coming forward to offer his condolences, though there was something else in his smile, a look of self-satisfaction. He held onto her hand too long. She had to pull it away, and a tremble of fear ran through her. Even Robert felt it and tucked her arm more tightly under his. She murmured, "So cold in here," and he said, "Yes, a miserable place."

Now here he is again, and she wonders if he will have the effrontery to knock and leave his card. She leans so close to the window that her hair sticks to the damp glass. Down on the pavement he cocks his head and lets his gaze run over the front of the house. Surely he can't suspect that she is watching. Nonetheless, she flinches back.

There's a knock at the front door. A few seconds pass, just long enough for him to leave his card, then the door thuds closed. He is gone. Even he would not insist on being admitted when the household is so newly in mourning.

She walks over to the fire and waits for a tap at the door. Sarah. "A card, ma'am. Mr. David Popham."

"You may leave it on the table."

"Yes, ma'am." She lays the card on the side table, then makes her way back to the door with a swing in her hips.

Mina looks down at the card as though she cannot bear to touch it. Then, with the tips of her fingers, she turns it over. There is nothing written on the back. Just leaving the card says all he wants to tell her: that he knows where she is, that he has found her out. She was certain it was so—that meeting in Mortimer's, the way he so quickly apologized for his mistake—of course that was all for show. Now all she can do is wait for him to make a move. He is not a clever man, but he is persistent, and he thinks enough of himself that he is unlikely to let an opportunity for revenge slip out of his grasp.

Damn him. She closes her fingers on his card, though the sharp corners of the pasteboard dig into her palm. Damn him. She lifts her hand to throw the bent card into the fire, but she stops herself. Anger will not protect her, only information will, and the capacity to think. So she sits down and flattens the card against her knee. It shows his name, his address, his club. Maybe he meant for her to know that he has moved, for her to find him. If she is clever she will be able to use this information against him. There must be a way.

The fire crackles and spits—snow coming down the chimney, dripping onto the hot coals. She sits and watches it. For a fortnight she is safe—they will not go out, they will not have guests, they will be shut up in the house to grieve. But after that—if only they could return to Paris. He wouldn't be able to reach her there. However, there is the matter of the failing Mrs. Bentley, who apparently is in no hurry to follow her son to the graveyard, and the newly widowed Mrs. Bentley, who has taken to her bed this afternoon, and who is in no hurry to leave this household either. Mina presses her hands hard onto her knees and forces herself to sit still because, at this moment, she would rather burst down the hallway and out into the street, and the snow, and the cold, than sit here in this room, waiting for whatever fate will bring her.

A fortnight to come up with a plan. She must think. The fire switches shadows across her face. She leans towards it though the heat prickles her skin. When she touches her cheek it feels too hot to her fingertips, and the crisp smell of hot fabric drifts up to her nose.

There's a knock at the door, and she turns quickly. "Yes?"

It's Jane, her body tilted against the weight of a bucket of coals gripped in one hand. She closes the door, then comes over to the fireplace.

Mina sits back a little and watches her. She still has that thinness of a young girl not quite a woman, and a certain softness in her face, but her hands are red and swollen, the skin cracked. For a girl like her, cleverness makes no difference. What counts is her ability to turn her body into a machine that cleans and carries. What, she wonders, does this girl think about when she is scrubbing floors and laying fires? Where does her mind go when her hands are busy?

She says, "Did you find out anything?"

"No, ma'am. At least, nothing you'd call found out exactly." She doesn't look up, as though even here with just the two of them in this room she must be careful.

"What did you learn, then?"

The coals rattle against the scuttle as she tips them in. "Well," she says, wiping her hands on her rough apron. "She's got a notebook, and in it is the address for Mr. Henry here, and addresses of people in India."

"What sort of people?"

"I don't know, ma'am. Just names and addresses." She sits back on her heels and looks at the fire. "It's been in water. The ink's run at the edges of the pages, but you can still read most of it."

"Is that all? Only names and addresses?"

"No," she says. "At the back she'd been doing her accounts. Her aunt couldn't have given her much of an allowance—she was working out if she could afford a new dress. They couldn't have been well off, could they? Maybe that's why she's not used to having a maid waiting on her. I'd say she's been in the habit of doing things for herself. Not just getting dressed and doing her hair, but keeping her room tidy."

"Has she been doing it herself?"

"Yes, ma'am." The bucket is empty, but Jane stays on her knees on the hearth rug. "There's something about her, ma'am, that's odd." She looks up. "If someone won't meet your eye, that means trouble. To me that's what it means, anyway."

"You've begun well." Mina nods. "Now you must be her friend—she'll tell you things about herself."

"She doesn't like me helping her."

Mina folds her hands together. "She's lonely and miserable. Be kind to her and she'll talk."

"Yes ma'am." She gets to her feet. "But if I don't know what I'm waiting to hear—"

"Tell me everything. That's all you need to do." She looks up into Jane's face and catches something—a flicker of distaste? Or at least of dislike? Of course, that's to be expected: she has caught this girl in a trap and she wants to wriggle free. But she's too useful to be let go so easily.

CHAPTER 13

His head feels big and unwieldy—all that wine last night. But he must think—think carefully of the words that will ask the question delicately, concisely, clearly. He takes a sip of his coffee and grimaces. Then he shifts a pile of papers to the side and takes up a pencil.

Cyril, he writes, *urgent query re Henry's widow.*

Should he direct him to find the aunt? Or simply acquaintances? From so far away, it is not easy to know the consequences of what he is requesting—and from a man he was at school with fifteen years ago and has not seen in more than eight.

His pencil hovers above the words, ready to dash a line through them. This whole business sickens him, to suspect the poor woman when she has been through so much. Where has this suspicion of Mina's come from? It worries him, for she won't let herself be talked out of it. Now it has worked its way into him, too. Last night at dinner he couldn't look at his brother's widow for more than a few moments at a time. She watched him with those pink-rimmed eyes of hers, a handkerchief clutched in her hand. A young woman caught up in a terrible grief.

And yet.

And yet, he cannot get past the fact that there *is* something odd about her. A slipperiness to all that she's told them. A way of looking off at the wrong moments.

He brings his pencil back to the paper.

❦ ❦ ❦

A half day off, though it is hardly worth the name, for Jane has had to hurry through her morning's work, and the evening's work will be waiting for her when she comes back. Even so—it is bliss. To put on her coat and hat and wrap her muffler around her neck, to come up the area steps and into Cursitor Road, where the snow has been trodden into an ugly slush, to be out of the house at last. At the top she hesitates: Which way to go? She has no idea, for in the month since she arrived she has barely left the house, and then only to come into the area. The world is so vast before her that she almost believes she can feel it curve under her feet as she turns to her right and takes off through the wet snow. How cold it is—melting snow leaking into her boots, the wind blustering up between the rows of houses and blowing into her face. She strides along; even in this weather it is a pleasure just to be able to walk when for so long she has been cramped inside the house. Down to the end of the street she goes, and into the next with its bare trees and a baked-potato man at the end with his cart. She turns again, this time into what she discovers to be a busier street. Not far away stands a row of shops, and she hurries across the road to them.

All she finds is an ironmonger's, a draper's, a butcher's, a baker's with cakes and buns and pies laid out in the window and the heady scent of hot bread escaping through the door. In her pocket she pinches the paper she wrapped her money in to hide it at the bottom of her box. The doorway offers a little shelter from the wind, and there she unwraps it. A sixpence, a couple of pennies. Nothing more. No half-sovereign. Shifting her feet, she looks at the ground, as though it could have fallen without her noticing. Nothing. How can that be? She tips the coins out of the creased paper and into her hand. And then she sees it: just above the fold is a crudely drawn noose, and inside it letters that spell *Martha Wilbred*.

Sarah. She has been through her box. She has stolen her money. And she has found out about her mother. Her mother, who was hanged before Jane was ever old enough to know her. Her mother who never had a husband, who worked in an inn, who plunged a kitchen knife into the chest of a Mr. Philip Granger, then ran for her life to the moors, and was only found after a week. It was all in the clippings the matron showed her—so Jane would know to govern herself more strictly than the other girls, she'd said, so she'd know she had the burden of bad blood to ask the Lord to help her overcome.

Now Sarah has found her out.

Not from the photograph, she's certain, for it is merely the picture of a young woman with a stern gaze. Not from anything she has let slip. She holds onto the wall, her head buzzing like a wasp nest at the end of summer. From Cartwright. From the warning he gave her that day when Sarah was going through Mrs. Robert's desk. Sarah overheard. She made him tell her more—and he did. Of course he did—Sarah has been gathering all of their secrets: hers, Cartwright's, Mrs. Johnson's. Out of them she's weaving a comfortable life for herself. Cartwright and Mrs. Johnson might snap at her, but they do nothing more. They are frightened of her.

She pushes herself away from the wall. She must find herself a new situation. No matter that the tazza cost five pounds, she will have to pay Sarah, and pay her, and pay her. There will be no end to it.

Her belly is still tight with the expectation of something from the baker's. It's not as though she is hungry, or that she hasn't eaten well at the Bentleys'. No, but to choose something to suit her fancy, to buy it herself and eat it when she likes—that is what she is hungry for. That was what she had intended when she stopped in this doorway.

Damn Sarah, she thinks. Damn the filthy, thieving bitch.

Her fingers touch the coins she has left—cold now. Enough to afford something, though the anger in her mouth will sour the taste of whatever she buys. She walks slowly to the window and lets her eyes linger on the trays of buns and pies and small cakes, half of which she's never seen the like of before. The wind threatens to tip off her hat, so she clamps a hand onto it. There is someone behind her, but she doesn't care; she takes her time before she makes up her mind and pushes the door open.

Someone follows her in—a man who stands behind her. But her eyes are on the baker's wife, a sallow woman with a turned-down mouth and thick eyebrows. She's polite enough, though. She looks to where Jane is pointing and picks out a Chelsea bun for her—not the best, for who knows if she'll be back?—but all the same, not one of the harder ones baked in the corner of the tray. Jane follows it from the woman's hand to the paper she wraps it in. Already saliva is pooling in her mouth, for she's imagining that glinting sugar and those plump raisins between her teeth. She pays and carries the bun outside, where the wind is a little colder than she remembered, and looks about her. Which way to go? Certainly not back towards Cursitor Road. So left then, into the wind, and towards the church that's tolling the hour, walking fast with her heels ringing out against the pavement.

She doesn't notice the man who comes out of the baker's shop glancing up and down the street, then takes off in a long-legged stride in her wake. In one hand he holds a bun wrapped in paper, but you'd think he'd forgotten all about it the way he weaves in and out between the people coming up the street towards him. He skips around a perambulator pushed by a nursemaid, knocking her shoulder, making her stumble. She sends a resentful stare at his back as he hurries off around a tall gentleman, then an old woman stabbing at the ground with her cane.

He's close behind Jane as she turns the corner into a broader street, and has to stop when she comes to a halt. There are more people here, but she stands in the midst of them like a branch caught in a river, and peers in both directions. She has a wrapped bun in her hand and this, he knows, is the problem. Where to eat it without walking along the street taking mouthfuls? After all, even a young servant like her has some sort of reputation to consider. This street does not look promising. Not even the smallest patch of green that would suggest a park where she might find a bench and, surreptitiously, bite into the bun. Nonetheless, she takes off across the road, and he has to dart in front of a carriage to keep up with her. The houses are more elegant here, and she walks awkwardly, staring up at them as though she has never seen buildings so tall.

He has been waiting for her to tire, or to tire at least of this searching for a quiet place to sit. Instead he finds himself beginning to flag, and wishes with all his might that the shabby little hat with its faded fabric flower that he has been following all this time would come to a rest.

They go another two miles before she shows any sign of despair, past a public house loud with the shouts of men that she turns her head away from, past vegetables trodden into the frozen mud left by a morning market. The wind has picked up and sends stinging specks of snow into her face and his, yet only when they come to a bridge does she slow.

In a couple of strides he comes abreast. He glances at her, then says, "Miss, I couldn't help noticing that maybe you need a place to sit down." He smiles—not too widely, he hopes—and tips his hat to her. "I'm not in the habit of approaching young ladies on the street, but if you would like directions to a park. It's not too far . . ."

"Well," she says, and blinks at him. She is cold, and feels emptied out by her anger. This city is not what she expected. It goes on forever in streets that resemble one another in that none of them provides a place for her to sit, as though stepping out of the doorway of one's house one cannot stop until one reaches one's destination. There are no grassy verges, no seawalls, no quiet churchyards, no hedges that one can sit behind.

She looks up at him, this young man with his gentle smile and long-lashed eyes. He is not a gentleman, but is too well-dressed to be a servant like her.

"Or perhaps you're too cold to sit in a park on a day like this. There's a tea shop close by, a very respectable place." He points, as though he has no intention of walking with her.

"Oh," she says, and follows the direction of his finger. She can see nothing promising in that direction either.

"I could accompany you." He notices that she stiffens at that. He lowers his head a little. "I know what it's like to come to London and not know anybody and not know where to go. I came here five years ago to be a gentleman's valet. I didn't want to stay, it's not a friendly place. Not like Devon—"

"Devon?" she says eagerly.

"Yes," he tells her, and he knows that he has got her now.

*M*other?" Robert sits in the chair by her bedside and pulls her hand from under the covers. It lies cold in his, so he lays his other hand on top. "Can you hear me?"

Her face is gaunt, as though the weeks of lying on her back have allowed gravity to leach the flesh from her nose and cheeks, to leave one beaky and the other hollow.

He leans towards her. Her breath is thick and stale, and this close he hears a crackling as her lungs fill and empty, fill and empty. "Mother?" he says again.

This time her eyelids lift enough for him to see her eyes swimming beneath them. She blinks, then her lips move and she swallows. He brings his ear close, but no words come. When he sits back her eyes widen, as though she doesn't understand who he is, or how she has come to be lying here like this.

A creak of the door behind him. Price. She comes close, takes her mistress's hand out of his and tucks it back beneath the covers. "We can't be having her catch cold." Her smile is narrow. He doesn't smile back, not even when she tells him, "Mrs. Bentley is doing a little better today."

He looks down at his mother lying there. Her eyes have closed again, and her mouth is cracked open. Her breath is louder now, a rustle that makes him press a hand to his own chest. Price is a fool, he thinks, then corrects himself—not a fool. No, she senses the end coming and cannot bear to watch it, for what will happen to her? A woman getting old herself, whose skills were good enough for his mother, who has barely changed her hair or the style of her dresses in twenty years, but are unlikely to get her another position. She must, he thinks, have savings. Isn't that what servants do? They open a savings account at the bank? After all, what can they spend their money on when they have food and a bed provided? Besides, his mother has left her a little money in her will.

He runs a hand over his moustache and opens his mouth to tell Price that yes, maybe his mother is looking a little better. Before the words leave his mouth she reaches in front of him to straighten the covers, erasing any sign of him having touched them. "Dr. James insists on quiet," she tells him. "Any excitement could be fatal." In her dark dress and with her hair plaited over the top of her head—how long ago was that style the fashion, he wonders—she looks like a bird of prey. Not an eagle, but something meaner and more drab.

"Of course," he says stiffly. With a sigh he stands and bends towards his mother, pressing a kiss to her forehead, then running his hands over the covers. When he turns he takes Price's elbow and walks her to the door. "Dr. James also warned us that she may not have long. If I were you, I would think about the future."

Her eyes widen a little, but he steps away and opens the door.

He makes his way down the stairs to the study. On a cabinet by the door sits the hat left by the intruder. A ridiculous incident— Michael Danforth sneaking into his house to look through his papers. And to leave his hat behind in the house of an expert on anthropometry! But then, for Danforth fingerprints are everything: they will match a man to his body once and for all. Yet, with no means to classify fingerprints, how would one sort through the thousands of prints that would be gathered over time? How would one specific set be found? No wonder the men who support the use of fingerprints talk in vague terms about a solution to this problem. As yet, there is no solution, and no sign of one. How else do they think Bertillon persuaded the French government to rely on anthropometry? A card with a convict's measurements—with fingerprints, too, and a photograph, for what they're worth—but the *measurements* are key. They mean each card can be classified, can be carefully filed, can be plucked out from amongst thousands of others with little effort.

Tomorrow, he will present before the Troup Committee. Rather than sit at the desk, he gets to his feet. From the back of the houses beyond, a lit-up window stands out. Past it comes a small boy jumping around like a wild pony until his nurse gathers him to her side with one arm. It is the sort of gentle gesture his mother would have used, and the sight of it heartens him.

But his mother is dying upstairs. He knew it was hopeless when he went to her room, yet he'd hoped that she would show some sign of improvement, of living the winter out at least. She is his mother, and she is slipping away from him, but it is not just the sadness of another death so soon after Henry's that occupies him: it is too late to change her will. When she dies he will have little time to discover who Henry's widow is and—if she leaves—she could disappear with half of what little money this family still possesses.

No, he thinks, he cannot let that happen.

He steps away, back to the desk, where he turns up the lamp.

A sullen morning. A low sky, and a chill wind out of the east that threatens more snow. This is a day much anticipated, however, and the man gives his hat an extra push to make sure the wind doesn't lift it away. He heads down the street in the shadow of the high wall that runs its length. No windows. No gates. Only a stone wall black with soot that looms over him.

His coat was never meant for a day as cold as this, and he has no gloves or scarf. Already his ears are red. He hides his hands in his pockets and hunches his shoulders against the wind. Not for long, though, he tells himself. He will buy himself a thick wool coat and the finest pigskin gloves, a new pair of boots—in fact, everything new, from his socks to his hat. By tomorrow he will be a new man with a new name.

For now, what he wants is a cup of tea and a bacon sandwich in the shop where Steiner will be waiting for him. He imagines the warmth of the place, and how the bacon will be salty in his mouth. Then when he knows he is safe, after he's had time to watch, and to slip around corners and into shops with Steiner keeping an eye out, then it'll be time to retrieve his money.

Down the street he hurries. As soon as a side street presents itself he takes it, never mind where it goes so long as it leads him away from the prison.

And so Flyte disappears from sight, a free man at last.

CHAPTER 14

When Robert arrives home he is in the foulest of tempers. His voice rings out in the hallway—"Miserable weather. . . . No, Cartwright, no, it was not"—then his footsteps thud up the stairs. A few moments later a door slams shut.

Mina looks up from the *Strand* she is reading. On the other side of the fire the widow is staring at a book of sermons, but all afternoon her eyes have been floating away from the page, so that every time Mina raises her eyes she catches her gazing around the room. Is she calculating the value of the house and its furnishings? Or is she looking for portable property that she can make off with before she is discovered? Now, though, she is watching the door—nervously, Mina thinks—and when she notices that she herself is being watched, her face twitches and she forces her eyes back to her book.

Mina lets her head rest against the antimacassar. So, things did not go well at the Troup Committee. How could that be? He was so confident—the case for anthropometry is a strong one, as he's often told her. What on earth could have so angered him? Nervousness like a tickle spreads through her gut, and she gets to her feet. Perhaps it was nothing to do with that. Maybe she was wrong—maybe Popham has already made his move and cornered Robert today. She can just imagine the way Popham would lean towards her husband, his fleshy lips shaping each word deliciously as he stripped away everything Robert thought he knew about her.

Why is she on her feet? She can't remember. Now she twists her hands together and tells the widow, "In this country one spends so much time sitting." She laughs—too harshly, she's sure. "It can't be healthy. Though neither is going outside when the air in this city is so filthy." She walks to the window, stares out as though idle curiosity has got the better of her. "More snow," she says. But her eyes are looking through the flurry. A few men hunched against the cold, none of them gentlemen, by the look of it. A woman wrapped in a sagging shawl who must be a servant. A wagon pulled by a white horse that is barely more than an outline against the snow. Across the road a bulky man reading a newspaper and stamping his feet. He is often there. Now she wonders—is he Popham's man? Of Popham himself there's no sign. She gives a sigh loud enough for the widow to hear. "The weather here never seems conducive to going out."

The widow's small face has turned to her. Those pale eyes. That pale hair. All of it paler yet against the black of her dress. "At home it was the heat," she says. "Or the rain. When the rains came you couldn't go out. You'd be drenched. Henry always—" and she trips. "Henry," she says more softly, "always used to hate the smell of dampness and mold. He made the servants have a clean shirt ready for him at midday, and always wanted it hot from the iron. That way he could be sure it was fresh and dry."

As Mina looks across at this young woman she forgets her suspicions. Oh yes, she thinks, early love is full of joy at idiosyncrasies, and she catches herself wondering how Victoria would have fared if Henry hadn't drowned. Would his particularities have become a burden? Or would she have been the sort of woman who devoted her life to them, so that a slightly damp shirt or dinner being served half an hour late would have counted as a catastrophe?

But then, she reminds herself, it is easy enough to feign knowledge of someone you scarcely know. You think of a person you know well and slip a new name and a new face onto them. Or you take a habit you have noticed and you build a world around it. It's not so hard.

Despite the fire and the lamps, the room seems gloomier than it ever does at night. She could abandon the widow here and ask for a fire to be lit in the morning room, but that would be little better. What she needs is to go outside—to walk, to sit at a table in a café or a restaurant, to see life going on around her. This room is too littered with small tables of figurines for her to be able to walk about it. Yet to sit back by the fire and close herself into the words of a story—no, she cannot do that when her guts are gripped by worry. So she comes near and holds her hands out to the warmth of the fire. She says, "I should see how Robert's day has been. Ring for tea if you want some before I am back." With a smile she turns and heads for the door.

The hallway is cold enough to make her shiver. If nothing else, she thinks, she should fetch her shawl. Up the stairs she goes, nodding to Sarah on the way, Sarah who merely stands to the side and kicks her dustpan out of the way. Such rudeness from a servant. She can't bear her, but neither can she dismiss her quite yet. To get rid of another servant so quickly after Lizzie—she knows that it would be enough to upset Mrs. Johnson and Cartwright, and if they gave notice the household would fold in on itself. For now, it has to stand firm. Not for long perhaps; when Robert's mother dies, as soon she surely will, there may be no reason to keep the household going.

He is in the bedroom, sitting on the bed dressed only in his shirt and socks. His head jerks up when she comes in, and he grimaces. "Soaked through and freezing cold. My best suit filthy. The damned fool of a driver got his hansom stuck between two carriages and I had to get out into a sea of freezing mud."

"Before the hearing?"

He unbuttons his shirt. "Naturally, before. And as though that were not enough, I found that the *insights* I was delivering to the committee were not new to them at all."

She sits beside him. He is still shivering, but she knows better than to touch him when he is in such a mood. Whatever is bothering him, it is nothing concerning her, and the pinch of her anxiety slackens. She says, "I thought they called on you as one of the leading authorities on the subject."

"It seems I was preceded by Dr. Taylor a couple of days ago."

"Dr. Taylor?"

"Sir Jonathan's colleague. We met at the British Institute of Anthropology." He tugs his arms free of the shirt. "Not only did he see it necessary to talk about his own work, he somehow managed to present my recommendations too."

"You told him enough for him to do that?"

His eyes look tired. "No," he grunts, and lets his shirt drop onto the carpet. "That would have been utter idiocy. He must have a sharper mind than I imagined. I gave him a few hints, and somehow he pieced together the entirety of my argument."

From the chest of drawers she takes a fresh shirt and holds it out for him. "Whatever happened to Sir Jonathan?"

"A *misunderstanding*. He was still in Edinburgh when he should have been here."

She hates it when he scowls as he is doing now. It makes him look like a petulant boy who cannot see beyond his own concerns. Standing in front of him, she cradles his face in her hands and brings her own to it so that his breath mixes with hers, and the warmth of her skin touches his. "My love," she says, "you are too fine a man for them. You should leave them behind."

"And let Sir Jonathan become the government's expert on anthropometry? When he can't even remember a meeting, and mistakes the day he is called to the Troup Committee?"

"Or," she whispers, "maybe Dr. Taylor will become their man."

He moves her to the side and stands up, his bare legs looking vulnerable below the bottom of his shirt. "I can't let that happen. The man's no expert—what has he done in the field? I can't leave the fate of anthropometry to a man like him."

"You'd be better off back in Paris."

"The battle's been won in France. It's here that I can make a difference."

"Robert—"

"Besides, there's the small matter of my soon having to earn an income. We have no choice but to live here now, for the time being at least."

She walks over to a chest of drawers rather than stand close to him a moment longer. She tugs out one drawer, then another, her hands busy while she thinks, thinks, what she must do. Her hands choose a pair of trousers, and she turns and tells him, "Then I should go back to Paris and arrange things. We'll have to dismiss Marie and Madame Pépin, and there are our belongings to pack."

"You can write to Marie. What else are servants for, my dear, if not to save us that sort of trouble?"

She brings the trousers over to where he waits. "I should go myself."

"No, my darling. Mother is dying. You must stay here."

She leans forward and kisses his cheek, dropping his trousers on the bed and closing her arms around him. Anything so that he doesn't see her face.

The water is wonderfully hot. Mina bends her back so that though her knees rise up through the steam like stark hills, the water wraps itself around her chin. Her eyes are closed and her breath sends a shiver of ripples across the surface. Soon she will have to get down to the business of washing herself. For now all she wants is for the warmth of the water to soak into muscles cramped tight and ease the discomfort in her belly. It is the thought of her letter that has done it: it is downstairs ready for the post, their Paris address written on the front, Marie's name at the top. By now it has gone out—Cartwright may have taken it, or Sarah. Sarah more likely. She imagines her holding it up to the light before slipping it into her pocket, and the jauntiness with which she put on her hat and coat and told Mrs. Johnson that there was a letter that needed to go out. Then she'd have climbed the area steps and taken off up the street to the postbox. She'd have stood there with it in her hands, reading the address, then, when she had it firmly in her head, she would have let it drop into the darkness of the box to wait for the postman's sack, and the sorting office, and the train to the coast, and the boat across the Channel.

The Dark Lantern

It won't take long to reach Paris, and Mina imagines Marie turning the key in the metal letterbox in the foyer and picking it out. A few minutes later, at the kitchen table with a cup of coffee and a *tartine* of bread and jam, she'll read it. Then she and Madame Pépin will start packing—the dresses, the shoes and hats, the books, the papers, the framed pictures, dusting off the trunks and arranging everything inside. What might slide out? She has been so careful, but she never anticipated other hands touching everything she left behind.

What is worse, she never imagined that it would all follow her here to London.

*T*he steam has left the letter damp. The crispness is gone from its folds and it lies on the counter like a dying thing.

Sarah's head appears around the scullery door. "Hurry up with it," she snaps.

"It's not in English," Jane tells her.

"Just copy it, for God's sake."

So Jane bends her head back over it. She runs one finger under the words and says the letters out loud to write them with her pencil. Her hands are alive with nervousness, and the pencil slides around awkwardly. Fortunately there is not much to the letter. It doesn't take her long to finish, and she folds it back into its envelope before slipping the copy and the pencil into her pocket. Then she hurries out into the kitchen where Elsie is chopping potatoes, and up the back stairs. On the landing Sarah is waiting.

"Let's be having it, then," she says.

When Jane hands her everything she clicks her tongue. "No no, just the copy." She plucks it away and heads up the stairs.

Jane still has Mina Bentley's letter in her hand. The flap is open and crinkled. "What about this?" she hisses.

"Better close it up and put it back on the table for Mr. Cartwright to take out," she says. "And be quick about it if you don't want to get caught."

CHAPTER 15

The four-wheeler lurches, and the two women facing him sway. From outside come a few indistinct words of song, and they both glance out the window, then away again, for the singer is a drunk idling his way up the street and his song is not fit for ladies' ears.

They pass a public house, a butcher's, a costermonger pushing a barrow of apples and another stirring chestnuts over coals—a dark, delicious smell. Not one of them has said a word, for what is there to say? The solicitor read the will. Everything to be left to Robert— he felt Mina's head shift slightly, saw the widow's twist towards him and her mouth open—except in the case of Henry having married, when everything should go to his widow or, if he had children, a third to his widow and two-thirds to his children. Of course, as the solicitor explained, these provisions do little more than abide by the law, for his marriage would have revoked any existing will.

Was that the moment to mention doubts? To demand proof of Henry's marriage? But Robert didn't say more than "I see." To have brought up such questions with the widow sitting beside him, and the solicitor peering at him over his papers—to suggest that the wid-owed Mrs. Bentley was an impostor—would have appeared ridicu-lously melodramatic. He could imagine the solicitor's pitying look: here was a poor fool muddling real life with the sensational stories sold in railway stations.

So Robert simply listened to the solicitor explain everything to the widow: he would ascertain Henry's property; he would contact Henry's insurance company, as he had insured his life for fifteen thousand pounds, with the money going to his brother or—Henry was nothing if not a careful man—to his widow and children, should he have the fortune to be so blessed. Of course, it might take a little while for the insurance money to be paid. And then—then there should be no problem. A death certificate had been provided, after all.

The widow's skin had flushed before turning pale, then she'd leaned to one side as though she might fall from her chair. When it was over Robert had taken her by the arm and followed Mina through the doorway. As they'd passed into the foyer with its dark panelling and potted aspidistras, he'd glanced at Victoria. Her chin was held a little too high for a recent widow—wasn't it?—and her mouth had a curious flatness to it, as though she were holding part of herself down.

"I've forgotten something," he'd blurted, "one moment."

He'd lifted the widow's arm from his to Mina's, turned quickly before he could catch the look on his wife's face, and strode back into the office. What had he said? Something like, "If one were to dispute the marriage, how would one ..." The solicitor had stared up at him from behind his glasses as Robert laid out his doubts like playing cards—the suddenness of the marriage, the fact that Henry had informed no one, the absence of any proof so that, in effect, they were simply taking the word of this young woman that she had ever been Henry's wife. Each one sounded ridiculous. Yet to have left that office without a protest, he could not do that.

As for the solicitor, he'd sucked at his lips. "Mr. Bentley," he'd said, "you will have to act quickly and discreetly. If the insurance company gets wind of this ... well, need I say more?" And he lifted both hands. "Further, you are in a position that requires the utmost delicacy. On the one hand, if you have suspicions you must act on them, and report them to the authorities. On the other, you risk compromising the character of a young woman it is your duty to protect at a time when she is most vulnerable. I wish you the judgment to act appropriately."

That, he realizes now, was a warning. He glances at where the widow sits, the cold light coming through the carriage window hard across her face. He must be careful if he is to come out of this without looking a fool or—worse yet—a blackguard. He finds himself studying her. She is ill at ease, looking out the window as though she is forcing herself to appear relaxed, her gloved fingers curled together in her lap.

"You will need someone to advise you," he says at last.

She looks at him. "Advise me?"

"Most women," he says, "have not had experience in handling their finances. After all—" he leans forward so that his elbows rest on his knees "—Henry's money must ensure your future. Properly managed, fifteen thousand pounds should be sufficient to keep you in comfort."

He watches her, but already her eyes have slid away to the window. Is she avoiding his gaze? Maybe, he thinks. Or maybe she thinks him insensitive. He looks over at Mina, but she gives him no clue as to whether he is handling this badly. No, instead she gives him a flash of a smile, and in response he pushes his foot against hers, hidden by her skirts.

The widow says, "When the time comes, you can be sure I'll be careful in how I manage Henry's money."

"Your money," says Robert gently. He watches her: her shining eyes, her jet earrings, the ghostly paleness of her face between the black of her hat and her coat. There is something different about her now, a determination behind her words that wasn't there when they set out for the solicitor's office only an hour and a half ago. Then she'd sat with her black-laced handkerchief pressed up against her nose and made noises that were half coughs, half sobs, that he found difficult to bear.

"You'll have to be wary," he tells her. "You're young, and you're suddenly financially independent. You will need—"

He catches a movement—Mina, raising a black-gloved hand to her mouth. He isn't sure if she is telling him to be more cautious.

She holds his eyes for a moment, then her foot moves away from his. She leans towards Victoria. "Everything's so new to you, including your circumstances."

The widow looks at the two of them. "You don't have to trouble yourselves. I'm quite able to take care of myself. In fact, I doubt I shall have to impose on you for much longer."

"My dear, you don't have to be in a hurry." Mina lays a hand on hers. "You have a home at Mother's for as long as you would like. I'm sure Henry would have wanted us to take good care of you." Her voice is deep with compassion. Robert holds his breath and watches as the widow shifts on the seat before sliding her hand free.

"Thank you." Her mouth clamps shut and she stares off into the street again.

Mina catches Robert's eye. He coughs into his hand. "Mina's perfectly right. It is our—our *duty*—to look after you. Henry would have expected nothing less."

The carriage slows. Cursitor Road, and the horse's footsteps ring out on the stones. The widow shuts her eyes. From the way her mouth moves it seems she is praying. But no. When she looks at Robert and Mina a few moments later, she tells them, "I'll be leaving shortly. In a week at the most, I imagine."

"My dear, the insurance company won't have had time to pay you."

"I plan to keep Henry's solicitor informed of my address."

Mina takes her hand and keeps hold of it. "But where will you go? Will you return to India?"

Already the cab has stopped, and the carriage shifts as the driver climbs down.

She pulls her hand free. "India?" she repeats. "I haven't decided."

She does not say more. Instead, she lets Robert hand her down to the pavement, where she peers about her, as if on the lookout for something that hasn't yet come into view. Robert reaches back to give Mina his hand, then leads the way up the steps to the front door and rings the bell.

It is not Cartwright who answers, not Sarah. Instead it is the new maid, Jane, her face flushed, her chest heaving. "Sir," she starts. "Sir—you need to go straight upstairs. It's Mrs. Bentley."

*I*n the end there was no need to hurry. She is dead. Price is kneeling by the bed with her face pressed into the blankets by her mistress's feet. The doctor is closing up his bag. "There was no hope," he says. "Even if I'd been called earlier, there would have been nothing I could have done."

Mina nods, and takes Robert's arm. He is shaking—the shock of it, the mounting up of death on death. "Come," she says to him gently. "My love, come and sit down."

"No." He pulls himself away and lifts both hands to his face. He stares out over the tops of his fingers at a world that has suddenly changed around him. It is too much. His brother gone, his mother too. He steps over to the window, where he closes his eyes, slowly, and keeps them closed.

The doctor pours water from a ewer into a basin and washes his hands. He is methodical, working up a lather, soaping each finger, rinsing not just once but twice. The floor creaks under Mina's feet as she picks a towel off the back of a chair and hands it to him. He gives her the smallest of smiles.

Then into the quiet breaks a high, haunting cry. Price. Price with her arms spread across the bed now, holding her mistress's feet through the bedclothes.

Mina lays a hand on her shoulder. "Calm yourself, please."

"My poor—my—my poor dear mistress. To meet her end like this—I was only out of the room a few minutes."

Mina bends close to her. She catches the smell of the woman's unwashed clothes, the cloying sickroom smell that hangs about her. "No one is blaming you," she says softly. "Now let Mr. Bentley grieve."

It does no good. Price falls to the floor, breathing hard. Soon she is sobbing, and lies on the carpet with her fingers pushed through her hair. Mina pulls at her arm, but the woman wrenches herself free. Is this grief, she wonders, or is it Price working herself up? "You must come with me. I insist. Your mistress would expect more of you than this."

Price twists at her feet as though in agony, and from her come noises like those of an injured dog. Mina can barely bring herself to touch her again, and when she does Price flings her hand away. Mina catches the doctor's eye. He comes forward and opens his bag.

"You'll have to hold her arm," he says, so she does. He fills a syringe and stabs the needle into the flesh of Price's forearm, though she thrashes and yells, her skirts riding up to show her dark stockings and her drawers.

Over by the window Robert turns. He was holding onto the curtains. Now he lets go. His face is grim. What choice is there but to step forward and grab Price by the ankles, to hold her fast until the doctor has finished? Then, when the needle has been put away and Price's yells are hoarse, Robert picks her up. She struggles and claws and kicks wildly. He comes close to dropping her until the doctor traps one foot, then the other, and between them they hold her like a calf at the county fair.

"Calm yourself, woman," the doctor yells. "You must calm yourself! You have no reason to carry on like this." Only then does she stop moving. She stares at him, at Mina, then closes her eyes and lets herself go limp, though surely whatever he gave her cannot have taken effect so quickly.

All this nonsense, thinks Mina, when what Price wants is pity. She hurries to the door and opens it. The doctor backs through it with Price's feet held high and her skirts sliding up her legs, and Robert follows with his arms looped under Price's. Perhaps Mina should go with them, but instead she shuts the door and leans against it.

She had forgotten about the widow. She is still in the room, by the bed, staring down at Mrs. Bentley's body.

"Victoria?" she says, and the widow looks up. Her eyes are large and glistening, not with tears, Mina thinks, but with anticipation.

CHAPTER 16

Jane has to take the dusters outside to shake them. More snow has fallen, and it illuminates the area, reflecting back the glow of the street lamps and what light escapes the house's curtains. It's too cold to linger out here, so she's quick to snap each of them through the air. She looks about her—once already Teddy has surprised her, waiting for her at the railings, and they managed to steal a few minutes to-gether before she heard Mrs. Johnson calling her back inside. This evening a movement up by the railings catches her eye. Someone standing close by, up in the street. Her eyes haven't adjusted to the dark but, as she watches, what appeared to be one body separates itself into two. One of them turns, and she sees the white of an apron and cap. The gate at the top of the steps squeals, and down comes Sarah. Jane looks past her. A dark coat, a tall hat. A large man hurrying away.

"Curiosity killed the cat," whispers Sarah as she draws close. "We've all got secrets, haven't we?" She gives Jane a wink and a sharp pinch on the arm.

Dinnertime, and Robert finds himself concentrating on his poached cod. Two days since Mother died. Two days of arranging a second funeral, of writing more letters with deep black borders, of living in the darkness of a closed-in house. It has made him realize: he too is a bag of flesh that will decay one of these days. He pushes his feet harder against the carpet under the table and takes another sip of wine.

By the sideboard Cartwright stands to attention, his hands tucked behind his back, staring into space as though he has not noticed the silences that seep into the conversation. At least he sent Sarah downstairs—she fidgeted and coughed and sighed as though disappointed that what little talk there was did not entertain her.

The cod has turned tepid and soft in the time it has taken to load it onto a serving dish, carry it upstairs, and ceremoniously lift it onto their plates. Mina, he notices, has barely touched hers, and is frowning as she pushes her potatoes around with her fork. As for the widow, she is not making any pretense about having an appetite and has arranged her knife and fork on the side of her plate. Why, he wonders, is he bothering? The mere thought of the cold fish in front of him while his mother lies dead in her coffin makes him gag. He pushes away his plate and reaches for his glass again. At least the wine is good.

From the front door comes the double *rat-a-tat* of the postman with a telegram. Robert listens, hears footsteps coming along the hallway, then the dining room door opening. Sarah whispers something, and Cartwright steps outside. He's back in a moment with a silver salver bearing a telegram.

The thought of more bad news makes Robert hesitate before he takes it. He cannot make out the first few words. They make no sense until he has read them twice and then—suddenly understanding who this is from—an "Ah!" escapes him and he lifts the telegram closer to his face. A reply from Cyril, who has, it seems, already made some enquiries. He has an acquaintance who knows the registrar in Bombay: there is no record of a marriage between Henry Bentley and Victoria Dawes. Further, although he has found many people who knew Henry, he has not yet found a single person who remembers a Miss Victoria Dawes, or indeed any young lady with whom he formed an attachment. Should he, he asks, pursue the matter?

Mina sets down her knife and fork and takes a sip of wine. "Good news?"

He looks up. Not only is she watching him, so too is the widow. He nods, says gravely, "Oh yes. For us, it is good news."

*H*is voice comes from nowhere. Jane stands in the cold afternoon air looking about her. "Up here," he calls before whistling a long, graceful note. And there he is, outlined against the railings around the area and the pale sky above.

All of a sudden she remembers herself—her filthy apron, her untidy hair, her face probably flushed and shiny from helping Elsie stir the copper full of laundry. "Teddy," she hisses back. "What on earth are you doing here?"

He gives a broad smile. "Couldn't wait to see you again."

With a glance over her shoulder, she starts towards the steps. She feels lighter, thanks to seeing Teddy amidst all the cleaning and carrying that began long before dawn. "You're going to land me in it," she says, "turning up like this. Anyway, how's it you've got the time to walk over here?"

"Master's out this afternoon. Got everything ready for when he gets back, and here I am."

Already she loves the way his cheeks crease when he smiles, and his way of lifting his hand to his face when he talks. Most of all, to hear someone who speaks the way she does, who was brought up by the sea, who knows Teignton, even if he's only been there once. And to think—if not for her buying that bun and finding nowhere to eat it, they'd simply have passed each other on the street and never spoken!

From the kitchen window comes the clatter of pans, and Mrs. Johnson calling for Elsie.

He beckons her closer. "Can you get another afternoon off?"

She glances behind her and comes up the first few steps. "Doubt it," she says, looking up at him. "The mistress just died."

"So I heard."

"It was the shock of Mr. Henry being drowned, that's what they say. One funeral already, and another any day now."

He nods. "Better to get them over with all together like that. Not as hard on the family, I reckon."

Maybe he's teasing. There's that about him, a tone she's not sure of, that makes her a little nervous.

"Come on up here," he whispers. "Quick now, before someone sees us."

"Why?"

He simply beckons with one long finger and, when she's close enough, he bends forward over the sharp ends of the railings and puts a kiss right on her lips.

"That's so you don't forget about me," he says. "Besides, it means you're mine now. So you watch yourself."

"Teddy!" The blood rushes to her face, and she turns away, down the steps. She hurries off without another look at him, though the unexpected softness of his lips stays with her for the rest of the day, and when eventually she goes up to the cold bedroom under the roof—later than usual because Price is still in bed and needs to be seen to—she summons it up so that it will be the last thing she remembers before she falls asleep.

Yet it's not Teddy's kiss that she dreams about, but Price lying in her narrow bed with her hair all undone, Price calling out for her mistress though she's nothing but a corpse.

CHAPTER 17

Cartwright clears his throat. The others turn to him, forks raised, slices of bread held aloft. However, he merely scoops up another forkful of hashed mutton and says not a word.

Things, he announced at the start of their lunch, have been getting too informal. With the mistress gone, it is their duty to act impeccably. He repeated that word for effect, then told Mrs. Johnson to serve up, which she did, lips pulled tight. All he has said since is that the hashed mutton isn't up to Mrs. Johnson's usual standard.

From outside comes the rattle of carriage wheels, then a man shouting, "Larry! Larry!" Down in the kitchen, though, there's nothing except for the angry roiling of hot water in a pot, the occasional hiss of drops onto the stove, the dull clatter of forks against plates. Even the knock of a mug being set down on the table draws attention.

Jane stares down into her plate. At times it's hard to breathe in this house, let alone eat. This is what you sell when you go into service, she thinks, freedoms that the family upstairs can't imagine being without. To talk when you choose to, to go out when you like, to decide what you will eat, to sit down with a book and spend a whole afternoon reading simply because you want to. A servant is not supposed to mind every minute of her day being laid out for her—this is what she will do at six in the morning, this is where she will be at half past nine, this is what she will eat for her supper, this is how she will spend the time before bed. Do ladies think their servants don't notice how they spend *their* time? Or that the very things servants are warned away from—reading novels, eating rich foods, making themselves beautiful so the men notice them—are the very occupations of their lives? But Mrs. Robert, she thinks, is different. Jane has found out enough about her to know that she lived in Paris for years and this, she has decided, is the reason why.

Though the hashed mutton is cold now, she shovels up a forkful. At the orphanage they had lessons between the sewing and cleaning—mopping the dormitory floors, sweeping the matron's rooms, for they were the only ones with carpet in the whole place and a servant must know how to do more than wash down a bare floor. They learnt to write, and to read—just enough to make themselves useful—and a little history. She remembers Mrs. Dougall with her hair the color of old leaves and her long jaw like a sheep's. She told them about kings and queens. All those Henrys and Georges so that it's hard to tell who's who, except for the Henry who had his wives' heads cut off so he could marry new ones. And there were wars upon wars so that the history of the country seemed little more than a succession of rulers who had to protect England with the blood of its men.

In all of this there came Mrs. Dougall's story of the wicked peasants in France who sliced off the heads of their king and queen. The girls were sewing as they listened, for their hands could not be idle even while their minds were being improved. But it also meant they could pretend to be intent on the aprons they were sewing as Mrs. Dougall's voice lilted its way through what happened. The king dead, his queen loaded onto a common cart—like so many lords and ladies before her!—and driven slowly to the square so that everyone could see her, the way she stepped on someone's foot and apologized—apologized!—as though she were on her way to a ball, not her execution. What dignity! What self-control! Jane glanced up to see Mrs. Dougall holding a handkerchief to her mouth, her cheeks trembling. She stood and looked around her. "Yes, girls," she said. "It was one of the greatest sins ever committed on this earth."

Beside Jane a girl shook, and it wasn't until she glanced into Jane's face that Jane understood the girl was barely able to control her laughter.

Mrs. Dougall's voice rose. "The terrible sinners who took up arms against their king and queen will burn in the fires of hell for ever more. Let it be a lesson to you girls; you already have a stain on your souls, but you can redeem yourselves if you make yourselves useful. You must serve your betters, because in doing so you are serving Our Lord. The consequences of not doing so—the terrible, *terrible* consequences—imagine . . ."

She couldn't finish. Instead she rushed from the room with her hands against her cheeks.

It took a moment for all those faces turned towards the door to find one another. But when eyes met eyes the girls could contain themselves no longer, and they rocked themselves on their benches, slapping their hands on the tables in front of them, reaching up to wipe tears from their eyes, pressing sleeves against mouths so that barely a sound escaped to ring out between the bare walls—after all, you never knew who'd be listening in the corridor.

As for Jane, she'd made herself laugh into her hands like the rest of them.

That was easy when her throat was tight and her eyes were stinging. To think of those noble people, dead. She'd carried the horror of it with her for days and imagined how she could have saved them. Maybe the queen could have been led to safety, or her execution stopped by someone—by her, but not her exactly, for Jane imagined herself as a young man who jumped onto the scaffold and made a speech that stirred the better nature of the crowd.

It was Mrs. Saunders who made her think differently. All that talk of how servants served their masters and mistresses, and how masters and mistresses served the queen, and how the queen served God, and this was the way it had been ordained by God—she remembers that word, *ordained,* for there seemed to be something dreadful to it— while she was mending Mrs. Saunders's linen and Mrs. Saunders was sipping a cup of her orange pekoe that she kept locked away because the cheapest tea was good enough for the servants, no matter that it tasted of dust. On and on she went, those white hands of hers holding that delicate teacup, her feet up on a footstool because she had been *rushing around half the day*—meaning she'd walked to the neighbors' to gossip—telling Jane that laziness was a sin she could not abide, that girls of her class must keep to their station, for there was nothing worse than taking on airs when they couldn't carry it off and they only made themselves look ridiculous. Jane had stabbed her needle into the cotton though she risked pricking her finger. She dragged the thread through it so quickly that she broke it, and Mrs. Saunders snapped at her to watch what she was about. So she'd forced herself to loosen her grip on the needle and pull it through the fabric gently, push it, gently, all the while imagining Mrs. Saunders in a cart being driven into the center of town and an angry crowd throwing horse droppings at her, and her being led up onto the platform, not with her head high but crying and pleading to no avail as no one was inclined to show her any mercy.

In France things must be better for servants, she thinks. Mistresses know what happens when they push them too far. Maybe that's why Mrs. Robert is different. Yet it is not that she is more considerate—no, she is more clever, more distrustful. She is a woman who understands deception, who doubts the word of a young woman nearly drowned in the wreck that killed her husband. What sort of a woman can she be? A woman with secrets? Without a doubt, yes, for when they discovered the burglar's intrusion, she'd turned deathly white. Anyone would think she has something to hide. And that could make her dangerous.

Is this why Jane hasn't told her about Teddy, even though Mrs. Robert has asked several times if she has a sweetheart? Even though she knows that Mrs. Robert will be angry to find out she's been lied to? And she will find out, for how can a secret be kept in a house like this? Just because Jane is supposed to be Mrs. Robert's eyes and ears does not mean she'll be safe from her. Mrs. Robert is clever, and despite her genteel manners, there's a hardness to her. So Jane will say nothing of Teddy until she's found out. At least until then, she will have a place to let her thoughts go when she is blacking grates and scrubbing floors—the warmth of his breath on her face, the press of his lips, the promise that her life will be more than this.

Above their heads a bell rings and startles her out of her thoughts. The study. No doubt it's Mr. Robert—or Mr. Bentley now, as he should be called. Jane notices Sarah smile into her plate, for Cartwright will have to answer it. He takes his time—chewing his mouthful of mutton, pushing back his chair, fetching his jacket and pulling it on so that the cuffs are aligned just so, walking deliberately to the door. This is not insolence, merely a way of showing Mr. Bentley that, at mealtimes downstairs, his calls intrude.

"I'll keep it warm for you," Mrs. Johnson calls after him.

Now that Cartwright is gone, the women sit back in their chairs and look at one another. "Well," says Sarah. "What's got into him all of a sudden?"

Mrs. Johnson takes up his plate and slides it into the oven. "He's taken it to heart, the mistress dying like that. He's worked here for longer than any of the rest of us, and she was always good to him."

"There's no need to make us sit at the table without a word."

Mrs. Johnson swings the oven door closed and lets herself drop down onto her chair again. "That's how things should be. You work in one of them big houses and you'll see—no one allowed to say a word unless the butler or the housekeeper asks them something first."

Sarah pushes away her plate. "I wouldn't stand for it." Elsie snorts but doesn't say anything. Sarah glares at her. "Well, it's not right," she says. "The family talk when they eat, don't they? Why not us?" She looks from Elsie to Jane to Mrs. Johnson.

Mrs. Johnson is pushing mutton onto her fork. "You should watch yourself. We've got a new mistress now and I'm sure she's going to have her own rules."

"What's that supposed to mean? I hope you don't think that—"

"The mistress is dead. All these weeks Mrs. Robert has been here and has had a hand in how things have gone but without being mistress. We haven't felt her being here, not really. Now it's her turn, and none of us can know what she'll be like."

Sarah snorts. "Of course we do. Soon we'll be on hashed mutton every day. Or maybe she'll want to us live off bread and cheese."

"There's the other Mrs. Bentley too," says Jane.

For a moment Sarah and Mrs. Johnson stare at her.

"That young thing?" Mrs. Johnson laughs.

"The house is just as much hers, isn't it?"

From Elsie comes a laugh. She hasn't swallowed the food in her mouth and it shows pale against her tongue. "That'll be a fine thing. Them two ladies both wanting to be mistress." She tears off a piece of bread and pushes it into her mouth. "Or p'raps they'll both go back where they came from and the whole lot of us'll be looking for new situations."

Mrs. Johnson bows her head at that and fiddles with her mutton. "No use worrying about it yet," she says.

Jane picks up her knife and fork and stares down at what's left of her food. To think that she could soon be thrown back onto the world, this time by a mistress who knows she is a liar. What's more, if Sarah should take it into her head to tell Mrs. Robert about her mother, she wouldn't be in this house longer than it would take to drag her to the door. Yet for now, why would Sarah tell when she can use the secret to make Jane open letters, to take on her work, to help herself to Jane's money? No, she thinks, Sarah won't tell, not yet.

And if Sarah won't tell yet, perhaps she should sway Mrs. Robert against her.

Sarah helps herself to another slice of bread, though Mrs. Johnson frowns at her. "Anyway," she says, "one thing's certain—we'll have to put up with Mrs. Robert for some time to come. Mr. Robert isn't going anywhere."

"Been listening at doors again, have you?"

Sarah laughs, but her eyes move quickly. "Can't help overhearing what they say sometimes, can we?" She shoves back her chair and the legs squeal over the floor. "They're having their things sent over from Paris." Her mouth twists into an odd smile as she turns away to the scullery.

This must be what the letter to Paris was about. Jane scrapes up what's left of her mutton. It lies unpleasantly cold against her tongue. Surely Sarah, she thinks, doesn't understand French. Maybe she *did* overhear it. Such a piece of information could easily slip out during the course of a conversation. No, that's not right, she tells herself. The way Sarah got up like that, and the look on her face. She can't help but show off what she knows.

But then, Jane wonders, how did she find out what was in the letter? As she wipes her mouth she thinks of Sarah's gentleman, who'd hurried away from the area railings. A gentleman would understand French, wouldn't he?

CHAPTER 18

Price does not even rouse herself for her mistress's funeral. When Mina, Robert, and the widow return, pale-faced and chilled, she is still nowhere to be seen. Mina takes off her coat and hands it to Cartwright. "Is she up yet?" she asks.

He folds her coat over his arm. "No, ma'am. Apparently she is still indisposed."

"I see." She lays a hand on the widow's arm. "Be a dear and come with me for a few minutes."

"Oh." Victoria's mouth twitches slightly. "Yes, if you think it necessary."

So Mina Bentley leads the way upstairs while Robert retreats to the study and Cartwright carries off their coats. She takes Victoria all the way up, up to where the stairs have no carpet and the paint has turned a dingy brown, then along a narrow corridor where their skirts brush against the walls. In the dim light doors are just visible. At the last one she knocks. Without waiting, she walks in.

Stretched out in the bed, looking suddenly old, lies Price. Her eyes are shut, though certainly she must have heard the knock at the door and the footsteps of the two women approaching.

"Price?" Mina pulls over the only chair in the room, a bare, straight-backed thing. She sits down on it and leans close to the bed. "Open your eyes, Price."

Instead she moans, and Mina glances up at the widow. This, her face says, is going too far.

"Price?" she calls again, more loudly this time. "Tell me what is the matter."

Price works her mouth, then licks her lips. "I can't move, ma'am."

"You've let yourself get too worked up. If only you'd get out of bed and eat a little food you'd feel better."

Price lets her head fall to the side and opens her eyes. "You wouldn't throw me out into the street in this state, would you, ma'am? I'd end up in the workhouse." Her voice is hoarse.

Mina moves the chair so that she is looking straight into Price's face. "I have a forgiving nature. But I can spot a deception with little effort." Beside her Victoria shifts. She reaches for the widow's arm and pulls her close. "Do you understand me, Price? I am giving you fair warning: I treat subterfuge without mercy."

Price's hands grip the bedcovers. "I have always been a faithful servant to Mrs. Bentley," she whispers. "I have devoted myself to her these last twelve years."

Mina feels the widow move, pulling away from her grip. "Victoria"—she glances at her—"we are prepared to be generous to Price, are we not?"

The widow nods, but her face has gone stiff.

"And your mistress was kind enough to leave you a small bequest, as you well know." Now she stands, all the better to look down at Price. "I expect that by tomorrow morning you will have the strength to get out of bed. Then we'll discuss the matter of your character, for I'm sure you'll want to look for a new situation immediately."

She leads the way back to the corridor, and to the narrow stairs down to the main floors of the house. On the landing she takes Victoria by the elbow. "I think I was more than fair, don't you? One cannot stand for being taken advantage of, though one hates to play the ogre. More than anything"—she touches the side of the widow's face with her fingertips—"it is being made a fool of that so offends, don't you think?"

The Dark Lantern

It has taken longer than expected, but five trunks arrive from Paris. They are lined up along the hallway like a train that has pulled in, and Mina walks the length of them until she finds it: an old battered thing secured with a leather strap, and with the marks of many paper labels that have been pasted on and torn off. "This one," she tells Cartwright. "The others can be taken to Mr. Bentley's study."

She watches as he hefts one end of it and Jane bends to lift the other. Of course, he makes Jane walk backwards up the stairs, and twice she trips because her feet catch in her skirts. Up they go, and Mina follows them at a dignified distance. This one, she thinks to herself. Surely this one, for she hid it in there herself just before she and Robert were married.

Carrying the trunk into the bedroom, Cartwright huffs like an old stallion. Yet when they set it down on the far side of the room beside the dressing table, it is Jane who stands unsteadily. "Come along," Cartwright tells her, "out of the way now."

The girl teeters, then holds her hands out in a way there is no mistaking. "Sit," commands Mina, and pushes a chair towards her. "I'll take care of her, Cartwright. I'm sure she'll be fine in a few minutes."

"Very good, ma'am."

Once the door has closed, Jane sits up straight. "You wanted me to be your eyes and ears, ma'am."

Mina stands on the carpet in front of the girl. "Yes."

"Sarah has a gentleman friend, ma'am."

She steps back to the mantelpiece. When the trunk is sitting right here, within reach, *now* the girl comes to her with stories—and not about the other Mrs. Bentley but about a downstairs romance?

"Thank you, Jane," she says. "You were right to bring the matter to my attention. I know that the late Mrs. Bentley did not permit her servants to form attachments. I, however, think there is nothing wrong in young women of the serving class finding a husband, provided that they do not resort to subterfuge." She gives a small smile. "I shall have a word with Sarah."

This will be the end of it. She will talk to Sarah, who no doubt will begin by denying any attachment but will eventually admit that there *is* someone, a perfectly respectable someone who works for the butcher or baker or draper. Then Mina will have to impress on her that there must be no sneaking around, no more excursions to the postbox at strange hours, no young men loitering at the area railings. Will Sarah catch her eye? Will she raise her chin ever so slightly? Mina imagines telling her that she cannot let out of the house a maid whom she does not trust. Not even on errands for Mrs. Johnson. Not even with urgent letters. From now on, she'll say, she will have to keep an eye on her because her good character might so easily be ruined. She'll let herself draw out that last word just a little, and surely that will be warning enough.

Jane must realize the impropriety of her sitting while her mistress is standing, for she gets to her feet. "Ma'am? He's not a follower, he's a *gentleman*. Except there's something odd about him."

"A gentleman? Meeting Sarah?" She smiles though she didn't quite mean to.

"Yes, ma'am."

"Do you mean he dresses like a gentleman? Have you met him?"

She fiddles with the edge of her apron. "I've seen him, ma'am. From a distance. He dresses like a gentleman."

"Yet you aren't sure?"

"His clothes—they didn't look like his own. And when he walks—"

Mina gives a small sigh and waves one hand through the air. "Yes, yes, very well. I'll talk to Sarah."

Jane licks her lips as though she's about to say more.

"I won't tell her how I found out, Jane, if that's what's worrying you."

It seems the maid has something else on her mind, for she opens her mouth. However, whatever it is remains unsaid, and she simply nods. "Thank you, ma'am."

At the door she turns back and asks, "Was I good, ma'am?" She lifts her chin towards the chair.

Mina says, "Oh yes, you're quite the actress."

"Thank you, ma'am."

As soon as the door closes Mina walks over and locks it. Sarah and her follower—a valet, no doubt, or perhaps even a butler, dressed in his master's castoffs—will have to wait.

She has to pull hard on the leather strap to undo the buckles, and the leather leaves her hands red and dusty. The top yawns open and the skirt of a dress she considered too bright for London spills out. She lays it on the bed, then another dress, and another. By the time she gets to the bottom the bed is heaped with dresses and shawls.

Since she has heaped everything pell-mell, it doesn't take much to send the top dresses cascading to the floor in a rustle of silk. And then she sees it: a letter, and for a moment her heart seems to stop. Then she reaches down. Across the front is written *Madame Bentley* in an uncertain hand. It is only a letter from Marie.

Still, she drops to her knees and reaches into the trunk. With her fingers she feels the corners, then the edges where one wall meets another. No one has tampered with it, and she sinks back onto her heels. "Thank God," she whispers. She was right—an unlocked, empty trunk, what interest would that have held for two bored servants? Now it can be stowed in the lumber room, out of the sight and minds of everyone in this household. She will call Sarah up to put away her dresses. She will tell her that sneaking about is uncalled for, that if she has a young man she is free to meet him on her half day off. Her tone will be enough to ensure that Sarah understands the consequences of disobeying.

She crosses to the window to read Marie's letter. Nothing much to say—she has packed everything, she hopes that Madame has been satisfied with her work, she is grieved that she will not see Madame again to say good-bye, but now she is engaged and will marry her fiancé just after Christmas. Not until the end of the letter does she mention something, a small occurrence. Just after she and Monsieur Bentley left, a large Englishman—*un gros anglais*—came calling for her. A strange man, not quite a gentleman. When he heard that Madame had remarried and was back in London he became angry and she had to shut the door in his face.

Mina finds her eyes tripping over the words—*un gros anglais*—*s'est fâché*. Then she rips the letter into strips and the strips into small squares, and she drops them into the fireplace—no fire now, for it is the middle of the day. So she takes a match from the holder nailed up by the mantelpiece and sets them on fire herself.

dow seems to haunt her. When Mina comes down for an
eakfast with Robert she finds Victoria already at the table.
there fiddling with her kippers, her eggs, her toast. In the
, soon after Mina calls for tea and takes the armchair across
obert, the widow appears, summoned by the quiet tread of
right's feet.

ight, even though the evening is getting late, the widow
't move from her chair across the fire. Instead she yawns and
through an old magazine without reading it. The possibility
es Mina that she is not just an impostor but something more. Is
here to keep watch? She bites her teeth together and looks into
fire. Ridiculous, she tells herself. All because of Marie's mention
un gros anglais who was looking for her. He could have been
yone—a chance acquaintance, an Englishman in search of En-
lish conversation.

No, she can't convince herself of that. Was it Popham? Or a man
n his pay? But if he knew she was in Paris, why wait so long to follow her? Maybe it was just by luck that she escaped him—
something had brought her to his notice and he pursued her to
France only to discover she'd just left. Is he so angry at how she
helped fool him all those years ago that he would go to those lengths
to find her? Is he clever enough to have tracked her down? Was
their encounter in Mortimer's not accidental after all?

No, she tells herself—he was surprised to see her there, she's certain of it. But then, perhaps he was surprised to pick up her trail again so easily after it came to a dead end in Paris.

She excuses herself to the widow—a headache, feeling exhausted because it has been too much, these funerals, this house to look after. Along the hallway she goes, to the study, where she gives Robert a quick kiss before she makes her way up to the bedroom. Upstairs she has to ring for Sarah, to wait for her, to stand patiently while Sarah unfastens her dress and helps her out of it, and her corset. Tonight the girl yanks hard on the lacings and drops corset on the chair like a dead thing. When Sarah catches gaze in the mirror she stares back for a moment too long. S that her follower has been discovered, that she is being Mina sends her back downstairs—she cannot bear to h around a moment longer. She puts her dress away herself, t by the fire and brushes her hair while she waits for Robert.

She has finished by the time he opens the door, and she sits as he undresses. She loves this—watching him remove his jack shirt and trousers, his body all long curves under his clothes. he pulls back the bedcovers and leans forward to blow out the dle, she stops him. She whispers, "We need to act quickly."

"Do we really need to whisper?"

She pulls the covers up over her belly, then sits back. "How you men stay so wonderfully innocent when it's your job to go i the corrupting world out there?" She nods towards the window. lies beside her, propped on one elbow, and she rests a hand on h thigh. "Haven't you noticed the way Sarah hangs around doors? C how she's always off on some errand or other?"

He lays a hand over hers. "Is she?"

"Apparently she has an admirer. I had to have a talk with her. Now she's angry, of course."

He gives a low laugh. "You aren't turning into one of those mistresses who objects to servants having a life of their own, are you? First poor Lizzie—"

"It isn't Sarah's admirer I mind, it's her way of sneaking around.

I know that she goes through our things—she even had the nerve
to look through my desk."

"Isn't that what servants do? If you leave something unlocked, curiosity gets the better of them. They don't have much else in their
lives, so it's no wonder they take an interest in ours."

"The usual curiosity I could put up with. Sarah goes too far."

"Then dismiss her."

Her hair is pulled back into a long rope, and she brings it over he
shoulder. "Am I the mistress of the house now?" She pulls a face
make him smile. "Should I be the one counting out dusters, ar
checking under the carpets for dirt, and making sure the co
doesn't sell our butter?"

He takes one of her hands and plants a kiss on the palm. "Y
would be perfect."

"Oh, you're so *gallant*." She slides down in the bed beside him
presses a kiss on his lips. "But we still have the widow to contend w

With a sigh he rolls onto his back. "Darling, what more can I
Cyril says he'll look into it. We need to be sure before we start r
ing accusations. Imagine if we are wrong. This poor young woma
the woman my brother loved—just think what we are doing to

She leans over him, her arms on his chest, and feels the wa
of his body against hers. "We've barely had three weeks to
know her. I wouldn't be surprised if she plans to sell the house
She's made no secret of the fact that she isn't going to stay."

He turns to her. In the candlelight his eyes look dark and m
ful. "If she's an impostor, why on earth would she do that? W
us that she's planning to flee? It doesn't make any sense."

"Yet if she's not an impostor, why can't Cyril find a record
marriage? Why hasn't anyone heard of her?"

"I don't know."

He blows out the candle on the chair beside the bed.
darkness he says, "What sort of woman would want to pro
death and misery? She'd have to have icewater in her veins

Mina rests her head in the hollow of his shoulder. "She'
be a ghoul, Robbie, a ghoul."

CHAPTER 20

Some mornings it is almost more than she can do to get out of bed. Six o'clock, and the air in the room is so cold that it stings her legs as she swings them out from under the covers. With one hand she feels for the matches and the candlestick. All those lessons on cleanliness at the orphanage, and now it is too cold to do more than splash water on her face, water covered with a thin crust of ice. What would it matter if they had a fire up here? Yet Mrs. Johnson and Mr. Cartwright have said no, as Mrs. Bentley wouldn't have allowed it— a waste of coal, for when are she and Sarah up here, except to sleep? Besides, don't they have covers enough on their beds to keep them warm? It's the *getting* warm that's the problem, though. Cold sheets, a cold mattress beneath, all of it so cold it feels damp.

She dresses fast, pulling on her flannel petticoat, her dress, her stockings, her cap, her apron. Then she knots her boots around her neck, picks up her chamber pot and candle, and leaves Sarah sleeping. She creeps along the corridor to the stairs so quietly that only the creaking floorboards give her away. No one will punish Sarah for not being downstairs on time. No one will tell Mrs. Robert, and Mrs. Robert is never up early enough to see for herself. After all, it's not for ladies to be out of bed before eight o'clock.

Or maybe even Mrs. Robert wouldn't dare say anything.

Sarah has been looking for something against her, and maybe

there is something to find. Is Sarah clever enough to win against a lady like her, though? Jane doubts it. At least, not on her own.

She makes her way down the last flight of stairs and along the corridor to the water closet. She sets down her candle and pours the contents of her pot down the toilet before settling herself onto the seat. It was Sarah who arranged for the burglar to knock at the door on that day, at that time, she is certain. Did he simply pay her? Was he looking for something of Mrs. Robert's? Has Sarah been spying on Mrs. Robert for him ever since? It could have been him at the area railings. If only it hadn't been so dark and she'd caught more than a glimpse of him.

There is little newspaper left for wiping—she'll have to cut more after Mr. Cartwright has finished with yesterday's paper. Another job to do. When she'd first arrived it seemed that there wasn't time for it all in a day, but now, on top of the cleaning and carrying, there is Price to be looked after, and the young widow. Mrs. Saunders once told her that with efficiency, anything was possible. Anything? To do the work of two or even three people? How would Mrs. Saunders know anyway?

At least, she thinks as she pulls down her skirts, she'll have an excuse to get out the newspaper and scissors, and who's to notice if she cuts out the classifieds and puts them in her pocket? She opens the door and creeps past Mr. Cartwright's room towards the kitchen. There must be other mistresses in need of maids in this city. Mistresses who will not make her spy on other ladies. Mistresses who run households in which one maid does not prey on another. In a few days she will be paid this month's wages. Will Sarah be waiting for her upstairs again? Will she give one of her narrow smiles and reach out her hand? What are the chances that she won't?

In the kitchen Elsie is busy lighting the stove. A candle sits on the table. Just outside the circle of its light, beetles cling to the ceiling. One falls and Elsie, quick as a hungry dog, stamps on it. Then she stoops to pick it up by a leg and flings it into the fire.

Jane sits down and pushes her feet into her boots. In a couple of hours she will see if the widow is ready to get up. By then she will need more questions, gentle ones that seem to arise out of nothing more than a maid's curiosity. Mrs. Robert is not satisfied, and it's not surprising—so far she has found out little.

Should she instead warn her about Sarah again? Should she be more insistent this time? Yet she has no evidence other than having seen Sarah go through her desk, and taking Mrs. Robert's letter and finding out what it means. The trouble is, to tell would be to tell on herself, too. As for the rest, she'd just be guessing, and guessing might look like trying to shift suspicion away from herself.

She fetches yesterday's tea leaves, the housemaid's box, a bucket of coal from the coal cellar, which she leaves by the foot of the stairs. Only then does she start up the steps with the familiar weight of the box banging against her calf and the candle stretching shadows over the walls. As she climbs she thinks up questions: Was it a big wedding, ma'am? Had you known each other long, ma'am? All of them ridiculous, all of them bound to fail to get anything out of the widow. She yawns and instead imagines herself in a church, Teddy beside her, this life of cleaning other people's dirt left behind because she and Teddy will—she and Teddy will do what? She has pictured the two of them coming out of the church, yet now she wonders—what then? To marry they'd have to leave service, and what would they do? Open a shop? That takes money. Teddy could go to work in someone else's shop. Yes, she thinks, to start with. And she'd be at home, with a baby, with a cat, with his dinner to cook and evenings with him by the fire to look forward to.

Her candle does little to dispel the gloom of the morning room. The pattern on the carpet is reduced to pale shapes against dark, and on the mantelpiece a small stuffed bird under its glass dome is poised menacingly. Its long blade of a beak is raised, its eyes intent as though, at any moment, it will launch itself at her. She can't help herself—every day she wastes precious time coming over to touch the dome, just to reassure herself of its substance. Yes, the bird is still trapped on its branch under the glass. A gruesome thing, she thinks— who would want to keep a dead bird to look at?

She smoothes the cushion of the armchair and picks off a stray thread. She'll be back here later, with Mrs. Robert sitting in this chair. She'll be standing on this carpet, staring down at her feet and saying, "No, ma'am, nothing more." The widow is like a winkle, and she needs a pin to pull her out, naked without her secrets and silences.

She ties on her rough apron and kneels in front of the hearth. Is it hot this time of year in India, ma'am? she thinks. Did you and Mr. Henry have many servants?

And so the early morning passes, a morning of sweeping ashes, shaking out cinders to be reused, blacking the grate, carrying buckets of ashes downstairs and others loaded with coal back up. Before long the stiffness in her hands is replaced by a dull ache, and her hands are filthy from the blacking, the soot, the coal. Has she touched her face? She isn't sure, so she stands on tiptoe in front of the mirror and raises the candle to her face. Her cap is askew, and a dark smudge runs from her nose across her cheek. She lifts her arm to her face and wipes at it with her sleeve. The dress is black, so who's to know? However, the smudge is stubborn, and she can only reduce it to a shadow. It'll take soap and water to remove it entirely, and that'll have to wait until she goes back down to the kitchen. She tries to fix in her mind exactly where it is. For who knows—Teddy might appear at the top of the area steps again. He might see her dishevelled and dirty and walk away without calling her name. And if he didn't come back? What would her life be except day after day of working herself into exhaustion just for food and a bed? What would be the point of that? If there's no hope for something better then . . . then you might as well just throw yourself in the river and be done with it.

She has to hurry to finish up the dining room and get downstairs after the clock in the hall strikes the hour. At least the kitchen is warm, and the air heavy with the smells of toast and bacon. She washes her hands and face, then sits down heavily, as though already the day has been too much. Mrs. Johnson pushes toast and a cup of tea towards her. "That'll keep you going," she says. "On a morning like this, we all need something warm inside us."

"What's it like out?"

"Bloomin' awful. Another freezing fog. Horrible stuff."

Jane takes her tea over to the area door and opens it a crack. Beyond the damp paving stones around her feet, the city has disappeared—this is how she imagines it must be underwater. The air has turned thick, muffling the clop of a horse's feet coming up the street. She steps out into a yellow murk and it makes her cough. Even here, only a couple of feet away from the kitchen, the light from the window is blurred and dirty. So much for worrying about what she looks like. Teddy won't be going out in this. She turns back and shuts the door behind her.

Barely has she taken a bite of her toast when the bell rings. Mr. Henry's room. The widow wanting to get dressed. It clangs again, though even if she'd leapt from the chair and run from the kitchen she could not have been upstairs yet. "Hold your horses," she mutters as she gets to her feet. Her stomach is cramped with hunger, so she takes a big bite of the toast, and a long gulp of tea that turns the bread soggy in her mouth.

She chews as she goes up the stairs and tries out new questions: Do your friends miss you, ma'am? Did you ever see a tiger? Were you happier in India, ma'am? As though coming to this dreary city as a widow could have given her the smallest pleasure.

She clenches her fists and knocks them against her knees as she climbs the last flight of stairs to the bedroom.

*I*t is an annoyance to have to work under lamplight in the middle of the day, but outside fog hangs like a curtain just beyond the windows. He'd forgotten how bad it could be, all those years in Paris, taking it for granted that a view from a tall building would be a view over the city. Not like London, where even on a clear day the haze from so much smoke obscures distant rooftops so that the city sits like an island on a pale sea. Then there's the reek of it—with the windows closed it still reaches his nose, a dark, unfinished smell.

The light from the gas lamp is exhausting to work by—already he has a headache. Candles, he thinks, he needs candles. Plus a day or two of quiet to finish the lecture. Sir Jonathan will be there, and Dr. Taylor, and, he has been told, Harry Roberts from the Troup Committee. It will be his moment to impress, to make up for the debacle of his presentation. Perhaps not a debacle—but certainly he felt a fool, being told to move on to a new point, something they hadn't already heard from Dr. Taylor.

What will he say to Taylor? The man is a blackguard. Will he have the audacity to ask questions after the lecture? Robert imagines himself at the podium taking a question from Taylor, a question that he can pull apart and show to be so wrongheaded that the man will look a fool. Yet he isn't a fool—that, indeed, is the problem. He's too clever to trust.

He turns back to the desk. He picks up his pen and stares at the last words he wrote. From along the hallway comes a knock at the front door—yet another caller leaving a card. The absurd ritual of mourning; he is supposed to be too grief stricken to see visitors. At least it means he has time to work undisturbed.

Stroking his moustache, he looks across the room, past the wallpaper and the walls, finding his way through a sentence that he has begun a dozen times already. There's a knock at the door, and he bellows, "Yes?"

It's Cartwright, his white hair luminous against the dimness of the hallway. "Sir, a Mr. Michael Danforth calling on urgent business. I explained the sad circumstances in which we find ourselves, but he insisted that he see you if at all possible."

Robert raises a hand to dismiss Cartwright, and the annoyance of the visitor, but he stops with his elbow just lifted from the desk. "Danforth, did you say?"

"Yes, sir."

"Michael Danforth? He's here? In the drawing room? Good Lord!" He laughs. "You can send him in—oh, but Cartwright?" He sits with his hand over his mouth, one finger tapping his nose, thinking. "Have Jane sent in—invent some pretext. But make sure she comes into the room while he's here."

Cartwright's brows are pulled down. "A pretext, sir?"

"Send her in with refreshments, or a message. Use your imagination, Cartwright."

"Very well, sir."

The absurdity of it delights him. Michael Danforth, daring to return after his audacious intrusion. He can reunite him with his hat—it is now sitting on the mantelpiece on a bust of Prince Albert that his father was fond of. He has to remind himself not to seem too gleeful; the house is in mourning, and Danforth will be bound to notice the incongruity.

Danforth turns out to be a grey stick of a man in spectacles, with a thick moustache that hangs over his mouth like an awning. He holds out a hand, says, "So sorry to intrude on you at a time like this, but it's unavoidable, I'm afraid. A case of great urgency has come to my attention."

Robert holds out his hand, feels Danforth's bony grip. From the mantelpiece beside them, Prince Albert peers out from under the brim of the burglar's hat that hangs loosely about his head. "My father," he says, and nods towards the bust, "was a great admirer of the prince."

"Ah," says Danforth. His gaze follows Robert's, and for a moment he says nothing more.

Robert feels himself tilt forward slightly, waiting.

But when Danforth turns back to him, it's with a smile. "Being an anthropometrist, sir, perhaps you could measure up His Highness for a better-fitting hat."

"Yes," he says quickly. He hopes Danforth doesn't notice the surge of blood to his face. "Quite so. Very good, very good." He indicates a chair by the fire, then takes its twin on the other side. Clever, he thinks, Danforth covering his own confusion by tripping him up like that. Why had he not noticed the ridiculousness of it himself? The prince's head, half swallowed by the dusty hat.

Danforth can barely sit down. Instead he perches on the very edge of the chair. "I won't beat about the bush. I've involved myself with a criminal case that could cause a sensation, however, I find myself unable to proceed without the aid of an anthropometrist."

Robert presses his fingertips against his lips. "I see," he says, but he's not sure that he does. Danforth asking for his help? This has to be a trick.

"Do you remember a case in Argentina last year? A dreadful murder in the offices of the Central Bank of Buenos Aires, and the discovery of the embezzlement of tens of thousands of pounds?"

"No," he says. "I have no recollection of such a case."

That is not the issue, however, and Danforth waves a hand as though to push the matter aside. "An awful case. A junior employee was arrested—one Arturo Villanova—and in the cellar of his house they found a bloody shirt, a hatchet with fingerprints that matched his, all manner of evidence pointing to him. He was put on trial, of course, but he was never convicted."

"No?" Robert pauses for a moment. "Was the evidence insufficient?"

Danforth lets out a snort of laughter. "He would have been found guilty, I'm positive. However, he escaped before the trial was over, and the money was never recovered. After his depredations, he was a wealthy fellow, and most likely he bought his way out of gaol."

"And now he has been caught again?"

"Not exactly." Danforth sucks at his lips. "Not yet, at least."

There's a gentle tapping at the door—Jane—and Robert calls, "Come in."

She's carrying a tray with two glasses of wine. She looks about her for a moment before approaching them where they sit by the fire. She seems unsure of herself, as though her feet might trip her on the carpet, or her hands become suddenly unable to bear this slight weight. Then she apparently makes up her mind and brings the tray close to Robert until he gives a shake of his head, and she understands and swings the tray towards Danforth.

"Sir?" she says.

"Ah," he says, and he takes a glass.

Her back is towards Robert, so he sees no startled recognition. She turns to him now and he lifts his eyes to hers. They are dark and wide, the lashes longer than he remembers having noticed before.

Maybe, he thinks, she is too well able to control herself, but he wants a sign. He holds her gaze, raises his eyebrows a little. However, she seems not to understand, for she looks back at him, then, as soon as he has lifted his glass off the tray, she takes off towards the door.

When he looks back, Danforth is licking drops of wine from his moustache. He cannot decide if the man looks villainous or simply self-satisfied. "Ah," Danforth says, and brings his gaze back to Robert, "where was I?" He swivels the glass in his hand and stares into it. "Ah yes—last night at my club, a gentleman from Argentina—Arturo Vilaseca—was introduced to me by a mutual acquaintance. In his thirties, clean-shaven, speaks with a slight Spanish accent. In short, he appears to be what he claims, a gentleman visitor from that country, embarking on a tour of Europe."

"Yet you have suspicions?"

"Yes, indeed I do." He coughs into his hand. "Naturally, I followed the Buenos Aires case with some interest because of the use of dactylographic evidence by the prosecution. I have to tell you that"—and he leans forward—"this gentleman, this Vilaseca, is sufficiently similar to the accused to have aroused my suspicions. He too is in his early thirties, he too is left-handed and walks with a slight limp. What's more, his name is uncannily close to that of the suspect: Arturo Villanova. Naturally, one could explain it all as a coincidence—but then again—" He raises his hands as though to suggest the balance of evidence is against such a conclusion.

Despite Robert's suspicions that this Michael Danforth is himself not above breaking the law, he finds himself strangely excited. "Have you gone to Scotland Yard? Surely they would be willing to arrest this fellow."

"My dear man," says Danforth, "the inspector I spoke to said, 'I can hardly arrest a man for being from Argentina.' I fear there will be little help from that quarter. No—" he raises his eyes to Robert's "—we'll have to catch this Vilaseca ourselves."

"If you are asking help from me, of all people, I imagine you have a plan."

Danforth gives a smile that lifts the ends of his thick moustache.

"Ah yes. In the interests of justice—and of clarifying the advantages and disadvantages of both anthropometry and dactylography—I have indeed come up with a plan."

"One that will show the advantages of anthropometry?"

"I could hardly expect your cooperation otherwise." He takes another sip of wine and frowns as he slides the glass onto the table. "I don't for a moment believe that anthropometry is without merit, just as I am sure that you see the advantages offered by dactylography. Naturally both systems are imperfect. We just happen to differ in our opinion on the relative significance of their drawbacks."

Robert allows himself a small smile. "Such as the lack of a system for classifying fingerprints?"

"Or the unavoidable fact that the human body alters as it grows to maturity? Or that it alters again as it ages?" He stares back at Robert, then blinks and turns away. From a bag by his side he extracts a small case, then, from inside the case, a wineglass, which he holds carefully by its base. "This," he says, lifting the glass, "is likely all the evidence needed to confirm Vilaseca's true identity." He points with one finger. "See the prints on the glass? One could hardly do better, except by fingerprinting the man."

Robert peers forward. "Yes, I see them. So if they match those left in Buenos Aires, you'll know you have your man."

"Exactly." Danforth sets the glass gently back into the case.

"And thus the case of dactylography will be advanced."

"Not quite, Mr. Bentley. Here is my problem. Vilaseca's leaving for Italy in a few days, and will be out of reach. I have his fingerprints. However, I have no way of sending them to Argentina for comparison before he departs."

At this Robert gives a small cry. "I see," he exclaims. "If only you could measure him and send the information to Argentina by the telegraph, the authorities there could confirm his identity, and Scotland Yard might act."

"Precisely."

"But how can you be certain the Buenos Aires police took his measurements?"

"One of the detectives on the case is an enthusiast."

"I see. Yes, yes." He sits back. "And yet we'd need a means of measuring him without arousing his suspicions."

With a sweep of his arm Danforth reaches for his wine and winks at Robert. "I believe, Mr. Bentley, that I have found a solution to that particular problem."

Climbing the stairs, Jane swallows to keep down the sour taste of fear. Her hands are not as clean as they might be. How could they be when she has spent the last hour on her knees scrubbing the linoleum up the back staircase? In the hall she pauses to wipe them on the back of her fresh apron. She knocks at the study door, then hears a brusque "Enter."

Mr. Robert is at the desk. He glances up, but she knows better than to expect him to hurry himself on her account. So she closes the door and stands a few feet from it, looking around the room with all its books and piles of papers and the ill-looking lamp that lights it. Maybe, she thinks, the Bentleys have found out about Teddy.

But if this were about Teddy, Mrs. Robert would have called her upstairs. No, this is not about him.

Her breathing sounds unnaturally loud to her. In and out, in and out, measuring out the seconds that are passing as she stands there. Her work for the afternoon is rising up around her—what with interruptions to carry wine in to Mr. Robert and being called to the study again now, she has fallen behind. That is not something that they taught you to manage at the orphanage. No, there was no mention of what to do when your employers make it difficult for you to do your work.

At last he sighs and sits back, tapping a pen against his teeth. "Come in, come in," he says. "There's no need to lurk by the door."

He doesn't sound angry, or terse, and that's a good sign. Still, he stares as she comes close, as though he is expecting something from her.

"Sir?" she says.

"Do you have anything to tell me?"

An awful stillness wells up through her belly, her chest, filling her throat. This must be what it's like to drown, she thinks. She opens her mouth, but nothing comes out. Has Sarah spoken to Mr. Robert? Has she told him what she's found out, that she's the daughter of a woman hanged for murder? But why would she when their wages will be paid in just a couple of days, and she's not above profiting from such a secret?

He puts down the pen. "Well?"

"No, sir," Jane says unsteadily.

"Nothing? Nothing at all?"

"No, sir."

He leans forward, elbows propped on the desk. "Think carefully now. You brought wine up here earlier today."

"Yes, sir."

"Did you notice anything?"

She noticed that he had a visitor, that he spoke excitedly, that it was odd for her to be called on to bring in wine when by rights that was a task for Mr. Cartwright or Sarah. She noticed, too, that the conversation paused while she was in the room—but it rarely failed to, unless it was about something of little interest.

"Sir, I didn't notice anything out of the ordinary." She keeps her face blank.

He runs his hands through his hair. "I thought you were an observant girl."

"I'm not sure what you want me to have noticed, sir."

"My visitor, Jane. Surely he looked familiar?"

"No, sir. I've never seen him before, as far as I know."

"This is important; very important, in fact. I want you to be absolutely sure."

"I am, sir."

"You didn't see him soon after you arrived? In this house?"

"You and Mrs. Robert haven't had many visitors, sir."

"Very true. But we had one unexpected and rather unwelcome visitor."

"The burglar, sir?"

He nods. "The burglar who seemed to take nothing. The burglar who brazened his way into this house by impersonating me."

So this, she thinks, is what it is all about. "But sir, your visitor was a different man."

"Think, Jane—it is possible to drastically alter one's appearance. Picture that burglar in your mind, then imagine him without his beard but in spectacles and with his hair grey."

She looks past him to the fog outside the window. A street lamp appears then, ghostly, the roofs of the houses opposite. In a few seconds they are gone again. Does she look as though she's imagining the burglar? She hopes so. She purses her lips, she tilts her head, waits for a few more seconds to pass. She'd know that fleshy face with its small, peering eyes anywhere. "It wasn't him, sir. I'm certain. The other gentleman had different eyes and a bigger face. Those aren't things a person could change."

"You're absolutely sure? It's easy to be mistaken."

"Yes, sir, I'm sure."

When he sits back he looks deflated. "Very well. Thank you, Jane."

"Sir? If I saw him I'd let you know. Even if I saw him in the house, I'd find a way to tell you."

"Thank you, Jane," he says, but already he has looked away.

So she turns on her heel and leaves him sitting there.

After all, there are the back stairs to finish scrubbing.

CHAPTER 21

As he follows Danforth down the hallway Robert Bentley feels a sense of unease. Behind him the porter is huffing under the weight of his boxes, his instruments clanging as the man knocks them about. "Steady on there," he tells him, but already the man's face is red from the effort of keeping up.

"We'll be in the Spencer Room," Danforth tells the porter. "And watch what you're about—those are delicate scientific instruments."

The porter struggles away, and Danforth turns on his heel. He leads Robert past a lounge of leather armchairs where men doze before a fire with newspapers spread over their bellies, past huge potted plants that half disguise the entrance to the dining room.

A table of men is waiting for them. Introductions are made all round: Thomas Richardson, Thomas Bennett, Harold Duplessy, John Clive, an American called Homer Schmidt, Francis Underwood, Cuthbert Whalen, and, of course, Whalen's acquaintance, Arturo Vilaseca. Vilaseca is a young man with slick black hair and glasses perched so far towards the end of his nose that they seem in danger of sliding off altogether. His nose is long and thin, and beneath it he wears a curved blade of a moustache that gives his face a rather villainous look.

Dinner is a fancy affair with plenty of wine. Danforth knows these men well, and inevitably the eddies of the conversation spin over their end of the table, while Robert Bentley and Vilaseca sit in near silence over their plates. Vilaseca peers at his food as though boiled potatoes and trout are entirely new to him. He has little to say, even in answer to Robert's queries. Yes, he has recently arrived in Britain to embark on a trip around Europe. No, he has never visited London before. No, he has not yet found time to view the museums, but he hopes to. As for his life in Argentina, Robert learns only that he was recently bereaved and is now heir to a fortune sufficient to enable him to travel at his leisure. He delivers all of this in perfect English with only a touch of an accent that makes his voice land too hard on some syllables.

As for Danforth, Robert has plenty of time to observe him when Vilaseca turns his attention back to his dinner. He speaks loudly in trimmed-down sentences, and pauses every now and again to look intently at the men around him. His face is creased, his spectacles flash in the glare of the lights, and Robert can't help wondering if the girl was wrong after all. There is something he doesn't quite trust about this man. Is he about to be made a fool of? he wonders. Was the girl so mistaken that she couldn't recognize Danforth through whatever disguise he used to gain entry to the house? Or was she somehow involved in that whole affair? The inspector who came to investigate certainly had his doubts about her honesty. She is a clever young thing, noticing so much about the burglar—but what better way to deflect suspicions? And after all, she was the one to let him in.

He takes a mouthful of wine and lets it pool under his tongue as he looks across the table. Danforth is certainly a man well-practiced in persuasion; he has convinced these men that Bentley and he are well acquainted, that it is possible, even with so small a number of men, to put both anthropometry and dactylography to the test. A ridiculous conceit. He has to remind himself that this is of no importance, for all they need is to measure Vilaseca, and to keep him from suspecting the ulterior purpose of the evening.

Slowly one course succeeds another, more wine is poured, and he is pulled into the circle of the conversation. He explains his years in Paris with Bertillon, he admits that yes, he did make a presentation before a government committee—the Troup Committee—only a fortnight ago.

"But look here, that is quite the coincidence," says Francis Underwood. He is a young man with a high, pale forehead and a way of lounging in his chair. "My cousin is serving on that committee—Alistair Renfrew, of the Home Office. He should be here tonight. I'll have him paged."

Before Robert can protest—a member of the Troup Committee sitting in on their "experiment"?—Underwood has called over a waiter, and the waiter has taken off across the dining room. It would have looked odd to have stopped him, would have appeared as though he lacked confidence in his method, yet as he pushes away his plate his hands feel large and unwieldy. He knots his fingers together on the tablecloth, then unknots them because he suspects it makes him look nervous. He takes a long gulp of wine. If he does well—if he shows beyond doubt that measurement is accurate, and enables a record to be easily retrieved and matched against its subject—then, he tells himself, this evening may accomplish more than his presentation before the committee.

The room hums with the conversations of more than a dozen tables. It's a low hum, for all the diners are male. It makes for a dull sight, he thinks: all those black jackets against the red of the wallpaper and the carpet, as though somewhere nearby is a drawing room full of women waiting for them to be finished with their port and cigars. Of course, the women *are* waiting—in houses throughout London, sitting at dinner tables with a butler or a maid to attend to them, but perhaps no one to talk to. Back in Cursitor Road Mina will be sitting across the table from the young widow. For all he knows she has used those questions of hers, asked so gently, so persistently, to pull the woman's secrets out of her. Maybe he'll return home to find the widow has fled—he imagines the door open, Henry's room empty, the house free of her presence.

The conversation has turned down a new avenue. Danforth is saying, "To spend a lifetime simply waiting, it quite staggers me."

Clive dabs at his mouth with his napkin. He has a high-cheeked face like a horse's, and through his greying hair his scalp shines. "The alternative would hardly have been a pleasant one. Now there's talk that he'll be passed over entirely."

Danforth chews at his moustache. "Not without protest." He has a way of darting looks towards Vilaseca, but the young man has been so slow with his dinner that even now he is still slicing up a piece of tart and feeding the neat triangles into his mouth. He doesn't seem to realize that Danforth has been paying him such close attention.

Underwood has been shifting in his seat, glancing around the dining room. Now he smiles broadly at a stout man who is approaching. "Ah," he calls out. "There you are at last, Renfrew. I was beginning to suspect that maybe for a change you were eating dinner with Alice."

Renfrew offers his hand. Danforth's mouth is tight, and he glances over at Robert as though to say, *Can you believe it? Renfrew right here to witness this.* Out loud he says, "Shall we start, then, gentlemen? I've requested a private room for our demonstration. By now everything should be ready."

He leads them away from the table, through the dining room and down a narrow passage lined with portraits and a mounted stag's head. Then he swings open the door and waits while they file in.

The room, notices Robert, is windowless. Chairs have been arranged in a semicircle, and two tables set up. On one sits his measuring equipment and his cabinet of cards; on the other, two boxes and a basin of water with soap and a towel. He takes a chair at the end, and looks at Vilaseca. If he suspects anything he is disguising it well, for he merely crosses one leg over the other.

Danforth does not sit down—there is no chair for him, anyway, with Renfrew added to their number. Instead he stands between the tables with his hands clasped behind his back, giving the impression that he is about to duck forward. "Gentlemen," he starts, "you have all expressed interest in the problem of identification, as we might call it. My dear friend Mr. Bentley has agreed to put on a demonstration this evening that will show the strengths and—admittedly—the weaknesses of the methods being considered by the Troup Committee." He smiles towards Renfrew, who merely nods. "We beg your patience and your cooperation—we will take you as our subjects. Mr. Bentley will measure you, and I will take your fingerprints. We will each make a duplicate set of records. Then"—with a flourish that surprises Robert, he indicates the cases standing on the tables—"we will insert one set in with the hundreds that we have collected in our research. From the other, you will select those of two individuals, and our task will be to retrieve their match from amongst the many records in our collections."

Even now Vilaseca shows little sign of alarm. His raised foot swings a little, and one end of his moustache is lifted. In derision? Robert is not sure. This could be the man who murdered one of his colleagues in cold blood, and made off with tens of thousands of pounds. Why would such a demonstration as tonight's cause him any alarm? If he understands its purpose, he surely also understands that he has adequate time to escape from England before Danforth can confirm his identity.

The men wait their turn good-naturedly. Naturally, Danforth is finished with the men before Robert; he has only to roll each man's fingers onto his inked pad, and to roll them again on the cards he has devised with a box for each finger. The men wash their hands and light cigars as they wait to be measured. They call for brandy, all except for Vilaseca, who asks instead for a glass of water. For tonight, Robert has simplified his measurements, though it will mean taking a little longer to retrieve the records. He will not ask them to remove their shoes and socks; he will only measure the length and width of their heads, the length of their left middle fingers and left forearms, and the length and width of their right ears. Still, there is soon restlessness amongst them as he slowly brings his callipers down to measure a head, then again, then again to make sure that he has measured accurately. Renfrew sits with his legs stretched out, and tugs his watch from his pocket. However, Robert cannot go more quickly, so he is pleased when Danforth, his work done, sits on the edge of the table and starts into an explanation of a famous case in which fingerprints were used to confirm the identity of a man who murdered his cousin and her two children.

It is not until Danforth explains how the evidence convinced the jury and led to a conviction that it strikes Robert: Vilaseca will surely understand the implications! He bends to note the length of Duplessy's ear and lets himself steal a glance at the Argentinean. He is paring his nails, the light of the lamps gleaming from his pomaded hair. The very picture of nonchalance—but is he acting?

When Robert has finished with Duplessy there is only Vilaseca left, and he finds himself hesitating before getting close enough to touch him. Ridiculous, he tells himself. He has measured men who have done far worse. Men who have cut the throats of their own wives; men who have thrown children into the sea, who have burned down houses full of people and stood by to watch. Those men were brutes, though. They would never have risen above the low nature of their lives. This man, this Vilaseca—he is a different creature altogether, sitting in front of him in his tailored jacket and gleaming hair, every inch the gentleman. His glasses give him the look of a thoughtful man, though if one looked closely, one might find evidence that those thoughts are of an unsettling nature—that narrowness of the eyes, that pinched look of the nose, that line of moustache like a sneer.

He takes more time over Vilaseca than the others, getting each measurement right to the millimeter. After all, success will do more for the cause of anthropometry than anything he could say in its favor. Or that Dr. Taylor could, come to that. Renfrew was watching, but his attention has drifted now, and he does not disguise a wide yawn as he sits with a glass of brandy held against the bulge of his belly. Robert reminds himself, this is the main shortcoming of anthropometry: the time it takes to measure a subject. Soon, though, when he files the cards, when he is able to produce the match from the hundreds he has brought with him—then he will spark Renfrew's interest.

When he has finished he separates the two sets of cards he has made for each man, and files one set in amongst the many others in the drawers of his case. Then he and Danforth step outside to the corridor. Danforth rubs his hands together. "We've got him," he whispers, "and he doesn't suspect a thing."

"Either that," says Robert, "or he's being careful to hide any sign he's detected the trap we've laid."

"No man could be that able to mask his anxiety. As I examined his hands I took the trouble to feel his pulse, a trick of mine. It was as slow and even as the ticking of that clock." He nods to a tall clock standing at the blind end of the corridor.

"Nevertheless—"

"Nevertheless, I will ask Whalen to tell me if he looks as though he is going to flee. If I inform him as to the nature of our suspicions, he'll be eager to help."

Robert is about to protest when the door opens. Renfrew—apparently it is he who has taken charge of the proceedings. He ushers them in, then hands them both two cards.

The room is silent while they work. Robert rifles through his drawers of cards, through *Heads: Length, Medium,* then *Right Ears: Long* and, within a few moments, has the first card pulled out. The second takes him a little longer. For a moment he looks through them to compare, then hands them to Renfrew, who makes a note of the time.

At the other table Danforth is still sorting through his records. He plucks out one, then slips it back in, his face a little flushed now. Indeed, it gets redder the longer he searches, flipping back and forth through the cards. Ten minutes, fifteen, and only then does he hand a card to Renfrew. One card, not two.

Robert has already taken a seat and helped himself to a glass of brandy. Renfrew checks the cards. All of them do indeed match, and he says as much. The men call out, "Bravo, bravo."

Danforth gives a small bow, and stretches out his hand to Robert. "You see," he says to their audience, "the two systems with their strengths and their weaknesses. With fingerprints, an efficient system of classification to allow easy retrieval is still lacking. But"—he raises a finger, looking at Renfrew—"collection of fingerprints is quick, and they offer another advantage: no two sets are alike. With fingerprints there can be no mistaking a man's identity—they are as much a part of him as his soul. He can burn his skin, he can cut it, but the new flesh will grow back in the same pattern."

It sounds like the speech of a man making excuses, thinks Robert. It must be apparent that without a classification system, fingerprints are useless for purposes of identification; they can do little more than confirm an identity found through anthropometry. All those prints to sort through to find a matching pair—the same problem that photographs posed—surely Danforth cannot expect that the Troup Committee will overlook this obstacle? Besides, and he stretches his chest, if after all these years no system has been devised, perhaps one will never be, or at least not soon enough to be of practical use.

The evening is soon over. In the foyer the men shake hands. Vilaseca steps through the doorway, and Danforth's eyes follow him, like those of a cat forced to let a mouse escape down a hole. Soon only Renfrew is left, and he shakes their hands again.

"Most interesting," he tells them. "To have had a demonstration is invaluable, absolutely invaluable."

Danforth rocks onto his toes. In his coat he looks like a well-dressed scarecrow, so thin and full of angles. "Well," he says in a hushed voice, "I have to admit that there is more riding on the demonstration than simply the good opinion of the Troup Committee, or the interest of our friends." He bends his head forward and flicks his tongue over his lips in a way that makes Robert uneasy. "Our young friend Vilaseca shares many characteristics with the infamous Villanova, you recall? The dreadful case at the Central Bank of Buenos Aires?"

"Who cut the throat of his colleague and escaped before he was convicted?"

"The very man."

Robert twists a button on his coat. He should have guessed that Danforth wouldn't be able to contain his excitement.

Renfrew splutters, "Good God, Danforth, what are you about? Shouldn't Scotland Yard be informed?"

"They can't act. They need more evidence than that of his nationality, his sudden wealth, and the similarity between the names. Hence this evening's demonstration—now we have information I can telegraph to Argentina." He pulls Robert's card from his pocket and taps one gloved finger against it. "We have him, I assure you."

Tilting back his head, Renfrew lets out a bark of a laugh. "You old dog, Danforth. Very clever. You had us all. Well done." He claps one hand on his back. "You'll let me know the minute an arrest is imminent, won't you?"

"Certainly."

Robert's boxes are by his feet. A porter picks them up and carries them to a hansom waiting outside. Robert shakes hands with Danforth and walks out into the street. The night is freezing, the fog thick enough to reduce the lights on the far side of the street to a vague glow. He climbs into the cab and breathes on his hands. The cold is a relief, a welcome diversion from the unease creeping through him. If Danforth's plan works they will share the glory, and the case for anthropometry will be difficult to assail. If it should not—they will share the shame of it.

CHAPTER 22

Once the doctor has peered into the chamber pot, Jane covers it with a cloth and carries it away. A stink seeps out of it, a filthy, thick stink that she turns her head from as she comes down the stairs. Perhaps Price is ill after all, despite the doctor's assurances to Mrs. Robert.

The smell clings to her, even when she has emptied the pot and wiped it clean with a rag. She's climbing back up the stairs when Sarah's head appears below her around the banister. "Hey," she calls softly, "down here."

So Jane comes down, pot in one hand, pushing a few strands of hair from her eyes with the back of the other. It's not often that Sarah seeks her out, and when she does it means trouble.

Sarah takes her by the arm and steers her down the rest of the stairs, all the way to the kitchen. Mrs. Johnson is not at the stove. She is not in sight at all. Only Elsie watches them, and she gives a sly smile from the end of the room as she sweeps a broom across the floor. Sarah nods her head to the area. "A visitor," she whispers, and opens the door for her.

Jane only just has the foresight to put down Price's pot and push her loose hair under her cap. In her dirty apron, her face most likely sweaty and red, what a sight she must be. She flaps her apron and the skirt of the dress, as though that will be enough to shake Price's reek from her. Of all the times, she thinks, of all the times in her day.

But if she didn't go out to him—then what would he think? For it is Teddy, it must be.

She steps outside and peers up to the railings. There he is, a red scarf loosely wrapped around his neck, his breath steaming out of his mouth. As he sees her he beckons. He has a new coat, by the look of it—one of his master's castoffs. And here she is, a maid with other people's dirt on her, stinking of their filth, as though this is all she is worth. Her throat is tight. She shouldn't have come out. Don't let yourself cry, she tells herself—for if nothing else she'll find out if he loves her, because what man who didn't would want her after seeing her like this?

A quick glance over her shoulder, but there's no Mrs. Johnson striding out of the door to catch her, no Mrs. Robert watching from a window, so she hurries up the steps, watching his face, seeing if it changes when he notices the soot on her clothes, the unkempt look about her. It doesn't. Instead he peels off one glove and, as she reaches the top, lays his warm palm against the side of her face. "I was just passing. I had to see you."

"Just passing?" she says.

"Well, a few streets away. It didn't take that long to walk here. My master sent me out with a couple of messages. I couldn't very well pass up the chance of giving you a message of my own."

"Oh?" She holds his hand against her cheek.

"Yes," he says. He tilts off his hat and, in its shelter, he touches his mouth to hers. A delicate kiss, then he reaches behind her and pulls her towards him, though the railings are between them. His mouth is warm and soft, and she lets him hold her like that, in full view of whoever from the house may be watching.

Mina has been expecting something, but not this: it arrives during breakfast, a letter that she lays down by her plate.

"Another letter of condolence?" Robert reaches for the toast. "Who's it from this time?"

She pokes through her scrambled eggs with her fork. She has no appetite, not since she recognized the handwriting on the envelope. "Oh," she says lightly, "I don't know." It wouldn't do to leave it there, unopened. To veer from the usual, that is to invite suspicion. So, with her hands feeling ungainly, as though they might knock over her coffee or send the small jug of milk flying across the tablecloth, she reaches for it. Robert passes her the letter opener. With a quick slit she has it open and unfolds it.

My dearest Nora,

I remember the feel of your lips on mine, the way your breast would be crushed against my chest. Do you? I thought I was dreaming when I saw you in Mortimer's—a married woman now. Does he send your heart racing in a way I never could? You made a fool out of me—it's not the money, it's the way you told me you longed for me and I believed you. However, you know that I do not easily give up, and I see no reason to now. I will still have you—you owe me that much.

Then his initials at the bottom of the page.

A hot rush of panic rises from her belly, but she has the foresight to fold up the letter, even as she pushes back her chair and mutters, "Excuse me—I'll be back in a few minutes."

Robert's mouth opens in surprise. She can still see it as she pulls the door closed behind her and climbs the stairs. Her legs carry her up, though she's barely aware of the fact that they are working, working. When the toe of her shoe hits a riser and she stumbles forward, it is all she can do to make them lift her the rest of the way, up and up and up—these bloody English houses with all their stairs—to the water closet on the half-landing. She pushes the door open, leans hard against it to close it. A key is in the lock—she turns it. Then she lifts her skirts and lets herself down on the toilet seat, head bent to breathe into her hands.

The Dark Lantern

Did she think she was going to escape? Did she really think she could pull herself free of her old life? She squeezes her eyes shut. There should be no tears, no pity for herself. Surely there is a way to fend off Popham, but she cannot think. The inside of her head is hot. Her thoughts run helter-skelter.

She knew he'd found her out—she tells herself that none of this should be a shock. Still—a letter that he must have known would arrive in front of Robert, the nature of what he wants. Not money, but her. The letter crumples in her hand as she tightens her fingers over it. He asks if she remembers. Oh yes, she remembers. The sour scent of his skin, the press of his tongue into her mouth. The way she'd sigh as if such pleasure was too much for her. How hard that was— winding herself around him, sliding a hand up his thigh, groaning when his hands wrung her breasts through the silk of her dress, promising him whatever he wanted because she had to. After all, she was the bait, and he was the fish Flyte wanted to reel in. And now? Now he wants revenge for her helping to make a fool out of him.

She hears footsteps outside the door, and she raises her head. It's Robert, his voice low and urgent. "My darling," he's saying, "what has happened?"

She takes a moment to pitch her voice just right: a little tremulous, yet bright nonetheless. She calls out, "I must have eaten something that was a little off."

"Should I call the doctor?"

"No, no. Please—I'll be fine."

Once his footsteps have retreated down the stairs she stands and rips the letter into shreds. They float in the toilet bowl, the ink bleeding into the water. Then she lowers herself back onto the seat and empties her bladder.

Opening the door, Jane peers through the half-light. In the bed she sees a hump—the widow, still in bed at this time of the morning. There is a noise, low and broken. "Ma'am?" she calls. "Ma'am, shall I get you ready for breakfast?"

The widow sits up suddenly, and Jane jumps. She is crying, letting out great spluttering sobs that shake her body. "Can't any of you just leave me alone?"

Jane comes closer to the bed. "Come on now, ma'am. You're with friends here."

"Friends?" She laughs, then pushes one hand against her mouth. It doesn't stay there. In a moment she pushes her fingers through her hair, hard, as though she wants to wrench it out by the roots. "Perhaps you're right. They're the only friends I have." She sinks forward, and from the shaking of her shoulders, it is evident she is crying again.

There is something distasteful about this young woman and her misery. It is almost more than Jane can do to touch her. Yet she does. She stretches out one hand—her red hand with its knuckles thickening from the heavy work that fills her days—and lays it on the widow's shoulder. It's no different, she thinks, than a piece of furniture. Hard to the touch yet a little warm, like wood.

The widow flinches but she doesn't pull away. "You've had a terrible time of it," whispers Jane. "No one could expect more of you." She's not sure whether she's said the right thing. What is the right thing? Words that wrap themselves warmly around the widow might stop her crying, but if they are pulled too tight she'll close up into herself.

Jane bends so close that her mouth is only inches from the widow's ear. "Ma'am? Maybe you could go home. Wouldn't that be better for you? To go back to your friends and your family? They'd take proper care of you, wouldn't they?"

The widow lifts her head and takes a shuddering breath. Her mouth's wide open. Strands of saliva hang between her teeth, and her face is slick with tears. "I have no one," she announces. "Do—do you understand that? Now I have no one at all."

Her head falls back and she lets out a wail. Jane hesitates, then she sits on the bed and pulls the widow into her arms. Her body is all bones, hard against her chest. Soon, though, the wailing softens, and the widow clings to her.

She leans her head against the widow's. "Tell me, ma'am," she whispers. "Tell me how it is you're so on your own."

With the telegram in one hand, Robert searches the house for Mina. He finds Sarah dusting in the study, Cartwright tidying the dining room, the widow sitting by the window in the drawing room, staring into the street. She jumps to her feet when he comes in, but he's startled too and shoves the telegram into his pocket, as though she'll be able to read it from across the room.

"Excuse me," he mutters. "I thought Mina might be here."

Her eyes look sore, as though she's been crying. "She's upstairs," she says.

"Thank you." He retreats, faster than he should, his feet carrying him up to the bedrooms. But she is not in their bedroom, so he takes the narrow stairs up to the dim corridor that passes the servants' rooms. He goes to the end, knocks, and gently opens the door. Price's head turns, but Mina is not there either. "Sorry," he says, as though he has intruded, when, as he tells himself as he closes the door, Price had no reason to look so affronted. Whose house does she think it is?

Belatedly he guesses where she must be: in his mother's room. Down the stairs he goes, Price's gaunt face floating before him in the half-light so that when he opens the door, the first thing he says to Mina is, "You really need to do something about that woman."

Over the bed are strewn dresses and petticoats and even a couple of corsets. Mina, though, is at the dressing table, his mother's jewelry box open in front of her. She raises her eyebrows. "Price, darling?"

"Of course, Price. There's nothing wrong with her. We've had the doctor out twice—how can it be her nerves? I thought women like her didn't *have* nerves."

From one hand dangles a pearl necklace. She studies it for a moment, then sets it down on the table. "She has nowhere to go, and no prospects. I've given her warning that she must get up, but the doctor intervened. What can I do? I can hardly throw her out of the house in the state she's in."

"She's worked herself up into it."

She comes across the carpet to him. "Yes, she certainly has. But it doesn't make it any easier to put her out the door."

He takes her in his arms though she's a little resistant. "She can't stay," he says softly. "She has nothing to do here, unless you take her on as your maid."

She jerks her head back. "She might just as well look after Victoria—and Victoria is unlikely to protest."

"Ah." He holds her out, at the ends of his arms. "But Victoria won't be with us much longer." He dips his hand into his pocket and pulls out the telegram. "See what's arrived? I've been all over the house looking for you."

She takes it over to the window to read. He watches her head shift slightly, as though the only way to absorb the message is to force her eyes over its lines again and again. Then she raises her head, light glinting red in her hair. "They were never married!"

"Cyril is nothing if not thorough. Not only can he find no record of a marriage between Henry and Victoria, he has not been able to trace Victoria Dawes. Other Dawes women, yes—but no *Victoria* Dawes. No one has heard of the woman—it's quite extraordinary." He takes the telegram from her and reads it again. "I hope you weren't thinking of dividing up Mother's jewelry just yet."

"Your mother left Price a brooch and a pearl necklace. As for Victoria—well, we'd need to get it all valued to divide everything equally. And that could take time, couldn't it?"

"Oh yes," he says. "Quite some time, I imagine." He smiles. "In the meantime we must confront her. It would be easiest if she just renounced all claim on Henry's money and left. What else can she do?"

"Yes," Mina says, "what else can she do?" Her smile, though, has a thinness to it that disturbs him. "Maybe she won't be got rid of so easily."

"Then it will be a matter for the police."

CHAPTER 23

Jane hurries along the street, her hands swinging back towards her body to touch her pocket and the letter inside. The afternoon is bitter. She bends her head against the sleet blowing into her face and only glances up when she has to, to see her way, to avoid dingy piles of snow, to slip past the few other people out this afternoon. Already her hands and face are burning from the cold, and under her boots the pavement is turning icy. She passes a hot-pie man, but she has no money. Not a single penny in her pocket.

Of all the afternoons to be sent out—but it is an urgent matter, said Mrs. Robert, and held out the envelope. There was no name on it, no address, and Mrs. Robert made her repeat over and over where it is to be taken, and into whose hands it is to be put—no one else's, only the master's, she is to be sure of that. She is also to linger if she can, to look tired and hungry and, if she is offered a cup of tea, to take it.

"What for, ma'am?" she asked.

"Because you are young and pretty," said Mrs. Robert, "and that can be useful."

She'd felt her face grow hot all of a sudden, and looked down. "I don't see how, ma'am." Mrs. Robert had lifted her chin with one hand—not brusquely, but not gently either. "You are my eyes and my ears," she said. "Now I need you to make yourself useful in Mr. Popham's household. Do you understand? He is sure to have a valet, or a footman. If he should ask when your half day will be, you can tell him tomorrow, or whichever day might be convenient for him." She went to the desk and gathered up a small pile of coins—Jane's wages for the month. "Well?" she'd said.

How could she protest? Yet when Mrs. Robert counted the coins into her palm and gave her a smile, she felt that she barely belonged to herself.

Of course, Sarah was waiting on the stairs again. "Got your wages, did you?" There was no point denying it with the money in her hand. Sarah's hand extended towards hers. "Thank you kindly," she said. She repeated it when Jane's hand didn't open. What choice was there but to give her the money? So she did, and then watched Sarah's skirts sway as she took the stairs up to their room to hide it.

Now she bows her head against the wind and tucks her scarf more securely around her neck. She read through the classifieds and imagined herself in a different household, as though she could just walk through a doorway and into a different life. Yet managing it has been more than she can think how to do: she has no writing paper, she has nowhere to sit and write her letter without someone— Sarah or Elsie or Mrs. Johnson—coming upon her. Perhaps Teddy could help. Does his master need a maid? Or one of his neighbors? Plus there is still the matter of her character. How can she write one for herself when any decent mistress in London would want to come and talk to Mrs. Robert?

Teddy. What would he do if he discovered what Mrs. Robert has asked her to do? Would it excuse it, that Mrs. Robert insisted she let another man—any man of this Mr. Popham's household—take her out? And, she wonders, would that half day be her only time off? Her eyes sting at the thought of it. Teddy wants to take her to Hyde Park, to the palace, to see the Tower of London where those queens had their heads chopped off back in the days when royalty could command that sort of thing.

Turning into a wider street, she finds more people to dodge, and when she has to cross the road, a pile of horse dirt that she comes close to stepping in. Everywhere lie the filthy remains of snow turned grey with soot. Nothing in this city can stay clean. Sooner or later—indeed, sooner rather than later—everything gets tainted, just from being here.

She has the route memorized: down to the end of the street and left, past the shops, across the street and right, past the church, past two more streets, to Howard Row, to number sixteen, where she is to ask for the master and to accept whatever refreshment is offered, down in the warmth of the kitchen.

Here is the church now. A shut-up-looking place, with its wooden doors facing onto the street. It doesn't do to be thinking about God at a time like this, she tells herself. She got set on the wrong path with that forged letter, and now look what has come of her, holding that young widow in her arms, her breath warm on her neck, urging her, "Tell me, ma'am. Tell me how it is you're so on your own." Then—barely an hour later—laying out everything she heard to Mrs. Robert: the widow is not really a lady, or at least only the very lowest kind. The orphan of missionaries in some small town in India, left on her own when they died of cholera, no one to care for her, so she became the paid companion of a spiteful old woman. She fetched and carried, she wrote the woman's letters, she managed the servants, she bathed the woman's wretched dog, she ate her meals between the blank walls of her room whenever there were guests. And every day she felt hope for her own life draining away.

She passes a street—Newham. A gentleman swears at her as she hurries in front of him. She thinks of how the gong for breakfast had sounded, and how the widow had turned to her. Her eyes looked small and afraid, and her hair clung to her face, limp as seaweed. "You won't tell, will you?" she said. "Who knows what they'd think of me." So she'd said no, she wouldn't tell, and the sound of her voice comes back to her now, its slight hoarseness, its firmness, all meant to convince the widow. She kept her eyes on the widow's and again told her no, and this time she'd come close to meaning it. No wonder the widow had believed her. Yet what was that promise in the face of Mrs. Robert's insistence that surely—surely after all those mornings and evenings helping the widow—she had found out something? It wasn't the words that made her stare down at her hands, it was the tone, so light, as though none of this was of much importance. Of no more importance than her own fate. If she was dismissed, she thought, it would be done like this—Mrs. Robert standing on the carpet by the fire, smiling, tilting her head just so, as though this were all a joke. So while the silence *tick-tick-ticked* between them she'd stared stupidly at her hands. "Well?" Mrs. Robert had said. "Don't you have anything to say?"

Was it wrong, what she'd done? She felt it was. Like a splinter under the skin, it bothered her. Though wasn't her first duty to Mrs. Robert and the household?

She has been walking so fast that now she has to make herself stop, look about her, notice that she has gone too far and turn around, knocking into someone—a large woman in bombazine. These days it seems everyone is in mourning.

The house, when she reaches it, is finer than any other she's yet seen in London, not that she's seen much. The steps climb from the street in a long, whitened rise, as though this is not a home but a temple. She works her way along the railings, down the steps, and across the area to the kitchen door, where she knocks.

A slightly fetid smell hangs on the air here, despite the cold. In a moment the door opens and a bedraggled maid in a wet apron says, "What d'ya want? No situations here."

She has to persuade her that she has a letter for the master, and when the maid's damp hand reaches for it she explains, it is for the *master,* and her mistress has told her it can only be given to him.

"Then you'll have to wait," she snaps.

At first she thinks she'll have to wait outside in the shadowy cold of the area, but the maid moves to the side and jerks her head to tell her to come in. The kitchen is bigger than the Bentleys', and brighter, too, though mostly because it has been painted more recently. At the table stands a small woman with a pale egg of a face and a cap on top of curly black hair. She looks up from the pile of onions she is slicing, knife poised, eyebrows raised. "What's this?" she says.

The maid bumps the door closed with her hip. "Maid with a message for the master. Has to put it in *his* hands, doesn't she?"

"Oh." The cook puts down the knife and wipes her hands on her apron. "The master trusts us," she says to Jane. "Isn't that good enough for you?"

"It's my mistress," she says. "I'm just doing it how she told me."

The cook leans onto the table. Her hands, Jane notices, are small, but her fingers are as thick and wrinkled as carrots. As for her pale eyes, they have a curious vacancy, like a cat's. Nevertheless, they watch Jane as she stands there, in her old hat and scarf, her coat that is not warm enough, her bare hands that have turned red from the cold. "Very well," she says. "Sit down, then. Fanny will fetch you a cup of tea when she has a minute."

So she sits and waits. She doesn't even unbutton her coat. Instead she perches on the edge of her chair, looking as though at any moment she expects to be turned out of this house to brave the winter day outside. The minutes pass. The cook drops the onions into a large pot and sets to work on a large cut of beef, salting and peppering it, dotting its sleek sides with butter. From the scullery two maids appear in rolled-up sleeves and grimy aprons. Fanny pours tea for them all from a large, stained teapot. She doles out milk, and sugar, and doesn't look at Jane when she pushes a cup towards her.

The tea is strong and barely sweet at all. Its sourness clings to her tongue. She blows on it though it isn't hot, just for something to do rather than look at the women around her. They're talking—about a butcher's boy who's been caught thieving, and his sweetheart who lives next door, poor thing, and whose mistress won't let her out of the house now, not even on her half day off.

When footsteps come thudding down the stairs they disperse like startled rabbits—the scullery maids back to their work out of sight, the cook to the stove. The door swings open. It is a butler with a shock of unruly yellow hair and a jacket a little too tight across the shoulders, his shoes loud across the floor. Strange, that, thinks Jane—a heavy-footed butler. He tugs off his jacket and sits at the end of the table. With his eyes on Jane he says, "What's this, then?"

She opens her mouth, but it is the cook who answers. "Delivering a message from her mistress. Has to wait to give it to the master herself."

"Does she now?" He taps his fingers on the edge of the table. "Well, how about that. Most of the master's acquaintances use Her Majesty's postal service if they are unable to call in person. Is your mistress familiar with the postal service?"

Is an explanation required of her? Jane isn't sure. What kind of servant would talk about Mrs. Robert like this? And what kind of a servant is she to sit here without a word in her mistress's defense? But what can she say when she isn't even sure why she has to deliver the message to the master himself? Is it simply to give her a reason to sit here and do as Mrs. Robert told her—to drink what she is given, to make herself *useful* by being free on her half day if she is asked? Who is to ask her, though? Certainly not this butler.

What is left of her tea has turned cold and she has not been offered more, though Fanny has poured a cup for the butler. He sips it loudly and watches Jane from over the rim. "Who," he says finally, "is your mistress?"

"Mrs. Robert Bentley, sir."

"Mrs. Robert Bentley? Who is this Mrs. Robert Bentley?"

"She's lately from France, sir."

"Ah, a French lady."

"No, sir. She's an English lady."

"Ah." He sets down his cup. "Indeed."

Somehow he implies that this is not quite as it should be—the thrusting out of his lips, the widening of his eyes. A moment later those eyes of his shift from Jane to the door, and it is lucky for her that they do, for there, hair slicked back, his jacket sharply pressed, stands Teddy. He catches sight of her and seems to falter. Then he collects himself and says, "Mr. Jarman—do you have a visitor?"

"A young person with a message for the master." He lifts his eyebrows as though there is something implausible about this story.

"Ah." Teddy comes forward, eyes hard on Jane's. "Very good. You won't have long to wait, miss. Mr. Popham is due back shortly, then I'll take you up to him." He gives a curt nod, then looks about him as if unsure what comes next.

Jane grips the edge of the table, says softly, "Thank you."

After he has taken off back upstairs she picks up the cold cup. Although it chills her hands, she lifts it to her lips and hides her smile in it. What luck, she thinks, what incredible luck. Mrs. Robert's order can be filled more pleasantly than she ever expected: she and Teddy can have an afternoon to themselves.

But even before she has put the cup back down her smile has fled. It cannot just be luck. The chances are too remote. No, she tells herself, there is something else going on here. She pushes the cup away. Is it her imagination, or can she feel the coldness of unfriendly eyes on her? She glances around. The butler is watching the cook, the cook is busy at the stove, and the maid is nowhere in sight. Still, as she waits for Teddy to come back, she cannot rid herself of the discomforting sensation that someone is spying on her.

CHAPTER 24

All afternoon he's been shut away making changes to his lecture—there has been no time to confront the widow, no time to think about it even, and now as he dresses he considers when it should be done. Will she flee while he is out tonight, giving his lecture? Has she sensed a shift in the atmosphere of the household? There could be something in their demeanor that has shifted, ever so slightly, but enough to alert her. A ladies' companion, passing herself off as a lady! As if his brother would marry such a person! Why on earth she confessed, to the maid of all people—what luck that the maid told Mina. But then, Mina has taken care to be kind to her.

Tomorrow, he decides. And they must take the widow by surprise. And then—then she will renounce all claim on Henry's property, and leave. How could she not?

There's a knock at the door—Cartwright with a salver, and a letter on it. A letter from Danforth. He takes it, gives Cartwright a cursory "Thank you," and puts the letter on the mantelpiece. His collar is too stiff and rubs against his throat, but it is too late now to change again. "Bloody thing," he mutters. In the mirror he looks absurd: collar and shirt, tie knotted under his chin, legs bare—scrawny pale things like a chicken's. He snatches up his trousers and sits on the bed to pull them on. He scrapes a hand through his hair fast before turning to the door. He hesitates—the letter. No time to read it now, but still, he crosses the room and folds it into his pocket. He'll have time for it later.

The Dark Lantern

It sits in his pocket in the darkness of the cab, in the bright, echoing hallway as Sir Jonathan's secretary escorts him to the lecture room. It must have shifted, for when he takes the chair that the secretary—Stallybrass—pushes forward for him, its corner digs into the soft flesh of his thigh. He presses a hand against it, listening as Sir Jonathan fumbles through his introduction, and to the soft pattering of applause that follows. Then he must stand at the lectern and read from his notes, glancing down at his audience, noticing the door swing open for a latecomer, resting his finger next to one point he feels he must come back to, but forgetting when a man in the front row loudly coughs into his hand.

Afterwards he answers questions, leaning forward as though that will help him through a tangled enquiry about measurement techniques, resting his hand on the letter every now and again through his trousers. His questioner nods—indeed many in the audience are nodding encouragingly—and he touches the letter again as he tells them that very soon, the benefits of anthropometry over dactylography will become dramatically evident. Of course they are intrigued, and he cannot help saying more—a dangerous criminal, an arrest imminent—then he lifts his hands and protests that he is in danger of jeopardizing the whole case and must stop there.

There is a press of people with more questions, and Stallybrass sniffing at his side and only belatedly rescuing him to lead him to where Sir Jonathan waits. Dinner at Sir Jonathan's club, a hansom back to Cursitor Road, and he might just as well have left the damned letter on the mantelpiece, because there is no opportunity to open it until he is back home. Thankfully, the widow is upstairs in her room, having excused herself with a headache.

The end of the evening is delicious in her absence. At least Mina knows better than to question him when he drops into his chair and rubs his brows. She asks Cartwright for a brandy for him, and sits quietly on the other side of the fire as he props his feet on the fender and lets his head sink back. It occurs to him that he and Mina have become an echo of his parents. Him in his father's chair, brooding; Mina with a book in her lap—not sewing as his mother would have, but silent and watchful nonetheless. He waits for the brandy, then allows himself a long sip before he sets down the glass and slides a finger under the edge of the envelope.

Having spent the evening in his pocket, the envelope is no longer crisp. The paper tears softly under his finger, and he pulls out the letter. He is so eager that he has to stop himself, force himself back to the start, read slowly enough to take in what Danforth has written. The damned man takes most of a page to get to the point. Indeed, he seems not to want to get to it at all, because the suspicious Vilaseca's ear length and head diameter are so different from those of the murderous Villanova that there is no chance they are the same man. Vilaseca is, apparently, merely a rich Argentinean.

"Robert?"

He looks up.

Mina has her shawl pulled tightly around her shoulders, her face pale above it. "Bad news, darling?"

He stares back at the letter and the dark sprawl of Danforth's handwriting. "Only the dashing of my hopes." He glances up and she seems to flinch away from his gaze. "Danforth," he explains quickly. "Danforth and his plans for glory. Now we're both to look like fools, thanks to him."

"He made a fool out of you?"

He folds the letter. "No. I believe I did that myself."

CHAPTER 25

It would not do to bring the matter up at dinner, when Cartwright and Sarah are in and out with trays and decanters every few minutes. Yet, Robert thinks, when else can they be assured that they will not be interrupted, their conversation not overheard, or any cries or shouts or frantic flights up the stairs not noticed? Leaving the house on a pretext when they are still in mourning would be unseemly, and so they have no choice but to seat themselves in the drawing room and to wait for Sarah to bring in the tea things, and for Mina to tell her, "That'll be all for now."

From the way Sarah raises her eyebrows ever so slightly, Robert suspects she will go no farther than the other side of the door. Even though he feels ridiculous, he waits a few moments after she's gone, then checks the hallway. Empty, but he catches the distant patter of footsteps going down to the kitchen.

The widow sits too stiffly to be at ease. She must, he thinks, know that something is afoot. He coughs and settles into the chair nearest the fire, and looks to Mina. She merely nods back as though, in her opinion, the time could not be better for him to begin.

"Victoria," he says, then coughs again. "Victoria, it has come to my attention—"

Her face swings towards him. "Yes?" she says quickly.

"Well." He pauses. He licks his lips and stares back at her, his words lost.

"What he means," says Mina, "is that we want to assure you that you are amongst friends." She sits forward a little, as though about to divulge a secret. "Please remember that. But in return we expect you to be our friend too."

The widow looks about her, then smiles uncertainly. "Haven't I been? If I have done something—"

"It is more a matter of what you haven't done. You haven't told us the whole truth, have you? About who you are."

It is remarkable, thinks Robert, that an accusation can sound so very charming. He glances at Mina, at her eyes so dark and welcoming, and the slight tilt to her head that somehow suggests that if there has been a deception, it can be cleared up with no unpleasantness.

The way the widow holds her hands together in her lap, you could be forgiven for thinking that her wrists were already manacled together, thinks Robert. Her mouth pulls tight, ready to ask *What?* or *Why?* But she seems unable to get out any word at all.

Mina turns her attention to the table between them, and to the teacups. She fusses with them, pouring milk and tea, spooning in sugar. Every few moments she looks up at the widow, and the silence of the room stretches wider. Then she lifts a saucer and the cup on it, and passes it to Victoria. "Why don't we begin with an account of your recent employment?" she says, and gives a little smile.

The widow appears unable to help herself—she takes the cup because it has been handed to her. It rattles unsettlingly. She tries to rest it on the black silk of her dress. It tilts and slops a little tea into the saucer, so she raises it—at an alarming angle—and sets it down on the arm of the chair. For a second it hangs there. Then the saucer slips, the cup overturns in the air, tumbling down to the hearth, where it shatters in a hiss of tea on hot coals.

Robert starts forward, though there is nothing he can do. He opens his mouth. He's ready to call for Sarah or Jane to clear up the mess. Mina, though, sits calmly stirring her tea. "And so?" she says. "Are you prepared to meet the kindness"—she glances at Robert, who nods—

The Dark Lantern

"the kindness that you must admit you have been shown here, by clearing up the matter of upon whom our kindness has been bestowed?"

The widow does not cover her face with her hands, or turn away. Her breathing is suddenly loud and wet, and when she blinks tears hurry down her face. "I meant no harm."

"But you are not exactly what you appear to be."

"What would you have thought of me? You, with your dresses from Paris, and ... and that *bearing* that so much is made of. I knew you'd look down on me." She snaps her mouth closed and swallows. "I can't help who I am. My parents didn't put stock in accomplishments. They wouldn't have sent me to school over here even if they could have afforded to. Do you understand? They left because they hated what England had become. They wanted to do God's work the way Our Lord would have done it. And they did—I believe they did."

"They were missionaries?"

The widow uses the back of her hand to wipe away a tear hanging from her chin. "We rarely saw anyone but Indians. We lived high in the hills. I wish I were still there—everything was better there!" She gulps and lets her eyes close.

"Where are they now?"

"With God," she whispers. "With God these last two years." She looks into the fire. "Cholera is a terrible disease. Dozens of people from the village—my parents, my sister. Even me. But I survived. They took me to a hospital, and after that, it was all over. They were dead. I couldn't go back on my own—what would I have done?"

Mina lifts one hand to shield her face from the heat of the fire. "So what did you do?"

"A lady took pity on me; she offered me a home, and in return I was to help her. I should have trusted in God—He provides if you let Him." She sighs. "It's like slavery, isn't it? You have no life of your own, no money because you can't pay a lady a real salary, no matter how far she has sunk. She even took away my name—she was called

229

Victoria too, so I became Cissy, from my middle name, Cecilia, which she thought *unsuited to my circumstances*."

"You were a paid companion, then?"

"Yes," she tells them sourly. "If you want to call it paid. And then when Henry came along—" She allows herself a brief smile. "You cannot imagine how that was, a man like him paying attention to me."

Robert props his elbows on his knees. This woman, he thinks, has been through so very much. Are they wronging her further? He watches Mina, hoping she'll look at him so that he can signal her to stop, but she pays him no attention. All this, he thinks, could end in humiliation, and he bites his teeth together as he thinks of Vilaseca. Danforth had seemed so sure. All those coincidences piling up until he couldn't see past them—there'd seemed no room for doubt.

His neck prickles. Maybe Danforth wanted to trick him, to encourage him to get involved in the case, to make a fool of himself and anthropometry. That can't be right, though—Danforth was the one to organize the demonstration, and who assured Renfrew that there was a compelling motive for it all. He's a clever man in a dogged way, but he's not cunning.

Once more, the question of who broke into the study nudges him. Perhaps it wasn't Danforth: the maid didn't recognize him. Could it have been someone connected to the widow? She's lied to them, maybe she's lying still. Maybe she's up to more than simply getting her hands on Henry's money.

Yet that, he thinks, is taking suspicion too far. Isn't it?

Across the hearth, Mina takes a sip of her tea. Her cup knocks ever so gently against the saucer. When she looks up it is with a slight smile. She sighs, says, "It's curious that there appears to be no record of your marriage."

The widow starts as though she has been stuck with a pin. Her face flushes a deep, uneven red. "How dare you," she lets out. "How dare you accuse me—"

"My dear, you appeared out of nowhere. Not a word about you from Henry. What should we have thought?" She lets her hand rest

against her chest. "Are we to believe that you married without bene-
fit of a clergyman or witnesses? Or without it being made a matter
of public record?"

The widow gets to her feet, her flushed face wild against the black
of her dress, her elbows clenched to her sides. "You can believe what
you'd like. The truth of the matter lies at the bottom of the sea,
doesn't it?" She stumbles against a small table, and its vase rattles
dangerously. For an instant she stares at it, then rushes across to the
door.

Robert gets up to close it behind her. He hears the drumming of
her feet across the landing, then up the stairs to the bedrooms, but
he doesn't catch the other footsteps, the ones that tread softly
downstairs to the kitchen.

*J*ane has brought up a bucket of coals and now she knocks.
"Ma'am?" she calls softly. "Will you let me in to make up the fire?"
No reply, but then she expected none.

After all, she has betrayed this woman.

Gently, she lays her hand on the doorknob and twists it, ever so
slowly. It is still locked. "Are you hungry, ma'am? Cook has made
pies today. Or can I bring you a cup of tea?" She waits, head inclined towards the door. Nothing. "I'll fetch some anyway, just in
case. Because you must be parched, ma'am."

So she goes down to the kitchen, and gets Elsie to put on water
for tea, though Mrs. Johnson says it's a bother at this time of the
day. Mrs. Johnson wants to know: Is the widow ill? Or is she in a
sulk over something? Jane shrugs and cuts a slice of ham pie.

She's back not more than a quarter of an hour later. The bucket of
coal is gone, a chamber pot modestly covered with a cloth of its
place. She sets down the tray, calls out, "Ma'am? Don't let the tea sit
too long or it'll stew." Her voice falls flat against the closed door.

She took such care to make the widow like her, and trust her, it is
hard to stop herself now. Is there comfort in tea and a slice of pie?

A small measure, perhaps, but as much as she can provide. If she could she would explain that she had no choice, because she has secrets of her own.

Instead she rests one hand against the wood of the door, as someone would who wants to calm a nervous horse. "I'm sorry," she whispers, then hurries away down the corridor.

CHAPTER 26

He has done his best to erase all suggestion that he may not be quite what he seems: he has had his hat reblocked, his gloves cleaned, though of course there is nothing like a new pair. Despite his efforts, the landlady looks at him with a face creased with suspicion. Is it the cut of his coat, which, he has to admit, is distinctly démodé? Or does something of prison life cling to him, like a bad odor that cannot be got rid of?

"Well, Mr. Fleet," she says, hands on her hips and her flaccid face a little red, "I don't usually take gentlemen"—in her mouth the word sounds like something spoiled—"without their being recommended."

He pulls himself up as straight as he can and gives her what he hopes is an avuncular smile. "My dear Mrs. Jasper, of course not. But as I think you will understand, since I have lived abroad for so long, it is difficult to furnish the sort of reassurances you require."

"I have to be careful, as I'm sure *you* understand. I wouldn't want anyone of a questionable character to lodge here." She sets her pale blue eyes on his, and he raises his eyebrows.

"Oh, indeed," he says, and looks around the bleak room with its bed crammed in next to a chest of drawers, and a murky window right above it that threatens to let in draughts. Could Steiner really find him nothing better? "I can appreciate that you would only want the best sort of gentleman here." He reaches into his pocket and pulls out a purse. "Would three months' rent in advance convince you of my character?" He smiles broadly, but not too broadly—he doesn't want a note of sarcasm to ruin everything.

"Plus payment in advance for your dinners? That will be acceptable." She has the nerve to hold out her hand right then and there.

He counts the coins into it with a lightness that almost convinces him that there are plenty more where they came from. Of course that's not possible, not after the expense of finding her—who would have imagined that after he was locked up, she'd have thought to show such initiative as to cheat *him*? She has led him a merry dance—he pictures her swinging her hips and glancing at him over her shoulder, keeping herself just out of reach. Not that she ever did such a thing; she's not the type. No, she is a serious woman and always was. Serious about robbing him too. Everything from their life together sold off as though he had died and left her to survive as best she could. And now it turns out, the strongbox—empty. He didn't think she even knew it existed, let alone where he'd hidden it away.

At last he has her now—or almost. Her house is only a short walk from here. Will he knock at the door and ask for her? The thought of it makes him smile. But that is not his way. It never was.

Mrs. Jasper's hand snaps shut on the coins. "Dinner at six sharp," she says. With that she's off, leaving him in possession of the dingy room with its weary wallpaper curling from the walls.

He goes to the window. With a few good shoves he opens it. Across the street are more houses like this one, houses trying to keep up an appearance of modest gentility. It is not these houses that interest him, though. He stands in the cold wind coming through the window and cranes his neck. A little down the hill a ridge of higher roofs stands out: Cursitor Road.

CHAPTER 27

These days when Jane comes out of Price's room it is all in a rush. She hasn't got used to it, that heavy smell of soiled linen and an unwashed body, of staleness and despair. Because that's what it is—Price has given up. On her own life, on the world at large. So she lies in the only place she can lay any claim to, drinking little, eating less, though Jane has taken the trouble to spoon broth between her cracked lips. No wonder the doctor won't let her be moved—have the Bentleys tried? Jane isn't sure. She overheard the doctor prescribe a tonic, but he added that Price would need rest until her strength is regained and her spirits restored.

As though there is any hope that Price's spirits can be restored.

It has occurred to her that Price's fate is that of any servant who outlives her usefulness. You devote yourself to your employer, you let your own life slip away, and one day you find yourself too old or sick or outmoded to be of use. Do your employers care for you? Do they tend to you as you have tended to them? No, of course they don't. They say there's not enough money, or not enough space—meaning none they want to spare. They would rather have you gone, even if it means the workhouse—or worse.

Jane's own room is painfully bright after the dimness of Price's room. It's cold, too, and as she changes into her best dress she shivers hard. Halfway through the day and there is still no warmth to it; frost lies thick on the window, and what sunshine comes through it has a brittle look. Down in the street Teddy will be waiting. The thought of him used to be a knot of warmth nestled deep inside her, but not now. Not since she saw him at Mr. Popham's and wondered: How could she be this lucky? Instead the idea of him has settled around her like a snake, coiled up, cold. Dangerous.

From the ewer she pours what little is left of the water and splashes it onto her face. At least the soot comes off with a little soap and a little rubbing, leaving her cheeks with a glow. As for her hands, there is not much help for them. They are red, the skin dry and rough, and on her right hand two scorch marks glisten wetly. A hot grate, and her not paying attention because her thoughts have been full of Teddy: how he leant towards her going up the stairs to see Mr. Popham, how he let the end of his nose brush her cheek, how he waited for her afterwards and eased her into a dark corner so he could land a warm kiss on her lips, then her neck, then behind her ear. "Teddy," she'd scolded, and laughed nervously. Not because he'd locked her in his arms, nor because they might be come upon at any moment. No, it was because she'd caught a glimpse of something in his face, a way of looking at her as a fox does a hen.

She knows she'll be cold outside. No gloves, only her old coat and scarf to protect her against the worst of the winter. Maybe they'll go somewhere warm—he knows London, he'll have somewhere picked out. So she makes sure her hat is on straight and hurries down the stairs, her hand on the banister, her feet a little too loud on the bare stairs. In the kitchen, Mrs. Johnson looks up from her pastry. "You'd better not be back late," she says. "You'll catch it if you are."

"She's got herself a young man," says Sarah. "Look how eager she is to get out, even though it's freezing today." Sarah gives her a tight smile. "Maybe if I make an effort, Mrs. Robert will give me an extra half day too. What do you think, Mrs. J.?"

"I wouldn't hold your breath."

Jane's head is down, and she fusses with a thread hanging from the cuff of her coat, as though they won't notice the blood rushing to her face. She should have known they'd be lying in wait for her. Now the first thing Teddy will see is her face burning. Will he wonder why, and distrust her just as she's started to distrust him?

"I'll be back on time," she tells Mrs. Johnson, and with that she makes for the door, though she hears a laugh—Sarah's? She thinks so. It's hard to imagine Mrs. Johnson laughing at anything.

He's there, back against the railings a couple of doors away, just far enough to look as though he isn't waiting for anyone from number thirty-two. Just to be safe.

He looks up and catches sight of her. He smiles. "Well, well, well, you must have shifted yourself to get out right on time like that."

She smiles too, then looks away quickly.

He steps closer, so close that she's standing in the mist of his breath. "Are you all right? What's up?"

"Nothing. Just tired out, is all. And feeling a bit down in the dumps."

"We all get that way," he says, and holds out his elbow so she can lock her arm through his. They take off down the street, like any lady and gentleman, she thinks. Like any girl and her sweetheart. Except her arm is pinned beneath his, and she's being steered along as though she's to have no hand in her fate.

This afternoon the city is dismal, passersby bowed against the stinging wind, cabdrivers wrapped in greatcoats, a costermonger with his thin jacket buttoned up tight, huffing as he pushes his barrow. A city of strangers and strange streets. And this man she's with—Teddy—what does she know of him? Not much, except that he comes from Devon, that he's Mr. Popham's valet, that he's eager to take her out. He picked her, didn't he? He picked her out from all the girls he must run into on the street.

The wind buffets past, and she presses her hat to her head. Maybe that wasn't an accident. Maybe he wants something from her, something more than to kiss her and push his body hard against hers in the few moments they can be alone.

She bends her head as though against the wind. A sob has pushed its way up her chest. When she opens her mouth and it escapes, the coldness of the wind rushes in. It finds a tooth, seems to work its way right inside it. She feels a shock of pain, and she lets out a small cry and covers her mouth.

Teddy stops. "What's wrong?" He bends his head towards hers.

"This tooth. It can't stand the cold. I never noticed it before. But then—" she lets herself lean into him so he can't see her face "—it was never cold like this in Teignton. Not like this."

"No, not nasty like this. This cold slices right into you. We'd better get in the warm somewhere. How about that?"

"As long as it's somewhere respectable."

"I'm a respectable man, I am," he says. He squeezes her arm a little too tightly. "You wouldn't catch the likes of me taking advantage of young maids. I wouldn't be caught kissing one of them on the stairs."

She makes herself laugh, though the wind sends a shiver of pain through her tooth. "People will hear," she hisses.

"Who?" He stops and looks around. He's right. Anyone who didn't have to venture out must have stayed home today, and the few who are on the streets are scurrying along with their heads dipped against the wind.

So they walk, a little faster than she would like, down the street, across to a road she doesn't know, and she hopes that wherever they're going it's somewhere close. In the cold his face looks harder, the angle of his chin more severe than she remembered.

"Couldn't hardly believe it when you said you could get the afternoon off," he says, then he looks at her.

"I'm in for it back at the house. It's put Mrs. Johnson's and Sarah's noses out of joint."

"So why'd your mistress do it? Out of the goodness of her heart?"

She's hurrying to keep up with him. Her heels hammer against the paving stones, and she listens to the empty sound of them. She wonders what she should say. She could tell him her mistress thought she deserved it from all the extra work she'd had—but what mistress ever paid attention to something like that? Still, she has no other explanation ready.

She blurts out, "I've been run off my feet fetching for the widow;

she's locked herself into her room and won't let me in. And I've got Price to care for, because she's taken to her bed."

Beside her he slows and swings her around him until they're face-to-face. "Come on," he says. "They don't give you an afternoon off because you've been working so hard." He hooks a finger under her chin. The leather of his glove feels cold. For a moment they stand like that, and her heart leaps uncomfortably against her ribs.

In the shadow of his hat his eyes move like fish underwater, crossing her face, quick. She lets her gaze slip from his eyes to his nose, his lips. She remembers their warmth and their surprising softness. She remembers how he kissed her gently, not greedily. His eyes are still on her face, and she wonders now if it's hardness she's seeing in them, or disappointment.

There's snow in the air, sharp flakes blowing against her cheeks.

"I'm sorry," she says.

"Sorry?" He lifts his eyebrows and rubs his thumb against her chin. "What on earth are you sorry for?"

"She's up to something. Mrs. Robert, I mean."

"I don't—"

"I'm supposed to tell her whatever I hear about Mr. Popham's household. That's why she wanted me to wait when I brought the letter, that's why I got an extra half day—I have to tell her whatever I hear from you."

She turns her head away because this must mean the end of things for them. As for Mrs. Robert, what will she tell her? Anything—anything at all, for what does that matter now?

He laughs. When she looks back she sees his head tipped back and his eyes narrow in delight. "Oh my Lord," he says, tucking her arm back under his. He's still laughing as he leads her along the street once more. "So you were supposed to let yourself be taken out by John the footman, or Jarman the butler? Was that the plan?"

The pain in her tooth pulses like an ember being blown on. She stares down at the paving stones. Specks of fresh snow are caught between them. "Except I wouldn't have. I'd have told her no one asked. Then I saw you, and I thought it was such luck—"

"So you were going to ask me all about Mr. Popham?"

"No, no. It was just a chance to see you." She runs her tongue over the tooth, feels the warmth of it against her gum.

They're close to the river now, and when she glances up she sees the balustrade along it, and the end of the bridge. Where tears have leaked onto her face her skin is icy.

There's a road to cross, and more traffic here. Hansom cabs, an omnibus, a cart carrying coal, a gentleman on a tall, delicate-legged bay horse.

Teddy turns to her. "What's she up to, then?"

"I don't know." She doesn't look at him but into the road, at the backside of the horse as it walks away.

"You must have some idea." He touches her face, rubbing away what's left of the tears. He's taken off his glove to do it, and his finger is warm. "What have you got yourself caught up in, Jane?" He says it so softly that the wind nearly pulls away the words before she catches them.

She shakes her head, then leans her face into his hand.

Of course they had to invent details. Over cups of tea and buns they laughed into their hands. Soon her tooth stopped hurting, and the cold wind and snow just beyond the window were forgotten. Teddy said she could tell her mistress that his master drinks too much port, and has a liking for quail eggs, and is scared of his old mother. She giggled, and let him rest his hand on hers. But now that she's standing on the hearth rug and Mrs. Robert is looking at her with her face all closed up in annoyance, Jane wishes she'd got something more from him.

"That's all you found out?"

She sniffs. Being out in that wind has given her the start of a cold, she's sure. "I don't know what you want, ma'am. I let him talk and tried to remember it all."

"Who comes to his house? Who are his associates? What are his bad habits?"

"I tried, ma'am. But I didn't want him to get suspicious."

With a snort Mrs. Robert turns away. "I'm sure you succeeded on that score, at least."

A few streets away a valet is standing by his master's chair. His master is in a freshly ironed shirt, for he's going out tonight.

"What sort of odd qualities?" he asks his valet.

"Apparently she is able to spot a forged letter from the ink."

His master slaps his leg. "Ha," he lets out. "Is that so? That's extraordinary."

"There's more, sir. She's so suspicious of her brother-in-law's widow that she's got this maid to spy on her."

"What's that?"

"From what I understand, sir, she is not convinced that the young lady is who she says she is, and other evidence is lacking. Of course, unless she is exposed she will inherit Mr. Henry Bentley's estate and collect his life insurance."

"An impostor? Extraordinary!" He chews at his moustache. "Well, well," he says, "you've done very well."

"Thank you, sir. She's a clever woman, by the sound of it—clever enough to ask that maid to spy on you."

His head jerks up at that. "Good Lord, do you think she suspects?"

"No, no, sir. But the coincidence is extraordinary."

He stretches out his legs and smiles at himself in the mirror. "Well, I think we shall have to oblige her with a little information, shan't we, Edward?"

CHAPTER 28

This morning Mina starts at every knock at the door. Surely it is a messenger with a note from Popham, agreeing to what she suggested. She will pay him back, every penny he was swindled out of. Isn't that reasonable? Of course, it cannot be all at once. She does not have such a sum saved; she will have to find it, here and there. Every month she will give him what she can. She does not ask for understanding, only for his patience.

Will it work? She's not sure. He may not want to be reasonable. She landed a blow to his heart, but also to where he was most vulnerable—to his pride. His mother wanted him to marry well, yet he chose her, a young thing with money and a certain kind of beauty, but with a family history that was—didn't he notice?—suspiciously curtailed. He'd had to argue, to convince the old lady that she wouldn't bring shame on their family, that this was a good match.

He didn't suspect a thing until too late, and then he was left with no fiancée, and nothing to show for the investments his fiancée's father had encouraged him to make. If he hadn't been so greedy he wouldn't have bought so many shares, and if he hadn't been so keen to boast he wouldn't have persuaded his cousin and friends into parting with their money too. So wasn't his undoing of his own making? Wasn't he a fool to want to believe that a silver-rich mine so many thousands of miles away existed? Wasn't he a fool to think he could have a woman like her?

The Dark Lantern

Mina looks at herself in the dressing-table mirror. Dark eyes that catch the black of her dress, a pointed chin, delicate cheeks, over her forehead hair in curls that catch the light. Not a doll's face—she never had that. A face that can be charming all the same, at least when she smiles. And when she doesn't? She leans forward now with a frown. When she doesn't, she looks like a woman who thinks too much for most men's liking.

His kisses were soft in an unpleasant way; they made her think of blind, underground creatures feeling their way with their formless bodies and their awful wetness. When he pushed his lips onto hers it felt as though part of him was seeping into her, dirtying her, and each evening when he left she'd rush upstairs and rinse out her mouth and wash her face and ears and neck, everywhere he'd left his traces.

It doesn't do to dwell on all of that. She stands and brushes her hands down her dress to smooth it, then crosses to the door. Her face is blank, her chin slightly raised, ready to meet whoever might be in the corridor—one of the servants; perhaps even the widow. Since she and Robert confronted her, the widow has been shut up in her room—in Henry's room. Trays of food have been left at her door. She is indisposed, Mina has explained to the servants, but she is certain they do not believe her. After all, it is evident that the widow has not taken to her bed. Her footsteps can be heard crossing and recrossing the floor, and once or twice the sound of crying has crept into the corridor.

Mina steps out of the bedroom. No one in sight, no sound. The floorboards creak as she makes her way along the carpet to the widow's door. She doesn't press her ear to it, simply stands and waits for what she might hear. This morning there is nothing. Has the widow gone? Now that she has been found out, has she fled before Henry's money could be hers? Does she know that Robert has gone to Scotland Yard this morning, and that she will no longer be able to hide?

Mina leans her head a little nearer the door.

A creak, as though the widow is on the other side, also listening.

‡ ‡ ‡

You have to develop a certain gait to carry a tray up stairs without tripping on the hem of your skirt. Lift your knee, kick your foot out and lift yourself up, over and over. One of these days, thinks Jane, she is going to fall. She has imagined it so many times that it has come close to taking on the solidity of a memory: her foot catches, she feels the tug of fabric as she tries to step forward, but with a tray in both hands—a heavy tray, loaded with a teapot and extra hot water—she cannot reach out to save herself. She falls forward as the tray tilts and the crockery slides onto the stairs. It shatters, and she lands on the sharp edge of a stair amongst shards of porcelain shiny in the spilt water.

Does she dream of such accidents? Maybe, because often as she falls asleep her foot kicks out and her arms flail, waking her. Certainly she has seen such accidents. In the orphanage a tall scarecrow of a girl tripped one day and fell on her face. She broke three teeth, all of them in the front. There was another who was working in the laundry and slipped on the wet floor and landed with her head against the copper. Jane heard it—that thud that meant the end for that girl, because she was never quite right afterwards; could barely even say her own name.

This corridor is brighter than the one outside the servants' rooms, but still it is gloomy with the doors closed. She knows her way without looking, and as soon as she has tapped on the door she bends to set the tray on the floor. No chamber pot waiting today, no empty coal scuttle. She's still wondering what this means when the door swings open. Brightness floods over her and into the corridor. There stands the widow against the light, her hair pulled back, her eyes blinking fast, looking for all the world like a fledgling on the brink of taking off into the world.

Jane straightens up. "Ma'am?"

"My dress," she says. She turns her back, because of course it is not fastened.

"Yes, ma'am." She carries the tray into the room.

The Dark Lantern

Outside a weak sun is shining through low clouds. Even this light is shockingly bright. It turns brilliant the roses woven into the carpet, the green cover of the neatly made bed, the underclothes folded on top of two black dresses.

The widow has thrown high the sashes of both windows. It is cold in here, a brisk cold alive with the smell of smoke from outside. Jane sets down the tray on the dressing table, then she fiddles with the cup, the bowl of sugar, the plate of eggs and bacon, because more than anything she wants to take in this sense of life going on outside. The hollow clop of horses' feet, the rumble of wheels, the echoing shout of a man selling pies. She leans towards the window. Out there the world looks fresh. Windows glinting, the walls of the houses opposite as white as laundered sheets and, down below, the outlines of people and horses as sharp as though they've been cut out with scissors.

The widow is still waiting. In the long gap of her open dress, the light catches the paleness of her underwear, her skin. Jane pulls the sides together and fastens them. She wonders—has the widow been in her corset since she shut herself away? How else did she get herself into it? But this lady seems to have more cunning than she'd ever have guessed. She has lied to the Bentleys—is lying still, no doubt. Now that she is so close to making off with whatever money Mr. Henry left, she knows the Bentleys no longer trust her. Who'd have thought that a pale young thing like her could be capable of so much?

Jane says, "Are you feeling better now, ma'am?"

"Better?" She turns away from her reflection in the mirror and looks at Jane. "Oh, yes," she says, "I am feeling much better."

"Well, I am pleased to hear that, ma'am." She gives a tiny smile, then looks around her—anywhere but into the widow's face, because there is something there she doesn't like. A quickness to her now that wasn't there before, and a tightness to her jaw that makes her look capable of desperate acts.

"In fact, I feel well enough to leave here. But I will have to rely on you." She steps towards Jane and lays one of her cold hands on her wrist. "You're still my friend, aren't you? You'll help me, won't you?"

Her voice has fallen to scarcely more than a whisper. "I can't stay here. The Bentleys can't believe Henry would have chosen a wife like me. I'm not good enough for them." Her face flickers. "Do you know what it's like to have no friend, and nowhere to turn? But even that is better than staying here."

Although Jane wants to pull her hand away, she knows she mustn't. "I'm sorry, ma'am."

"This—" the widow points to the bed—"is all I have. I'll need a small trunk for it."

"A trunk?"

"Mine's at the bottom of the sea."

"Yes, ma'am." Jane looks at the clothes on the bed. They will not fill a trunk. "Excuse me for saying so, ma'am, but what do you need a trunk for?"

"For respectability's sake." The widow gives her wrist a slight squeeze. "You can't travel without luggage. People will suspect you. I've learnt that much about the world."

"Where will you go?"

She lets go of Jane's wrist. "As far from here as I can."

Of course the widow doesn't trust her. She must know Jane was the one who told the secret of her past to the Bentleys. Who else does she have to help her, though?

Jane says she knows there are trunks in the lumber room upstairs, and that most likely it is either unlocked or the key is hanging up in the kitchen.

Along the corridor and up the back stairs she goes, up to the top floor. She has no reason to be up here at this time of the day, unless she is looking in on Price, so she makes her way to Price's door. Inside the dim room the air is stale. A small fire is glowing in the grate—a fire she lit a couple of hours ago. Now it has burnt down to its embers. As for the tray she left on a chair by Price's bed, it looks untouched. The broth has a greasy, cold look, and the dripping has sunk into the bread. "Mrs. Price," she calls, but Price doesn't move.

She bends over her. All of the color has disappeared from Price's face so that the darkness of her hair stands out unnaturally. Her breathing is slow, but loud enough for Jane to hear it without leaning closer.

She sits on the edge of the bed. At the end of the corridor the lumber room waits, and with it the widow's hope for escape. She could easily bring down a trunk. She could help the widow lay her clothes in it; she could even carry it down the stairs to the hallway for her. But they would be discovered before the widow could be carried off in a hansom. Besides, she can't be Mr. Henry's widow if there was no marriage, and there cannot have been a marriage if there is no proof of one—that much Jane has overheard through the drawing room door. So the widow deserves what she gets for pretending to be what she is not, for trying to profit from Mr. Henry's death.

Even as she tells herself this she feels doubt seeping in around her heart. The woman hardly looks like a criminal. And hasn't Jane heard her crying in her room, great wrenching sobs that must have come from deep inside her?

She hears footsteps in the corridor, and she starts to her feet. With both hands she smoothes the covers, hiding any sign that she has been sitting.

Mrs. Robert is standing in the doorway. "Jane—what are you doing here?"

"Looking in on Mrs. Price, ma'am. I thought perhaps her fire was burning low." She nods to the hearth.

Mrs. Robert's skirts rustle as she closes the door. She looks over at Price. "How is she today?"

"Much the same, ma'am."

"Has she eaten?"

"I don't think so, ma'am. I brought her up a tray, but she hasn't touched any of it."

"At this rate she'll soon be following her mistress into the grave."

"Let's hope not, ma'am."

Mrs. Robert looks about her, then gestures to the fire. "Hurry up with that. I don't know what you've been about this morning to be so behind."

The coal scuttle is half full. Jane crouches beside it and picks out lumps to feed to the fire. "Mrs. Victoria Bentley asked me to help her get dressed," she says.

"Did she indeed? Then it's possible she's thinking of leaving us."

"Yes, ma'am."

"Is she, Jane? Is she making plans?"

She keeps her face turned to the fire. She blows on the embers and they pulse with heat like something alive. "Yes, ma'am."

"I see."

Jane hears her moving about the room, those skirts of hers rustling. The tongs clang as she hangs them back up with the poker and the brush, then she rubs her hands to get rid of the coal dust.

Mrs. Robert comes close. "For the moment, oblige her. Do you understand? Help her with whatever she wants. But tell me the moment she tries to leave the house."

"Yes, ma'am."

*M*ina can't bear the feeling of Price's skin lingering on hers, or the rough texture of her unwashed hair. She stands at the basin rubbing soap over her fingers and across her palms, finding every crevice, then she plunges them into the water. Price barely opened her eyes at the sight of the jewelry, though Mina told her, "Look what your mistress left you. There's fifty pounds too. You can't say she didn't provide for you. Come on now, sit up. Sit up, Price." Instead Price let her eyes close and turned away, as though whatever her mistress had left her was not enough.

Cartwright knocks on the door, then enters, carrying a salver and a single letter on it. "For you, ma'am." He holds it towards her though her hands are wet. She takes a towel from the stand and carefully dries them, never mind that Cartwright is standing there, not watching but waiting certainly, his face expressionless, his thoughts apparently far away. She has often wondered what he thinks about while he stands at attention, as is so often required of him.

The moment she catches sight of the writing, she knows the letter is from Popham. She takes it and keeps her voice steady. "Thank you, Cartwright."

"Ma'am?" he says. "Excuse me for intruding, but I have noticed our second housemaid in the lumber room. She says she has your authority. Is that indeed the case, or has there been a misunderstanding?"

She holds the letter against her chest, as though she might drop it. "In the lumber room, Cartwright?"

"Yes, ma'am. Apparently Mrs. Victoria Bentley requested a trunk."

"She has my permission. Thank you, Cartwright."

The door closes behind him, and she carries the letter over to the dressing table. With one finger she rips open the envelope and reads: *You cannot expect me, my dear lady, to think of our past merely in financial terms, and your behavior was such that I laid myself open to humiliation in the eyes of my family and friends.* She reads to the bottom of the page, and the blood rushes to her face. *You are no longer my luscious rosebud. The bloom has gone off you a little, has it not? However, I am prepared to overlook such deterioration. I will send a hansom for you on Thursday evening at seven o'clock. You may give your husband whatever excuses you think necessary. Naturally, if you are unable to be free at that time, I will be happy to explain to him the exact nature of our acquaintance, and provide unassailable proof.*

She has two days. She tears up the letter and drops it into the grate.

*T*he trunk is bulkier than Jane expected, and lifting it by one handle is awkward. She could ask Sarah for help, or even Elsie, but that would mean going all the way down to the kitchen. It is the smallest of the trunks—surely she can manage it. So she tries again and kicks the door wider as she comes close. She misjudges and staggers, falling against the doorframe. The trunk slips through her arms and hits the floor. There is sure to be someone coming to investigate again—already Cartwright has poked his head around the door and told her that he is sure she can have no business in here.

She should hurry. She turns the trunk back the right way up. Its lid hangs open, and something flaps loose. Has she broken it? She peers inside, and with one hand feels around. The bottom lining of the trunk has come unstuck, and she tries to press it back again. It won't lie flat, so she tips the trunk towards the light. Underneath she sees a flat packet of some kind. She gets to her feet and stands listening in the doorway. No one is coming. Slowly she pushes the door closed on its dry hinges, so slowly that its squeals barely reach her ears. It doesn't take much to pull the packet free. Papers by the look of it, tied up with string. She carries the packet past the boxes, past the furniture draped in dust sheets, over to the grimy window, and there she tugs on the knot.

CHAPTER 29

Apparently the matter is not one of great urgency, for it is three hours before Robert returns with a detective. For Mina it has been three hours of sitting, of remembering the way the shreds of Popham's letter curled as they burnt. Of listening for sounds from the hallway. The widow is clever—but is she clever enough to buy Jane's loyalty? To somehow escape from the house undetected? Mina pictured herself standing in the hallway with her arms outstretched, blocking her path; she imagined herself hurrying into the street just in time to see the widow disappear into a cab that took off with a clatter of wheels. She let herself taste how it would be to take off in that cab, to rush away from this house, and the widow, and Popham. But try as she might, she could not come up with a way to have Robert beside her. So she sat, waiting, listening, until she heard Robert return from the police station.

Now Dixon the detective is here, though he isn't much to look at. That was her first impression: a shrunken man with a habit of sniffing that pulls his face all to one side, and a coat that looks in need of a good cleaning. He has come, he says, merely "to make enquiries," and he perches on the edge of the sofa with his notebook and his stub of a pencil, though Robert isn't yet down with the widow. He refuses the tea Mina offers to ring for and looks about him as though this room contains clues he should take note of.

She wonders if she should make conversation, but what does one talk about with a detective? So instead she watches as he peers about, eyes flitting from the landscape on the wall, to the novel she was holding when he was shown in, to the bust of the queen on a high shelf. The silence is measured out by the clock on the mantelpiece. How long could it take for Robert to walk upstairs and knock at the widow's door? Under the hem of her dress, one foot starts tapping. Dixon sniffs, a great rippling sniff that makes one eye wink and the end of his moustache lurch upwards. He looks like the sort of man who eats bacon sandwiches and drinks tea by the mugful in cheap shops. Probably he lives in a boardinghouse, or if he's married it's to a bossy woman who commands their house in the suburbs with its cramped square of garden and its sullen maid-of-all-work. There's something small and dingy about it all, just as there is about the man himself. If you spend your life rooting around in the wrongdoing of others, well, some of it will rub off on you, won't it?

Now he's looking at her, and she smiles, though those eyes of his track unabashedly over her face, her hair, her black dress, as though she's merely part of the furnishings and he must get his bearings. Then they rise back to her eyes, not once but twice. It's unnerving, the way his eyes meet hers while seeming to focus on something beyond them. She holds his gaze, but wonders—is that a sign of guilt? The ability to stare back at a detective? When he does look away— Robert is coming through the doorway—she lets out a silent sigh of relief.

"She will not come down," Robert announces. His cheeks are flushed, his shoulders held stiffly.

"Perhaps, then," says Dixon, "I should go up. The lady may find it more difficult to refuse when she's faced by the Law."

It takes Mina a moment to realize he is referring to himself. The Law, apparently, is this man in a worn coat.

"Very good," says Robert, and steps aside.

The two of them head up the stairs. She hears the creaking of the boards under their feet, then knocking and voices. Dixon, most likely, telling the widow that she now has to answer to the Law.

The Dark Lantern

Along the hallway comes a shadow. Mina leans forward. It's Jane, craning her head to catch every word of what is going on above her. Was she waiting for the widow? she wonders. Or is this mere curiosity?

It's difficult to walk quietly in the rustling skirts of a lady, and Jane hears Mina before she gets close. "Is it the police, ma'am?"

She meets Jane's eyes until Jane glances away, back up the stairs. "Yes, it is."

"Are they taking her away?"

Mina looks up the stairs, too, up to the landing, though there is nothing to see. "It hasn't come to that. Not yet at least."

They wait, listening. Soon the widow will be brought downstairs to answer Dixon's questions. The thought of it makes Mina shiver. A lady—however dubious her past—made to explain herself to a man like him who has grubbed through the sad secrets of so many lives. All compassion, gone. His job is to knit evidence together into a tight net.

The widow is an impostor, Mina tells herself. She has come into this household to take what she can. To have let her succeed— wouldn't that have been foolish? Especially when the ruse was one so easy to detect? It's unlikely she came up with it herself. Some- where a man is waiting for her to come to him with the money. An older man. A man who has some hold over her, who sends her out into the world and expects her to return with all she has managed to steal for him. Isn't that what thieves in India train monkeys to do? Yes, she thinks, and it was the widow who told her about them— monkeys dressed in dapper outfits who skitter up your arm and press a bristly kiss onto your cheek, and before you have recovered yourself their small hands have lifted the earrings from your ears or the necklace from around your neck, and they're gone.

Was that what she once was herself, she wonders, nothing more than a trained monkey? She wraps her arms around herself.

Jane points up the stairs. "Here they come," she whispers.

"Then get back to your work."

"Yes, ma'am." She hurries through the doorway to the stairs down to the kitchen.

The widow is between the two men, as though she has already been arrested. Her face is a ghastly white, and she trips. Robert reaches for her shoulder to steady her, but she flinches away. Down the stairs she comes, down to the hallway, where they lead her into the drawing room. Mina follows. Hardly has she set foot across the threshold when Dixon spins on his heel.

"This is no place for a lady like you, Mrs. Bentley."

She looks beyond him to Robert. "I believe I can be of help."

Dixon is between them. He says, "Help a detective from Scotland Yard?" He has the effrontery to laugh. "I believe I can handle things from here, madam."

Then the door swings shut in her face.

CHAPTER 30

Flyte is a patient man. For over four hours now he has walked up and down this street, smoking, reading a newspaper, standing in a dark doorway to eat the hot potato Steiner brought him. At times he has had to blow on his fingers to warm them, and when his bladder ached he had to take off down the street and into a dark alley to relieve himself.

You need stamina for this sort of waiting. Days can pass with no reward. Today he has been in luck, though. The door opened and out came Mr. Bentley. Here he looks small and vulnerable. Funny that, how prison can make a perfectly ordinary gentleman seem more elegant and poised. Coming down the steps, Mr. Bentley looked about him. The last place Mr. Bentley would expect to see him would be standing in his street in a greatcoat. However, one cannot be too careful, so Flyte turned away.

By the time he turned back there was a woman at a window on the first floor—was it her? He can't be sure. A pale face, a dark dress. He thought she was watching the street. Does she know that he has found her? If she does she'll be worried enough to make an escape, no matter how comfortable that house has been for her.

How would she have guessed, though? From Mr. Bentley? His name slipping out in the course of a conversation? A description of the curious man who was so attentive an assistant, and who she somehow recognized as him? Or was Steiner not sufficiently incon-spicuous, loitering in the street day after day? Not a remarkable man, but one who might be noticed as not belonging. And of course, there was that ill-advised burglary when the new maid started. Steiner never was a man for caution.

Three hours later Mr. Bentley came back with a shabby man in a bowler hat who has not yet come out. A man with the air of soiled working-class respectability he's familiar with. The air of a detective. He knows he has lingered here too long. Now he feels noticeable, but how can he leave? Has Bentley found her out? Has the detective come to arrest her? Then how will he get what is his?

There's a movement in front of the house, and he follows it with his eyes while seeming to have his attention on a dog sniffing along the gutter. Just a maid in a tight coat and a cheap hat scurrying up the area steps and along the pavement. Off she goes, rushing along with her arms folded across her chest and a nervous look about her. Has she been sent on an urgent errand? She might be worth follow-ing. Yet—what is going on in the house? He watches the maid hun-grily as she makes her way down the street, then forces his gaze back to the windows.

*T*he cold air burns her chest. From inside come noises—pans clattering and a burst of song in a woman's voice. Then the same woman calling, "You going t'get that, Doris? I've got me hands full here."

Jane still has her arms folded across her chest and they ache. The trouble is that if she moves them the packet could fall out from under her coat and into the filth of coal dust and mold and trodden-down snow that covers the area's paving stones.

A woman opens the door a few inches—the maid from last time. "You again?" she says.

"Yes."

The woman sighs loudly. "Come in, then." She leaves Jane just inside the door and calls into a backroom, "Ted? Ted? Got a job for you." Then she nods at one of the kitchen chairs for Jane to sit down. "He'll take you up in a minute."

So she sits with her hands folded into her lap. What a piece of luck—the woman assuming she needs to see the master again, and calling Teddy like that. Just as well she didn't call the butler, or Jane would have had to explain herself.

The scullery maids are shelling boiled eggs at the table, backs to her, but they steal glances over their shoulders. A servant with a message from her mistress to their master, twice in a week—now that is the sort of thing that tempts the imagination. Jane avoids their eyes, concentrating on the grain of the floorboards at her feet and an arc of bread crumbs missed by whoever swept up.

Teddy comes out with his sleeves rolled up and a mug of tea in one hand. His mouth snaps closed in surprise.

"Got another message from her mistress, hasn't she?" says the maid.

"Oh?" He comes closer and sets his mug on the table. He folds his sleeves down carefully, and takes his jacket from the back of a chair. "Mr. Jarman not around?"

"Gone to the postbox."

"I see."

He doesn't seem pleased to see her. She is a chore, a person to be escorted upstairs when evidently he is busy. Is he pretending for the sake of the maids, or has she caught him off guard? Jane stares into his face. He coolly looks back at her.

"Come on, then," he says, and he jerks his head to indicate she should come with him.

The air is chilly in the stairwell, and they only make it as far as the landing before he spins around and forces her against the wall and pushes his face against hers. "What on earth are you doing here?"

"Got a message, haven't I?" His mouth is hot on her neck, almost too hot. "Not for him, though. For you."

"For me?"

She's glad the light is dim, because all the way here she imagined how he was going to look at her, and what she would tell him, and whether she should tell him at all. "She wants to see you."

"Your mistress?"

"Yes."

He leans back, away from her. "She wants to see *me*? Why?"

"I haven't been doing a good enough job. Finding out about your master." He's looking away, up the stairs. "She sent me here to ask you. And I thought you'd—well, that you'd want to know." Her voice fades.

"Yes," he says, but she can tell he's thinking of something else.

She waits, her back still against the wall. At last she says, "So will you?"

"All right, then. Tonight. I'll come tonight. Tell her that. I don't know what time, so she'll just have to wait." His face swings back towards her. "And you?" he says more gently. "Are you going to wait for me too?"

"Yes."

His head tips towards hers, but he doesn't kiss her. Instead his lips brush her cheek, then she feels the warmth of his tongue across her skin and the coolness of the moisture it leaves. It moves down to her mouth, over her lips, across the ledge of her chin and to her neck. He pulls her hard against him, and from between them comes the crackle of stiff paper. He pulls back. "What's this?"

"Something for you to keep safe for me." She pulls the packet out from under her coat. "I haven't got anywhere to hide it."

He takes it from her. "What on earth have you been up to?"

Mina comes into the study and stands beside him at the desk. "Well?" she says.

Robert leans back in the chair. "Well? Well, he says he'll 'look into it,' whatever that means."

"And what did she have to say for herself?"

He reaches for her hand and holds it in his. "I hope you're right about her, my darling. Because she told a good story."

"She's had plenty of time to think of one." She squeezes his hand. "So what was it, this story of hers?"

"That they got married on board the steamer. They met the first day of the voyage and Henry was so taken with her that he proposed soon afterwards. She says she was eager to escape her dreadful employer, whom she was accompanying on a trip home—an unbearable woman, she says, who detested Henry and whom he detested in turn. So they got married, right there on the ship."

"Did the detective believe her?"

"Dixon? What's not to believe? He never met Henry. He doesn't have any idea how unlikely the whole thing is."

"It's preposterous. She can't provide any proof."

"Dixon said he'd investigate. The ship's log is lost, so the best he can do is to chase up the other survivors and see if they've heard of this marriage."

She pulls her hand free and sits on the edge of the desk. "Even if he bothers, I know what will happen. None of them will remember a marriage, and for lack of other evidence we'll be told to presume they *were* married. How will we be able to protest without looking heartless?"

"We can't assume she's guilty. We have to let him look into it."

"Oh, Robert." She gives one hard shake of her head. "Do you really think she's what she says? The scheme is a clever one, but she could have come up with it herself. Or perhaps someone else did, someone else who stands to profit from it."

"Now really, Mina—"

"Don't you read the paper? The world is full of swindlers. The good ones succeed because they appear to be what they claim."

"Darling, I've come across many criminals in my work. I think I can tell—"

"You've only seen them once they've been found out. They're they ones who've failed. How about all the ones still out there, undiscovered?" She gestures towards the window. "Why is it so impossible to believe that we could be harboring one?"

"You should join the detective force, my darling. You look at a respectable woman and see a criminal."

"No, Robert. It's rather that she's not a practiced liar. Maybe this is the first time she's attempted something like this—do you see why I suspect someone put her up to it, someone who's kept out of sight, letting her take the risk but who's waiting for the insurance company to pay her? Fifteen thousand pounds, Robert, that's quite a prize, even if they don't wait for this house to be sold and Henry's share of it."

"Dixon advised her not to do anything rash." He weaves his fingers together and lays them on his belly. "So she's going to be on our hands for a little while longer. Leaving now would make her look suspicious."

"Then let's hope she keeps to her room. I don't think I could bear to eat dinner with her again, knowing she's lied and not being able to do a thing about it."

He sighs. "Mina, we don't have proof."

"Isn't that the beauty of the scheme? There's little chance that there's any proof to be had." She crosses to the window, where she stares out into the dimness of the winter afternoon.

Is it the widow she is thinking of? Perhaps. Or perhaps it is the fact that she sent Jane off over an hour ago, yet Popham's valet still hasn't come to see her. Of course, he must be working. But tomorrow is Thursday, and at seven o'clock Popham's carriage will stop in front of this house, and he will step down, and she will have no choice but to go with him.

Still, it is only Wednesday. There is still time.

And she is sure the valet is nothing if not greedy.

*T*here's something more tempting about gold than banknotes, and something more usefully anonymous. Mina spills the sovereigns onto the desk between them—no point being coy when so much is at stake. One rolls off and falls silently to the carpet.

She sees him move ever so slightly, as though instinctively he must pick it up. But he doesn't; he merely follows it to where it has come to rest, somewhere by his feet.

"You're generous, Mrs. Bentley," he says. "But you still haven't said what you want from me."

She lets her head rest against the back of the chair. He's a younger man than she expected, and more handsome, too, with dark hair combed back and a narrow nose. No wonder Jane didn't object to letting him befriend her. It occurs to her that maybe the maid has been *too* eager to please this young man, and him her. As soon as this is over, she will have to make sure that Jane leaves her service. How could she keep a maid who's become friendly with the valet of a man who means her harm? How, for that matter, could she let her take a position in the house of anyone whose path she and Robert might cross? These things, though, are not difficult to arrange. An accusation of a small theft, the proof found in Jane's box—a pair of earrings, or silver spoons—the police called in. After that no respectable lady will hire her.

She rests her hands on the edge of the desk. "Your master has something belonging to my family that he has declined to return."

"Let me guess—you'd like it back, would you?"

Already he is a little too at ease. She mustn't let him see how this annoys her. Instead she lays one hand on the other on the desk. "Indeed I would. Some letters. Probably a dozen at most."

There is the slightest suggestion of a smile around his mouth. "Love letters, Mrs. Bentley?"

She bites the side of her tongue and stretches her fingers, slowly. "Naturally," she says. "And naturally, the person who wrote them is unable or unwilling to arrange for their safe return herself. I will pay you for your time and the risk that you will no doubt take in locating them and getting them to me."

She nods at the coins on the table. "Since the matter is urgent, I will pay you the same amount again when the letters are in my hand."

"All right then. But how will I recognize these letters, Mrs. Bentley?"

"Oh," she says, "you'll recognize them."

A smile pulls his mouth to one side. "I see. Then if you double what you've got there"—he points at the coins scattered over the desktop—"and pay me that much again when you get the letters, we've got an agreement."

She expected as much. Still, she sees him differently now: his eyes are alive with a sense of his own cleverness.

"Very well," she says. From where she's kept it out of sight on her lap, she opens her purse and counts more sovereigns onto the desk. There will be nothing left to pay the butcher, or the grocer. For now that cannot matter. "Tomorrow is Thursday—the letters must be here by this time tomorrow at the latest. Do you understand?"

"Oh yes." He starts scooping the coins off the desk and into his hand, then looks up with a wink. "I understand perfectly."

CHAPTER 31

Thursday, and it is what Robert calls filthy weather. The city has turned ghostly since a foul, yellow fog settled down on them again, muffling sounds, blurring the carriages passing slowly along the street. The reek of it seeps into the house so that even sitting by the fire, Mina would swear she can smell it.

All afternoon she's been uneasy. She's trapped in this house—how to go out when she has nowhere to go, no reason to be anywhere? Yet to sit still—to let her fate be decided by a self-satisfied valet who will, no doubt, read the letters and smirk over the passions the words shape, yet understand nothing at all—is almost more than she can bear.

But sit still she must. She has kept her composure through breakfast with Robert, and pretended to be busy all morning with the household accounts and menus for Mrs. Johnson, and bills to be paid—as though she still has the money to pay them. That way she could be silent, could seem occupied without having to explain. At lunch when Cartwright stepped out of the room, Robert leaned over and said she looked pale. The fog, she told him—it depressed the spirits and had given her a headache. Plus all this business with the widow was a strain. He stroked the delicate skin between her thumb and index finger, said, "My poor darling."

Now, eventually, she has persuaded him that he should venture through the fog for his meeting with Sir Jonathan. So here she sits alone, a shawl wrapped around her shoulders, staring into the fire. Again and again she asks herself whether there really is nothing else to be done. No, she thinks, there is not. Popham has the letters. That is his hold over her, the handwriting that will give her away, the name at the bottom that Robert won't recognize: Nora. Was she ever really Nora? No. After all she has done to pull herself onto the high ground of respectability, the waters are rising and threatening to sweep her away again. She shivers as though she already feels the coldness of the tide. How could it have crept up so far? She'd imagined she was safe. Instead she's been foolish. She should never have let Robert convince her to come to London; she should have found any reason to stay away.

She hasn't lost yet, though. She has sent the valet off to find the letters. Now she must hope that they are not too well hidden, and that he won't see if Popham will pay more to keep them than she can to retrieve them.

Perhaps he agreed to help her too easily. He could keep the letters and slowly, painfully, bleed money from her over months, or years even. For that, he'd have to understand why she's willing to pay to have them back. Is he clever enough for that? She presses her hands together because they are so very cold.

Jane is shaking out the dusters when she hears a voice: a man's, light, cheerful, and although she knows it's not Teddy's, she looks up. From out of the fog leans a small man in a hat that threatens to swallow his head, and a greatcoat wrapped around him.

He bends over the railings and calls out again. "Young missy— young missy down there. Would you be kind enough to help me?"

What harm is there in helping the gentleman? She snaps the last duster through the air, then comes up the steps towards him. He might be lost, in which case she won't be of much help; or he might want to find a family that lives hereabouts, in which case she won't be of any help at all. Instead, he tips his hat to her and says, "I'm a friend of your mistress, but it's a little hard to visit at a time like this."

"Yes, sir." She nods, watching his thin face.

"I don't mean to be indelicate—I have been away for several years and feel I would intrude to ask the family—but has there been a recent bereavement?"

"Oh sir." She shifts her weight and leans against the railings. "First it was Mr. Henry, then the shock of it killed his mother."

His eyebrows arch up in surprise. "Two deaths? Good Lord, how terribly unfortunate." His hands come out of his pockets and settle on his chest, a strange womanly gesture.

"Yes, sir. We're all awfully upset by it."

His hands can't stay still. Now they dance along the pointed tops of the railings. "Yes indeed, yes, quite so. I hope this doesn't mean the household will be broken up?"

"I wouldn't know, sir."

"No." He gives a gentle smile. "Naturally. Then in that case—" he fiddles with his gloves "—I shall have to pay my respects sooner rather than later."

"Yes, sir."

"You have been most helpful. I'll be certain to tell your mistress when I see her."

"Thank you, sir."

Then he's gone, back into the sea of fog that fills the street. The air is dank, and Jane shivers. Down in the area the light from the kitchen spills out, warm and hopeful. It seems to shine out across a great distance, like a far-off cottage's windows at night. She folds the dusters and takes off down the steps to see what Mrs. Johnson is cooking for dinner.

She has until seven o'clock.

By then the valet will have come, and she will be safe.

At times it seems the fog will lift, for occasionally it parts and the houses opposite suddenly appear, carriages passing in front of them that soon vanish back into the dingy white, as though only this part of the street exists. Something closer catches her eye. A man—a man in a too-big hat and an odd way of holding his hands to his chest. He is at the railings, and her breath catches painfully in her chest. That bulky coat, that tilt to his head that makes it seem he's looking in one direction when he's looking in another. She'd know him anywhere. He's a stain on her memory she'll never be rid of. Flyte.

He has been released, then, and already he has found her. Somehow, despite the tricks she used to cover her trail, he has put his nose to the ground and followed her scent over so many miles and so many years.

He's not looking up at the house but down into the area. Talking to someone, she realizes. Someone standing on the area steps—a white cap, an apron over a black dress. Jane.

Mina stumbles towards the fire and lets herself down into an armchair. How can this be? Flyte outside the house, talking to her maid, on the very day that Popham is coming for her. Was it Flyte who betrayed her to Popham? Because he would, she's certain—he might be so furious over his lost money. Yet it can't be that. Popham was in Mortimer's, he found her by accident, and Flyte was still in prison.

So what is he doing outside the house? He wants his money back. He has discovered the strongbox is empty, his fortune gone. To find his money, he believes he must find her.

She has been betrayed, she is sure. *Jane.*

The idea of it sinks inside her, a cold stone that settles in her belly.

Flyte has been more clever than she has; she should have guessed he would be. Why did she assume he wouldn't win himself an early release from prison? Or that hiring a maid from the country would be safe? Indeed, she'd congratulated herself on finding one who'd lied and so had every reason to be loyal to her: at one stroke, she could reduce her to the sort of despair that makes women of her sort throw themselves into the dark waters of the Thames. Yet, what has she just seen but this very maid talking to him?

He has paid her. He must have.

Jane Wilbred has taken his money and spilled everything she knows about the household into his ear. Everything about her mistress lately from France, whose past only goes back so far, then mysteriously stops. Was it Jane who managed things to let the burglar in? Has Jane been working for him all along? Is she not the real Jane Wilbred? She must be, Mina tells herself, for she was careful in hiring her. Wasn't she?

The lumber room. Jane was up there. Cartwright told her, yet she paid him no attention. She'd had Popham's letter in her hands, could hardly think of anything else. Now she wonders—are the papers still in the trunk? Or has Jane found them and handed them over to him? What else could she have been up to?

She hurries from the room into the cold of the hallway, then up the stairs, past the bedrooms, to the stairway that leads up to the servants' rooms. Along the corridor she rushes, right to the end, where she unlocks the door of the lumber room and looks about her. The light is so dim that she feels with her hands, but soon it is clear to her: out of the trunks that came from France, the smallest is missing. With it is gone the packet of shares in mines from Argentina to the Yukon that the police missed when they came for Flyte, documents drawn up by Flyte himself and that looked so very much like the real thing. Documents that would earn him another stretch in prison. They are gone—the only security she had against him.

The glow of a street lamp floats disembodied in the fog. Soon Jane has run beneath it, is searching for the next, running, running. No coat to keep off the cold, no hat, just the white cap and apron that she's worn all day and that are smeared with coal dust and polish. As she runs her hair comes loose, the soles of her boots thud against the pavement. What a sight she must look—respectable people will shy away from her, for such despair, they will think, must be of her own doing.

Her shoulder knocks against something—someone—a man. He yells out and she stumbles, falls to the slick pavement, but in a moment is up again, rushing on despite the pain raging through her knee. How can she keep going? Her lungs are burning, her throat tight. The taste of the filthy air is everywhere inside her. She'd cry if she could, but she can't yet, not when she must run as fast as she can though she can hardly see three paces in front of her. She must find Teddy. He'll know what to do. He'll know a place where she can stay, he'll lend her a few shillings to tide her over. He'll find her a shelter in this terrible city, because, of all the shadowy people fumbling their way through the fog, she must be the only one who has been thrown out onto the streets and has nowhere to call home.

Such fury! Mrs. Robert's face drawn in on itself, her spittle landing on Jane's cheeks as she hissed that she was the worst sort of traitor, a spy in her own house. That she'd trusted her and now she'd been made a fool of; that Jane couldn't understand the enormity of what she had done, all for the sake of a little money. On and on. She'd felt her knees give way, had held onto the back of an armchair, though Mrs. Robert had told her to move her filthy hands—she remembers that now as she runs—*filthy hands.* And whose filth was it?

Even as Mrs. Robert dragged her from the room and towards the front door she hadn't understood what was happening. How could she be so angry? A litany of accusations: letting in the burglar, breaking the tazza—so had she noticed, or had Sarah told her? Talking to a gentleman this afternoon, but what could one expect from a liar and a thief, a girl rotten through and through? With that Mrs. Robert had swung open the door and pushed her outside. Behind her the door had slammed shut.

She'd stood staring at it. From the other side came the hollow sound of retreating footsteps. Then silence. She'd knocked. She'd beaten the door so hard that she'd bruised her hands. No one had come. She'd forced herself down the front steps and past the railings, down into the area. They must have heard her and been given instructions. A key grated in the lock. Against the kitchen window an arm appeared and swept the light behind a curtain. Sarah's arm, she thought.

There was no point calling out. There was no point waiting but she did, though she didn't know for what. How long had she stood there? Long enough to grow cold. Long enough to understand that the moment she walked back up the area steps, she'd be alone and penniless.

So now she runs, for what else can she do? She runs through the fog, stumbling into gutters of slush, coming close to being hit by an omnibus, going wrong because on a night like this the streets all look the same. She retraces her steps, then dashes on, up the next street and the next because somewhere close by is Mr. Popham's house, where Teddy, surely, will fold her into his arms. Perhaps Mr. Popham needs a housemaid, and as she trips over the edge of the pavement she imagines the bliss of that—seeing Teddy every day, being able to steal moments together without having to see Mrs. Robert afterwards to explain that no, she didn't know much more about Mr. Popham's household than before though yes, she'd tried, but please, what was it she was supposed to be finding out?

When Mr. Popham's kitchen door swings open the cook's eyes slide down—from Jane's face with her hair come loose from under her cap to her dirty apron. She declares that Teddy is not home and she has no idea when he will be back. With that she closes the door in Jane's face.

She waits. A church bell chimes out the half hour. Then the hour. She presses her hands under her arms and her arms against her body, and crouches against the wall. It's of little help against the cold. Occasionally she calls out, "Please—can I just warm myself? Only for a minute. Please!"

At last the door opens. The cook. She hefts a pan of water at Jane. It slaps her in the chest, then its coldness spreads over her skin. The cook shouts, "Hook it. Go on, off with you," as though Jane is a stray cat.

Her legs are stiff and cramped, but she stands as best she can. Her wet dress clings to her. She backs away, up the steps to the street. There's no point running now, even if she could. No, she walks slowly, as though she is carrying a weight across her shoulders, back along the street and towards the river.

CHAPTER 32

Teddy has had to hurry to make it by six o'clock. Now he gives a smart rap at the kitchen door. His breath curls around him and hangs in the damp air like his own ghost. He sweeps his hands through it, then huffs onto his gloved fingers to warm them. It's the butler who answers, shirtsleeves folded up and his face red.

"Yes?" he says.

"Your mistress wants to see me."

The old man doesn't step out of the way. "Indeed?"

"Yes, indeed. You can tell her that Edward is here, from Mr. Popham's."

"I can, can I?" He looks down his stub of a nose at Teddy.

"It's an urgent matter. You can ask her yourself, if you like."

Without a word Cartwright steps back and jerks his head towards the kitchen. Then he takes his time—folding down his sleeves, looking about him for his jacket, plucking off stray hairs and pieces of lint until, finally, he shrugs himself into it. Even walking to the door he is slow, each step deliberate as he makes his way along the corridor and towards the stairs, until the sound of them can no longer be heard.

The cook is at the table rolling out pastry. From the scullery comes a maid in a filthy apron, her hair askew. She gives him a scowl. Only the housemaid pays him any attention, and she's all smiles as she sets down a tray. A pretty thing, fair hair, a delicate curve to her chin, and a sway in her hips as she walks towards him. "You're Jane's young man, aren't you?" she says. "I remember you calling around for her not so long ago." She nods in the direction of the area. She steps closer and her smile narrows. "She's not here, though."

"No?" he says.

"No." She keeps her eyes on him. "Been thrown out, for spying on the mistress. Terrible to-do there was. Like you wouldn't believe."

"Spying?" he says. "What, does your mistress have secrets?"

She gives a laugh. "They all do, don't they? Only some more than others."

Behind her the cook turns around. "Sarah," she snaps.

"It's all right, Mrs. J.—I haven't been gossiping when I shouldn't." She licks her lips and leans against the table. "Got caught, didn't she? Talking to some gent, apparently. Mrs. Robert saw her and wouldn't have her in the house a moment longer."

Teddy stares back at her. "Oh yeah?" he says.

"Oh yes," Sarah tells him.

For a few moments he seems to be thinking. His eyes look as though they're fixed on some faraway point, and his jaw tightens. "Well then," he says at last, "I ought to be getting along." The chair scrapes over the floor as he stands and buttons his coat. Then he nods and opens the door.

He takes the area steps two at a time, and hesitates at the top with one hand on the railing. A wind has picked up, dragging at the fog, pulling it loose so that he gets glimpses of the houses opposite and the half moon high above. Soon it will be gone, but the air's hard with frost and he hunches his shoulders.

As he starts up the street the wind rushes against his face. He bends his head and pushes his hands into his pockets. In the right one his hand comes up against the stiff paper of the letters. They are tied with string—ordinary string, for he thought it wise to leave the brown paper and the ribbon in which he'd found them wrapped apparently intact in the locked drawer of his master's desk. As he walks away he presses the letters against his hip, as though they are dangerous enough to need holding down.

Mina waits. Beside her the fire crackles and sends out sparks, and she stamps on them before they burn the carpet. He should be here by now—where could he have got to? She imagines Cartwright's laborious re-ascent of the stairs, the young man close behind him. They could have climbed those stairs three times already, and yet he still isn't here.

The gold is heavy in her hand. She'll ring the bell, get Cartwright to hurry up, for no doubt Mrs. Johnson has given the young man a cup of tea and a slice of pie. She can just see him—taking his time, telling Cartwright that he will only be a minute or two longer, that he's sure the mistress won't mind waiting.

Her hand is on the bellpull when she hears the creak of a floorboard in the hallway. There's a rap at the door, but it's only Cartwright, standing there alone. He coughs into his hand, as though he must excuse himself.

"Yes?" she says.

"Ma'am, he appears to have gone."

"Appears to have gone?" Her fingers curl towards her palms. "What on earth do you mean?"

"While I was enquiring whether the young man had an appointment with you, he apparently changed his mind about the necessity of his visit."

Her lungs feel stiff, her breath gone. She has words ready to hurl at him—such incompetence, such formality masking his ineptitude. Popham's valet was here, and Cartwright has let him escape. But she finds herself unable to say a word.

He's looking at her. Slowly, she sits down in her chair by the fire and breathes in as deeply as she can. "If he—if he returns you may show him up to me. Immediately. Thank you, Cartwright."

"Very good, ma'am."

When the door has clicked shut behind him, her hands fly to her face. Already it is after six o'clock. Popham will be here at seven, and she is defenseless. Her skin feels oddly cold, and in her ears comes a strange hissing—the sound, she's sure, of a terrible misfortune winging its way towards her.

CHAPTER 33

Dread is a terrible creature, cold-blooded, sharp-toothed, with a grip one cannot escape.

It is dread that takes hold of her as the clock tolls out the hour— seven o'clock, and she wishes she hadn't persuaded Robert to go to the lecture tonight. She could have confessed everything to him. He loves her, so wouldn't he have forgiven her? In the end, at least?

The valet has not come back.

Her ears reach for every sound. The echo of a laugh from someone going down the stairs—not Jane, for she's gone. Sarah, surely. From outside, the clatter of a carriage going too fast, then a shout. She holds her breath, but there's nothing more. It has passed on down the street.

Dinner is being prepared, as though she will be here to eat it, as though she would be able to swallow a single mouthful even if she were. Her hands are damp and she wipes them on her handkerchief, then balls it into her palm. She glances to the mantelpiece. The minute hand creeps past the twelve to the one. Soon it has reached the two, then the three. Perhaps the danger is past, perhaps there is no carriage coming for her, for Popham was always prompt. A man too literal for his own good, who did not look beyond the surface of things—wasn't that his undoing? Believing that she was Flyte's daughter, that Flyte would make him rich?

Yet even if by some miracle Popham is not coming, somewhere

outside Flyte is waiting for her. He will not be put off. Can she run from him? Perhaps. Or, given a little time, perhaps she will find another way to elude him. After all, as he always told her, she is devious. From downstairs the gong sounds for dinner. Her legs feel weak, yet she stands and makes her way to the door. The air is strangely thin, as though a violent storm has passed overhead leaving her unscathed. "Thank God," she mutters. "Thank God."

Across the carpet she goes, past the end tables with their figurines, over the floorboards to the door. She steps into the hallway. And then it comes. A sharp knocking at the front door, and she has to lean against the wall. Cartwright crossing the hallway to answer it. His head turning, his voice low but insistent, then he turns towards her.

If he notices that something is wrong he does not mention it— surely she is pale, her eyes wide, and she is gripping the doorjamb as though otherwise she would fall. All he says is, "A gentleman—on an urgent matter, he says, ma'am."

It is more than she can do to reply. Instead she nods and waves him away.

*I*t is, after all, an ordinary carriage carrying an ordinary man. Merely Popham, with his way of leaning too close when he talks, that dry odor of soap and cigars that lingers about him. Still, his hand on her wrist is tight as a cuff, and in the dim light she catches the twitching of his eyes, the wetness of his lips. He is excited, sure of himself. She can't bear to watch him any longer. Instead she looks out the window—they are crossing the Thames, and she thinks to herself that she should take note of their route, though he seems not to care that she sees it. In places the fog lingers over the river that rushes beneath them, slick and dark, glinting with the lights of the bridge.

So much spit in her mouth. She's tempted to send it flying into his face, but how would that help matters? No, she must seem calm. She swallows it and it slides down to her stomach.

He clears his throat, as though it is necessary to get her attention when his leg is pressed against hers, his hand clenched on her wrist. "You were so convincing," he says, "that you almost made me doubt myself. Can you believe that? I wasn't sure if I could trust my eyes. Such coincidences are not impossible, that's what I told myself."

"No, not impossible," she says. Merely that, for what he wants is her interest, not her conversation. He has had no one else to tell this story to, so he tells it to her: the story of how he found and trapped her. She wonders if he knows that she tried to bribe his valet—surely he must. Perhaps he instructed his man to promise her he'd steal the letters. Is he that cunning? He never struck as her as a clever man. Now, though, she isn't sure.

He's squeezing her wrist harder now and looks past her out the window. He gives a snort of a laugh. "But you did it—you got off scotfree while your father went to prison. Such devotion—protecting you like that." He laughs. "Protecting his golden goose. And now you've landed Robert Bentley—though I have to admit, I thought you'd have picked a wealthier husband. Maybe Bentley wasn't your father's idea—he's still quite young and handsome, isn't he? Not like me. Isn't that right, Nora?" His face swings towards hers. "Nora—now what have you been calling yourself?"

"Mina," she tells him.

"Ah yes, Mina," he says on a sigh. "A good choice."

His breath touches her cheek and she can't stop herself shivering. He notices, of course.

"Cold, my darling?" He wraps his arm around her shoulders, never mind that now she must sit forward awkwardly. "Don't worry. I've found us a warm place to spend the night. A private place. I know you'll appreciate that, although you hardly deserve such consideration."

His arm tightens around her and she winces.

"You left me looking a prize fool, didn't you? No fiancée, those shares worth absolutely nothing." His voice is brittle. "Can you imagine the disgrace? Having to explain to everyone from my cousin to the fellows at the club that I'd helped make them owners of a silver mine that didn't exist? In some quarters my name is still mud."

Outside the streets have become narrower and dirtier. If only they could drive along these streets forever, she could put up with this: his hands on her, his breath on her, this shame of her past held up for examination.

He must have noticed that her attention has wandered. He whispers into her ear, "Don't even consider trying to run, my darling. You wouldn't get far, and in streets like these you'd be in considerable danger."

He's right. Everything is darker here. They pass a public house of the worst sort, its stench of old beer hanging on the air of the street. By its door shadowy shapes cling together, moaning. Are they fighting or—and she turns away—is it a man and a woman too drunk to have any shame? This is the sort of street in which men with thin knives lie in wait. Here she would be robbed—or worse. She presses her tongue against the roof of her mouth to stop any sound escaping her. Yet perhaps even having her throat cut might be better than her fate with Popham. She imagines her body limp in the gutter. What are the chances it would be recognized? If she failed to return home, would Robert track her down to whatever place her body ended up? That she couldn't bear: for him to find what was left of her here, for him to find out what she'd been and to suspect that their marriage had been a sham. Because no matter what their marriage was, it wasn't that. It was all a marriage was supposed to be— the union of two souls, the binding of two loves.

Is it her fault that Flyte snatched her up before she ever met Robert? How could it be? And yet, look what has come of it: here she is sitting in a carriage with a man intent on revenge. If she survives what he has planned for her, there is always Flyte. He is not the sort of man to let go of what is his.

She has to stop herself before Popham notices that she is blinking away the wetness in her eyes. This is not a time for weakness. Perhaps there is still a means of escape and of leaving Popham to whatever fate these streets would hold for him.

The Dark Lantern

He pulls a handkerchief from his pocket and blows loudly. "All those years in prison—I wonder, how has your father survived it, a man like him? But it's only right, isn't it, that criminals pay for what they've done? He must be due for release sometime soon, hey?" He wipes the handkerchief across his nose, then stuffs it in his pocket.

Did she flinch? A little, and she hopes he didn't notice, though how could he not with his arm gripping her so tightly? She wonders now—is she bait for Flyte? Is Popham that clever? Maybe there's still a chance for her, if it's Flyte he wants. She'll get back to Robert, they'll leave for France, and everything will be back the way that it should be.

Occasional lights in the street—from another public house that has its door thrown open despite the cold, from a pawnbroker's shop, from a steamed-up window from which the smell of fried fish escapes, from the doorways of houses that have a seedy grandeur about them.

Popham perches forward to glance out the window. "Nearly there."

His voice is taut with excitement, like a wire pulled tight. She looks at the houses they're passing. There's something furtive about them, the way their lights announce their presence yet seem not to be inviting. Of course—they're brothels. What had she expected? Those long kisses she'd allowed him all those years ago when she'd let him push his crotch hard against her leg and press his hand on the part of her corset that overlaid her breasts. That had been enough for him only because the way she let him hold her promised so much more, and she was to make good on that promise on their wedding night. The wedding night that never came because it was never meant to come, for it was merely the bait on the hook designed to reel him in.

Or rather, she thinks, she was the bait and Flyte was the hook. Flyte, who is too cunning to be caught by the likes of Popham.

Where is Robert now? She imagines him sitting with his legs crossed and his arms folded across his chest, his head a little tilted as he listens to the lecture; she imagines him in a sea of other men in dark jackets: her Robert, with his way of pulling his lips together when he thinks, the delicate, warm scent of his skin when she pushes her face into his neck.

With a lurch the carriage stops. Popham lets out a sigh like a man about to indulge himself, and for a moment his grip loosens. Could she pull away and run? How far would she get before he caught up? Not far, she thinks. And the coachman is in his pay. He'd probably be more than willing to chase her down for a few shillings extra.

The carriage door swings open and Popham gets down. Not for one moment does he let go, so that getting out of the carriage is a graceless dance, him stepping down first, his hand on her wrist and dragging her down after him.

A cold wind is blowing, catching scraps of paper and spinning them down the gutter, pushing along an empty bottle that rattles jarringly as it rolls across the street.

Popham pulls her up the front steps to a dark door where he knocks. It opens immediately. They are expected.

A maid in cap and apron opens the door, looking for all the world like a maid in any respectable home, except for the scar that runs from her eyebrow to her chin and puckers the skin into a furrow.

Along the walls hang pictures. There's a hat stand, an umbrella stand, a large mirror. All of it a little too grand for so mean a hallway.

"Ah," says Popham. "Is everything ready?"

"The red room, sir."

"Very good."

"Any refreshment, sir?"

He pauses, looks at Mina as though she has any say in the matter, then purses his lips. "A bottle of champagne, if you please." Then he pushes her gently in the back towards the stairs.

So this, she thinks, is the best he can come up with. To bed her in a place like this so as to add to her humiliation. It shows a little imagination—but only a little. This is not a trap for Flyte; this is revenge against her, that is all. He will heft himself on top of her and shove himself into her over and over for as long as he is able, and then will he feel satisfied? What, she thinks, will come after that? Is she to be left here? She keeps her hands crossed in front of her, anything so as not to touch this place, not even the banister. The wall-paper is flocked and red, the light fittings brass, the pictures on the wall mostly of naked women chased by centaurs and satyrs. On the landing waits a pale statue of a girl entwined around a naked man, her cheek against his thigh, her head just obscuring his genitals.

She looks away. The taste of Popham in her mouth—the thought of it brings the burning of bile into her throat.

Along the corridor they go, his hands pushing her, finding their way down to her buttocks, though through the layers of her coat and dress and petticoats it must be more the idea of her body that excites him. She hears his breath—it rasps a little, and when he speaks his voice has a tremble to it. "In here," he tells her, and turns her to the right.

He knows this place well.

Of course, she thinks, a man like him.

He reaches past her to open the door. A cacophony of color—red wallpaper, a carpet in reds, oranges, and yellows, curtains in a shade only slightly less bright than scarlet, and, in the center like a stage waiting for actors, a bed behind its four posts, closed in behind curtains. He sweeps the drapery to one side and there, in a vibrant shade of violet, waits a dress. A dress for her, she realizes, that will barely cover her breasts, that is trimmed with fur. A whore's dress.

"Let me help you," he says, almost gently.

She shivers as he pulls off her coat, then sets to work on the fasteners running down the back of her dress. It sinks to the floor, deflated, and he turns her around and stares without shame at the tops of her breasts. He can barely contain himself—she sees that. He reaches out and snatches at her crotch, squeezing it hard and shoving his face against hers. For a moment it seems he will forego the whore's dress—he lifts her petticoats and spreads his other hand over her buttocks to pull her close. Then he lets go. "I've waited too long," he says. "I'm going to have you the way I've imagined it."

He nods to the dress, but when she doesn't move he picks it up and holds it out.

"You ladies," he says, "are so helpless." He nudges her so that she will step out of the mourning dress still pooled around her feet and into the violet one. "But as you will notice, women who earn their own keep can get themselves dressed."

This dress fastens down the front. Naturally it would. "I'll give you ten minutes. Don't forget"—he points to a dressing table in the corner—"to make yourself beautiful. I'm sure you'll get the idea."

His smile flickers, then he turns away and hurries out of the room. A key squeals in the lock behind him and she's left alone to make of herself what she will.

The curtains are drawn, but when she pulls them back she finds no window, only a blank expanse of wall. So she tries the door—it doesn't budge. She kneels down and spies the key left in the lock. Popham was never a man who managed details well. Over on the dressing table are powders and brushes and combs. With her fingers she snaps the teeth off one of the combs to make a sharp end, then she plucks one of the prints off the wall—a nymph covered only by a twist of ivy—and rips it out of its frame. She shoves it under the door, then pokes around in the keyhole with the end of the comb.

Her hands are shaking. She must hurry. How many minutes have passed? Two? Three? She is still locked in here. If he should return—well, what would he do that is any worse than what he has already planned? She can't imagine, yet dread makes her hands stiff, and she has to stop and breathe slowly before working the comb in the lock again.

The end of the comb slips. It slips again. At last it catches the side of the key just enough to straighten it. She peers into the lock, then, with one push, sends the comb back into it. With a dull clatter the key falls out on the other side of the door, onto the print.

She hears footsteps.

She tugs at the print, but it doesn't move.

She waits.

There's a creak of the floorboard, then a rustle. She presses her eye to the keyhole and sees a man's dark clothes. She starts to her feet. Her arms rise up across her chest to protect herself. She hears the clatter of the key going into the lock, its scrape as it turns, the slow swing of the door opening. She flings out her arm for the candlestick on the mantelpiece, grabs it and holds it high.

For a moment there is only the doorway, empty, and she steps forward.

Then he's around the door so fast that she has no time to bring the candlestick down. Her hands are in his. Even as they struggle he kicks the door closed with his foot. Then it's over. She's on the floor, the weight of him on top of her.

"You?" she says.

For it is not Popham who has her by the wrists now, but Flyte.

CHAPTER 34

Along the corridor they run, to a door almost invisible under its coat of wallpaper. Flyte wrenches it open. No carpet here, just bare boards that resound with the hammering of their shoes. From the bottom a woman's face stares up at them, but he doesn't let that slow them down. Down the last flight of stairs they come, Flyte leading the way. He lets go of her wrist, draws back his hand, and lands it squarely in the woman's face. She staggers, then falls against the wall with her arms lifted to shield herself.

But there are no more blows. The two of them take off, up the short corridor and out through the dank kitchen, leaving the door open in their wake.

Behind them the woman, screams, "Mrs. *Archer!* Mrs. *Archer!*"

The alley is as dark as a well. They dash blindly. He pulls her by the arm, hard, despite the fact that she is running as fast as she can on legs stiff with shock and cold. Behind them, voices and footsteps are coming fast.

Flyte calls out, "Steiner? Where the hell are you?"

Up ahead a man appears with a lantern. She stumbles, but Flyte wrenches her on. Her lungs are aching. She can barely fill them. Her foot catches on something—the edge of a paving stone? A foot stuck out to trip her? Flyte won't let go and she falls awkwardly, her temple smacking against the stones. She lies there. Her head is filled with the sound of bees. Then Flyte has his hands under her arms and is dragging her along. A lantern. Swinging. Shouts from close by. The smell of wine on Flyte's breath, for his face is close to hers. Someone grabbing her feet and lifting her. The echoing dark of a four-wheeler and she's lying on the floor. A lurch—Flyte climbing in.

But there is trouble. A horse whinnies, and the carriage rolls back. Men's voices raised, then Flyte's. "Get out of here, Popham! Get back to your whores!" he's shouting.

"She owes me—*you* owe me."

"You got what you deserved, you fool." The carriage trembles. She lifts her head and sees Flyte kicking out, hands on the doorframe.

Popham roars, "I'm going to teach her a lesson. And you. You're not going to prey on anyone else when I've finished with you."

There's a gasp from close by and she sees Flyte hanging onto the frame by his fingers, his body hanging out of the carriage door. He yells, "Steiner! *Steiner!*" He is being pulled so hard that he groans, but he won't let go. His hat thuds to the floor next to her.

The carriage pitches, and Flyte's gone. The doorway is empty. A moment later the shape of a man appears, hefting himself up. Outside Flyte is crying out, "Steiner—get him. Get the stupid bastard."

She lets her head back down to the floor. Her future hangs there in front of her. She could pull back her legs and launch a kick at Popham, sending him flying if she's lucky, giving Flyte a chance to rescue her. Or she could go with Popham, for that way she may have a chance—there has to be a chance, doesn't there?—of getting back to Robert. Yet even if they fled to Paris, what chance would she have against Flyte?

Popham can't help himself. Just when he is so close to victory he stands in the doorway and yells, "I've got your daughter, Flyte, and you're both going to be sorry now."

She hears Flyte bellow, "She's not for you, Popham. She's my *wife.*"

Of course Popham has his back to her and doesn't see her raise her legs. He doesn't catch the swift motion of her feet coming at him until she has kicked him so hard on the buttocks that he stumbles.

Hands reach towards him from outside, pull at him until he is plucked away. She hears the thud of bone hitting the ground, and a grunt of pain.

Lifting herself on her elbows, she peers at the shadows outside. Someone is moaning, someone else getting to his feet—she hears the scrape of boots against stone, and Flyte calling again for Steiner.

Steiner. She catches sight of him in the light of a lantern—whose lantern? She doesn't know. A broad man, a man with bow legs and a clean-shaven face. The man who has loitered in Cursitor Road all these weeks.

Of course. Not Popham's man. Flyte's man.

The awful thudding of fists and feet into flesh, then Flyte's head appears in the doorway. He's breathing hard, but he pulls himself up into the carriage, then drops onto the seat, though his legs have to arch over her where she lies on the floor. With one fist he knocks on the carriage ceiling, yells out, "Get moving, Steiner, get moving." The movement jolts her this way and that, and she closes her eyes. *Robert!* she wants to call out, *Robert!* But he is far away, back home by now most likely, and wondering where she could have got to.

Flyte shifts his legs. "All right, Kitty?" he asks. "Persistent bugger, wasn't he? But then, he always was. Now, my love." He bends over her. "We need to have a little talk, don't we? There's that small matter of the money gone missing."

CHAPTER 35

He was in too much of a hurry to dress warmly, and the cold of the night soaks through his flesh into his bones and threatens to slow him. He's asked the servants, people on the street, everyone he's come across if they have seen her and they've pointed this way and that, and he's followed their fingers to these awful streets. He's in a part of town he's unfamiliar with. The streets are crooked and dark, the few streetlights dim against the night. Here there are no more clues. No one has seen her; it is as though she has sunk without a trace into this city.

He has a dark lantern. He raises it when he sees a movement, slides open its panel and releases a shaft of light. Two small boys, filthy and shoeless, with newspapers spread over them. One of them spits at his boots. He doesn't bother to ask if they have seen her. She couldn't be here, could she? Why would she have come here? Maybe he has gone wrong.

He walks a little farther into a dark soon impenetrable. What choice is there but to open the panel of the lantern again and shine it around to get his bearings? Still, it is an unwise choice, for here a bright light is irresistible. He hears footsteps, delicate as a woman's, and feels a hand grabbing at his coat. He wrenches his arm away and turns, has to dodge another shadow. The lantern clatters use-lessly into the gutter. Was that the glint of a blade? Was that whis-per the sound of it slicing through the air? He jumps back and kicks, shoving with all his might past whatever it is that is stalking him, and takes off down the street at a run.

*H*e is cruel. She's always known that, but for him to do this—it is beyond anything she imagined. The slap of water just behind her like the lap of a hungry creature, the stinking breeze its breath. Down here on the dock the wind has to find its way through the docked ships and stacked crates. Flyte seems to know his way around—is this another place from his past?

The rope around her wrists scratches her skin. Steiner wound it around and around, but, she wonders, what of the knot? He tied it too quickly for it to be secure.

A few feet away Flyte sits on a bollard and picks at his nails with a knife. "My love," he says, "it would be so very much easier if you told me where it is."

In the dark it is impossible to see his expression. She imagines it—sweet yet exasperated, the look a father might give a child when she has disappointed him. Isn't that about right? In those first weeks of their life together she'd called him Father a few times and felt the force of his hand against her cheek. "No," he'd said gently, "I'm not your father. Don't you understand?" So she'd asked him what he meant to do with her—what did he want with claiming her from the orphanage when he was no relation of hers? An abandoned child— unwanted, left behind. So he'd shown her what he wanted—in slow steps because he wasn't, he told her, a brute. First his hand undoing her dress, then the next week lifting it off her, a few days later peeling off her underclothes so that she sat shivering on the edge of the bed, the small buds of her breasts hard in the cold. He could hardly restrain himself then. But he had. By Christmas, though, he'd had her, and had her every night from then on. Always he'd called her "my love," and the day she was old enough he'd taken her to Scotland and married her.

She was a clever thing; he'd told her so because she'd picked up his tricks quickly. That's surely why he'd put his claim on her before they went in search of men for her to lure—couldn't go actually marrying one of them while she was married to him, could she? A pretty thing, not what she seemed, not his daughter, not a young girl in search of love and a husband. No, indeed. How many foolish young men did they take? She can't even remember. Who'd have thought that it would have been Popham who'd bring it all to an end, when he was the dullest of all of them?

She's so cold that her flesh feels dead to her. He could have given her his coat, but he didn't. Instead he forced her down here still in her underthings. A clever trick, she realizes, for even if someone she could appeal to should happen by, what would they make of her, undressed like this?

"It's all spent," she says.

"My love, even you couldn't be so foolish."

She shifts her weight, tries to feel behind her with one foot for the edge of the dock. "I lived on it. How else was I supposed to get by?"

He clicks his knife closed and stands. "Kitty, Kitty, please don't try my patience. I didn't bring you up to be a fool, did I? You made do very nicely, found yourself a proper English gent to *marry*, in Paris of all places. Well well well; what more could you want? I was out of sight and out of mind, wasn't I? Did you think I wouldn't find you?"

"I had to eat." She turns her wrists this way and that though the rope burns them. Has it loosened? A little, just a little.

He comes close and lays one hand on her arm. "My love, I *understand* that you had to eat. I *even* understand that you'd go through a sham of a marriage to give yourself a home. But"—he grips her more tightly—"where the *hell* did my money go? I earned it, didn't I? All those years in the clink, I stayed true to you. Didn't tell them what I knew about you, did I, or where you were?"

"You didn't bloody know where I was." She pulls herself away but he grabs her, and it's as well he does—reaching back, her foot has found only air.

He shoves his face into hers, his nose hard against her cheek. "Now, tell me where you hid it. If you don't, I'll be no worse off without you. I'll get into that house, I'll rip it apart, and I'll find it."

If he loosens his hold now she'll fall, the water will rise over her head. She can't swim, not really, can barely stay afloat, and won't even manage that with her hands tied. Even with them free her chances wouldn't be good: the water is cold, and filthy, and full of hazards that could cut her, or entangle her, or pull her under.

He hugs her to him. He even presses his lips against her neck.

"Darling Kitty," he says, "my love, my heart. I'd hate to lose you. You know that, don't you? You'd sink like a stone, right to the bottom. A terrible accident. Oh yes, tragic."

She shudders, says quietly, "It's all spent on him. He didn't have much—we lived on it." She works her wrists, twisting, pulling. Although the rope is loose, she can't pull her hands free.

He holds her more tightly. His coat is warm against her skin. "No," he whispers into her ear. "No, no, that's not how it was."

"Yes." She leans her head back, away from his shoulder. "Every last farthing. All spent on him."

"Oh, Kitty." He kisses the corner of her mouth. "My lovely Kitty, what a fool you've been." Then he opens his arms and lets her fall.

She doesn't make a sound until the water takes her.

CHAPTER 36

The river has an oily look to it. For a quarter hour by the chimes of the church clock Jane has stood here staring into it. One old soul— a woman so bent that she walks as though searching for something lost on the ground—stops and says, "That's the way, isn't it? A man gets you in trouble, and that's how you end it."

Jane looks around. The wind whips her hair around her face, for her cap is long gone, lying trodden into the dirt somewhere between here and Cursitor Road. "It's all gone wrong."

"You can put it right, or have someone do it for you. Unless"— she nods as best she can at Jane's belly—"it's too late for that."

"What do you think I am?" She glares at her, this crooked old thing with her shawls and her wrinkled sack of a face. "It's not like that."

She lets out a rough laugh. "Go on, jump if you're going to. It's painless, so they say." She limps away along the bridge, this thin strip of city stretching over the river. Mist gives the lamps the glow of halos, marking her path. Soon her figure is indistinct, her footsteps erased by the rumble of a grand carriage coming over the bridge. Jane turns away. She leans onto the parapet and stares at the water rushing beneath her.

It is late now, very late indeed.

CHAPTER 37

He's gone. She's gone too. The widow comes downstairs and looks about her. No one in the morning room, or the study. Not even a servant. No one in the dining room either. Did everyone disappear overnight? She rings the bell and waits.

It is Cartwright who eventually comes up the stairs, slowly, stately, as though nothing about this morning is unusual. "Cartwright," she says. "I'll need breakfast, and then I'd like my trunk brought down and a cab."

His cheeks flutter slightly. "Yes, ma'am?"

"Yes, indeed." She folds her hands together. Shouldn't he go, now that he has his instructions? What does she need to do next?

He stands on the corner of the carpet, silent and unmoving.

"Go on then," she says, and pushes her hands through the air, shooing him away.

"Very good, ma'am."

He closes the door, then walks away to the back stairs, where he pauses and raises his eyebrows. He blows his breath through his teeth and mutters to himself, "Blimey, not losing any time, are you, young miss?"

Down in the kitchen Mrs. Johnson is cracking eggs into a pan. She says over her shoulder, "Her, was it?"

"Wants breakfast. Then a cab."

"Told you," she says. "Guilty conscience, isn't it? Wanting to take off like that just when Mrs. Robert is gone missing and Mr. Robert is at his wits' end?"

Sarah comes in, carrying the housemaid's box. "I can't do it all on my own, you know."

Mrs. Johnson tosses an eggshell into a bucket, then starts beating the eggs. "We can't be letting everything go, just because the household's all upset."

"Who's going to notice?"

"Mr. Robert when he comes back, that's who."

Sarah lets herself drop into a chair and shakes her head. "He's got his mind on other things. He's not going to be worried about whether the rooms are all made up."

"He won't want to be worried about it on top of everything else." Mrs. Johnson taps her fork on the edge of the pan.

Cartwright pulls out a chair and sits down too. "He'll be calling in the police, I'll bet. Not much more he can do on his own, is there? Wasn't much point trying, if you ask me."

Sarah props her elbows on the table. "Run off, hasn't she. Told you she was a dark one."

Mrs. Johnson lifts the fork and points it at her. "That's enough of that. You hear me? Now, get on with you, and be grateful the widow's off today, or there'd be her to see to as well."

Sarah scowls, but she gets to her feet and picks up the box again. She doesn't say another word, and that's unusual for her. Mrs. Johnson doesn't notice, and neither does Cartwright, for she's saying to him, "Maybe we should tell the police about her taking off like this. Can't let her just go, can we? Not without Mr. Robert knowing about it."

Just before ten o'clock, when the cab pulls up in front of thirty-two Cursitor Road, Cartwright calls for Sarah to help him with the trunk. She doesn't answer. In fact, she cannot be found. In the end he has to shout down to the kitchen for Elsie, and she slouches her way upstairs in an ill humor. Together they carry it, and though it is small they knock it against the banister one moment, the wall the next, because Elsie falters and shifts and complains all the way down to the hall.

Mrs. Johnson is standing there, hands knotted together and hair unkempt from taking off her hat too quickly. With neither apron nor cap she looks odd, as though she's missing a layer of herself. "Well?" hisses Cartwright as he struggles with the trunk.

"No," she says. "They won't come."

"Bleeding idiots," he huffs. "What are we supposed to do?"

She shrugs.

The three of them are still standing there when the widow makes her way down the stairs. She comes close to missing her footing when she notices them—the cook, the butler, and an ugly young girl who must be one of the maids, all standing next to her trunk as though they mean to delay her.

She lifts her chin and walks along the hallway to where they wait. They do not move. They do not speak. "Thank you," she says, but her hands stay folded together at her waist—no handshakes, no tips to thank them for their trouble.

She looks towards the door and the seconds pass, doled out by the tall clock in the hallway. She fiddles with her gloves. She touches her hat, her coat—all black, of course. When the clock chimes out the hour they all turn.

Cartwright nods for Elsie to get the door, and together they carry the trunk outside.

The widow follows at a respectable distance, as a lady would. Once the trunk has been stowed by the driver, she climbs in. Not a word more to Cartwright or Elsie, no smile of thanks. They walk back up the steps to where Mrs. Johnson is watching. For a moment the widow's face looks out at them, then she disappears and the cab moves away.

"Good riddance," says Mrs. Johnson. "Never did trust that one."

Cartwright looks at her. "Still going to get Mr. Henry's money, isn't she?"

"Not necessarily. Mr. Robert will know what to do." She makes to wipe her hands on her apron, but it's not there. "Better get myself dressed," she says. "And you'd better find Sarah. If she's taken off, she's in for it this time."

But they don't find her. Instead Cartwright, who makes the rounds of the bedrooms, finds Mrs. Robert's jewelry box forced open.

*W*hen Sarah comes in, Cartwright and Mrs. Johnson wheel around where they are sitting, spoons held high. "You!" they say together.

Elsie merely glances at her, then goes back to her plate of stew. She mutters, "You're really in for it now," and gives a snort that sounds like a laugh cut off too soon.

Sarah stares back at them. "What?" she says. "What's up with you lot?"

"Been out somewhere important, have we?" Mrs. Johnson sets down her spoon.

"It's not like I was that long."

Cartwright gets to his feet. "Over two hours. I'd call that long. Wouldn't you, Mrs. Johnson? Enough time to get up to all sorts of no good." He folds his arms.

She goes a little pale and reaches for a chair. She's still in her coat, but she doesn't try to undo it. "Never minded before, have you?"

Mrs. Johnson looks down at her plate.

"Have you?" Sarah says more loudly. "But then, it was convenient not to notice, wasn't it? Just like I didn't notice things either. All those joints of beef from the butcher's he charges us for—we could have been feeding an army, couldn't we? All those bottles of port we buy and Mr. and Mrs. Robert hardly touch. I never told them what was going on, did I? I didn't say a word because I know how it is— got to get through each day, haven't you? Got to save a bit for a rainy day?"

"Well." Mrs. Johnson lifts her head, though her cheeks have turned a deep pink. "You've put by more than a bit, haven't you, love? Can't turn a blind eye to that."

Cartwright moves forward, edging behind Sarah in case she makes a dash for it. "Might as well admit it," he says, and she starts.

"What am I supposed to admit to?" She gets to her feet and leans her fists on the table. "Why don't you tell me what this is all about?"

"Think we wouldn't notice?" says Cartwright. "Mrs. Robert disappeared off somewhere and the widow fled, and everything all topsy-turvy. When I went to look for you, what did I find? Mrs. Robert's jewelry box, empty as an orphan's pocket."

The news seems to catch her off guard, for she stammers, "What? Well then." She looks about her. "The widow—it was her, must have been."

Of course, the police are called in so they can decide the matter.

They arrive, a detective and the same young constable who came after the burglary. The detective sucks at his teeth and listens to the story, says, "So your mistress has gone and run off? Maybe she took 'em herself."

Cartwright has to point out that she had the key; why go to the bother of breaking open the box? Yet though the detective and his constable find it all bizarre—that's the word the two of them use again and again, *bizarre*—they decide to take Sarah with them, despite her protests. After all, of the possible culprits, she's the one they have to hand.

Mrs. Johnson follows them to the door. They're already in the street before she calls out, "How about the widow—it could have been her, couldn't it?"

The policemen don't hear her: she hasn't shouted loudly enough for that. The only one who turns around is Sarah, then she bends her head and lets herself be taken away. As for Mrs. Johnson, she sighs and closes the door. A shame that this should happen, a crying shame. Yet as she busies herself at the stove she whistles a delicate tune that was a favorite of hers when she was a girl and that hasn't come to mind in years.

The Dark Lantern

Such is the chaos of the day that it is not until after dark that Mrs. Johnson thinks to send Elsie upstairs to Price with a bowl of broth and some tea. The girl comes back five minutes later.

"Gone, in't she?" she announces, and slides the tray back on the table.

Mrs. Johnson is preparing a roast chicken—for whom it is uncertain, since Mr. Robert has only come back for long enough to change his clothes and drink a few glasses of wine. Then, his face haggard, he took off again with no word as to when they might expect him.

"What?" says Mrs. Johnson.

"Price—gone. Bed's empty, clothes all gone too."

"Blimey," says Mrs. Johnson, and shoves the chicken back into the oven.

CHAPTER 38

Sunday afternoon, and the gloom of a heavy sky has settled over the city. A man in a ragged jacket is maneuvering a boat under a bridge, for he has noticed something breaking the flow of the water. The current is strong enough to make this a tricky task, especially here between the pillars where the twisting water can capsize a small boat and whisk it off in a matter of seconds.

Now that he's pushed the boat far enough over, he lets the current move it and readies his hook. He'll only have one chance, so he crouches like a harpooner coming up on a whale. As the boat swoops under the bridge he stabs with his hook. It catches and the sudden wrench nearly pulls him into the water. The boat takes off down the river and he staggers, his catch floating along behind him. Only when he's regained his balance can he look back and see exactly what it is. A woman's body, bobbing along on his hook with the water curving up around it.

He smiles—a good catch—and sets about securing it so he can row to shore.

She must have been caught under a ship to come up so battered and torn—at least, that's what Dr. McPhee says as he leads Robert to the table and the covered figure on it. No jewelry on her, though that doesn't mean much, because the sort of men who retrieve bodies from the river—well, they have their own way of making a living.

Robert steels himself; it's going to be her, but he won't break down, not in front of these men. He must control himself, no matter how bad it is, and it seems it will be bad. Still, he feels weak, as though every ounce of strength he ever had has been drained away in the last three days—has it only been three days?—since she went. In a carriage, when she'd given him no word that she'd be leaving the house, and told the servants only that she was going on an urgent errand and would be back late.

Every time he's arrived home after his frantic search for her, after his alerting the police that she was gone and having to impress on them that she wouldn't run off—why would she?—even after falling asleep in his armchair in front of the fire, he's imagined that she would be back: dozing in their bed, perhaps, with a story about getting lost, or kidnapped, or hurt in some terrible accident. The trouble is that she is nowhere to be found. He has checked. Even the police, after he insisted, have checked. This is the best they could come up with, this body found by one of the men who trawl the waters of the Thames.

The doctor is a Scot with a red moustache and a military bearing. He leans over the figure on the table, then says, "Brace yourself, Mr. Bentley," and lifts away the sheet.

It is worse than he could ever have imagined.

The head is a broken egg with no face, the torso sliced open and the entrails hanging loose, purple and red, as though snakes have invaded the cavity. One arm is missing—the left—but the other is surprisingly undamaged, as are the feet. He stares at them, but it is hard to find anything to recognize. The flesh has turned white and waxy from being in the water, and the fingers and toes are swollen.

"Perhaps," says Dr. McPhee, "if you concentrated on looking for those little marks that we know so well on those we love. The moles, the scars."

Mina had three moles in a line on her left arm, but that arm is gone. Robert shifts his gaze, finds it resting on the mass of hair. This, a voice from inside tells him, used to be a woman. Perhaps his wife. The breast hanging by a flap of skin may be hers, the thighs that are swollen and white, those that he has run his tongue against so many times. His head is tight. The room shifts. He reaches out, but the only thing to hold on to is the table with the corpse. There's a whistling in his ears like a storm wind, blackness rising up.

Then a chair underneath him, his head thrust down onto his knees, and the doctor's voice breaking through the noise in his ears. "Steady there, Mr. Bentley. Now, breathe deeply, come on."

When finally he is able to stand, the doctor helps him into his office, then arranges for a cup of tea to be brought. It takes a few minutes, and they sit in silence, Robert with his head down until the doctor tells him, "Drink this, man, it'll make you feel more like yourself."

The tea's too sweet, but he takes a long gulp, then sets down the saucer and holds the cup between his hands.

McPhee leans onto his elbows. "Did you recognize anything?"

The cup is hot, too hot, but then he is colder than he has ever felt before. He shakes his head.

"Well then, are you sure it is *not* Mrs. Bentley?"

"No."

The doctor comes around the desk. "Wait here, then. We can do this without putting you through that ordeal a second time."

He lays a hand on Robert's shoulder in a friendly manner, but it makes him jump.

It cannot be her, he tells himself. It must be her. With his mind he feels out into the world, trying to sense which is right—whether he is a widower, or a deserted husband, or merely a man whose wife has met with some misfortune from which she cannot free herself. Recently she was distracted and her temper easily sparked. Was she worried by something? Did she know trouble was coming for her?

She'd never said much about her first husband, as though she wanted to wipe away every last memory of him. Not a happy marriage, of that he was sure. To an older man, a man who loved her with a passion but kept her too close. What woman would want such a marriage? But then, she's told him, she was a respectable but poor girl, brought up by an aunt in the country who died suddenly, and there he was—Mr. Fleet—with the means of giving her an easier life.

Strange, he thinks, how her life was so much like the widow's. Or at least, the story the widow invented.

She's gone too. Cartwright told him so when he got home last night, worn out and filthy from another day of searching. He hadn't cared. Let her go. Let her take what she likes and be gone. Price too. What did any of it matter if Mina was lost? Here in the doctor's office he feels as though he's sitting on the highest point of the earth and might fall. The brown linoleum is distant beyond his feet, the desk out of reach. Farther away, out of sight, the world is running along strange paths, all out of kilter.

With a squeal the door opens. The doctor is carrying something in a metal dish. "Here, now," he says. "This should be easier on you."

He looks at what the doctor sets in front of him. A dish of hair. He must have made some effort to dry it, because it no longer has the slick look of the mass tangled under the corpse. Dark hair. Dark brown. It could be hers. It could be. He rests his face in his hands.

"Mr. Bentley? Mr. Bentley? Is it hers?"

"I don't know," he says, letting his hands drop. "I can't be sure."

Dr. McPhee sits down behind his desk. "Yes," he says, "I understand the difficulty." He nods to himself, then stares past Robert. "Do you feel up to another look?"

Robert shakes his head. "Not right now. Besides, what good would it do? There isn't much . . . there isn't much left to recognize."

He realizes the irony of this situation, even if Dr. McPhee doesn't say a word. An expert on the Bertillonage techniques of identification, unable to identify a body that could be his own wife's. He never measured her—why would he have? He's measured convicts and servants, but to use those callipers on Mina, what reason could there have been for that?

How to keep searching when this might be her? Wouldn't it be better to know, by whatever means?

"There is a way," he says at last, and the doctor looks over at him. "We'll have to call in Danforth, the fingerprint expert."

CHAPTER 39

Despite the awfulness of the circumstances, Robert detects a certain smugness about Danforth. He strides about the bedroom with his magnifying glass as though he is Sherlock Holmes, looking at a hairbrush, looking at the small pot used for hair taken from the brush.

"Just as well," he says, "that your servants have been less than assiduous." He bends to peer at the edge of the dressing table. "Generally, the greatest obstacle to my work is a housemaid trained to remove every last trace of dirt. In my business, polishing is the enemy."

Robert sits on the edge of the bed. "The household has been in an uproar. My wife missing, the jewelry taken, the police—" He waves his hand in the air.

"Understandable. Very understandable." Danforth points at the jewelry box, raises his eyebrows in question, though how could there be any doubt that this was the box broken into when it sits on the dressing table with its wood splintered?

"It was the maid," Robert says flatly. "The police have taken her away."

"Ah, the maid," says Danforth. "Possibly so." He huffs as he bends down for a better look. "Promising. Certainly the culprit did not expect the box to be examined for fingerprints. There seems to have been no attempt to wipe them away."

He straightens up, then gives his waistcoat a tug to smooth it.

Gerri Brightwell

"I'm hoping that if I identify the thief, it will lead us to your wife. After all, there is every chance that the theft and your wife's disappearance are related."

Robert looks away to the window. He has hardly slept in days, has drunk too much brandy when the house was quiet. This room seems starkly bright. Not with sunshine, thanks to the low clouds hanging over the city, but too bright nonetheless. Light glares off the pillow where she laid her head until a few days ago, the polished arms of the chair where she sat to brush her hair. Now it all looks a little shabby.

"I don't see how that could be so." He gets to his feet, crosses to the window and looks out. Two horses pulling a carriage that gleams darkly, a maid across the road coming up from the area in a hat that, he notices even from here, is bright with dyed feathers.

"Well." Danforth clears his throat. "There are lots of possibilities. But for now—"

Mina arranging the theft herself? Is that what he means? Robert leans against the window frame. "Look here," he says, "my wife had absolutely no reason—"

"Yes, yes. I didn't mean to offend you." Danforth takes a breath. "I am here to help you get to the bottom of this affair."

"Thank you." Yet he cannot stay in this room with this man for a moment longer. "I have other business to attend to," he tells him. "If you cannot find my wife's fingerprints here and need to examine other rooms, Cartwright will be able to assist you."

Danforth frowns. "I see. Well." He pulls at his ear. He looks about him, at the dressing table, at the bed. "Yes," he says more quietly, "perhaps that would be better."

Robert makes his way downstairs. The house is cold—he is cold, having eaten a breakfast that was nothing more than toast and a kipper, for with so much else to do this was all that Mrs. Johnson could manage. Even the doorknob of the study is cold to the touch—not surprising, given that the room is as he left it the night before when he sat here with a decanter of brandy and his feet propped close to the fire. The decanter is still on the table, empty, and the glass is clouded with his fingerprints. As for the fire, it is dead, the hearth choked with ashes. He pulls back the curtains and the room looks more miserable. He could ring for the maid—or rather, Elsie, for it is she who has been suddenly elevated to house-maid for the time being, clattering up and down the stairs with buckets of coal and the housemaid's box.

He has been waiting: for Mina to return, for this home to be filled again. Soon, though, it could be more empty yet. Will Mrs. Johnson and Cartwright stay in a place like this? Will Elsie? For now, it is only the four of them in this big house, and they are not enough to make it feel alive. So he sits. He doesn't ring for Elsie, who would fumble at the hearth and spill ashes and coal. He merely sits, and waits.

By the time there is a knock at the door he is thoroughly chilled. "Come in," he calls.

Cartwright opens the door wide to let Danforth in.

"Good God, it's freezing in here, Bentley." He hunches his shoulders. "Need to take care of yourself, or you'll be coming down with something."

Robert shrugs and looks to where the fire should be, sees the ashes, looks away again. "Do you have news?"

"I do." He settles himself on a chair. He has a notebook, as though he fancies himself a detective, and flips it open. "The body is not that of your wife."

Robert sinks forward. "Thank God."

"The number of souls that meet their end in the Thames is astonishing. However, this particular one is not that of your wife. Of that I am certain. The fingerprints of the drowned woman show no similarity to any that I found upstairs."

"I see." He doesn't even look at Danforth. He's thinking only that the corpse was never one he'd held close, never one he'd caressed. Somehow that helps, as though the grip it has had on him has been loosened. But what of Mina? What has become of her?

"As for the thief, that is a more difficult matter."

"The jewelry thief?"

"The jewelry box has been handled by a number of people—including the police, I presume. What few prints I could find that belonged to persons in this household were those of your wife and the lady's maid."

"Price?"

"I would not make an accusation based on the incomplete evidence I found. The police have made that impossible."

Robert lets his head rest against the back of the chair. "So my wife is alive."

"Your wife? All I can say is that the body is not hers."

"You're certain?"

"It's impossible for it to be hers."

It is Danforth who will call on Dr. McPhee, who is eager to take onto himself whatever he can of this business of the body from the river. As for Robert, he sits in the study with his hands under his arms for warmth and looks at the work he has spent so many years on. His equipment, his papers, his cabinet of cards that have the measurements of convicts and servants and even a few friends, all neatly ordered in their drawers—but not hers. What use has it been? What use will it ever be?

CHAPTER 40

From here England almost looks appealing—the low, green hills of the coast that drop away to white cliffs, the fishing boats with their abrupt prows breaking into the waves, as honest-looking and determined as one could wish. Soon these last signs of land are gone, and she is left gazing at an expanse of sea that's grey and empty. That's a better way to remember England, she thinks—for what were those weeks at the Bentleys'? And the days upon days she spent in a boardinghouse, not daring to go out, waiting for her check? Nothing more than a wretched half life, shut into overstuffed rooms in a dour city.

She lets go of the railing and starts back. There's still her trunk to unpack in that miserable little cabin. Her cabin, though. Not to be shared with any vicious-tongued Mrs. Thomas, who believes that a companion is a slave to wait on her at any time of the day or night, someone to be tortured, gently, by having her hopes picked away, one by one. Now the trunk is full: a new trunk, holding three dresses—all black, of course, but of her own choosing—hats, underwear. For she is a young lady of means now. Fifteen thousand pounds. Not everything she could have got, for there was the house, and the jewelry, but more than enough to live on. To have tried for more would have meant risking everything.

She's tied on her hat, but the wind catches the brim and lifts it from her head. With both hands she reaches for it. The ship rolls and, before she can find her balance, she has been thrown to the deck.

"My good lady," cries a voice. "Are you injured?" Hands take hold of her and she's lifted, ever so gingerly, to her feet. An older man with a huge moustache. Now he will not let go of her, but steers her to the railings, where she can hold on.

"Thank you," she says, and turns a smile on him. She means, of course, that he can release his hold, but it is only when she glances down at his hands that he understands.

He gives a sharp laugh. "Sorry, dear lady." Then, "Sorry," on a sigh this time. He holds the railings, too, and looks at the sea swelling around the ship. "Awful business with the *Star of the Orient*. Makes me think about this sea travel quite differently. Lost a dear friend." He glances at her. "But you, my dear, have also suffered a loss."

"The *Star of the Orient*," she says. "I was aboard when she went down."

"Good Lord!" He blinks at her in the wind. "So sorry."

They stand like that, contemplating the chop of the waves while seagulls cry over their heads, until he says, "My nephew. Gordon Douglas. Did you—?"

She shakes her head. "I lost my husband—Henry Bentley."

"Bentley?" he says. "That regional administrator chappie? Good Lord. Had no idea he'd tied the knot."

"On the *Star of the Orient*," she tells him. "We met on the *Star*. Both returning home, though for me it was my first time to England." She's said it often enough now that the story slides off her tongue without her having to think. Even so, she'll have to be careful. She was not the only survivor, and it's possible that one day she will come across someone who'll remember that there was no wedding on the *Star of the Orient*. Because that's something one would remember, isn't it?

He must have jammed his hat down hard on his head, for even the gusts that fling spray into her face do not shift it. "A terrible loss, my dear lady. To find happiness, and then to lose it." He lowers his head, as though the weight of this tragedy is more than he can bear. "Now you're on your way back?"

The sea smells of salt, a good, clean smell. "Yes. I couldn't imagine what else to do. Nothing in England was familiar. I just couldn't—"

He nods. "I understand. You are not travelling on your own, I hope?" By the way he has his eyebrows raised, he evidently expects that she is.

"Yes," she tells him. "I have no one—no one to—"

"We can't have that. I'll introduce you to my wife and son. You'll be part of the family."

A few minutes later she is escorted to his cabin to meet a stout woman in a black dress, and a young man with a look about him that suggests that, in a few years, he too will be stout. He's friendly enough, though, and seems more so when his father introduces this young woman as a widow who has suffered the most tragic of losses.

It's not so far from the truth, is it? After all, she and Henry did take long walks along the deck, and on one of those walks he did propose. She needed a little time to make up her mind, she told him. Although she liked him he wasn't quite what she expected in a lover, being so formal even when they were alone. And while she was thinking about what her answer would be, the ship foundered and sank.

If it hadn't been for that, she might well have been Mrs. Henry Bentley.

CHAPTER 41

The train snakes between the dreary houses, puffing out smoke that will leave smuts on sheets and petticoats and aprons hung out to dry. It's only half past three in the afternoon, but evening is coming. At least the train is heading in a direction that will stretch the day, nosing its way west from Paddington.

As yet it has hardly begun its journey. It winds along between the backs of houses cramped together, past gloomy yards hardly large enough for a washing line, rattling everything from cups on tables— no saucers here—to the floor beneath a small boy batting at beetles with a ladle. In windows faces turn—who can resist the sight of such power, such speed, such promise of other places one could be and the other lives one might be leading? Then they look away to the walls of their houses, or to pots of potatoes boiling on stoves, or to the remains of meager dinners.

Through the train's windows only a few faces stare out at the city rushing past. Others are shielded behind newspapers, or bowed over books, or glowering at their children, who will not sit still. In a third-class carriage, amongst the din of a crying baby and the chesty coughing of an old woman wrapped in a shawl, sits a young woman. All that she owns is in a small bag stowed in the netting above her head, and there is not much in the bag. A dress, a change of undergarments. Nothing more, as though she sprang into being only a few days ago, with no past to carry with her. She leans towards the window. It's misted already, so she wipes a peephole and lowers her eye to it. It is like looking out of a porthole onto a stormy sea: all those roofs, all those bridges like waves breaking overhead. She reaches out beside her, finds a warm hand and squeezes it. "Tell me again—how far did you go?" she asks.

He says, "All over. Down to the docks, up to Hampstead. You wouldn't believe some of the places I went. I wouldn't give up."

She turns. "I nearly did."

His thumb strokes the back of her hand. "Don't say that."

The train jolts and her shoulder presses against his. "It's true."

He lets go of her hand and puts his arm around her, though for that he earns a glare from the old woman, who sets to coughing more loudly.

"You should have waited for me," he says. "Anything could have happened to you out on your own like that."

She lets her head fall against his shoulder. Those words of Mrs. Robert's have stuck like burrs: *Traitor, spy, fool. Don't you understand? You've been used to get to me—what else did you imagine? That he'd want a girl like you?* She'd picked through them as she'd run to Popham's, as she'd fled, soaked to the skin, as she'd stood on the bridge and watched the Thames slide past, undoing her hopes with every last one of them until she'd understood that she was alone, and friendless, and cold, and that the river was only a few feet away.

She'd remembered the warmth of his breath on her neck, the way he'd always held the door open for her, even going into the dismal tea shop by the river—as though she was a lady—the way he'd sat across from her with his tea going cold and looked at her and looked as though it would never be enough. So she'd walked back over the bridge, and up the road, and to the uneven street where the tea shop stood, and there she'd settled down on her haunches to wait for morning in the narrow space of the doorway. To her surprise she'd been woken by a gentle shake and made to sit in the kitchen with a blanket around her, and as much hot tea as she could manage, and the cook hurrying a small boy around to Mr. Popham's to fetch Teddy.

She says, "I nearly didn't trust you, not after all that the mistress said."

For that she gets a kiss at the corner of her jaw. "We're going to have stories for our kids," he tells her. "They'll know better than to go into service, won't they?"

The train gives a blast and, clear of the city proper now, picks up speed. The carriages are chilly, but huddled together, Jane and Teddy stay warm.

1901

Nowadays meals are a silent affair, just him and Cartwright, him picking through his food, Cartwright standing at attention by the sideboard. The house has closed up around him, just like his life. The bedrooms ghostly in dust sheets, the morning room too. All he needs is the bedroom—Henry's old room, because he could never bring himself to sleep in the bed he'd shared with Mina—a place to eat, and his study. Though mostly he just sits and reads the paper.

He sets down what's left of his toast, and pushes the scrambled egg around his plate. Overcooked. What else can one expect of a young girl with no one to train her? Maybe he should get himself a housekeeper, and he dabs at his lips with his napkin, then runs a hand over his beard. No. Not another one, not after the fiasco with Mrs. Rogers, who installed herself in his house like its mistress and pressed his hand between hers and called him a *dear man* at every chance. Two years of that, and he was saved only by the butcher proposing to her.

He tucks the paper under his arm and shoves back the chair. He's grown a belly in these last years. Not from the food—he barely eats—but from his evenings sitting in front of the fire with a bottle of brandy. It has given his face a flushed look it never loses, just enough so that he seems like a healthy, active sort while inside he is slowly rotting.

It's a bright July morning, but the girl has built up the fire in the study—the brightness never reaches the back of the house, and there's no point skimping when he'll be in here most of the day. He settles into his armchair and opens the paper. The king off on a visit to Scotland. A schoolmaster murdered by his own wife. The owner of a small guesthouse in Torquay handsomely rewarded for reporting a suspicious guest found to be an infamous jewel thief. The Belper Committee's recommendation that fingerprints be used as the primary means of identification of criminals finally adopted by the police forces of England and Wales.

He settles his glasses a little higher up his nose and lifts the paper. So much for the Troup Committee's decision for the country to use anthropometry—eight years ago now. A lifetime ago.

Well, he thinks, Danforth will be pleased. He's made a point of calling around every few months, taking him to his club—as though the place would not spark memories of the unfortunate Argentinean affair—having him around for Christmas dinner a few times. A well-meaning man, if somewhat too dogged to inspire much in the way of real friendship. That woman pulled from the Thames turned out to be a shopgirl—her father identified her. For months Danforth went to the morgue on Robert's behalf, armed with Mina's fingerprints, and compared them to numerous other unfortunate women who'd met their end in the river.

But Mina is gone, and no clue about her whereabouts has ever turned up. His hopes that she would return to ask forgiveness—oh yes, Popham made sure to tell him what he knew of her, he couldn't restrain himself, and Robert had to be pulled off him—those hopes have withered. So he lets himself die, day by day, for what life can there be without her?

In a small guesthouse in Torquay, Mrs. Edward Knight sits in the kitchen sipping a cup of tea. With one finger she points at the newspaper, says, "Look, Teddy—it's in here."

He pulls out a chair and sits down opposite her, though the table in front of them is crammed with dirty plates and cutlery. His face has grown thinner in the seven years they have been married. After all, it hasn't been easy—scraping together money, doing so much of the work of running this place themselves. Not so very different from being in service, he's thought at times, not that he would ever tell her so.

Now he pulls the newspaper towards him and props it against the teapot. She watches him read, the way his lips move slightly, the hunch of his shoulders. Then he sits back and sniffs, says, "Got it wrong, didn't they?"

"Wrong?" She frowns at him.

"They make it sound as though I was the one to find him out."

She tilts her cup to drink the last of her tea. "Maybe you would have, if you'd been the one cleaning his room."

"Three hundred pounds. All because you thought he was *suspicious* and poked around a bit in his things." He gives a smile. "We could retire."

"We could move to a bigger place and hire a couple of girls to help us out."

He reaches over the dirty plates and takes her hand. "There's no stopping you, is there? You're going to have us moving up in the world. Next thing you know we'll have a hotel on the promenade. People will be calling us sir and madam and doffing their hats to us."

She gives a small laugh. "What would be so wrong with that?"

From upstairs comes a knock at the front door. Teddy gets to his feet. "No rest for the wicked, hey love?" He buttons up his jacket and is about to head up the stairs when he ducks his head towards hers and kisses her cheek.

The feel of it lingers even after his footsteps have faded up the stairs. From the sink comes the slow drip of the tap into a half-empty pan of water. It intrudes into her thoughts as she reads the story over again. Three hundred pounds. Just in the nick of time. Slowly, she gets to her feet. Her belly is swollen. One more month until their child is born—at last, when they'd long lost hope of having a child at all—and they'll need to have someone helping out.

From a drawer she takes a pair of scissors and cuts out the story. Something to save. Something to show their child one day. Then she lifts down a wooden box from a high shelf and opens the lid. Papers upon papers pressed in together. She pushes them back and slides in the clipping. She's about to swing the lid closed again when she hesitates. Her fingers travel over the papers crammed against one another. The last letter Teddy's father wrote to him before he died. A portrait of her and Teddy at a photographer's studio, looking stiff-faced and unlike themselves. Packets of papers that came with them from London, hidden in Teddy's pockets. She pulls them out and looks over them again. Love letters from a woman called Nora to Mr. Popham that Mrs. Robert had been willing to pay very generously for. She'd never got them, though. Instead Teddy had left the Bentleys' house with them still in his pocket, and Mrs. Robert had disappeared. It had been in the papers. A mystery. A lingering question for weeks. Yet surely Mrs. Robert had simply run away and not wanted to be found. Surely she was Nora.

Jane sets down the letters and pulls out another packet. Ornately inscribed certificates for shares in a diamond mine in Rhodesia—Arnold Flyte, prop.—and silver mines in Argentina owned by Arthur Fleet, and gold mines in the United States, and Siam, all in different names that are uncannily similar. She and Teddy have puzzled over them many times. They have even considered cashing them in.

Now she unfolds one of them. Of course, they might well be worth something. Teddy has told her so, many times. But then again—those names. Flyte. Fleet. Echoes of each other. There is something wrong here, something that spells trouble.

The baby kicks, and she winces. Her ribs are sore from those feet pushing against her bones, eager to be out in the world. "It's all right," she whispers, and rubs her belly with one hand. With the other she picks it all up—the certificates, the letters. Then she swings open the stove door and throws the whole lot into the flames.

A gentleman of his acquaintance recommended her—an efficient woman, if cold in a rather British way, one who would keep to herself. A Madame Dumontet, a widow, a respectable lady, even if a foreigner.

He waves his hand at her to sit down, and she does, perched on the edge of the chair. "So," he says, "you have been with Monsieur Clavier for four years?"

"Yes," she says. "Four years."

"But he has not written a character for you?"

"No, monsieur. He died."

"Ah." He puts on his glasses and looks over her letter again. "Where are you from?"

"From Norfolk."

"In England? I see. Parents?"

"An orphan."

"Ah." He takes a cigarette from the box on his desk. "And your husband?"

"My first husband was a good-for-nothing. My second died just before our fourth anniversary."

"No children?"

"No."

He nods, as though this is good news, though of course it is only good for him. No children invading his home, no requests for time off to visit them. "I live a quiet life, madame. You will have one day off a week, you will cook and supervise the woman who comes in to clean. Occasionally you will be woken in the night if patients need me, or to provide food at odd hours. The wages I can afford won't make you rich, but, if you're careful, they'll give you enough to live on in your old age."

"Very good."

He takes off his glasses and lays them on the blotter. "You want to bury yourself here? I have to tell you"—he gives her a long stare—"your chances of finding another husband in a place like this are not good. If that's what you wanted."

"No," she says.

"Very well. You may start as soon as you wish."

Outside she stands in the shadow of the house and shades her eyes. She has had the foresight to arrange for her trunk to come with her as far as the station. Now it only needs to be brought the few miles through the crushing heat of this summer's day. The land seems to tremble. It shakes and ripples as though it will fall apart.

Of course, that's merely an illusion of the heat, and of her exhaustion.

A quiet place. Safer than Paris. Safer than Lyon or Nancy. She had worried, in those cities, that he would find her, for her husband was nothing if not a persistent man. He may have assumed that her body was carried out to sea. Or he may have noticed that the wife of Mr. Robert Bentley was never found, drowned or otherwise.

The air smells sweet. In the garden stands a mirabelle tree, its fruit overripe, plums scattered through the grass. No one has bothered to pick them up. Already some are rotting on the ground. She steps over them, bending down to gather those that are still good, plucking more from the branches overhead.

In the years to come she'll make jam from them, and tarts. She'll send her favorites amongst Dr. Lambert's patients home with them, and that will make them kinder in their gossip: that it's strange, the doctor and his housekeeper, the two of them living together like that. And hasn't old Beauvais seen her in her underwear at the window—not her own window, but the doctor's—throwing open the shutters?

Of course, they are right. A man, a woman who is by no means unattractive—despite the sharpness of her face, and the shortness of everything she says, so that one gets the impression she thinks herself superior. Some nights she spends in his bed. It's a comfortable existence, though when she falls asleep it's not him she thinks about. You can't conjure love where it doesn't exist. However, you must live as best you can.

For now, she wipes her forehead with her sleeve and watches the cart turn up the road, off to fetch her trunk. She takes one of the plums, still warm from the sun, and slides it into her mouth. It bursts with juice, and she shuts her eyes to savor it.